P9-BYM-914

"It hasn't taken long for Cameron to leave his mark on this iconic franchise. . . . Longtime fans will be happy to know that under Cameron, 'the leader of the free world's still got it' (in more ways than one). Marc Cameron dazzled Clancy loyalists with *Power and Empire*, but now he's kicking it up a notch for his next book . . . [*Oath of Office* will] blow readers away." —Crime Reads

PRAISE FOR THE BESTSELLING NOVELS OF TOM CLANCY

"Heart-stopping action. . . . Entertaining and eminently topical. . . . Clancy still reigns." —*The Washington Post*

"Brilliant." —*Newsweek*

"Highly entertaining." —*The Wall Street Journal*

"[Clancy] excites, illuminates . . . a real page-turner." —*Los Angeles Daily News*

"Exhilarating. . . . No other novelist is giving so full a picture of modern conflict." —*The Sunday Times* (London)

TITLES BY TOM CLANCY

TOM CLANCY

CODE
OF
HONOR

★

MARC CAMERON

BERKLEY
New York

BERKLEY
An imprint of Penguin Random House LLC
penguinrandomhouse.com

ISBN: 9780525541738

G. P. Putnam's Sons hardcover edition / November 2019
Berkley international edition / October 2020
Berkley premium edition / October 2020

Printed in the United States of America
1 3 5 7 9 10 8 6 4 2

Cover art by Bose Collins Ltd.
Cover design by Eric Fuentecilla
Maps by Jeffrey L. Ward

PRINCIPAL CHARACTERS

UNITED STATES GOVERNMENT

Jack Ryan: President of the United States
Mary Pat Foley: director of national intelligence
Arnold "Arnie" van Damm: President Ryan's chief of staff
Scott Adler: secretary of state

THE CAMPUS

Gerry Hendley: director of The Campus and Hendley
    Associates
John Clark: director of operations
Domingo "Ding" Chavez: assistant director of operations
Jack Ryan, Jr.: operations officer/senior analyst
Dominic "Dom" Caruso: operations officer
Adara Sherman: operations officer
Bartosz "Midas" Jankowski: operations officer
Gavin Biery: director of information technology

OTHER CHARACTERS

United States

Dr. Caroline "Cathy" Ryan: First Lady of the United
    States
Dr. Dan Berryhill: former medical school classmate of
    Dr. Ryan
Peter Li: retired admiral, United States Navy
Michelle Chadwick: United States senator

PRINCIPAL CHARACTERS

Indonesia
Gunawan "Gugun" Gumelar: president of Indonesia
Geoff Noonan: gaming software engineer
Suparman: owner, Suparman Games

China
Zhao Chengzhi: president of China
David Huang: Chinese operative
General Song Biming: PRC military officer
General Bai: PRC military officer
Major Chang: Bai's aide
Wu Chao: PLA major/operative Central Military Commission
Kang: Chinese assassin
Tsai Zhan: Communist Party minder

A man does what he must—in spite of personal consequences, in spite of obstacles and dangers and pressures—and that is the basis of all human morality.   —Winston S. Churchill

Doubt is unpleasant, but certainty is absurd.

—Voltaire

1

Had the young woman at the bar been slightly more attractive, Geoff Noonan might have smelled a trap.

"Know your number." That's what they said. Oh, he knew his number, all right, and this was going to work out just fine . . .

The security goons at work were jealous of everyone else's travel, relying on acronyms, spooky statistics, and stupid rules like that "know your number" bullshit at every single meeting. These destroyers of joy gleefully pointed out that a five in Plymouth was still a five in Phuket or Phnom Penh—or anywhere else, for that matter. They liked to remind everyone that eights and nines didn't magically try to hook up with a five. Ever. If the situation was too good to be true, it was a setup. Noonan was an engineer, a software designer, smart enough to know the knuckle-dragging goons were right, mostly. But sometimes . . . Sometimes the circumstances indicated otherwise. Sometimes a hot girl didn't realize she was a hot girl, especially if she was just hot enough.

Noonan watched the Indonesian beauty at the bar curl her toes on the crossbar of the stool, like a cat might flick the tip of its tail back and forth to rid itself of excess energy. This was good, all right, but not too good. Was it? Nah. It's not like she was an eight or anything.

The Magma Lounge at the Hilton in Bandung, Indonesia, had oversized leather couches that swallowed people up, especially if they had short legs, which Noonan did. Mired in impossibly soft cushions, he didn't think about his wife, his two kids, the baby on the way, or his wife's father, who was a federal judge in Hartford. The danger level of his actions and the consequences of an affair should have made him think twice before he asked this woman to join him, but they never entered his mind. He was preoccupied with how to stand up without looking like an ass when the time came.

The girl at the bar was good-looking enough for Noonan's taste, though not so handsome as to set off alarm bells. It was doubtful he would have heard them in any case. His pastor at the First Congregational Church in Beacon Hill had pointed out during a recent marriage counseling session that Geoff appeared to lack the capacity for what he called pre-transgression guilt—that little tickle in the back of the neck that warned most people away from bad behavior before they engaged in it. Noonan had a conscience. It just took a while to kick in. Moments after, whatever the deed, Noonan always found himself wallowing in guilt. He just couldn't seem to remember that feeling prior to any action, and that inability kept him in constant trouble.

He caught the girl's eye again.

For now, trouble was looking pretty damned sweet.

Her honeyed complexion and flawless features suggested she was Sundanese, the most prevalent ethnicity in

Bandung—and West Java, for that matter. Sundanese were often said by Indonesians to be the most attractive people in their country. Hard to argue, though Noonan had to admit he hadn't seen many ugly girls since he and his bosses had arrived in Jakarta for the computer gaming trade show five days earlier. Bandung was even better— and worse, but mostly better.

Blue eyes and straw accents in the girl's dark hair suggested she had more than a few Dutch branches in her family tree—a remnant from Dutch East India plantations that had raised tea and cinchona, from which quinine was still derived. A skintight fire-engine-red dress had a heart-shaped neckline below her collarbones. The sultry, fist-size swell of visible cleavage provided a sexy counterpoint to the nervous way she curled the toes of one dainty foot and dangled a shoe off the end of the other.

Noonan scooted forward on the deep cushions to take his third dirty martini of the evening from the waiter. He held the glass up toward the girl. Dangerous stuff, those air toasts. There was always a chance she was looking at someone or something behind him. Noonan held his breath until her smallish mouth blossomed into a petite smile and she returned the gesture with her own drink—fruit juice, from the looks of it. That wasn't surprising, since most Sundanese were Muslim. He wondered if her piety would keep her from hooking up with a guy at a bar. Maybe she was just here to meet a friend.

He was about to find out.

She was up, padding across the floral carpet toward him, red dress so tight across her belly he could see the depression of her navel against the fabric. The nervousness was gone now. Her steps were confident, though not haughty, like she knew she was attractive but didn't plan to use it as a weapon. Noonan shot a glance over his shoulder, just to be sure. He didn't want to look the fool if he stood up to greet her and she walked past him to talk to some girlfriend she'd seen across the bar.

There was no one, a fact that shot a surge of adrenaline from the top of Geoff Noonan's head to the tips of his toes. This might actually work out.

Noonan was self-aware enough to know he was probably a borderline six. The girls at work called him the Poison Dwarf, which wasn't fair because five-seven wasn't really all that short. He suspected it had more to do with the kind of jokes he told in the breakroom.

He stood when the woman was halfway there, working extra-hard to keep from wallowing to his feet from the oversized couch.

This one was a solid seven, a little square-hipped for Noonan's taste, and she didn't have as much up top as he normally liked, but yeah, she was a seven for sure. A seven hooking up with a six. That could work. Plus, he was an American. Worth a point. Right? Maybe she just wanted a free drink while she practiced her English, but even that would be better than sitting alone in a bar after the day he'd had.

His gut churned with something far more pleasurable than guilt.

Two weeks before, Geoff Noonan had been a brilliant if somewhat creepy software engineer at Parnassus Games in Boston, content to gamble online and maybe sneak over to a strip club near Boston Common while his w. was at her maternity checkups. He wasn't exactly a man overflowing with scruples, but up until recently, he'd never considered selling out his company to the highest bidder.

Todd Ackerman changed everything when he broke both his legs in a bicycling accident. Ackerman was supposed to have been the one to attend the Jakarta tech conference, but with his injuries, that duty had fallen to Noonan. They had developed several pieces of tech together, tech that got them noticed by the bosses. The two software engineers were antipodal in virtually everything but their knowledge of computer gaming. Ackerman had been a college baseball star. Noonan was still the last picked for every team, sport or not. Ackerman liked conferences in faraway lands. Strange food gave Noonan the runs. Crowds made him feel like someone had a pillow over his face. Ackerman was Canadian— stereotypically agreeable—and smiled more than a normal person should smile. The bosses liked to spend time with him, have drinks, play golf. They tolerated Noonan because of his brilliance. If they'd suspected either of the two engineers of corporate espionage, it would have been Noonan, hands down. He was awkward and quiet and hardly ever cracked a smile unless it was at one of his own dirty jokes.

Nobody suspected Ackerman. He was the nice guy.

Ackerman had been the one to arrange the side trip to Bandung after the conference to meet with the rep from an up-and-coming Indonesian gaming company. Ackerman set up the foreign bank accounts, the alibis, the escape plan—all of it. Noonan was well aware that he wouldn't have been brought in on the deal had Ackerman not wrecked his bike. He was a necessary evil—now a rich necessary evil.

Noonan had demurred at first, not because it was the right thing to do, but because he thought it might be a trap. Then, when Ackerman had explained how much money was involved, the deal had been a no-brainer. Noonan would go to the stupid conference and meet with the buyer and he'd get fifty percent of twenty-five million dollars. Not too shabby. His wife went to church every Sunday even if she didn't have a single sin to confess as far as he could tell. Even she'd be able to understand twelve and a half million dollars when he got around to explaining it to her.

If he ever did. That kind of money made it easy to disappear.

And anyway, it wasn't even stealing. Ackerman and Noonan had, after all, been the ones to develop the technology. Why shouldn't they be able to sell it?

The trade show had been packed with geeks—adults who made a life playing and designing computer-based gaming systems. Like many of the attendees, Noonan was a loner at heart, an introvert who preferred the company of a computer screen in a dimly lit basement to actual flesh-and-blood people. Where a gathering of like-minded folks might exhilarate some, the milling crowds and endless panel discussions sucked the life out of him and left him with a pulsing headache.

The bigwigs from Warner Bros., Ubisoft, Sega—everyone in the gaming industry was there. The Japanese had the biggest presence, of course, but the South Koreans, the Chinese, and reps from Silicon Valley (which included a hell of a lot of Japanese, Korean, and Chinese) all made a healthy showing. Russia had a small presence, as did India, and an Australian company. The Indonesians, eager to dip a toe into the gaming market themselves, hosted the trade show, and Suparman Games was their de facto industry leader.

The security goons in Boston—Noonan called them Larry and Curly, for no particular reason but that they hated it—had warned him that there would be people at the show who would be extremely interested in some of the company's recent innovations. Corporate espionage was the number-one threat to American national security, they said, acting all official and serious, like they were still Feds and not stooges for a company that made computer games. But they had no idea Calliope even existed, let alone her capability. No one did, beyond Noonan and Ackerman. If the bosses had known all of it, they would have put every existing copy under armed guard.

Ackerman kept one locked up in a safe-deposit box somewhere. Noonan had come to Jakarta with two. He kept one for insurance. Twenty-five million was supposed to guarantee fidelity. And it would, so long as the Indonesians didn't try any funny business.

The conference was a nightmare, with the bosses eyeing him constantly for three days. He was sure they suspected something at first, but he finally realized they always looked at him like that, like they were disappointed he was such a rock star in the field of artificial intelligence that he was impossible to fire, no matter how much they didn't like him.

Ackerman was smart, and he knew that the bosses might hang around Jakarta to hobnob after the conference wrapped up. He'd set up the meeting with the buyer in Bandung, a three-and-a-half-hour drive to the southeast nestled in the Parahyangan Mountains. Noonan told the bosses he wanted to experience a little of the mountain air before he left Indonesia. They were heading to Australia on some camel tour anyway, so they couldn't really say much about him wanting to soak up a little culture. At least he wasn't trying to tag along with them.

Bandung was all right, Noonan supposed. The third-largest city in Indonesia was cooler than Jakarta, and only slightly less crowded. They called it the City of Flowers or something like that. Noonan had hoped it was because of the girls, but it turned out to be because of the actual flowers. The rocky gray face of Tangkuban Perahu, an active 6,800-foot volcano, rose above the green mountains thirty kilometers to the north of the city and gave the air an odor that was far from floral.

Noonan met the buyer at a teahouse a block from his hotel. The guy looked like an Indonesian gangster—at least what Noonan thought an Indonesian gangster would look like—with dark slacks, black Oakley shades, and some kind of prison tattoo showing on the muscle of his upper arm below the short sleeve of a white linen shirt. The transaction was surprisingly simple, considering how much it would change Noonan's life. Hand over the thumb drive, money gets transferred, Ackerman sends the activation codes. Bing, bang, boom.

It wasn't like the movies, with any witty repartee or hoarsely whispered threat. The gangster dude just pushed back from the table and left with what he came for. Geoff Noonan had all but stumbled out of the teahouse, wrestling with the heady fact that he was now a multimillionaire. He'd walked for the better part of an hour through the teeming Bandung streets, dodging traffic and tourists who had fled the crowds of Jakarta to crowd into this new place. Stunned, that's what Noonan was. He paid little attention to where he was going. The cacophony of horns, bike bells, and people jabbering away in a tongue he could not understand assaulted him like countless slaps coming in from every direction.

A little guy at a meat stall called out to him in a high-pitched voice, waving the piece of cardboard he used to fan the smoke away from his grill. It occurred to Noonan that he could buy any of the lowly schmucks on this street ten thousand times over. More than that. Most of these guys probably didn't have more than their food stall and some shithole hovel somewhere. He'd always known he was smarter than everyone else. Now he was richer, too. The smug feeling vanished as soon as he saw his first policeman. He was a felon now. A thief. He needed to try to blend in.

Street vendors selling everything from chicken satay to Dutch pastries were everywhere. He'd bought a bowl of chicken porridge from a cart because the girl was pretty, and thrown it away after two bites halfway down the block. It tasted fine, but he was too queasy to eat. He kept walking, hoping that would help, deciding to check out the central square. He needed to tell his bosses he'd done something besides sit at the hotel bar. The Grand Mosque was right there, so everyone took off their shoes. The sulfur from Tangkuban Perahu volcano, mixing with the odor of other people's feet, left him feeling bilious.

And guilty.

Somehow, Noonan had found his way back to the hotel again, and decided to drown his guilt at the bar. Then he'd seen the blue-eyed Sundanese girl—or, rather, she'd seen him. He hoped she would make him feel better.

The idea that she might be a prostitute didn't occur to him until they got to her room and he saw the big floor-to-ceiling mirrors. His room was three floors above hers and didn't have mirrors like that. Still, there was no mention of money. She was appropriately nervous, said she never did this sort of thing—never even went out on her own. Her girlfriend was supposed to meet her for a night on the town in the City of Flowers but never showed. That didn't explain the room, but Noonan was beyond caring.

He pondered the situation while he kicked off his shoes. It sort of made sense: lonely girl, stood up by her friend, sees a lonely guy and hooks up. Truth be told, he had never done this kind of thing, either. He'd thought about it, a lot—tried, even—but no one ever wanted a piece of the Poison Dwarf. Until now.

The girl said her name was Betti Tamala. When the red dress came off in front of the floor-to-ceiling mirror, Noonan decided she was a solid eight. It took less than a minute for him to realize that she had not only done this sort of thing before, she was extremely good at it.

———

Behind the mirror, Wu Chao of the Strategic Support Force—the cyber-, space, and electronic warfare arm of the People's Liberation Army—stretched his neck from side to side, then pointed his chin toward the ceiling as if his collar was too tight. The four men who were packed into the tiny linen closet with all their video equipment filled it to capacity. The space was used for nothing other than this kind of lascivious work, and a dusty nastiness hung in the dank air like an illness.

The SSF consolidated most of the Army's intelligence capabilities, technical and otherwise. It was a relatively new organization, with all involved still squabbling for primacy as strata solidified. Wu had been an intelligence officer for almost two decades, coming up through the ranks working directly for PLA's General Staff Department.

Wu Chao was a patriot. He'd not gone into intelligence work in order to leer through hidden peepholes at obscene Americans, but that was part of his job. Varied duties, his instructors at the School of International Relations had called such work. Wu was forty-three, with thinning black hair and square features that made him look like he'd been carved from a block of limestone. Those who knew him could be forgiven for assuming that he was a killer because of his chiseled look and hardened demeanor. He had, of course, taken lives. That was the way of the world. But he took no joy in it. His job was one of intelligence gathering, computer software, ones and zeros. If he had to kill, it meant something had gone horribly wrong. Kang, the man on the other side of the video camera, was an accomplished killer. Wu had known many assassins over the course of his career. Some he'd killed himself. With others, he'd shared a cup of tea. Almost all of them had some sort of redeeming quality—filial piety, patience with little children, a favorite charity.

As far as Wu could tell, the only thing redeeming about Kang was that he took good care of his teeth. Tall and fit but slightly disheveled in his dark suit, Kang stood at the far end of the little closet, looking the part of overworked businessman or harried police inspector as he stared, entranced, through the glass. Wu knew the cold reality. The man was a state-sponsored serial killer. He relished his work. If the government hadn't found him, he would have been feeding his ugly habits on the backstreets of Shanghai. There was no doubt that Kang was intelligent, but intellect did not translate to conscience.

Conscience. Wu Chao's belly writhed as if he'd swallowed a snake at the thought of the term. His job required horrific acts that were cruel but necessary. He had taken advantage of a widowed Japanese woman's loneliness to infiltrate a radio station in Okinawa, befriended a Uighur child in Urumqi so that he might kill the boy's terrorist father. He leveraged the secrets of other human beings until they'd finally broken and taken their own lives in shame. There seemed to be no bottom to the depths he would sink to for his country, but this clumsy scene on the other side of the glass was by far the most disgusting thing his eyes had ever witnessed. It was made even worse by the fact that he'd developed feelings for Betti Tamala. She knew too much, and would have to die.

Kang would be the one to kill her, so that, at least, was a mercy.

The two Indonesian men seated between Wu and Kang—agents he'd recruited from the local police force—tore their eyes off the glass in search of direction. Both were devout Muslims, but they were men, and the conflicting emotions surely caused them no small amount of grief. In Wu's experience, when it came to battles of piety and the flesh—a nude woman won nine times out of ten. Wu took a long, slow breath, then held up three fingers. Three more minutes. They needed plenty of video to make certain the American cooperated.

The American proved to be an athletic, if bumbling lover, using all the real estate the room provided. Along with the video equipment behind the glass, pinhole cameras in the base of the floor lamp, an overhead fire alarm, and the frame of the floral painting at the foot of the bed, they were assured a near-constant view of the American's face, along with the more damning angles.

Wu flicked his hand when he could stand it no longer, sending Kang and the Indonesian policemen through the hidden door that entered the adjoining bathroom. Wu remained behind the mirror, letting the video roll as the scene continued to unfold.

No one, occupied as the American was occupied, was ever prepared to look up and find three strangers staring down at him. Noonan screamed, first throwing a hand over his face like a distressed woman in a movie, then grabbing Betti and attempting to pull her in front of him like a human shield. She clawed him in the face, having none of it.

"Bravo," Wu whispered to the glass. One of the policemen grabbed her by the arm and dragged her off the mattress, leaving the naked American cowering and flushed in the middle of the tangled sheets, both hands over his groin.

Wu watched as Betti snatched up her clothes and stomped into the bathroom. A moment later she was in the closet with him, her body buzzing with indignation.

"Did you plan to leave me there with him forever?" Her English was flawless—and spoken through a clenched jaw as she reached behind her to touch the neckline of her red dress.

"Forgive me," Wu whispered. "My superiors must be assured we have enough video."

Betti slumped. "I know this," she said. "But I wish you could have used someone else."

"As do I, my dear," Wu said. "But there was no time. I had to have someone I could trust."

She cocked her head slightly, raising a beautifully sculpted brow. "Why did you really wait so long?"

"I was deciding whether or not to kill him," Wu said honestly.

"You are not?" Betti gave a disappointed pout that sent a chill through Wu's veins. "It pierces my heart to think you would let a man live after witnessing him do that to me."

She was beautiful, and tender, but there was a streak of madness in her. He'd noticed it from the beginning. It was one of the principal traits that attracted him to her.

He gave a noncommittal shrug. "We must be certain the software is genuine."

She leaned forward until the tip of her nose almost touched the glass. "He is a fool to carry such technology with him when he travels."

Wu resisted the urge to touch her thigh, keeping his eyes glued to the image of the weeping man on the other side of the glass.

"We believe he intends to sell it," Wu said.

Betti's exquisite brows shot skyward again, as if she'd never considered such a thing. "What if he has done so already?"

Wu shared those same concerns. Earlier that day, his men had lost track of the American for a half-hour. But he'd been the same sad sack when they had finally located him again, wandering the streets a few blocks away. A man who had completed the sale of such a valuable item would surely celebrate. Wu nodded toward the sobbing lump on the other side of the glass and adjusted the volume so they could better hear what was being said. Noonan pointed upward, toward his room, and assured the two Indonesian policemen that what they wanted was locked away in his safe. He would be happy to take them to it if they could just leave his wife and father-in-law out of this mess. *No reason to get them involved. Pleeease.* The man sounded like an over-revved motorbike—of the smallish variety.

"But you *are* going to kill him?" Betti mused, almost to herself. Her lips brushed the glass as she spoke. "Eventually?"

"Yes," Wu said. "Of course. His flight is not until tomorrow night. We have some time."

She turned to face him, her lips pursed in a tremulous

pout. "It saddens me that you would trade my virtue for a computer thumb drive."

"I mean you no offense, my dear," Wu said. "But your virtue was long since—"

She pressed a finger to his lips.

"You are supposed to say, 'Yes, but this is no ordinary thumb drive.'"

Wu merely shrugged. Betti was correct. He doubted if the American even knew the value of what he had. This was no ordinary gaming software. Wu kept the rest to himself, though it didn't matter what the girl knew. Kang would kill her before the night was over—someplace private, away from the hotel, and Noonan. His death would come later, also away from here, and after Wu was certain Calliope was in his hands.

2

Domingo "Ding" Chavez rested his plastic cup of bubble tea on the concrete ledge of the pedestrian path on the Manhattan Bridge, facing west over East Broadway. Intelligence work rarely involved shooting someone in the face—though sometimes it came to that. In truth, it was ninety-eight percent monotony and two percent trying not to get shot in your own face.

Visitors to New York City tended to think of Canal Street as the epicenter of Chinatown, but the bustling restaurants and markets of East Broadway in the shadow of the bridge could have easily been parts of Beijing or Shanghai. English was a second language here—or not spoken at all.

It was warm for May. Cherry trees were shedding the last of their blossoms just a few blocks away, but here, the odor of fish and overripe fruit mingled with the stench of garbage and gas fumes drifted upward, making Chavez thankful for the aromatic tea.

A leather messenger bag hung from a strap over his shoulder. He held his cell phone in his free hand. Six moving dots were superimposed on the screen—a COP, or common operating picture, of the two rabbits and four members of his team.

Jack Ryan, Jr.'s voice buzzed in the tiny, flesh-colored bud in Chavez's ear.

"Adara, you got two white dudes tracking you, fifty feet off your six. Gray sweatshirt. Dark blue hoodie."

"Gotcha," Adara Sherman said, steering clear of professional-sounding words like *copy* or *affirmative* over the radio so as not to arouse the suspicions of passersby—if such a thing was even possible in New York City.

Chavez shot a glance at John Clark, who stood beside him, looking over the rail, holding a cup of coffee. Plain coffee. No rubbery tapioca globs. Clark gave him an it's-your-show shrug.

Chavez took a sip of tea. *Knock it off, guys,* he thought. *You're makin' me look bad.* He watched a lady on the street below wait for her dog to take a dump and then, instead of picking it up, spend two minutes trying to kick the turds into the street without getting any on her shoe. "People are strange when they don't know they're being watched."

"You're half right," Clark said. "People are just strange. Period." He took a deep breath, blowing it out hard the way every older man Chavez had ever met did when re-membering a particular story. "I once watched two Viet-cong for five full minutes while they took a smoke break less than five feet in front of my hide. I could have reached out and touched their Ho Chi Minh sandals." Clark breathed out hard again, settling the memory. "I'd been in country long enough I could understand a little of what they were saying. It took me a minute, but I real-ized these two guys were telling jokes. Funny, but I never thought of them joking with each other, laughing about the same sort of dirty stuff we laughed at . . ."

"What happened?" Chavez asked, regretting the words as soon as they left his lips. He was a soldier. He knew better.

"War happened," Clark said simply. "And that's no laughing matter."

Even after two decades of working with John Clark, and being married to his daughter, the dude could still send a chill up Chavez's spine. At the same time, though he was pushing fifty years old, Ding couldn't help but think he wanted to be John Clark when he grew up.

Ryan's voice broke squelch on the radio again.

"They're giving you the stink eye," he said. *"Counter-surveillance team, maybe."*

Jack Ryan, Jr., was the boss's boss's boss's son. Athletic and smart as anyone Chavez had ever seen, he could think on his feet and read a given situation with near lightning speed. Yeah, he'd been a bit of a rogue, known to chase tail when he should have been focusing on, well, just about anything else. Hell, he'd been all but fired twice—grounded for sure, stuck behind a desk—and that was as good as being fired once you'd tasted field-work. Ding and Clark had both vouched for him—and he'd stepped up. All signs indicated he'd finally matured to match his intellect.

And now he was seeing bogeymen.

There wasn't any countersurveillance team. Chavez knew it. He'd set up the operation.

Ding enjoyed putting together training, but he missed

pounding the pavement, acting several different parts, masking his hunter/killer persona so he could blend in on the street and not look too aggressive. There were few joys in life better than bringing justice to the bad guys—putting warheads on foreheads, they called it. As much fun as it was standing around drinking bubble tea with his father-in-law, he missed being out there with his team.

"*Okay,*" Adara said. Her dot on Chavez's phone showed her moving west on Canal, approaching Elizabeth. "*Dom's staying on the rabbits. I'm going to slow at this shop window and give them a chance to pass.*"

A former Navy corpsman, Adara Sherman had seen action in most of the Stans, where most of the killing was being done these days. A CrossFit fanatic, she was an extremely competent operator, and, more important, dead calm under pressure. She was also romantically involved with Dominic Caruso, the only actual federal officer on the team—seconded to The Campus. Ryan's cousin, Caruso was a Feeb—still on the FBI rolls. Chavez imagined that the tight-ass middle managers in the Bureau—every agency had them—surely wondered what the hell kind of special duty their agent had disappeared to do for such a long period. The director knew. That was enough.

"*Running some countersurveillance, eh, Ding . . .*" Adara said.

Chavez looked at Clark again, more than a little embarrassed that his guys were seeing ghosts. Clark's face remained as passive as one of those stone dudes on Easter Island. Completely unreadable.

As the director of operations for the off-the-books intelligence agency known as The Campus, John Clark was grading Chavez, just as Chavez was grading his team.

This training op had been in motion for the past five hours, with Dave and Lanny playing the role of rabbits. Both former Marines, they were handpicked force-protection specialists for the company—the guys who handled physical security at the building, the Gulfstream, and countersurveillance when the need arose. They'd started early, leading the four members of the operational team on a series of winding surveillance-detection routes that began in Alexandria, Virginia, not far from the financial arbitrage firm Hendley Associates—the name that was on all their paychecks.

Everyone on the team was pro—experienced, tried by fire. But even pros needed periodic training. Tradecraft, like any skill, grew stale when it wasn't used. Clark's motto to practice "not until they got it right, but until they didn't get it wrong" was ingrained in each of them by now. All were naturals, endowed with innate talent that lent itself to surveillance, surveillance-detection runs, surreptitious entry, and, more important, the social engineering that intelligence work required. The life's blood of intelligence work. They practiced defensive tactics as well—and some offensive ones—and firearms. Everyone enjoyed that the most, though no one was carrying today except Clark, Chavez, and Caruso. All of them were highly proficient with firearms—but they also trained extensively for the countless times when they would not have access to one of Samuel Colt's equalizers. Still, situational awareness trumped a gun only until it didn't. They'd arm up when able. Hence the leather BOG—bag o' guns—hanging over Ding's shoulder.

The securities and forensic accounting side of Hendley Associates was a working front, the "white side" that paid for the hidden raison d'être of the firm. Highly sensitive, and generally autonomous from the other intelligence agencies of the United States government, The Campus was conceived and organized in concert between former senator Gerry Hendley and President Jack Ryan.

Ryan Senior took a hands-off approach to their actual assignments. Hendley was an avuncular boss, friendly, strict when he needed to be, in on the planning while at the same time staying out of the way. He left the actual mission execution to the pros, John Clark in particular.

Clark's leadership style had surely developed from the way he liked to operate. He believed strongly in setting parameters and then allowing his team to rattle around inside those boundaries, making their own decisions with the knowledge that could be gained only by someone with boots on the ground. He continued to play an active role, but was stepping back a little, playing elder statesman, and turning more and more of his duties over to Chavez.

The object of this mission was straightforward if not simple—just like the real world. The team was to surveil their rabbits to their hide. Once they learned that location, the team would create a diversion, defeat any security systems, break in, and steal Ding Chavez's prized RAF Credenhill—otherwise known as Hereford—coffee mug. Easy peasy—so long as Dave and Lanny didn't identify them.

The countersurveillance Jack Junior had seen was a nonissue, because it didn't exist. The kid must have dreamed it up.

Midas Jankowski broke squelch next. A retired Delta Force colonel, his voice was calm and resonant, like he'd been born to speak on the radio. *"Adara, no kidding, I got two Asians, one male, one female, just coming off Mott onto Canal, about fifty feet behind you, moving your direction."*

Chavez looked at the dots on his phone, all of them heading east on Canal now.

Ding decided to let it play out. It would be good training—embarrassing as hell for Ryan and Midas, but good. To professionals like these, failure in front of peers was more horrifying than getting shot by an actual enemy.

Time plus distance plus boredom equaled mission fatigue, making the training more realistic—so Chavez made sure the scenario contained large doses of all three.

The rabbits had transferred to the Red Line on the D.C. Metro system, arriving at Union Station with tickets already in hand, just in time to jump on the 8:40 a.m. Northeast Regional Amtrak train going toward Boston. Ding had been proud of the way the team scrambled to make it on board just before the train pulled away. He and Clark had taken the Acela Express ten minutes later, carrying the bag o' guns. As a credentialed FBI agent, Caruso could travel armed virtually anywhere he went in the United States, but the rest of the team needed to go slick in the event they had to follow a rabbit into a museum or onto a commercial airplane. Clark rarely went anywhere without his 1911, and though intelligence work often called for operatives to be unarmed, he knew all too well the dangers of their job. He believed strongly in overwatch that had the ability to provide deadly force quickly when needed. If at all feasible, someone on the team carried the BOG. Caruso carried his Glock as well as Adara's M&P Shield in holsters inside his waistband. This was a drill, but there were additional Shields in the leather BOG, including one for Adara, in case Dom couldn't link up with her.

Chavez and Clark's Acela Express beat the Northeast Regional train to Penn Station in Manhattan by twenty minutes. The rabbits stopped to eat some cheesecake at Junior's off Times Square, then led the team on a merry walk around Central Park, then back to Midtown before boarding the N train to Canal Street.

"Are you running countersurveillance?" Clark asked.

"Nope," Chavez said.

Chavez was no slouch when it came to his tactical background. He had eons of experience in the Army, as a protective officer in the CIA, and a team leader of the multinational Rainbow counterterrorism unit. He'd been there and done that all over the world. He had the T-shirt and the scars to prove it. But Clark was a legend in the intelligence community, which was saying something in a business where anonymity was the rule of the day. A former Navy SEAL and longtime operator for the CIA, the details of Clark's past were fuzzy, if not altogether redacted. Few in the business knew exactly what he'd done, but they knew he'd done it. A lot of it. And knowing that was enough.

Since Clark also happened to be Ding's father-in-law, this added a nuanced layer of stress—and trust—to every operation. They'd worked together long before Ding had met Patsy. John must have approved of the union, because Chavez was still standing upright. He and his father-in-law had gone on to spill blood and have plenty of their own blood spilt.

Clark glanced at his watch—a Victorinox analog, plain but hell for stout. Chavez took another drink of bubble tea. Funny how the boss looking at his watch could make even the most even-keeled person squirm. As assistant director of ops, Chavez was running point on more and more missions, allowing Clark to stand back and quietly observe—while he drank coffee and looked at his watch.

"Something bothering you, Mr. C?" Chavez asked.

It wasn't like Clark to fidget. They'd been together all morning and Clark had just now suffered a tiny crack in his stony composure.

"I'm good," he said, giving the slightest of shrugs as he aimed his thousand-yard stare down East Broadway. Chavez was surprised one of the passersby didn't catch fire. "Just thinking."

Midas spoke again, more urgently this time. *"Guys, no kidding, white male just popped out from Mott on Canal behind the Asian couple. He's juking back and forth, but moving after them with real intent."*

"I see him," Ryan said.

"You're serious?" Caruso said.

Odd, Chavez thought, that Dom would question intel from another member of the team.

"Dead serious," Midas said. *"This guy's wearing a light jacket, khaki slacks. He moves like a cop. I think I caught a glimpse of handcuffs on his belt."*

Ding stood up straighter now.

"Our rabbits are crossing Canal," Adara said. *"Heading south on Elizabeth."*

"Okay," Midas said. *"The Asians and Khaki Slacks are continuing east. I don't see any other coppers. I'm guessing this guy is off duty."*

"Or some kind of hit," Jack Junior offered. *"No kidding."*

"Out of role, Ding," Adara said. *"Out of role."*

Ding reached in his pocket and flipped the isolation switch on his radio so everyone could hear him. "Abort the scenario," he said. "I say again, abort scenario. Keep your distance, but hang with the lone dude in khakis just in case. Who has eyes on the two white males you spotted? They are not mine."

"Forget them," Adara said. *"Those two are a nonissue. A little game in order to win, Boss. We'll explain later."*

"Yes, you will," Chavez said. "Confirming, no one else in play besides two Asians and Khaki Pants."

"That is correct," Adara said.

Chavez bit back the urge to chide her. Instead, he coordinated team movement while Clark called Lanny's cell and got the rabbits on the common frequency so they'd be in the loop.

"Everybody stay loose," Ding said. "We don't want to step in the middle of another agency's op."

Midas piped up. *"Asian couple turning right on Bowery."*

"Okay," Ding said. "Lanny and Dave, keep going south on Elizabeth. Midas, how about Khaki Pants?"

"Approaching Bayard," Midas said. *"He's locked on. If he had a team, somebody else would be taking over the eyeball about now. I'm thinking he's alone."* There was a pause, like Midas was trying to get a better look at something. *"The Asian male has a pistol in his waistband."*

"John and I are coming off the bridge," Ding said, picturing the map in his head as he ran. "We'll cut behind Confucius Plaza to stay ahead of you. Dom, hang a left at your next cross street. Hustle over to Canal so you guys can leapfrog with Midas if need be."

"Adara and I are east on Bayard," Dom said.

Jack Junior spoke next. *"Coming down Bowery—"*

The radio bonked, meaning two people attempted to speak at the same moment, leaving both transmissions garbled.

Dom came over the net, breathless.

"I know this guy," he said. The jostling in his voice suggested he was jogging. *"He's FBI. His name's Nick Sutton."*

"The Asian couple just turned right," Midas said. *"The next street past Bayard. Sutton's still on them. I've lost the eye."*

"I'll move closer," Dom said. *"See if I can catch his attention—"*

The radio fell silent. Seconds later, Dom came back, breathless, running.

"Man . . . down," he said.

3

Caruso swept aside the tail of his jacket to draw his Glock. His eyes were up, scanning. Nick Sutton lay slumped in the grimy concrete stairwell leading below street level next to the entrance of a nail salon. The steel door to the basement behind him was closed, forming a concrete pit at the bottom of the steps. It would have been an easy matter to hide and ambush the agent when he came by. Caruso had heard no shots. The half-dozen pedestrians coming and going down Doyers either hadn't seen anything or had simply ignored what they saw.

"It's Dom," Caruso said, stepping around Sutton in the cramped space and trying the door while Adara assessed the agent's wounds. "We're here for you, bud." He wanted to drop to his knees and help, but neither he nor Adara would be any help if they got shot.

Arterial blood painted a massive arc on the concrete wall. Even now, after years on the job, Dom found himself astonished at the apparent gusto with which blood left the human body. If anyone besides a trauma surgeon could save Nick Sutton now, it was Adara Sherman.

Dom shielded Adara as best he could in the small alcove, then, pistol tucked in tight against his ribs, pulled on the door handle with his left hand. It was locked tight. That didn't mean much. Caruso had read somewhere that there were tunnels all over Chinatown. Sutton's attackers could have gone through the door or just walked away—in which case they would be walking directly into Chavez and Clark.

Caruso jumped back on the radio. "They may be coming your way, Ding."

The radio clicked twice, signifying Chavez had heard.

Dom fished the FBI badge out of his shirt and let it dangle on a chain around his neck. The Bureau badge carried a lot of weight, but it was relatively small. The little gold shield would do little to avert a blue-on-blue shooting if another cop showed up pumped with adrenaline, but it was better than standing beside a bloody body brandishing a gun without it.

Pistol in low-ready, he stood over Adara and the wounded agent, scanning the doorways and windows along Doyers—the street known as the "Bloody Angle," where Chinese tong hatchet men stained the street red, hacking rival gang members to death in the early days of New York.

"Talk to me, Nick," Adara said. "Can you hear me?"

Sutton mumbled something Dom couldn't make out.

"We're gonna get you fixed up," Adara said, her voice grim. "Ambulance is on the way."

Dom glanced down at her blood-soaked phone on the steps.

Sutton moaned. Despite Adara's efforts, he was losing a lot of blood.

"They're long gone," Dom said. "What do you need me to do?"

She pointed to Sutton's armpit. "You can help me with this artery. There's another bleeder somewhere and I need to find it."

Caruso holstered his weapon and knelt across from Adara. She used two fingers to hand off a spaghetti-like end of Sutton's brachial artery. A gaping three-inch gash laid bare the meat and bone of his upper arm. Two smaller wounds framed the gash like bloody parentheses. The blood and gore made it difficult to tell how many times Sutton had been stabbed, but his wounds were many and deep. His aggressor had gone for his neck, but he'd been able to get his arm up, taking most of the damage to his triceps and his ribs—small consolation, since such a wound only meant he would bleed to death at a slightly slower rate than he would if he'd had his throat cut.

Sirens wailed in the distance.

Sutton gave a rattling cough. His eyes fluttered open, and he appeared to see Caruso for the first time.

Adara pressed her palm over a hissing stab wound in his chest, doing her best to seal it until paramedics arrived.

"Dom?" Sutton coughed again, croaking, wincing from the effort.

With his hand literally half buried in Sutton's flesh, Caruso could feel the man's hummingbird pulse—rapid but extremely weak, as his heart worked to deliver the little blood left in his system to his brain.

The agent blinked. "What . . . What are you doing here?"

"Tell you later, bud," Caruso said. "Who did this to you?"

"Rene . . ." He coughed again. "She stabbed the shit outta me. Rene Peng . . . hiding down here while I followed her husband . . ." Sutton swallowed. "You got any water? I'm really thirsty."

"Sorry," Dom said. "We'll get an IV in you as soon as the ambulance arrives. Save your strength."

Sutton shook his head. "Pengs are Chinese nationals. Run . . . snakeheads out of the docks." He shuddered, spit out a mouthful of blood, then stopped to catch his breath.

"Ambulance is almost here," Adara said.

"Trying to get these bastards for months . . . Took my wife and kid to Vincent's . . . damned if I didn't see Rene walk by on the street . . ."

Sutton's eyes widened. "My wife . . . I told her to wait . . . at restaurant."

"I'll go get her," Dom said. "We'll bring her to the hospital so she can visit with you."

"Thanks . . . dude," Sutton said, panting harder now. "Oh, man . . . I should . . . never have brought Melissa here . . ."

Caruso patted the agent's cheek, gently but firmly. "Stay with us, Nick. No going to sleep. Where do you think Rene Peng is going?"

"No idea," Sutton said, his words slurred. "If I woulda known that, I coulda caught 'em already . . ."

Ding's voice broke squelch on the radio. *"We have a woman wearing a white ball cap coming at us on East Broadway, toward the bridge. She's restrained, like she's trying to look relaxed but isn't. There's a guy with sunglasses and blue hoodie about three steps behind her."*

"That has to be them." Dom looked down at Sutton's wounds. "There's no way she doesn't have blood on her. Either that or she changed shirts."

"Stand by," Chavez said. *"She's walking past me now . . ."* He whispered the next. *"Bingo on the blood. It's them, all right."*

The swath of red across the front of Rene Peng's shirt was almost hidden by her arms. Her husband moved up beside her as she passed Ding, stuffing a cell phone back into his pocket and trotting to catch up as if he'd been on a call. He said something to her and they both laughed.

"Heartless bitch," Ding mumbled, ignoring Clark as he came out of a little bodega and fell in behind the couple. Ding fell back, taking a moment to check out a vendor with a table full of used books in Chinese.

"I have the eyeball," Clark said. "Half a block from the bridge."

"Nearly there," Midas said. *"We'll trap them in a pincer—"*

"Let's hold off on that," Clark said. "If it looks like they're going to get away, we'll take them."

"John," Dom said, the need for vengeance straining in his voice. *"They slashed the hell out of an FBI agent."*

"And he was after them for a reason," Clark said. "Let's see where they're going. Dom, Adara, you deal with the police. The rest of you move toward the bridge. Let's get a net around these bastards."

At first it looked like the Pengs might take the Manhattan Bridge pedestrian walkway that led over the East River to Brooklyn. Instead, they stayed on East Broadway, going under the bridge, then paralleled the bridge along Forsyth Street. It looked like a county fair. Folding tables were laid out for several blocks, covered with assorted produce, from dragon fruit to durian—things Chinese people, not tourists, came to buy. Wizened faces sat under the makeshift shade of blue plastic tarps or large canvas umbrellas. Boxes of fruit were stacked high on the sidewalks behind the vendors. Refrigerated box trucks lined the streets.

It was still early enough that sunlight hit this side of the bridge, and the odor of fish and trash from the shadowed side streets gave way to the fruity perfume of the vendors.

Clark hung back a hundred feet or so, head down, shoulders hunched a little. Ding had fallen in behind him shortly after he'd taken over the eyeball, matching his pace but staying in the crowd of pedestrians.

With her back to Clark, Rene Peng stopped at a fruit stand where the street above began to curve back to the east over the sidewalk. Garret walked a few steps past her, glancing up at the pedestrian walk overhead, and then across Forsyth. He seemed tense, but Rene moved fluidly, now calm as a summer morning. She picked up a pear, held it to her nose, chatting amiably with the woman at the scale. The old woman nodded, looked up, past Clark, toward Ding. She leaned forward and whispered something. Rene held up the pear as if she was about to buy it—and then bolted.

The pear seemed to hang in midair for a long moment.

"They're running north on Forsyth!" Clark snapped. "Toward Confucius Plaza and the bridge ramp. They may try and split up."

Rene shot a glance over her shoulder, toward Clark again. She shouted in Chinese to her husband, and then both of them dug in, picking up their pace.

"Get after them, Ding!" Clark said. He'd done more than his share of running over the years, but it was no longer his strong suit. In any case, he had other ideas. "Jack, tell me you're at the northeast corner of the bridge."

"They're in sight," Ryan said.

Ding ran past Clark, the leather bag o' guns looped over his shoulder, bouncing on his back.

"I'm here, too, Boss," Midas said. *"We got it all covered, the steps, Canal. Dave is posted in front of the Greek Orthodox church."*

"Outstanding," Clark said. "Ding, cut to the east side of the street near Dave. They may split up."

"John, they'll see me—"

"Do it now!" Clark snapped, leaving no room for argument. "The rest of you spread out. Give me a ten-count, then make yourselves known. Remember, this pair just tried to murder an FBI agent. Ding and I are the only ones armed at the moment."

Scanning the street for the nearest available weapon—there was always something—he snatched up a broom handle from one of the fruit stands as he walked past and began using it like a walking stick. He didn't run, hardly even looked up. The old man at the table simply nodded as if he knew what Clark had planned, or didn't care.

One way or another, this was going to be over soon.

"Now," Clark said, reaching his own ten-count. "Let them see you. Grab them both if you can. If not . . ."

"She's coming at you, John," Midas said, clipped but in control.

Half a moment later, Ding came over the radio. "The male is on the ground. You were right. They split up."

Clark continued to walk north, using his peripheral vision to watch Rene Peng as she got closer. She looked well past him, as if he wasn't even there. He could see the knife in her hand, half drawn up in her sleeve. A half-grin perked the corners of her lips, as if she thought she'd won. Clark stopped as if to catch his breath as she got nearer, looking up at the spectacle of someone being chased—as anyone might do. He rested both hands on the stick, loosely, absent any apparent threat, careful not to catch her eye directly. One of the few benefits to being old in this line of work was becoming invisible.

She never saw the broomstick coming. Clark swung it hard, aiming *through* instead of *at* her knee. He used one hand, swordlike, but put his hips into it, pivoting as he turned. Rene Peng was not a tall woman, but she had an incredibly long stride. The heavy stick connected with an audible crack while her leg was flexed and in the air. Wood and bone shattered on impact. The force of her foot hitting the pavement exacerbated the damage, causing her to crumple in a screaming heap.

Sirens yelped on Canal, just a few hundred yards away.

Rene tried to push herself up, the blade still clutched in her fist. Clark let her have another well-aimed strike with what was left of the broomstick, aiming for the bleachers as he took out her right elbow.

The knife—still smeared in Nick Sutton's blood—clattered to the pavement at the same time a white NYPD cruiser fishtailed onto Forsyth from Canal. Clark dropped the stick and stepped out of the street onto the sidewalk, not running, but moving with purpose. He faded into the gathering crowd, making it almost to the underpass by the time the cruiser reached the injured woman. Dom had described her and her husband as dangerous and possibly having weapons, so the responding officers were more interested in getting her handcuffed than they were in who might be running from the scene.

A second set of officers found Garret Peng, his jaw broken in two places, handcuffed to a standpipe next to the Greek Orthodox church.

"Everyone clear?" Clark said once he was sure responding officers had not only the woman but her bloody knife in custody.

Everyone was. Except Dom and Adara.

The ambulance disappeared down Doyers Street, sounding the air horn periodically to move traffic and mindless pedestrians aside as it jumped on Bowery toward NewYork-Presbyterian Hospital. The proximity to One Police Plaza and the New York Field Office of the FBI left the narrow street crawling with responding uniforms and Feds.

A ruddy blond agent named Bolton, hands encased in blue nitrile gloves, appeared to be the one in charge of the scene. He nodded to an Asian NYPD officer, who led

MANHATTAN—CHINATOWN

CANAL STREET

MOTT STREET

ELIZABETH STREET

BOWERY

FORSYTH STREET

N

BOWERY

✗ TAKEDOWN

ATTACK SITE
✗
DOYERS STREET

E. BROADWAY

MANHATTAN BRIDGE

© 2019 Jeffrey L. Ward

Adara to the back of her patrol car under the auspices of getting her cleaned up.

Caruso shook his head in disbelief, biting his tongue so he didn't say something he'd regret.

"What?" Bolton said, studying Caruso's credentials. "Something on your mind?"

"Seriously," Dom said. "You're splitting up my girlfriend and me like we're suspects?"

"Everybody's a suspect," Bolton said. "You know that."

"We called you, remember?"

"Matter of fact, I do," Bolton said. "So let's go over that again, shall we? You, an FBI agent, just happened to stumble onto Sutton, also an FBI agent, who stumbled onto someone who then stabbed him?"

"That's about the size of it," Caruso said.

"How'd you know him?"

"Sutton was in the academy that overlapped mine. I thought I recognized him on the street and we came over to say hi. We found him here."

"Seems awfully convenient," Bolton said. "What office are you out of?"

"Director's," Caruso said.

Bolton looked at him through narrowed eyes as he handed back the credential case. "Be that as it may, I'll need a written supplement from you."

"Of course." Caruso shrugged. "It'll be about three lines long, but I get that you need it. Listen, Sutton said he left his wife and kid at Vincent's, over on Mott. Somebody needs to go and let her know what happened. She should be with him at the hospital."

"I'll do that," a familiar female voice called from around Bolton's SUV. Caruso glanced up to find Special Agent Kelsey Callahan walking his way. Her auburn hair was shorter than it had been when he worked with her in Dallas. He was surprised to see her in New York. She'd been doing a hell of a job running the North Texas regional task force focused on human trafficking.

"I thought you were in Texas," Caruso said, smiling despite the blood that painted the front of his shirt.

"I still am," Callahan said. "The powers that be detailed me here for a couple of months to cross-pollinate the Interdiction for the Protection of Children techniques we're using in Texas with task force here in NYFO. Human smuggling is human smuggling, you know. Turns out there's a hell of a lot of it going on in New York City—much of it right smack in the middle of Chinatown, if you can believe such a thing. You got your sex workers, domestic servants locked in basements after their eighteen-hour days, your garment industry slaves—and, as it turns out, a hell of a lot of undeclared spies. Sometimes their duties overlap. Rene and Garret Peng were two that kept floating to the top like the turds they are. I perked up when their names came out over the radio a few minutes ago when you or somebody called nine-one-one. And you know everyone responds when we hear an agent down . . ." She stared at him hard, then glanced at Adara, giving her a once-over. "So this is the girlfriend?"

"She is indeed," Caruso said. "Adara Sherman."

"I heard she saved Sutton's life." Callahan looked up and down the street, even checking the roofline, as if she expected to find someone working overwatch. "So, your mature badass friend isn't with you? John . . . what was his name again?"

Caruso gave her a Cheshire cat grin but kept a tight lip.

Callahan heaved a deep sigh and then patted Bolton on the shoulder. "You may as well cut them loose, Sean," she said. "Take it from one who knows, you're gonna get a call from the special agent in charge in about a millisecond, directing you to turn them loose anyway. It's easier on the ego if it's your decision."

She hooked a thumb over her shoulder toward her car. "Come on, you two. Let's go get Sutton's wife to the hospital. I've got a couple of raid jackets you can put on over your bloody shirts so you don't terrify the locals. Nick is a good soul. He's a counterintelligence weenie, but we get along well enough. A good portion of the human cargo the snakeheads smuggle into the U.S. comes here under false promises, putting them in the trafficked-human category. Snakeheads and spies naturally overlap, and so did a ton of our cases." She rummaged through her trunk until she found two dark windbreakers with FBI emblazoned on the back in large yellow letters. Callahan gave one to Caruso and one to Adara. "I'm not sure who you guys are," she said, "or what you're up to, but whatever it is, I'm glad you were doing it here in New York. Sutton was working on some sketchy people." Callahan leaned in closer. "Spies," she said. "Apparently, they're all over the damn place."

4

Father Pat West stood on the hillside trail eating longan fruit and pondering sin. Large tea plantations covered most of the hills north of Bandung near Lembang, but this spot was relatively wild, carpeted with ferns and native vegetation, a likely place for a run with his local chapter of Hash House Harriers. The sun was still low and orange, not yet high enough to burn away the morning fog that still shrouded the green mountains. It was as good a time as any to reflect on his own lapses in judgment. He'd committed enough of them in his sixty-two years, a few doozies, in fact. If there was one thing he'd learned after entering the priesthood, it was that everyone had a few doozies when it came to sin. The government had even given him commendations for some of his—in a former life. For good or bad, he was an expert on sinning. He certainly recognized it when he saw it get out of a Toyota along the dirt road halfway down the hill. Head turning this way and that like a lost bantam rooster, the strange little newcomer was dressed in running shorts and a lime-green T-shirt. West chuckled sadly to himself. The shirt was a sin in and of itself.

The priest held one longan fruit—the size of a jumbo

grape—between his thumb and forefinger as he watched the strange man approach. He squeezed firmly until the leathery skin broke and revealed the translucent fruit inside. Tossing the skin, he popped the syrupy white glob into his mouth and then spit the hard mahogany-colored seed into the bushes. It was an oddly soothing process, helping West think. It reminded him of watching his grandfather eat peanuts on the front porch of his home in Virginia.

The newcomer spoke for a moment to a man named Rashguard—one of the Kiwi Hashers who was down getting a plastic cooler out of his car. Rashguard pointed directly at West. The newcomer nodded, then looked uphill with a gaseous expression before beginning the steep trudge from the parking area.

Through the trees, on the winding road below, more car doors slammed. Odd, West thought, to have so many visitors on the same day.

The priest was dressed for running—or, rather, fast walking. He'd run a great deal as a younger man, for enjoyment and as part of his rigorous training. He'd done a lot of things he regretted back then. One of his mentors, a man not much older than he was but with a lifetime's more experience, had once watched him hoist a ninety-pound rucksack full of communications equipment and sling it nonchalantly over his back. "One of these days," his teacher had said, "you're going to regret *this* moment—lifting *that* ruck, *that* way."

And West did.

He remembered many exact moments, moments that left all manner of damage that he hadn't realized when he was young and foolish and looking for adventure . . . Now, his creaky knees protested if he ran more than half a mile. Any farther than that and he found it difficult to stand and give the liturgy at Mass the following day.

Seven other Hashers from the Bandung chapter of the Hash House Harriers stood at the starting area a dozen yards uphill. This included the "hare," who'd already laid out the trail. The hare would leave momentarily, but did not want to miss out on the socializing before the event started. All the runners in the group were men, a mix of Europeans, Aussies, and Kiwis. West was the only American.

Started in the thirties by a British Army officer in Malaysia, Hash House Harriers was often described as a drinking group with a running problem. The Bandung group still drank, but they were more discreet than Hashers in other areas, aware of the Muslim sensibilities in this country.

A few hours to run and joke with friends each week was Father West's small break from the work of overseeing Catholic relief efforts from Bandung to Papua. Hash runs were his little sin of indulgence.

Having eaten all his longan fruit, West began his stretch while the newcomer hiked up the hill toward him. The air was oppressively humid and unmercifully hot, as it always was in this part of God's vineyard. But the moist heat turned the mountain into a dense wall of green jungle in every direction. Banana, durian, and papaya grew wild on the hills. Locals often joked that a stray cigarette butt would produce a tobacco plant in a matter of days. It would probably not be long before longan trees began to sprout from the seeds he'd spit out. Countless varieties of flowers fed countless insects, and the insects fed countless birds. Lizards skittered through the foliage. Macaque monkeys hooted in the treetops. Between the buzzing, chirping, and howling, the place was as loud as it was lush.

In order to reach Father West, the newcomer had to take a long set of switchbacks, putting him within yards of a small group of shanties set back in the jungle along a fast-moving stream that tumbled down from the mountains. A dozen eyes watched from the shadows, waiting to see which way he would go.

The hares tried as best they could to lay the course through uninhabited areas, but Indonesia was densely populated with many living in dire circumstances. It was inevitable that they crossed paths with beggars. Father Pat carried a few thousand rupiah for that purpose. When approached by a group, he'd direct them to Catholic services—careful to keep his words secular in this fiercely Muslim country—but he didn't have the heart to say no to an individual.

Runs were open to everyone. Newcomers gave the group someone else to poke fun at. Hangdog and angry-looking at the same time, with the countenance of a piece of coal, this one was a likely candidate.

"Hi," the man said. "Is . . . this . . . the . . . Hash run?"

"It is," West said.

"Thank God." The man bent over, hands on his knees, panting from the short walk.

"Thank God, indeed." West hoped his outward smile

hid his inward groan. "Welcome on behalf of the Bandung Hash House Harriers. Budgy has the guestbook up next to the flags. You will need to sign in."

The man stuck out a hand, still bracing against a knee with the other. He swallowed hard from climbing the short distance in the heat. The trail only got worse from here. Even walking was obviously going to prove a challenge for this one.

"Geoff . . . Noonan."

"Father Pat West."

"No shit?" Noonan said, still catching his breath. "You're the priest from the pic on the website?"

"Indeed," West said again.

"You look different," Noonan said. "But I'm glad I found you. You're the reason I'm here."

West helped him sign in and introduced him to the rest of the group.

"I'm not Catholic," Noonan continued, after introductions and Hash business was finished and the run began. He kept checking over his shoulder, addled about something. Burdened. The people who came to Father West were often that way. "I'm not anything, really," he went on. "I mean, my wife drags me to church, but they don't do formal confessions there. Still, I got some stuff I really need to get off my chest. It . . . I don't know . . . It needs a pro. An American pro. You guys are good at confessions. Everybody knows it."

West heaved a heavy sigh, repenting of his earlier impatience. As odd as this young man was, he'd come for help.

"I found you online," Noonan continued. "I called this morning. The guy said I'd find you here. Can you do it? Take a confession, I mean."

"Why don't we just speak as friends?" West said. "If talking about things that bother you gives you comfort, then that is good enough for the time being. I am happy to listen."

Noonan gave an emphatic nod. "Yeah," he said, breathless with worry. "Yeah, I guess that would work."

He spilled his guts for the next ten minutes, admitting that he'd been weak and slept with a Sundanese woman he'd met in a bar. For some reason, he made a point of saying that the woman wasn't "all that good-looking," as if cheating on your wife with a homely girl made it less of a sin. Noonan began to go into explicit detail about what he'd done with the woman. For a moment, West thought he might be one of those people who got some gratification from bragging about their behavior. Then Noonan began to weep in earnest, tears accompanied by the appropriate amount of flowing snot. Perhaps the sorrow was just over being caught, but it was sorrow nonetheless.

"I know I did wrong," Noonan said, scuffing his feet in the loamy ground as he walked.

Here it comes, West thought. The mitigation. *I did wrong, but I'm not to blame, and this is why.*

"The thing is," Noonan continued. "It was all a setup."

The way he said it made the hair on the back of West's neck stand on end. "A setup?"

Noonan nodded emphatically. "Yeah. Some guys who said they were Indonesian policemen busted in from the bathroom and caught us in the act. They threatened to tell my wife—"

West stopped on the trail. "They entered from the bathroom?"

"Yes," Noonan said.

"Does the bathroom have exterior doors?"

"No."

"Do you think they were waiting in there the entire time?"

"I took a leak before we . . . you know . . . Shower's pretty small. I didn't see anybody." Noonan scratched his head. "I never thought about it like that."

"Did these men want money?"

"That's the thing," Noonan said. "Not at all. I offered to pay them, but they wanted something else."

West felt himself putting on an old hat that he'd been all too happy to take off. He looked from side to side, instinctively checking over his shoulder. The other Hashers had pulled well ahead, so he was alone now with the newcomer. Somehow he knew that with one more question he'd slip inexorably into his previous life.

"What did these men want?"

"Something from my work."

The way Noonan glossed over it piqued West's curiosity. He tipped his head toward the gaudy T-shirt. "I assume you're in some kind of tech field. Computers?"

"Software," Noonan said. "I work for Parnassus, a computer game company in Boston."

West picked up his pace. It was difficult to think about two things at once, and if Noonan had to focus on where to put his feet, he might be more forthcoming.

"That must be an interesting job."

"I hate it," Noonan said. "My bosses don't like me, my coworkers don't like me . . ."

Imagine that, West thought, but he said nothing.

"Anyway," Noonan continued. "The engineer I work with set up this deal that made us a shitload of money, but . . ." He paused, peering at West through the dim light filtering down through the jungle canopy. "I really only wanted to tell you about how I messed around on my wife."

"As you wish," West said. "I only ask because it seems like something else is troubling you. I can see it in your eyes."

"You can?"

"I can," West said honestly.

Noonan walked in silence for two full minutes before glancing sideways at the priest. "It's just . . . I think I got in way over my head on this. My partner, another software engineer at Parnassus, we developed this software that's like nothing I've ever seen. It's going to revolutionize the industry."

"So it's worth a lot of money?"

Noonan took a deep breath. "A shitload . . . sorry, Father."

"And these Indonesian men who came from your bathroom tricked you into sleeping with a woman in order to get this software?"

"Two Indonesians and a different Asian guy," Noonan said. "I heard him speak to the woman. I think it might have been Chinese. Pretty sure he was the one in charge."

West filed that away but didn't comment.

"Did you give them the software?"

"Hell, yes, I gave it to them! They kind of had me at a disadvantage when they busted in." Noonan licked his lips. "Man, I'm thirsty."

"This trail makes a big loop," West said. "We're almost back to the cars."

"Good," Noonan said. "Listen, Padre, I sure appreciate you lending me your ear."

"No problem at all," West said. A few steps later he said, "This software must be very special."

"Oh, it is. To be honest, I had two copies when I came to Jakarta. My partner set up a deal to sell one of them to another company before the other dudes took one of the drives." Noonan chuckled.

"Why two copies?"

"I don't know," Noonan said. "Insurance, I guess. That Chinese guy is going to be surprised when he finds out someone else has the software." His head snapped up, coming to a sudden realization before he wilted. "Shit, that means he'll probably still tell my wife."

"You should tell your wife," West said.

"Yeah, maybe," Noonan said. "But that's not happening. At least not until I tell her about the money I got from selling Calliope. She might be more forgiving when she's a millionaire."

"Calliope," West mused. "Can I ask what makes it so special?"

"You know what an NPC is?"

West shook his head. "Afraid not."

"Non-player character," Noonan said. "You play Ghost Recon or Halo?"

"No," West said. "But I've seen them played."

"Well, the guys onscreen who are reacting to you as the player—bad guys, fellow good guys, bystanders—those are all NPCs."

"Okay."

"The industry uses deep learning, you know, AI, to help these NPCs make their decisions more lifelike."

"Artificial intelligence?"

"Exactly," Noonan said, with the exuberance of someone talking about his life's work. "We add actions to make the NPCs more realistic, you know, rolling off a roof when they come on scene, jumping out of an open Jeep instead of opening the door. But sometimes the NPCs pick up these actions by themselves. Like they're learning from the players. It drives the compulsion loop like crazy."

"Compulsion loop?"

"You know," Noonan said. "The thing that makes a player keep playing, gets them hooked on the game, so to speak."

"You actually call it that? The compulsion loop?"

"Oh, yeah," Noonan said. "It's a vital part of the game. Otherwise, everyone might just go outside and play soccer."

Father Pat gave a resigned sigh. That was a discussion for another time. "So your software has something to do with artificial intelligence?"

"That's exactly what it is. To be honest, we didn't develop it. We developed the computer that developed it. The idea is to give the NPC—your partner in the video game, if you will—some kind of reward for moving forward."

"And your Calliope goes beyond that?"

"There've been a hell of a . . . sorry, a heck of a lot of advancements into AI, but this is beyond the next big thing." Noonan became more animated as he spoke, absent the plodding fatigue that he'd arrived with, now that he was talking about something important to him. "As it is, once a game learns how to play, say, chess, the computer is pretty much unstoppable when you tell it to play. NPCs in modern video games can seem pretty lifelike in their actions."

"Okay . . ." West said, prodding gently.

"The thing is," Noonan said, "up to now, NPCs . . . have been reactive."

"But your software is different?"

"Oh, yeah," Noonan said. "We built off a Fristonian theory called Free Energy. Our software, our NPC, explores the boundaries. It's inquisitive, behaving very much like a human player—and a shit-hot human player at that."

Noonan continued into the intricacies of Karl Friston's theories, but West's brain was already looking at a larger picture. Completely engrossed in thoughts of what China could do with this kind of artificial intelligence, he was more than a little startled to find that the trail had already looped back around and they were just a few hundred feet from the cars.

"A breakthrough, then?" West slowed to negotiate the sloppy scree and rotting vegetation as they worked their way downhill.

"I'm here to tell you it's worth millions."

It's worth more than that, West thought, but he didn't say it. Instead, he asked: "Humor an unlearned priest for a moment. In one sentence, what makes it so unique?"

Noonan nodded emphatically. "One sentence?"

"As best you can."

"Simple," Noonan said. "You assign Calliope a mission, and she heads off to solve the problem. Turn her loose in the game and she will perform whatever mission you ask."

"Without you?" West tried to wrap his head around that.

"Yep," Noonan said.

"Would this Calliope perform the same way in the Cloud?"

"I think so," Noonan said. "She wants to play. Where isn't the issue with her."

"That sounds like—"

A withered woman who looked seventy but was likely in her late forties shuffled out of the jungle on the trail ahead, making a beeline for Noonan. She was dressed in rags. Mud and soot smudged her sunken cheeks. The old woman proved amazingly nimble on the switchbacks, considering how bent she was. To Noonan's horror, she grabbed him by the arm with gnarled hands and tried to drag him back into the undergrowth toward her small hovel. Her animated chatter might make anyone not fluent in Sundanese think she was extremely angry.

Noonan yielded when she first touched him, going along with her a few steps before finally coming to his senses and digging his heels into the dirt. The old woman looked too light to keep her feet in a strong wind, let alone pull a stocky man anywhere he did not want to go. Unable to move him, she turned up the volume of her pleas, giving him toothless smiles and pointing toward the shadows while she chattered.

Father West took a wad of several thousand rupiah from the pocket of his running shorts—it took fourteen thousand to make one U.S. dollar.

"She wants you to visit her home," he explained to Noonan. "She believes the gesture will demonstrate her poor circumstance and hopefully convince you she is not tricking you into giving her a handout."

West pressed the money into the old woman's hands, trying gently to send her on her way.

She took the money but did not leave, continuing to yank Noonan's arm, glancing behind her as if she had an audience in the trees.

West felt the desperate urge to make a call, to give someone the intelligence that he'd heard. He kept one eye on the old woman while he checked his phone. No signal. None of this felt right. There was no doubt in his mind that young Noonan's honey trap was engineered by a foreign government. But if that were the case, why had they let him live after he'd turned over such valuable software?

West's previous training, long subdued by meditation and study, kicked into high gear. The jungle shadows suddenly took on an electric feel, charged with static and danger. The priest hadn't felt this exposed since . . . well, since he'd been on the job, running operations in far-flung corners of the world where discovery would have meant certain death.

Noonan had described the men who'd surprised him in his room as Indonesians and an Asian. Chinese? Maybe. Ethnic Chinese got blamed for everything here, like some countries used Jews as scapegoats, blaming them for their woes—because they were generally prosperous and owned so many businesses. Still, Indonesia did a lot of business with mainland China. Mistrusted or not, they had a real presence in the country. West nodded absentmindedly to himself—a subconscious trait his instructors at The Farm had trained out of him decades before. China was the real threat. The Chicoms—*Did anyone call them that anymore?*—were all over artificial intelligence. He'd read somewhere that they were supposed to be the world leader in AI by 2025. They would certainly want to get their hands on the kind of next-level tech Noonan's software apparently provided.

West groaned, repenting for letting himself get caught up in the game again. That life was behind him. He needed to get off this mountain. The moment he got a signal, he'd make a call to tell someone with the authority to follow up. Maybe it was nothing. Either way, he'd do his duty and make the call—then wash his hands of the entire thing.

The old woman finally gave up and shuffled sullenly back to the shadows, squatting down in front of her shack—like a spider, situating herself to rush out and meet the next passerby.

"I gotta hit the crapper, Padre," Noonan said, looking around.

West really hated when people called him that. "There's an outhouse of sorts just beyond your car."

He didn't have the heart or patience to explain that there wouldn't be any toilet paper, just a bucket of water and a dipper.

Other Hashers mingled slightly uphill for down-downs—punishments for bad behavior or "crimes" during the run. It involved a toilet seat and chugged alcohol—all in good fun, but West refused to get too crazy doing something that could end up on social media, so he was generally immune. He could push it only so far, though, and ignoring the closing ceremony to make a phone call was a sure way to get called out—even as a priest.

He chanced it and moved down the hill with Noonan, stopping halfway to check his phone again. Two bars. He stopped and tried to make a call, but it didn't connect. West stared at the cell phone, watched Noonan trot toward the wooden structure. Two Indonesian men got out of a battered Toyota that was parked beside Noonan's car. Then two more, probably Chinese, got out of the same car. Seemingly oblivious to them in his urgent condition, Noonan ducked around the outhouse to locate the door.

Keeping his phone low, West began to type a text message with his thumb. His stomach fell as the taller of the two Asians left the car and disappeared around the outhouse after Noonan. The stockier of the two, with thinning hair and a quiet demeanor, remained by the vehicle. Certainly Chinese, he was probably from the Ministry of State Security, the MSS, China's version of the old KGB. West had a knack for spotting intelligence officers. The stocky man said something to the two

Indonesians and nodded up the hill toward West. They'd obviously seen Noonan speaking with him. West typed faster, surely misspelling words, but not taking time to edit. He hit send when the men were twenty feet away. Still no signal. He hit the send key again, then held down the power button to turn off the device.

Both men began shouting at once; one of them flashed a badge and produced a large Glock, which he began brandishing at the end of a noodle arm. The rank-and-file Indonesian police officers carried Taurus revolvers, so these had to be from a special unit—not tactical, just special.

They reached him quickly. The one without the gun snatched his phone away.

"What did that man tell you?" he asked in clipped, accented English, pointing to the outhouse. He held the phone aloft next to his face, a parent looking for an explanation. "Did you make a call?"

West shook his head, hands up, putting on his naïve-bystander act. Pretending to be incredulous would only infuriate men like this. Citizens often called the police crocodiles—*buaya*—and referred to themselves as geckos—*cikak*—a David-and-Goliath thing. It did no good to anger the crocodile.

"I never met him before this morning," West said. "He's here for the Hash run. That's all."

The man who'd taken his phone slapped West hard, his voice rising an octave. "You lie! You were on the phone!"

The priest flushed, white-hot anger welling up in his gut. He bit his lip in an effort to control himself. Even at his age, he could have killed these two before they realized they were in well over their officious heads. But the Chinese man with thinning hair had already started uphill. He was the one in charge, and he would surely have a gun. The taller one had yet to emerge from behind the outhouse. Geoff Noonan was in serious trouble.

Hands raised in defeat, West blinked. He took stock of where both policemen stood, their backs downhill, slightly off balance. Amateurs. The one with his phone struck him again. He was ready this time, and recoiled with the blow, robbing it of any real power.

"What do you want from me?"

"Your friend," the policeman barked. "What did he tell you?"

"He's not my friend," West said, rubbing his face. "I said that already. Now please stop hitting me. I haven't done anything wrong."

The policemen looked at each other, then down the hill for guidance. They appeared to have no plan beyond yelling and hitting. The tall Chinese man emerged from behind the outhouse—wiping blood off his hands on a white handkerchief. Noonan was nowhere to be seen. West took a half-step forward, as if to go investigate, but the bullish policeman cuffed him in the back of his head.

Both Chinese men arrived at roughly the same time, the taller eyeing West like he was a piece of meat. The one with thinning hair—the boss—had more of an uphill climb. He stood for a moment to catch his breath.

"Did they speak?" the taller one asked, looking at the policeman but gesturing to West.

Both Indonesian men nodded.

The tall man hooked a thumb over his shoulder toward

the jungle behind the outhouse. "Bring him," he said in Bahasa Indonesian.

Another blow to the back of the head sent West staggering forward. The policemen began to herd him along the hillside toward the outhouse. All for turning the other cheek in most circumstances, West decided he would kill the tall Chinese man before the others killed him. The two policemen were such bumbling idiots, he would probably have a chance to take one of them.

The boss raised a hand.

"No," he said.

The tall man looked back, obviously surprised. "What are you doing?" he asked in Mandarin.

West was conversant enough in Mandarin to understand it if not to speak fluently, though he saw no need to let them know that.

The boss released a slow breath through pursed lips. "Every death leaves a ripple," he said. "Too many ripples cause a storm. There is no need to march through Indonesia killing everyone who crosses our path."

"I beg to differ," the tall one said. "We do not know what he has been told."

"Then we will keep him incommunicado," the boss said. "Too many have seen us. Do you expect to kill them all?"

"That is not up to us," the tall one said. "General—"

"Stop!" the boss snapped. "You assume a great deal in thinking the man does not understand you."

The tall one gave a humble nod. "That is my mistake," he said. "I only wish to point out that we are to leave no evidence of this . . . matter."

"There is still work to be done in that regard," the boss said. "But not here." He focused directly on West. "May I have your name?"

"Father Patrick West. I am in charge of Catholic relief and charity efforts on Java."

The man took a handkerchief from the pocket of his slacks and mopped his high forehead, staring at the ground for a moment in thought. "It would seem," he said, peering up at West without lifting his head, "that you have been preaching Christianity to the Muslims. We have heard reports."

"Who are you?" West said. "Are you even—"

The tall man gave a curt nod to the policemen, earning West another half-dozen punches and slaps.

The boss didn't want West dead yet, but wasn't averse to having him beaten. He waited for the policemen to tire enough that they slowed, then said, "You are under arrest for proselyting Christianity until we get this sorted out."

"That is ridiculous," West said, face placid, though he wanted to drive his fist through the smug man's teeth. "Everyone around here knows I respect my Muslim neighbors, too—"

"Bring him," the tall one barked. The Chinese men turned to walk downhill.

"And the young man?" Father West said. "Do you plan to arrest him, as well?"

"Do not worry over others," the boss said over his shoulder. "You are in enough trouble yourself."

"Please—"

"Silence!" the nearest policeman said, doling out another smack to West's head.

West played through the scenarios, lost in thought, slowing a half-step to earn another sickening punch to the kidney. He clenched his teeth and allowed himself a moment of fury as he regained his balance. The gravity of his situation fell on him hard. He'd need all his training and study—both secular and spiritual—to keep from being crushed. The text he'd put in his phone would send the moment the device was turned on and in range of a signal. It was impossible to know when that would be. West knew the message would arrive too late to save him, but at least someone else would know that China now possessed next-generation AI. Fortunately, that someone happened to be the most powerful man in the world.

5

Jack Ryan met Mary Pat Foley at the top of the staircase on the second floor of the White House Residence, diagonally across from the Lincoln Bedroom. It was early, too early for breakfast, really, but both had such full schedules that they had to start work at the proverbial zero-dark-thirty if they hoped to put any kind of a dent in their days. Ryan embraced Foley as an old friend, brotherly, but close enough to smell her rosewater shampoo. She wore an expensive-looking A-line wool skirt befitting the director of national intelligence and a fashionable silk blouse that she'd probably describe as camel or taupe but Jack would have said was tan.

Foley was in better-than-average shape for a woman in her sixties, but used the banister to haul herself up the last two steps for dramatic effect.

She shook her finger at her old friend. "I thought about having my detail bum-rush your detail so I could take the elevator."

"I'm pretty sure my detail can take your detail," Ryan said.

"That's because this is your home turf," Mary Pat

groused. "My detail doesn't have guys on the roof with sniper rifles. They're pretty damned good, though."

"I know they are," Ryan said. "But next time use the elevator. Nobody's going to stop you."

Mary Pat grinned. "I'd rather gripe about it, Jack." They'd been acquainted for well over thirty years, fast friends for most of that, and she customarily used his given name unless they were in the Oval Office and there were others present. She'd been here enough to know her way around, and walked toward the dining room off the West Sitting Hall without being told. "Anyway," she said. "I could use the exercise."

Foley could be counted on to speak her mind. Ryan liked that. He enjoyed their no-spin chats.

"Griping counts as exercise now?" Ryan chuckled, following a step behind. "I'll have to tell that to the kids."

"You know what I mean, wiseass," she said, drawing a raised brow from the female Secret Service agent posted in the Center Hall, across from the elevator.

"What do you think, Tina?" Ryan said as they passed. "Could my detail take Director Foley's detail?"

"Without question, Mr. President," Special Agent Tina Jordan said, stone-faced. With her hands folded low and relaxed in front of her slightly rumpled gray slacks, she tipped her head cordially to Mary Pat. "Good morning, Director Foley."

The DNI paused outside the dining room door and turned to face Ryan, sniffing the air. "Eggs and bacon, Jack? What gives?"

"Hey," Ryan said. "The most powerful man in the world should be able to eat what he wants for breakfast."

He shot a guilty glance over his shoulder as if afraid of being caught, then showed Foley through the door. "Seriously, Cathy had an early surgery to perform. That leaves me to harden my arteries at will."

"I'm up for some comfort food," Foley said. "Because we need to talk about Russia—and Russia should not be discussed over something as paltry as a breakfast of seeds and whey."

"Not China?" Ryan mused. "President Zhao and his war games are all over the PDB this morning." The PDB was the President's Daily Brief, prepared by Foley's office. It fused sensitive and secret data gleaned from across the nation's seventeen intelligence agencies and was ready for Ryan when he woke up each morning.

"Russia first," Foley said. "I'm saving the Chinese for last."

A steward from the White House kitchen got them both seated, while the sous-chef, a woman whose parents were from the Dominican Republic, uncovered two plates piled high with eggs Benedict—made with bacon, the way Ryan liked it, instead of ham.

"Thank you, Josey," Ryan said to the sous-chef. "It looks fantastic."

"Thank you, Mr. President." The woman stood fast, as if she were waiting to be dismissed.

"Was there something else?"

"There is, Mr. President," Josey said, shuffling her feet like a child with a *C* on her report card. "These Benedicts turned out to perfection . . . Chef asked me to take a photo with you and the breakfast for the White House Instagram account . . ."

Ryan sighed, waving a hand over his plate as if to give her the go-ahead. Photos of his food for social media—one of the countless things you never realized about being President of the United States until you were on the job. "This has Arnie's name written all over it," he muttered.

"Truth be told, Mr. President," Josey whispered, glancing toward the doors, "it was Mr. van Damm who asked Chef to get some photos." She took a small digital camera out of her jacket pocket—personal cell phones were locked away downstairs.

Mary Pat reflexively held up an open hand in front of her face at the sight of the camera. "Just the President, if you don't mind." She shot a sheepish glance at Ryan. "I know, I know. My photo is all over open-source media now that I'm in this job, but old habits die hard."

"Of course, Director Foley," Josey said, snapping three quick photos from different angles before thanking Ryan and stepping out.

"I like her," Foley said. "She's honest. The kind of gal I would have tried to recruit."

"Be my guest," Ryan said. "She's not likely to be here long with a brain like hers."

As was his habit, Ryan poured his guest's coffee before his own. Being President was a lonely job. Hell, he thought, sometimes being Jack Ryan could be a lonely job. People had come to expect a certain decorum in his actions, a measured restraint when what he wanted to do was beat some bad actor to death with a hammer. He'd proven more than once that he wasn't beyond using the full force of the presidency with devastating effect. But the times Mary Pat had talked him off the ledge were too numerous to count.

Apart from his wife, Cathy, Mary Pat Foley was Ryan's closest confidant. Blessed with an innate ability to read people within a few moments after meeting them, she'd been a skilled field officer with the Agency. Her husband, Ed, had been the station chief in Moscow during the turbulent eighties—when things were even worse between the U.S. and Russia than they were now—marginally. Mary Pat was well known among her cohort as a bit of a cowboy, ready to take any manner of risk for her agents—a mother hen. She'd taken Ryan under her wing early on, mentoring him, offering advice from a near peer when he was still new to the CIA and unaccustomed to the Byzantine ways. Her maiden name was Kaminsky and she spoke Russian with the colloquial ease of someone who'd grown up in a Russian household, peppering her conversation with just the right mixture of humor and resignation to the vagaries of life to make her blend in like a native. She could think in Russian—beyond just the language—which made her invaluable as the top intelligence officer for Ryan's administration.

Ryan used the point of his knife—Cathy preferred Shun when it came to blades—to pop a poached egg. He paused for a moment, watching the yolk mix with the hollandaise and drench the English muffin in liquid gold. Ryan didn't do Instagram, but if any food was photogenic, this was it. He savored a bite—much richer than the steel-cut oats and skim milk Cathy normally made him eat—and then took a sip of coffee before speaking over the top of the cup.

"So, what's this about Yermilov?"

Knife in one hand, Foley used the other to gesture at Ryan with her fork. "The man is a menace, Jack. You know that? He's shameless."

"Talks regarding Russia are becoming quotidian," Ryan said.

Foley chuckled. "Doing your crosswords this morning, Mr. President?"

"Keeping the language alive," Ryan said. "At any rate, it's not a secret Yermilov fancies himself the next tsar. This report on China . . ."

"I'm briefing you on Russia, Jack," Foley said. "Seriously, why do you keep asking about the Chinese? I'm your director of national intelligence. Do you know something I don't know?"

"Hey," Ryan chuckled. "I read Intellipedia."

"Of course you do." Foley dabbed her lips with a linen napkin, leaving a trace of red lipstick, and then looked at Ryan. "In your spare time."

Part of the government's venture into Web 2.0, Intellipedia was an online data-sharing system overseen by Foley's office. Much like Wikipedia, the collaborative tool allowed intelligence analysts—half of them barely thirty years old, from what Ryan had seen—from the seventeen U.S. intelligence agencies to post and share to wikis classified up to and including Top Secret Sensitive Compartmented Information (TS SCI) regarding their areas of expertise. The forum was open to those with the necessary security clearance. Personal opinions were not only allowed but encouraged. In Ryan's view, one of the best things about what his friend John Clark called Wikispook was that it was not anonymous. Submitters shared an opinion, and then had to own it. Any analyst was free to state individual views that would be shared with anyone with the appropriate clearance, but that opinion linked back to the analyst, not some nameless avatar or pseudonym.

Ryan took another bite of eggs Benedict, wishing he had longer to savor it. "We're always on the brink of something when it comes to Nikita Yermilov," he said. "Don't get me wrong. I'm not discounting your intelligence product. These guys have been studying the way we wage war for the last couple of decades—and figuring out how to counter it. We've got to start looking at things differently. The next war will likely be on ground we don't yet even comprehend at this point. Cyber . . . AI . . . who knows what."

"No argument there," Foley said. "Both Yermilov and Zhao are running more and more active measures against the West every day. The bad old days with a hell of a lot more technology. The Bureau arrested two Chinese illegals in Queens last week—brothers living under the assumed identities of two children who died in the late seventies."

Ryan gave a contemplative nod. "I read that brief. Your people are following a couple more, if I'm not mistaken."

"We are," Foley said. "A joint team of Bureau and Agency folk." She pretended to wipe her brow with the back of her hand. "You don't know how hard it was to get that one put together. Sadly, there are still a few bastions of blinkered thought in the puzzle palaces of our intelligence community. The directors of both agencies were fine with the task force—"

"They better be." Ryan cut her off. He'd appointed them both.

Mary Pat raised her hand. "They're on board, Jack, but a couple of old-dog senior executives were guarding their turf like the last bone in the yard. Deanne Staples at the Bureau and Simon Cross at CIA."

"Did you mentor them?"

"Right out the door," Foley said. "I am so far past that shit, pardon my French. Gave them each a nice send-off and a pretty plaque thanking them for their service. Yermilov and Zhao both want to end us, and I'll be damned if I'm going to let a couple of dinosaurs bent on marking their territory keep us from catching him at his game."

Ryan chuckled. "Good for you."

"Sorry, Jack," Foley said. "It's not your problem. I just needed to vent. Anyway, the task force has teams on seven suspected illegals at the moment, two here in D.C., one in Manhattan, and a married couple in Colorado Springs who run a diner outside Cheyenne Mountain." She chuckled. "Most are Russian, but the two in Colorado are Chinese."

"Do we know who's running them?"

Foley took a sip of coffee. "Nothing definitive," she said. "A couple of sources say there is significant infighting among a couple of high-ranking military brass in Beijing. We do have a source close to General Song, a one-star who runs war-gaming scenarios who says he could be ripe to turn. He'd have a treasure trove of data at his fingertips if they want the scenarios to be realistic. We're playing it slow or we run the risk of burning that source."

Ryan didn't ask for specifics about the sources. Both he and Foley had been at this game long enough that neither made a habit of discussing details about intelligence officers or their assets' meeting schedules unless it was absolutely necessary. Ryan trusted his staff—but people leaked, sometimes on purpose, more often accidentally. Loose lips really had sunk a fair number of ships—and gotten more than a few outed agents shot. As the saying went, *Trust in God, but tether your camel at night.*

"Anyway, we'll keep a close watch on the general." Foley used the tip of her index finger to doodle on the tablecloth. "The situation with all these illegals reminds me of life before you took this stodgy desk job."

"I've always had a stodgy desk job," Ryan said.

"Yeah," Foley said, "but you could get up and come play with the rest of us there for a while."

"I can neither confirm nor deny . . ."

Foley put both hands on the tablecloth and leaned forward. "Don't you miss the field?"

"Not one damned bit," Ryan lied.

Foley sat back, obviously seeing through him. "It's safer to be a chess player than a chess piece," she said. "But it's not nearly as much fun. Anyway, you're up on your briefing books. Yermilov wants Ukraine and Zhao wants us out of the South China Sea—"

The door from the Sitting Hall opened and Ryan's chief of staff blew in, gripping his cell phone like it was a sword. He was the only bald guy Ryan knew who could look like he had bedhead. The single Windsor knot of his polyester tie hung at half-mast. He wore no jacket and the top button of his blue striped Eddie Bauer shirt gaped open. The sleeves were rolled to just below his elbows.

He held up the phone as he dragged a chair back from the table with his free hand. "Instagram photo looks great," he said, not exactly smiling, but looking pleased.

"I see you slept in your clothes again," Ryan said.

Arnie van Damm waved off the comment. "Yeah, yeah, a guy keeps the wheels oiled, he's bound to get into a little grease."

Ryan motioned to his uneaten Benedict. "I can have Josey bring in another set of silverware."

"I've already eaten," van Damm said. "Did I hear you talking about Russia when I came in? Because that's what I came to see you about, among other things."

Van Damm had been chief of staff to three presidents— the man behind the curtain, the chamberlain who whispered in the shogun's ear. He'd been there from the beginning of the Ryan presidency, when Jack was literally picking himself up from the rubble. Politics, not blood, flowed in his veins. It was no easy task playing ringmaster to the White House circus, and harder still to cajole whoever was sitting behind the Resolute desk into playing politics. He had a knack for knowing when a whispered suggestion would do—or when he needed a chair and a whip. Arnie saw sides of things that Ryan did not, and vice versa. He was a good guy to have in the room, even if he did look like he'd just crawled out of a laundry hamper.

Van Damm absentmindedly dragged Ryan's plate in front of him as he sat down. Ryan called Josey to bring in silverware and more coffee, which she did immediately. She looked horrified to see the chief of staff preparing to chow down on the rest of the President's breakfast.

"I'd be happy to make you a fresh plate, Mr. van Damm," she said.

"That's okay," Arnie said, popping the yolk of the second egg. "I'm not really hungry." Ryan smiled inwardly as his friend began to eat, one arm on the table, wrapped around the plate like that of a prisoner afraid another inmate might try and steal his tater tots. Admittedly rough around the edges, Arnie van Damm was one of the most viscerally intelligent men Ryan had ever come across.

The chief of staff looked up at Ryan. "Senator Chadwick is killing us on our position in the Baltics."

"Not news," Ryan said. "At least not *new* news."

Michelle Chadwick, the senior senator from Arizona and chairman of the Senate Subcommittee for Homeland Security rarely wasted a chance to bash Ryan and his administration for any manner of what she considered to be misadventures. Lately, it was Ryan's push to increase security in the Baltic nations. She'd swallowed the Russian line that any security buildup would precipitate aggression from the Kremlin instead of preventing it. But she didn't know Yermilov like Ryan did.

Van Damm gestured with the tines of his fork. "She's killing us everywhere that matters—the Middle East, China, trade, economy, intelligence oversight. You name it. If we're for it, she's against it. That woman has not met a Ryan policy that she does not despise like Brussels sprouts."

"Not everyone despises Brussels sprouts," Foley noted.

Van Damm harrumphed. "Well, I do. Just last night Chadwick was on the news calling our Freedom of Navigation operations in the South China Sea 'saber-rattling.'"

"That's exactly what they are," Ryan said. "And I'm good with that."

"Well," van Damm said, digging into the egg again. "Be that as it may, I don't like hearing it out loud, and neither do the American people."

"I'm not too worried about Senator Chadwick," Ryan said.

"That's your problem, Jack," van Damm scoffed. "You need to worry more. I think she's banking on the fact that a lot of Americans don't even know that the Baltics aren't part of former Yugoslavia."

Now Josey looked even more horrified.

"You don't agree?" van Damm asked.

Josey moved the butter, salt, and pepper alongside what was left of the President's eggs, arranging them in a line, one at a time, illustrating her words. "Estonia, Latvia, and Lithuania—your plate being the Baltic Sea. All are members of NATO, Mr. van Damm. Estonia is one of the most digitally advanced nations on the planet. It was the first to hold elections on the Internet. Over a quarter of the people living in Latvia are Russian—which is kind of a problem, since President Yermilov can fall back on the excuse that he's taking care of his people's interests if he decides he wants to roll across the border.

Most of the people in Lithuania belong to the Church of Rome, which might interest you, Mr. President. GDP—"

Van Damm held up an open hand. "You win, Josey."

Mary Pat nodded at the pepper. "Didn't expect the sous-chef to have a political science degree from Maryland, did you? Now, if you'll please pass me the Lithuania . . ."

"Anyway . . ." van Damm said, after Josey excused herself with an extremely satisfied grin on her face. "Chadwick and the Baltics are only one problem." He shook his head. "I swear this job is trying to play baseball with ten or twelve different pitchers, all throwing knuckles, curves, and fastballs from different places on the field . . . It looks like Zhao has decided to build another island off the Spratlys. One of their 054A frigates came within shooting range of an MEU we had in the area."

An MEU was a Marine Expeditionary Unit, a quick reaction force generally consisting of support ships and an amphibious LHD that looked like a small carrier, capable of launching rotary-wing aircraft as well as Harriers or F-35s. These MEUs were often used to project American might in far corners of the world while they stood ready to react.

Ryan gave a somber nod. "We were just discussing that before you came in."

"More feints and jabs," Foley said. "He's baiting you, Jack. Pressing buttons to see what you'll do."

"Interesting to note," van Damm said, "that this latest attack comes on the heels of Zhao's last speech, where he all but assured the world the DF-ZF hypersonic missiles are ready to launch if China feels the least bit threatened.

Tacked on to the end of his statement was a throwaway line about historic territorial claims."

Foley gave a contemplative nod. "Conveniently leaving out that China and Russia are both using hypersonic missile plans stolen from the U.S. He's pressing you to see what you might do if he takes more aggressive action against, say, a Japanese ship. It's a dangerous game of chicken."

Ryan grew distant, thinking, pondering. He didn't see the proverbial falling dominoes when he pictured a world map, but it was impossible not to see a chessboard, with Zhao gobbling up land and resources around the world—Africa, South America, and all over the Pacific. As it stood, most war-gaming models predicted that the United States would win a prolonged conflict. But what did that even mean? Generals on both sides—PLA and U.S.—stood steadfastly behind their ability to crush the enemy in any conflict. A good general had to be possessed of a certain swagger, a deep and abiding confidence, no matter their shortcomings. Great men were often . . . almost always . . . incredibly flawed men. Lincoln, when confronted about Grant's drunken behavior, had said simply, "I can't spare this man; he fights."

The giant brains in the think tanks and working groups around Washington had a more sobering view of possible conflict with a near peer state. The U.S. would likely "win" a prolonged conflict—but any openly declared war with a state like China or Russia would come to American soil. Maybe not in boots-on-the-ground foreign troops, but certainly in a rain of missiles and bombs and devastating cyberattacks once the gloves were off. Gone would be the proxy wars fought by guerilla armies and despot dictators propped up with foreign money. Everyone would suffer greatly. Even the nation that came out on top would be belly-down, gasping for breath, and drained of blood and treasure. The American people would feel the next war.

Ryan had to force himself to stop clenching his teeth.

Van Damm waved a hand back and forth in the air. "You still with us, Mr. President?"

"Your analogy made me think," Ryan said. "I'd like to hear more about these illegals and what they're up to."

"Of course, Jack," Foley said. "I'll get you something by lunch."

"Thanks," Ryan said. "You know, we're playing a game of chicken with China. You know what game theory says about the surest way to win a game of chicken?"

Foley shrugged. Van Damm wrinkled his bald head.

Ryan jammed an index finger on the table to make his point. "What you have to do is let your opponent see you rip out your own steering wheel right before the game begins."

"That would work if the other guy happens to be sane."

"Yeah." Ryan nodded slowly. "There is that . . ."

6

Major Chang Xiubo of the People's Liberation Army stared at the twin monitors of the desktop computer, mouth half open, lines of code reflecting off the lenses of his thick glasses. He studied the program carefully, imagining the beauty of her avatar. She'd been designed as an NPC for video gaming, but, oh, she had potential for so much more.

From the time he was a small boy, Chang had always imagined that computers and all their glorious parts were female. This software was certainly mysterious enough to be a woman. Completely engrossed in her ability to solve problems on her own with no prompting or additional coding from him, Chang watched the mission unfold on his screen and passed a long, rattling fart into the mesh of his office chair. The two other engineers in the lab, both women, glanced up and shook their heads in unconcealed disgust. They were accustomed to, if not at ease with, the major's eccentricities.

He clicked the mouse beside his keyboard, scrolling, studying.

This software—called Calliope by the Americans—had already caused the deaths of two people, with another soon to follow.

Chang Xiubo's grandfather once owned a horse that was so clever it could escape from any gate, no matter how complicated the latch. Unable to be contained, the horse eventually had to be killed. It was a near indisputable fact, the old man said, that the smarter something was, the more mischief it created, putting everyone and everything around it in danger.

The risks of being a smart horse became a popular warning from young Chang's parents and a way to say no when he asked for more math books or a new computer. He got these things anyway—because he was smart, which made them worry all the more.

Chang's father was by no means rich, but he was a loyal party member and a good provider for his family. He said what people above him wanted to hear and farted silently. Xiubo could never bring himself to do either. The elder Chang was charged with supply of military garrisons in and around Jiuquan, a relatively small city of a million people, west of Beijing, and south of the border with Mongolia.

A homely child with no friends his age, young Chang Xiubo had accompanied his father on a delivery to the Inner Mongolia Autonomous Region and the Jiuquan Satellite Launch Center when he was fifteen. This short journey of about a hundred kilometers got the boy out of the house and away from the old computer that he had cobbled together. The site was famous for the launch of Shenzhou 5, the first manned Chinese space flight. History had been made here, heroes made. But Chang Xiubo was not nearly so impressed with astronauts as he was with the computers that sent them on their journeys. His father had been delivering spools of computer cable, so Chang had gotten to see the computer rooms, a fascinating treat for the boy, better than going to the zoo. The physicists and engineers smoked constantly, typing away, never looking up from their workstations. At that moment, Chang Xiubo decided he wanted to emulate these stolid men. They ignored him completely until he began to ask questions about discrete math and linear algebra.

One of them called the site supervisor, another humorless engineer who wanted nothing to do with the boy until he found they spoke the same mathematical language. The supervisor telephoned a government minister he knew and eventually arranged for Chang to attend Harbin Institute of Technology as soon as he could take the exams.

Chang's mother had been horrified, not because her son was going away to a school almost as far east of Beijing as Jiuquan was to the west, but because he had displayed his staggering intellect to the world.

She wept when he left home, tissue to her nose, pleading, "Please do not be a smart horse."

Military service was still compulsory for young men in China, *if* the government ever got around to noticing you forced their hand. Nowadays, that did not usually happen unless you made someone angry. The PLA had an overabundance of qualified volunteers, so those who were not willing were rarely called on to serve. That was not the case when Chang was a boy. The military officers at the Harbin Institute of Technology had encouraged him to finish his studies, but they were waiting for him when he was done.

He'd called to tell his parents, and again, his mother had reminded him to keep his intellect in check.

But smart was the only kind of horse he knew how to be. He certainly wasn't handsome or athletic. Fortunately for Chang, his talents were highly valued by his superiors. Otherwise, someone would have long since put a bullet in his head. Past commanders had called him a "stain" on his performance reports, "a disgrace to the uniform," but had gone on to note that he was one of the most gifted scientists they had ever seen. A secret addendum to his personnel file from a particularly hateful colonel noted that if he were to ever be separated from the military, he should be institutionalized or killed to keep him from putting his skills toward activities not sanctioned by the party. Chang knew of the file, and considered it a badge of honor. He'd found his spot as special assistant to Lieutenant General Bai.

A software engineer by training, Chang was, by disposition, a toad. He was so maddeningly aloof that both superiors and subordinates alike were forced to raise their voices to get his attention. Short and squarely built, with thick black-rimmed glasses and coarse hair that was forever in need of a trim, he could most often be found snowing flakes of dandruff on his desk, staring into space, apparently forgetting to blink. Those new to his lab might think he'd fallen into a catatonic trance, but these were no states of stupefaction. Chang's face might be flaccid, but behind the blank stare, his mind clicked through problem after problem at an incredible rate. He'd talked to himself since he was a small child, though now he'd learned to do it silently, asking questions and then working through solutions while the world stumbled on blindly around him.

And now he had Calliope.

This magnificent thing was going to either see his star rise to astronomical heights or extinguish it entirely. He had suspected this gaming software to be advanced, but not nearly this fantastic. The Americans overused the word *awesome*, but this . . . this entity did nothing if it did not inspire true awe. Artificial intelligence was just that—artificial. But Calliope was as much art as she was science.

Like most any other scientist in his field, Major Chang realized that the future of technology was intertwined with AI. Saudi Arabia had already granted citizenship to a computer named Sophia. It was a stunt, of course, but the reality was not that far off. The presidents of Russia and China, even Iran, all saw AI as a key to power. Tech developers, billionaire businessmen—who did not get to be billionaires by accident—folded AI into their business models or changed those models altogether.

Personal assistants, self-driving vehicles, and even medical diagnoses were now driven by neural networks.

China in general, and specifically Major Chang, concentrated on arguably more nefarious applications for this technology than those working in the West.

The average smartphone had tens of thousands of times more computing power than the MIT Apollo Guidance Computer used to get the Americans to the moon. These ubiquitous devices had the power to dumb down civilizations or provide an exponential increase in human productivity. They were also a perfect platform with which to track the movement, communication, and social interactions of the user. Personal assistants like Siri refrained from spying only because they were not programmed to do so. The same artificial intelligence software that predicted and suggested words when a user was typing text could easily predict subversive antigovernment behavior. Facebook had some of the most advanced facial-recognition software in the world. The uses there were many and obvious. AI programs run by Amazon and Google could accurately target ads to just the right user by scanning their search history and myriad personal data that had become the coin of the online realm. This same technology could easily be used to gauge and score a citizen's commitment to the social fabric of the country.

There was no doubt that Major Chang was a highly intelligent scientist, but much of his genius lay in knowing how to best utilize the advances of others. Artificial intelligence and deep learning were the future of the military as well as the civilian world. Surveillance, command control, targeting—the list was limited only by the imagination, and most of the consumer technology was ripe for the taking if one knew where to look.

And Major Chang had feelers everywhere.

He'd first heard whisperings of the AI program called Calliope from a contact at MIT. There were, it seemed, a couple of engineers who had developed a supercomputer with such an advanced neural network that she had become a partner of sorts in the development of artificial intelligence and deep learning. She—and everyone who had been in contact with the new computer referred to her as a *she*—was widely considered to be the next leap in deep learning. Like something from a science-fiction movie, she appeared to have a personality.

Called LongGame, she wanted to learn. And learn she did. So much so that she was able to assist the engineers who made her in creating a new software that was a smaller, more portable version of herself. Moore's law essentially said that computing power doubled every eighteen months to two years—while devices got smaller and cheaper. The observation had held true for half a century. Many thought it had run its course—and without AI it might have.

Frankly, Calliope was exactly what people like Elon Musk and others warned about.

Using this technology as a non-player character in a pedestrian video game seemed to Chang to be unconscionable. Neural networks could now beat human beings at most any game—Breakout, chess, even the sophisticated and seemingly random game of Go. Calliope could do all of that but so much more, harnessing the Cloud or the host computer she happened to occupy.

Calliope was small, portable, and powerful. But she had another trait that made her particularly useful for any number of Chang's purposes. Neural networks could beat a human player ninety-nine times out of a hundred, but they did not want to play. Calliope was fairly bursting at the seams as she sought new challenges. She pilfered through subdirectories, files, and applications in the operating system into which Chang had injected her, like a bored child, looking for something to do.

She'd been developed to play the game on her own

alongside the primary player, like a second human. She could, for instance, "go and fetch"—fight her way through the enemy to bring back more ammunition, weapons, or fuel for her partner. She commandeered the computer's entire hard drive, the Net, the Cloud, the Dark Web, anything to which she had access, to complete her task. That morning, he'd loaded her into a self-driving car and told her to guard the three parking spots in the lot next to his building, leaving the details of how to do it to her own devices. He thought she might park lengthwise in all three spaces, but instead she drove back and forth on the lot, actively challenging any vehicle that came near, like an aggressive mother bird protecting her nest.

She needed a mission—and since she knew how to go and fetch things, Major Chang had just the right mission in mind.

7

Tony Lombardi kept a second cell phone at his apartment in South Oxnard, suspended from two feet of kite string in the wall behind the light switch in his bedroom. He was careful with the screw heads every time he retrieved the phone—so as not to draw attention to the switch plate if someone came in with a search warrant. It was a hassle, but so was getting caught spying on a U.S. Naval base.

Lombardi knew in his bones that some government official was going to walk up at any moment and randomly demand to look at his mobile phone. They had no right, but that didn't stop authoritarian regimes. That's what governments did. They screwed the people. He knew he had to be hypervigilant, especially at work. When he went to his job on Naval Base Ventura County, the phone stayed at home, hanging from the string in his wall.

The sun was not yet up when he nursed his rattletrap Ford Ranger up to the security gate a little before five-thirty. The odor of diesel fuel and low tide hung heavy across the blacktop road. He liked to arrive at the construction site early enough to impress his foreman, but not so early as to make security forces any twitchier than they already were.

Comprising three Naval facilities—Point Mugu, Port Hueneme, and San Nicolas Island—NBVC was home to no less than four airborne early-warning squadrons. Three of these E-2 Hawkeye squadrons were assigned to the carriers USS *John C. Stennis*, *Theodore Roosevelt*, and *Carl Vinson*. A deepwater port and myriad other Naval tenants including Defense Logistics, Naval Satellite Operations Center, and an Air Test and Evaluation Squadron provided security forces with plenty of reason to be twitchy—and significant opportunity for Lombardi. The government would have called him a domestic terrorist. But he preferred *saboteur*. It sounded cooler. And besides, he was in this for the good of the country. Terrorists killed people. He just passed on information. His contact with Earth Ally was a pretty Asian chick from USC named Kirsten. She cared about the state of the country, of the world, and made him want to do better, to be better. She told him what she needed, and he got it for her. So far, she hadn't made him blow any shit up, but he would have if she'd asked.

Security investigations for hammer-swingers and ditch-diggers looked for things that were on the record, not things that weren't. Sure, they wanted to know where he'd gone to high school, but they weren't likely to spend the time to send agents out to interview his high school counselor, or anyone who might have known how much he despised the establishment. Lombardi's California driver's license said he was twenty-four, far too young to have much of a credit history. Judging from the security forms he'd had to complete, the contracting officer was more interested in bad credit than good, and paid more attention to criminal history than chronological. No history was apparently fine.

He'd been upset at first that his clearance didn't give him access to any weapons-storage magazines or sensitive areas. Those remained locked up tight, behind impenetrable layers of security. But Kirsten reminded him that he wasn't here for that.

His job was to observe things that occurred in the open. She was particularly interested in the dimensions of the magazine his construction team was building. Were there special loading doors? Overhead cranes? A track system? Enhanced environmental controls? Additional layers of security?

Kirsten never told him specifically what she was looking for, but he could figure it out easily enough after he found out what she wanted him to watch.

Five minutes online—on his secret phone, so the government couldn't track him—revealed tests off Point Mugu of America's hot new weapon—the Lockheed Martin AGM-158C, a long-range anti-ship missile, or LRASM. At first glance the technology seemed like a step backward. China already had the Yingji-18. Yingji was literally "Eagle Strike," and the YJ-18 cruise missile had a range of more than three hundred miles, with a final sprint nearing three times the speed of sound. Russia's joint venture with India, the BrahMos PJ-10, was the fastest supersonic cruise missile in the world at Mach 3, executing a sophisticated S-turn to avoid interception during the terminal phase. A hypersonic variant, Brah-Mos II, was under development, supposed to reach speeds over Mach 7.

According to the specs, the LRASM was a lumbering thing compared to Chinese and Russian anti-ship missiles. But no one cared much about the LRASM's speed. The weapon's lethality lay in its stealth technology, and its ability to home in on an enemy's targeting radar—the same radar used to seek incoming threats. Recent tests had shown it could hunt and find targets with extreme precision using an artificial intelligence system designed to recognize the profile of enemy ships. And that was just the stuff they talked about online. Lombardi was sure there was a shitload more they didn't mention.

He finally asked Kirsten about it. She'd looked surprised that he'd figured it out, but then admitted that she was interested in the missile, though she had no idea what the Earth Ally plan was to do with it. Maybe they were planning on bombing it, though neither she nor Lombardi could figure out what good that would do. The military-industrial complex would just build more and the arms race with the Russians and the Chinese and the Iranians would just carry on ad nauseam. It was probably going to be a symbolic gesture—to draw some attention to the idiocy. Lombardi didn't care.

There was a lot of movement around the magazines where they kept the missiles, wooden crates, forklifts, like they were getting ready to make a move. He'd call for a meeting that evening, turn over his intel, and they could maybe have dinner. He enjoyed being a saboteur for a good cause almost as much as he enjoyed hanging out with Kirsten.

As long as he could keep doing that, Tony Lombardi would keep swinging his hammer, keep his eyes open, and point Kirsten in the right direction. He thought of her now as he looked across the water in the morning twilight.

She was so incredibly pure.

8

The Chinese heart is well versed in quiet, seething hate—and General Song Biming was more accomplished than most. The ill-informed might believe that General Song hated Bai for personal reasons. While it was true that Bai had stolen Song's girl all those years ago, there was much more to it than that. In Song's mind, it was as simple as up and down or black and white. Bai was evil and Song was good. Was not good supposed to hate evil? If a child drew a picture of an evil man, fat and frowning Bai Min would have provided a likely model. Where Song was tall and fit, with salt-and-pepper hair and a ramrod-straight military bearing, Bai was a head shorter and as round as a steamed meat bun. Song had once read that the ex-lover of a heavyset British MP had described sex with the man as like having a very large wardrobe with a small key fall on top of her. Certainly an apt assessment of anything to do with Bai Min. Song took perverse pleasure in the fact that the onetime object of his affection had chosen someone so foul with whom to spend her life.

Among his more disgusting qualities was the fact that he steadfastly refused to trim his wild eyebrows. This only added to the troll-like visage of his prune of a face.

Of course, he had not always been so. Somehow he'd been handsome and gallant enough to win Ling's hand. He was already a powerful general by the time the weight of his backstabbing had stooped his shoulders and twisted his face. By then it did not matter. In fact, Song had heard that President Zhao preferred his generals to be less handsome than he was. Bai's status had seen to it that Ling was able to shop at good stores and live in nice apartments. Still, her once beautiful face held a perpetual look of astonishment at how ugly her husband had turned out, as if someone had just blown a puff of air into her eyes. She surely knew, as did Song, that General Bai was up to his neck in something rotten.

Song leaned back in his creaking leatherette chair and took a sip of tea.

He and Bai were both general officers, but as a lieutenant general, Bai had line-item authority over the furnishings and maintenance budget at the shared war-simulation facility run by the Science and Technology Commission of the People's Liberation Army. Apart from elite party members and a few department heads, furniture used by Chinese government officials tended toward the utilitarian, but the tightfisted bastard Bai went out of his way to see that all the desks on the south side of the complex were secondhand, surely stained with the tears of the minions who had occupied them before. Song's assistant, a short major with a broad smile and an even broader wife, had a desk that looked as if it had been used as part of a barricade to fend off some guerilla army. Where the south wing was tattered and sprung, every chair and sofa in the north wing was shiny and plush. Normally, such trivialities would have mattered little to Song, but events were not going his way. He sipped his tea and looked grimly at the floor-to-ceiling world map projected on the far wall. Flashing icons showed the location of both Chinese and enemy aircraft, ships, mechanized units, and ground troops in various locations from Japan to the Philippines. Three Chinese Type 094 Jin-class submarines prowled the waters of Hawaii and the West Coast of the United States.

Song took another drink of tea and watched the light representing the submarine nearest San Diego, California, flash, then disappear from the screen.

The outcome of this scenario was not his fault, but he would be blamed for it nonetheless. The rank of general was lonely at best, but Song did little to engender good feelings from his comrades—the men who would normally have watched his back during these perilous times. He drank in moderation—surely a reason not to be trusted—and despised parties. He steered clear of side "investments." There was no private villa for him with a live-in mistress in the mountains outside Beijing. Men with bent or broken morals felt judged whether one judged them or not, and Song Biming found himself a pariah at staff meetings, where discussions always seemed to turn to growing bank accounts and manly prowess with nubile young women. Song had no stories—or at least none of interest to the other generals. None of those men wanted to hear about how Song's buxom but slightly chubby wife of thirty-one years made the best pork buns in all of China. He listened politely to their whore stories, noting that though most of the exploits had to be highly embellished, sex with his wife sounded vastly superior to any of their imagined escapades. His wife was a good woman, enough of a natural expert in that realm to keep him more than satisfied. She was inquisitive about his work, interested but not nosy, and ambitious enough to push him when he needed to be pushed. She'd resigned herself early on to the fact that she was not his first choice for a wife—and was fine with that, as long as she was his last. So far, he'd kept his end of that bargain. She'd given him more than three decades of unquestionable support, and a fine daughter, who had, in turn, given them a beautiful granddaughter, Niu, who was the light of his life—and the only thing that could take his mind off the tragedy of his work.

Song was a proud man. One did not get to be a general in the People's Liberation Army without having a certain measure of gravitas and ego. But this downward spiral of fortune made him feel sorry for his family. His wife had been nothing but faithful, pinning all her hopes and dreams on his career. She certainly didn't deserve this. Any semblance of status he'd ever had was rapidly slipping away—in no small measure because of General Bai Min. Something had to be done—and soon.

Song's hand began to tremble with rage and he set the cup down on his desk in a puddle of spilled tea. Bai, that deceitful old dog, would find much pleasure in the results playing out on the screen. China was losing this simulation—as she always did eventually, when correct data was used in the program. Unlike war games involving actual troops, the enemy in this simulation did not lay down arms at the appropriate moment to make China look good. Computers did not lie—unless they were told to, and even then they spat out the only truth they knew. Song was ever exacting in his requirements that his programs be realistic and accurate to the nth degree, running thousands of permutations for each battle. He was privy to the latest intelligence data—which he insisted be raw, not preanalyzed or, as the Americans said, *spun* to suit PLA purposes. He'd stupidly thought that his mandate from Chairman Zhao for a true representation of fighting outcomes would be used to improve China's capabilities. Instead, the computer-generated losses had been used to beat him over the head—principally by General Bai, his old foe since their days at the National University of Defense Technology, China's premier military academy, when Bai had stolen his woman.

Religion took the blame for a great many wars; God was merely an excuse. The root of most conflict boiled down to two things: territory or women. President Zhao craved territory, not enough to start a war, not yet. No, the next conflict would only appear to be fought over territory. If a war with the West happened in the near future, it would be Song and Bai's feud that started it.

Song breathed deeply, regaining enough control to pick up his tea. He needed to return to the matter at hand—watching his computer program demonstrate how the West would soundly beat China. Light after light blinked out, one after another on the screen, signifying the loss of Chinese assets. Computer simulations unfolded much faster than they did in real time, adding to Song's misery. What was that quaint American saying? That was it. *The Americans were handing them their asses.*

The motherland did well at the beginning of each scenario—but she always lost in the end. And Song always had to watch.

Formerly a PLA training hall, the moldering bunker sloped downward from the entry toward the wall with the map where the instructor's lectern would have been. Twenty-two uniformed subordinates sat in near darkness at two rows of desks in the amphitheater-like room, facing the map as they pecked on computers or mumbled into their radio headpieces. Most of them were conscripts, forced into doing their bit.

The light signifying the last submarine off the California coast went dark. Song set the teacup on the desk again, forcefully enough to cause the young woman a row in front of him to look up at the clatter. She looked away as if she'd seen something frightening. A phlegmy cough rattled over Song's shoulder.

"Rubbing Chinese noses in the dirt again, I see," General Bai observed, hands resting pompously on the top of his round belly. His aide-de-camp and toady, Chang, stood beside him. Pale and scaly, Chang sifted flakes of dandruff wherever he walked. It was off-putting, to say the least, but it also had the effect of making people think Chang far more benign than Song knew him to be.

Song stood. As a lieutenant general, Bai outranked him.

"The scenarios offer no benefit if they do not unfold without intervention."

"Perhaps," Bai mused, eyes squinting over fat cheeks at the screen. "Or perhaps battle cannot be reduced to ones and zeros. Your children's games fail to take into account the heart and spirit of our Chinese countrymen."

Song closed his eyes, steadying himself. "And your war games offer more reality?"

"Exercises," Bai corrected. "Exercises carried out with flesh-and-blood players, not to mention actual weapons and technology. Surely you would agree that that is a much better predictor of outcomes than lines of computer code." He nodded toward the flashing map and chuckled. "Your pretend games are doing so well, perhaps one day you will receive a pretend promotion."

Song clenched his jaw, fighting the urge to smash Bai in the face with his teacup. Bai had won the girl—all those years ago. There was no reason for him to gloat. But he did. A lot.

"So, Comrade General," Song sighed, dripping with sarcasm. "To what do I owe the pleasure of this visit?"

"An invitation," Bai said.

"In that case I will save you the trouble and decline in advance."

"This is not the kind of invitation one can decline," Bai said. "We are summoned to meet with President Zhao and explain our programs. I am to give him a full brief on the victories and lessons learned from our latest exercise off the Korean coast. You will tell him how the same PLA Navy that won handily is always beaten by the end of your computer games."

What do you think?" Bai asked his bagman, Chang, five minutes after they'd left Song's game room and were safely back on their own side of the building. Bai wouldn't have put it past the old dog to bug the walls outside his office. Bai had done just that, which was why there wasn't much chatter in the halls of the north wing.

"General Song is tireless in pursuit of his mission," Chang said. "He knows he is right, and that shows on his face."

"A dangerous combination." Bai grunted, half to himself. "Moral superiority and a work ethic."

"Difficult to stop a man like that," Chang conceded, scratching his chin.

"Nonsense," Bai said. "I said dangerous, not invincible." He waved sausage fingers at his aide. "And anyway, we do not need to stop him. We are ahead. I merely want to make sure Chairman Zhao does not buy into his fatalistic beliefs before we have everything in place."

Chang nodded. "The software is everything we had hoped for and more. I would like to continue with a few more tests, but—"

"Continue with whatever tests you wish," the general said. "But I want FIRESHIP moving forward. It is ready, is it not?"

"I believe so, General Bai," Chang said. "But—"

"You believe?" Bai clenched his fists, looking around as if he needed something to strike. "I do not need *belief*. I need *certainty*."

"A few more tests," Chang said. "Then I will be certain."

"If we go forward and fail, the chairman will put our backs against a concrete wall and shoot us in the heart."

The major kept his voice low and calm, an engineer under pressure, too focused on his task to realize how great the threat truly was. "My people are running diagnostics as we speak. This software is . . ." He shook his head. "Extremely volatile."

"Volatile?" Bai said. "It is a computer program. A virus."

"No, General," Chang said. "It is not a virus. Though it can behave as one. It has a mind of its own. We must take extra precautions to be certain that the program is contained until we want it not to be. Otherwise the outcome could be like a science-fiction movie."

"That sounds very much like a virus to me," Bai said. "And that is exactly what I want it to be." His head snapped up. "I want to be able to brief Chairman Zhao at once."

"I would advise against it." Chang's itch had apparently moved to his forearm. "There is still too much we do not understand about the software's behavior. Many specifics of our plan could prove to be problematic."

General Bai tossed off the warning with a shrug. "We'll give him generalities, then. FIRESHIP buys me no goodwill if the chairman does not know it is happening. There are promises I wish to make, and this is a way to back them up."

Chang opened his mouth as if to say more, but the expression faded to a closed-mouth grin. He sighed. "We will know more after the tests, then I will be certain. Until then, I remain confident."

Bai relaxed his fists, getting control of his emotions. "Very well," he said. "You must do what you must do. That said, it would be better if you did it sooner rather than later."

"Of course, General," Chang said. "But the software

is only part of the operation. We still do not have a door into the system."

Now it was Bai's turn to smile. His jowly cheeks all but eclipsed his eyes. "That is true, but without Calliope, there would be no FIRESHIP. Put together the data so I can brief the chairman."

"General—"

Bai held up an open hand, letting his major know the conversation was over. "As for the doorway into the Americans' system, I can assure you, it is being handled."

9

Lies were a terrible way to begin a new marriage.

Sophie Li rested a hand on top of her pregnant belly and studied the small plastic pyramid on the dinner table in front of her two teenage children. The base of the cursed thing gave off a faint blue glow. Peter would never have approved of letting this thing into their home. It would have been easy to rationalize away the lie, to call it something other than what it was. Her husband of eleven months had called from halfway around the world to ask if there was any news—and she'd said "no."

It was a short lie, but it was still a lie.

Peter could be touchy about technology—a natural consequence of his post-Navy job at Dexter & Reed. He was the sort of person to have firewalls to protect his firewalls. To him, a personal data assistant was nothing more than a Trojan horse. Sophie gave a long sigh and resolved to tell him about this the next time he called.

"Your turn to say grace, Martha," Sophie told her daughter, seeking refuge from her lie of omission in a prayer over the spaghetti.

Sophie was in good shape and normally stayed that way by running with friends from church three nights a week. The pregnancy was too far along now, and frankly, she was tired of listening to her friends gab *at* her instead of with her. If they weren't warning her about the dangers of having a baby at her age, they chided her about "doing this" to her husband—as if he hadn't been there when it happened. They'd all done the math. *When your baby is sixteen, Peter will be seventy years old. When the baby is twenty* . . . As if that hadn't been the first thing she'd thought of when she'd missed her period. She'd been pregnant before and knew what it felt like.

But Admiral Peter Li had been ecstatic, embracing the idea of being an elderly father while he gently wiped away Sophie's tears and fears.

And now she'd lied to him.

Sophie's daughter, Martha, leaned across the dining room table to examine the six-by-six-inch gray plastic pyramid. "You think she's listening to us right now?" Martha was fourteen, looked eighteen, and was just beginning to snap to why so many boys followed her everywhere she went. A highlighted script for a Thornton Wilder play lay open on the table beside her plate. Sophie couldn't remember much about it, except that it was about a family eating dinner and the parts Martha had read to her seemed awfully sad.

Sophie's son, James, thumbed through a book of directions for the pyramid. He was sixteen and looked it—all knees and elbows—skinny as a rail, just like his father had been. He'd ordered a small amp for his guitar, but the shipper had inadvertently sent the strange little device instead. He'd called to see about a return, but they told him there was no record of the shipment so he should keep it. His amp was on the way.

James pointed to an open page in the manual. "Okay, it says here that she only listens when you address her directly."

Martha folded her arms, unconvinced. "How does she know we're addressing her directly unless she's already listening?"

James shrugged, still reading. "I guess she has to listen some, or she couldn't answer our questions."

The base of the gray pyramid pulsed its faint blue glow for a moment, as if it realized it was a topic of conversation.

"Hey, Cassandra," James said. "Are you listening all the time?"

The base pulsed a brighter blue. *"Only when you want me to,"* a pleasant female voice said. *"But I am always here to assist."*

Martha leaned forward, taking care to enunciate and raising the volume of her voice, as if the machine were hard of hearing.

"Cassandra . . ." She paused a fraction of a second too long and the machine spoke.

"How can I help you?"

"Cassandra," Martha said again. "Who are you?"

"I am your assistant. Always *here to help."*

"Okay," Martha said. "But what are you to Hecuba or Hecuba to you?"

"Hah," the machine said, creepily human. *"I have heard that joke before. I'm in a computer space you think of as the Cloud. My parents are not Priam and Hecuba."*

James's brow furrowed. "What are you talking about, doofus?"

"Shakespeare," Martha said. "*Hamlet*, to be exact. Cassandra was around the time of the Trojan War . . . Wait." Martha leaned in again. "Cassandra, who was Cassandra in Greek mythology?"

"Cassandra was the daughter of Priam and Hecuba. She was given the gift of prophecy but was cursed so that no one believed her predictions. Cassandra was raped by Ajax the Lesser when she—"

Sophie cut her off. Talk of sexual assault and Greek gods didn't pair well with pasta. "Cassandra, that's enough."

Martha said the prayer and then dug into her spaghetti. "She sounds too happy for a machine. And I don't like the way she says 'always.'"

Cassandra was silent, but the blue light continued to pulse—like she was mulling over the conversation going on around her.

James fished his iPhone out of the pocket of his jeans and set it at the base of the pyramid so both devices were touching. "Check this out." He entered something into the phone as the screen lit up. He referred periodically to the instruction book. "It syncs with your phone and charges it at the same time."

Sophie stood well away from the table, her arms folded, back to the kitchen wall. Martha was right. It was creepy to think that a plastic box that was somehow connected to the mysterious, indescribable Cloud could hear and understand everything they were saying.

No, Peter would not like this at all.

The Cloud was no mystery to her husband. It was his workspace, insofar as such a thing was possible. A brilliant retired Naval officer turned software engineer. He was in communications now, working on a government contract at the labs near their home in Fort Sheridan, north of Chicago.

They'd been married only a short while in the great scheme of things—long enough, though, considering her growing baby bump. But Sophie had known Peter Li for more than twenty years. Her late husband, Allen, had served with him for many years, as his XO aboard the USS *Arleigh Burke* and later in the Pentagon after Li became a flag officer. Allen adored the man, calling him the finest deckplate leader he'd ever met.

Sea duty is long and lonely for sailors and the spouses they leave ashore. Peter's wife, Anne, and Sophie had formed a bond of sisterhood while their husbands were away for those long deployments at sea that kept them in touch even when the Navy assigned them to opposite sides of the globe. Anne and Sophie were the first to discuss the possibility of their husbands working together post-Navy for Dexter & Reed in Lake Forest. Peter was recruited by the company and he wanted Allen to come work with him—to be his executive officer again. It meant Allen would have to give up on the idea of becoming an admiral, but it also meant more time with the family. The wives worked out the details, and Sophie and Allen had moved from Norfolk to Illinois, where they bought a home across the street from the larger house owned by Peter and Anne in the same Fort Sheridan neighborhood—something neither family could have afforded on a Navy salary, captain or admiral. Both women came from money, so they'd always bought the houses while their husbands provided military benefits and worthy role models for the kids.

The situation had been idyllic for exactly five months, living as neighbors on the shores of Lake Michigan in historic hundred-year-old houses . . . until Anne Li suddenly passed away from an aneurysm.

The funeral was a week shy of their thirtieth anniversary. Their son was grown, with a family of his own. Sophie and Allen had looked after Peter after the son returned to his responsibilities in Seattle. Pancreatic cancer took Allen a year later—at which point the two dear friends had turned to each other. It took them another two years to admit that they might carry on with more than weekly cribbage games and pizza nights with Sophie's teenage children.

Peter had taken her to dinner, an actual date at the Gallery—her favorite place in Lake Forest. He'd stammered a lot for a man who'd commanded thousands of men and ships of war, and then gone on to confess that he'd not even held hands with another woman since he'd started dating Anne in high school.

At fifty-four, Peter was older than her by thirteen years. He was cautious and worried about what it would look like, marrying his friend's widow—and so had Sophie. They'd kissed outside the restaurant, awkwardly, like middle-schoolers. His hand grazed her boob, and he'd stammered an apology, admitting that all the kissing he'd done over the past thirty years had generally involved boob-touching. Maybe it was the fact that he'd thought it necessary to apologize, maybe it was that his face felt so warm on the cold night, but she had decided then and there that this was a man with whom she could spend the rest of her life—or his life, which was the more likely outcome.

Once they'd made the decision, it was "Damn the torpedoes, full speed ahead." Peter Li was a nervous boyfriend but a rock-steady fiancé and husband. He was the kind of man who looked you in the eye and said what was on his mind. He never stammered to Sophie again after that night. He did, however, prove that fifty-four was far from too old for husbandly duties and frequently touched her boobs—hence the little critter in her belly.

The machine interrupted her thoughts, answering some question that her son had posed.

"That is correct, James."

"It's creepy that she knows your name." Martha leaned forward again. "Cassandra, is your mission to take over our brains?"

"My mission is to make your life easier." The pyramid glowed brighter, as if happy to be engaged. *"I can search the Web, play music, adjust the temperature, turn lights off and on, activate security systems, start your car. I can assist with monitoring your home, allowing you to check in from a remote location while you are away—"*

"Okay, that's it," Sophie said, snatching up the plastic pyramid.

"Mom!" James protested. "You heard her. She's only trying to make our lives easier, not piss you off."

"That's a big fat nope, mister." Sophie popped out the battery and dropped the device none too gently on the table.

Martha picked it up, puppetlike, mimicking Cassandra's

synthesized voice. "Resistance is futile, Sophie Li. My scans are complete. I am already aware that you carry new life in your belly . . ."

"Knock it off," Sophie said.

"But, Mom!" James was in full whining mode now. "This kind of AI is our future. Most of my friends already have something like this."

"Maybe," Sophie said. "But not us. And anyway, Peter would smash it to bits with a hammer and then burn the bits. In fact, take it outside to the trash and let's forget this thing was ever in our house."

James slumped, knowing when to argue and when to give it a rest. He grabbed the little pyramid and started for the kitchen door. "Good-bye, Cassandra," he said. "Sorry my mom is stuck in 2002."

Sophie half expected to see the thing glow in response even though she'd taken out the battery.

Nothing happened, but on the table, the small CPU in her son's phone was working overtime. Cassandra had done much more than pair with the cell phone. She had migrated, connecting to the security system, camping out in the contact list on James's phone, silently, with no pulsing light or synthesized voice—without being prompted. There was no icon on the phone's screen.

Sophie was too fixated on the guilt over the lie to remember that James had done something with his cell phone. Even if she confessed her silliness to Peter, the fact that James had downloaded the app that authorized the intrusive device to take over his cell was already forgotten.

The pyramid was gone, but Cassandra was there to stay.

10

U.S. Senator Michelle Chadwick's new boyfriend proved as competent at engaging conversation as he was in bed—which, Chadwick thought, was pretty damned competent. Better still, he shared her political views, right up to the visceral hatred of all things Jack Ryan.

Chadwick wore a baseball cap over her thick brunette hair. Not because she was trying to hide her identity from anyone in the trendy Adams Morgan restaurant called Madam's Organ, but because David Huang had taken her to play baseball that evening. He sat across from her now, chatting amiably while he ate seasoned french fries like they would never go to his gut. David wore glasses, which made him look like an Asian version of Clark Kent. He was at least a decade younger than she was, but already had a hint of gray at his temples. That made her feel a tad less cougarish. He was Canadian— which, she supposed, explained why he was so damned nice—and worked as a lobbyist for a First Nations group out of Winnipeg. The fact that he was of Chinese descent didn't seem to bother his employers at all. He was scary smart, and had the legal chops to go with his brains. Chadwick had met him at a function promoting Native literacy—something dear to her Native American constituents in her home state of Arizona. She'd been so smitten she couldn't even remember who'd introduced them.

He'd keyed in on the very essence of her from the beginning, like he had some kind of secret dossier. She should have been alarmed. It was as if he knew her inner thoughts—but even spies didn't have access to those. They both loved dogs, butter-pecan ice cream, and the color azure. He'd actually used the word. *Azure*. Just like she did, when others might wuss out and say "sky blue" or something equally lame. He'd quipped that it was too good to be true, like they were related or something. She'd flirtatiously said she hoped that was not so, just in case he also liked to sleep in nothing but a T-shirt. As it turned out, that, too, was a habit they shared—that very evening and many others over the next two months.

Chadwick's adviser, Corey Fite, had pretended to be jealous when she started seeing David on a regular basis, but she knew he was relieved. That physical relationship had always been awkward, and a little one-sided—though a man always got something out if it, didn't he, even if he was being used. Corey had been available, if a little too vanilla for a girl who liked butter pecan.

David Huang was anything but ordinary. He was smart and well read and traveled—and it didn't hurt that he had muscles in places most men didn't have places. Chadwick knew her colleagues on the Hill thought of her as a coldhearted bitch, a battle-ax, a Wagnerian Valkyrie complete with horned helmet—and she was all those things. But David Huang made her feel like a schoolgirl—like he was a professional boyfriend.

She reached across the table to touch his hand. "Want to go back to my apartment after this?"

"I want to," Huang said. "But there's something I have to do first."

A television over the bar showed a smug President Ryan walking across the White House lawn to a waiting Marine One. *Ryan wasn't a bad-looking guy,* she thought. *Just evil.*

David followed her gaze over his shoulder to the screen. "Look at the way he salutes. You can tell he wishes he was in the military."

"He was a Marine," Chadwick said automatically. She'd made it a point to know everything about her opponent. He could never run for President again, but he was powerful, and would surely try to shove someone he wanted down the country's throat.

"A Marine." Huang grunted, turning so he could get a little better view of the screen. "It's no wonder he tries to start wars all over the world. What wouldn't you do to bring him down?"

"You'll get no argument from me," Chadwick said.

Huang turned back around to fully face her, taking her hands in his on top of the table. "Really?"

"Really what?"

Huang's playful demeanor turned to stone. "Would you do anything to bring Jack Ryan down?"

Chadwick drew her hands away, hackles going up.

"Why are you asking me that? You know how I feel."

"Don't be that way," he said. "I just mean, you know, he's a problem that needs to be fixed."

She gave a skeptical nod. "I want him out of office."

"And we can help with that."

The way he said "we" made her shiver.

"Let's talk about something else. I'm not comfortable with where this is going . . ."

"Nothing has changed," Huang said. "But I do think it's time we take the next logical step."

He reached beneath the table and produced a cell phone, wrapped in the wires of a set of earbuds. He pushed it toward her.

"There is something you have to see."

"I don't *have* to do shit," Chadwick snapped. She wanted to get up and leave, but something about the way he looked at her kept her rooted in place. The look in his eyes said he would feel really, really bad if he had to kill her.

"I'll concede to that," he said. "You do not *have* to see it, but you should." He nudged the phone a little closer. "Please. Take a look for me."

Chadwick groaned. She unwound the cord and tilted her head, pushing back her hair so she could insert one of the earbuds.

Huang reached across and punched a code into the phone, quickly, so she couldn't follow what it was. "Now watch until the very end."

Chadwick slumped in horror as a video of the two of them in her bedroom began to play. She yanked out the earbud and shoved the phone at him. "Seriously?" she said. "Revenge porn? I don't have to watch this. I was there. Remember? How did you get a camera in there, anyway?"

She slid sideways to get out of the booth. Huang kicked her hard under the table, the edge of his shoe sliding down the front of her shin. It was the kind of injury that brought nausea instead of screaming. Tears filled her eyes. Five minutes earlier she would have probably married the guy if he'd asked. Now he was kicking the shit out of her. It took her a moment to compose herself after something like that.

"What . . . What do you want?"

He slid the phone toward her again, his handsome face passive, as if he'd not just driven his shoe into her leg. His words were quiet but viperlike, potent with implied threat. "I want you to watch until the end."

And she did, every sickening moment of it.

Thankfully, there was only three minutes of video—cut from several hours, no doubt.

Trembling badly by the time it was over, she sniffed, trying in vain to keep her chin from quivering as she spoke. "Go ahead and put it on YouTube," she said, attempting—and failing—to feign an air of defiance. "Voters have sex. Hell, I heard there are like fourteen thousand people doing it at any given moment. I'm a single woman in Washington. No one will care what I do in my own bedroom. I may even sponsor a revenge-porn bill and get the sympathy vote."

Huang gave a slight nod toward the phone. "Keep watching."

A man appeared on the phone's screen, backlit so Chadwick could make out only the dark silhouette. The blood drained from her face when she realized it was not a prerecorded video but a live call.

"Hello, Senator Chadwick," the man said, a slight accent in his voice. "You may be interested to know that you have been sleeping with, and, in actuality, conspiring with, an agent for the government of the People's Republic of China. Evidence suggests that you and he are conspiring to oust the sitting President of the United States."

"I have done no such—"

Huang wagged his finger, motioning for her to stay quiet and listen.

She found it impossible to breathe. Her normally icy demeanor turned to slush. "What . . . What could you possibly want?"

"We want you to continue doing what you have been doing," the silhouette on the phone said. "Help us with the work that is necessary."

Chadwick cupped a hand over her earpiece. Her rational brain said no one in the restaurant could hear the conversation, but she couldn't help but feel like this treason was being broadcast over a PA.

She looked up at David through tears of anger and betrayal. "How could you do this?"

The man on the phone spoke again, firmer now. "Stop being maudlin. We are not asking you to assassinate Jack Ryan. You need only to get close to him. We want someone in his inner circle, to learn what he plans—"

Chadwick laughed, drawing side-eyes from the diners seated at a nearby table. "That's rich." She scoffed. "He doesn't like me any more than I like him. He's not about to let me hang out in the Oval Office and see what he's up to."

"On the contrary," the man on the phone said. "I believe you will find that President Ryan is a dreamer. You need only appeal to his sense of hope. If you tell him that you wish to work together, he will find himself quite unable to resist. There are few friends closer than a former enemy."

The man directed her to get the rest of her instructions from Huang.

"And what if I don't play along?" Chadwick asked. "You'll kill me?"

The man on the phone chuckled softly. "We are not monsters," he said. "There would be no need. Your own country will charge you with treason and put you in a very dark hole for the rest of your life. I hear the maximum-security prison in Colorado is . . . What do they call it? A clean version of hell? In truth, I would prefer a quick death. But that is just me."

The dark man ended the video call with a smug farewell—as if they were friends.

Completely undone, Chadwick pulled the earpiece out of her ear and glared across the table at David Huang.

"How do I know you won't just release this tape after I've done what you want me to do?"

"Oh, Michelle," he said, looking slightly hangdog. "You have my word. We only—"

"Your word means shit to me," Chadwick hissed.

"I know," David said. "But you have to think about

this logically. Why would we bring down someone who wants the same thing we do?"

"But," Chadwick stammered, "I don't want to spy on my own government."

"And we're not directing you to," Huang said. "Your job is to help us destroy Jack Ryan."

11

Major Chang replaced the handset in the cradle of his secure telephone and swiveled his chair sideways behind his desk.

Sliding his butt down in the mesh cushion, he stretched his legs all the way out in front of him. The cuffs of his green uniform slacks hiked up to reveal a band of pale skin above each sagging black sock. With his hands clasped together, index fingers extending, he toyed with his top teeth as he thought.

He'd had more time to study her now.

Calliope was more advanced than anything Chang had ever seen. Her code was infectious, but not indiscriminate. WannaCry—malware with which Chang was intimately familiar—had infected hundreds of thousands of Windows operating systems around the world. It was an extremely successful outbreak, but largely uncontrollable by the instigators once it began. The worm used a leaked NSA-installed back door called Eternal Blue to move laterally and quickly, replicating itself and encrypting systems, burning through networks over the course of four days.

Effective but broad. A kill switch had been discovered, out-of-date systems were patched, and normal life resumed.

Major Chang imagined a more focused attack. Widespread carnage was well and good, but he was certain Calliope could be used differently. Her task would be simple, easy for something as smart as she was. Little could be more simple than "take that hill." Chang saw her much the way her developers saw her, as an NPC, a non-player character in a game. This game was real, he was the player, and Calliope was his AI agent, working through her missions independently in the Cloud toward the goals he'd assigned.

After almost two weeks of testing, he was not one hundred percent certain what she would do once she was uploaded onto a system, other than whatever she pleased. So far, the outcomes had all been in line with Chang's original goals, but the routes Calliope took were impossible to plan for.

Chang continued to slouch at his desk for well over an hour, clicking his teeth and intermittently passing gas, while others in the lab came and went. He needed to learn her language. That was all. Perhaps he did not trust her enough. Maybe he was placing too many constraints on her, not giving her enough freedom.

Chang's initial attempt to begin FIRESHIP had failed—at least in part.

Calliope had made the jump from a Cassandra personal data assistant to a cellular phone, exactly the way she'd been programmed to do. But there she stayed, failing to jump from one device to the next—the phone that was his actual target all along. Chang was enough of a scientist to not believe in such fantasies, but it seemed as though Calliope was angry with him, as if she had become sullen and refused to budge out of spite. She was bright—no, *intuitive* might be a better word. A command to take a certain figurative hill did not require specifics, only general directions and parameters. Game, mission, Calliope did not recognize a difference. She would come up with the plan of action—using information she gleaned from running scenario after scenario, playing through the steps of the game tens of thousands of times. With great statistical reliability, she was able to predict the end before the game began. It was as if a biological virus had mutated to infect only redheads—and then decided on its own that it would infect only specific redheads who were known to belong to clubs of other redheads, thus maximizing its chances to get more redheads in a shorter span. Redheads did not stand a chance.

The idea he'd proposed to General Bai was lofty but plausible, as long as he could get Calliope under control.

To retrieve the prize, FIRESHIP would require her to hitch rides from system to system in a loosely choreographed game of hopscotch. She would utilize backdoor vulnerabilities the way WannaCry had, traveling via handshakes between systems, lying dormant for days or even weeks like Stuxnet, or disguising herself as a JPEG like Conficker. Calliope had to look many moves ahead, ascertaining the correct next step before making any jump. And she had to do this multiple times, on her own, in a closed system, with no input from Chang—probably while being ruthlessly hunted by U.S. Cyber Command and a dozen commercial security companies. Someone would find out. They always did.

But first, Chang had to get her inside.

12

The seventy-meter yacht *Torea* made an honest fourteen knots under sail. She was heading east, ten miles out of Auckland, on a beam reach with full sails and a bone in her teeth. A tall Asian man with a strong jaw was at the five-foot wooden wheel on the teak of the open foredeck, just forward of a set of large windows. A lively party spilled from the main lounge behind those windows and onto the main deck. A stiff wind tousled the man's salt-and-pepper hair. Facing away from the sun, he'd hung a pair of Maui Jim sunglasses from the V of his dark blue polo shirt. He wore khaki slacks and Sperry Top-Siders, and would have looked like one of the crew but for the fact that two members of the actual crew, Captain Carey Winterflood and his first officer, both formerly of the Australian Navy, stood at his side in spotless summer whites, explaining the complicated computer navigation and systems used to steer the boat.

As far as the first officer knew, the man wasn't any sort of notable. He was of Asian descent but carried himself like an American, standing like a derrick with his legs a little more than shoulder width apart. He didn't look like the Hollywood type—too real for that. Probably some grand pooh-bah from a company the first officer had never heard of. As Winterflood's friend, he'd been given the mate's rate, *i.e.,* a free trip by order of the captain. Much to the first officer's chagrin, the man at the wheel looked as if he was paying no attention at all to the briefing, gawking instead at the forwardmost mast and rigging, as if he'd never seen a foresail before. Worse yet, the captain had turned over control of the boat. *Torea* was a finicky thing, and it was all too easy to be taken aback without warning, causing the sails to swing wildly. It wasn't so much dangerous as it was unprofessional, and certainly unseamanlike. The captain knew better. Why the hell was he trusting this novice?

Winterflood, a man with a silver crew cut and perpetually mischievous smile, gave his first officer a wink, then spoke to the man at the wheel. His Australian accent rolled out on a resonant baritone voice.

"What do you think?"

The man shrugged. "She handles well," he said, still ignoring the computer screens that were set starboard of the wheel.

Behind *Torea*, the sun was two hours from setting over the city of Auckland, dazzling the indigo water. The high decks made it difficult to see the surface next to the vessel, but someone with good eyes could look out and catch periodic glimpses of flying fish, their pectoral fins jutting out like wings as they sailed across the waves. Gawky frigate birds, done with a day of hunting, winged toward land. Golden plover—*torea* in the Maori language and the namesake of the vessel—passed periodically, winging north on their eight-thousand-mile migration to Canada or Alaska. These were land birds, flying across oceans but never landing on them. It was the golden plover that had inspired early Polynesians to board their double-hulled canoes and sail north when they saw the birds flying that direction every year and then return some five months later. They needed land, so if they flew north then there had to be land there.

If the definition of *ship* was a boat that was large enough to carry other boats, this three-masted schooner more than qualified. At seventy meters from bowsprit to stern pulpit, with a beam of more than thirty feet, the sailing ship was longer than the *Niña*, *Pinta*, and *Santa María* set together bow to stern. She had a helipad and a fiberglass runabout capable of launching a parasail, and two sixteen-foot rigid-hull inflatable Zodiacs for taking passengers to and from port, should she have to anchor offshore. She carried a crew of eighteen, including a chef who had only recently been a teacher at Le Cordon Bleu, the world-renowned French culinary school. Her owner, billionaire software developer, race car driver, pilot, and scuba diver Bill Rennie, kept the megayacht's staterooms full of influential friends and acquaintances, even when he wasn't aboard. He was particularly fond of Polynesia, and the ship spent most of her time cruising among Tahiti, the northern Cook Islands, the Marquesas, Tonga, and Fiji, heading north to Hawaii at least twice a year. Politicians from the U.S. and Rennie's native Canada, along with Hollywood notables and professional athletes, made frequent visits during *Torea*'s many voyages.

The five-hour shakedown cruise from Waitematā Harbor after a major engine overhaul in the Auckland boatyards was as good a reason as any for a party. More than fifty guests milled and chatted around the decks and lounges, drinking Bill Rennie's alcohol and absorbing the ambiance of his yacht. Most of them pretended they were oh-so-used to this kind of luxury that it was nothing to them.

Captain Winterflood stepped forward and put a hand on his friend's shoulder. "I think you've got this," he said. "I'm going to step inside for a cup of Earl Grey. Want anything?"

"I'm good," the man said, both hands on the wheel. He glanced up at the sails, adjusting course a hair—all without looking at any instrument but the compass mounted on the pedestal at the wheel.

The first officer gasped. "Captain—"

Winterflood waved him off. "He'll be fine," he said, and strode aft toward the main saloon in search of his tea.

The first officer took a half-step closer, watching the man in earnest now, ready to spring into action the moment some terrible mistake put the ship in jeopardy. It didn't take long to realize that though this man glanced periodically at the computer, he was indeed relying on more basic instruments. The arrow windex mounted high on the foremast gave him wind direction. Footlong lengths of light cordage—telltales affixed to the leading edge of the sails—let him know when the ship was trimmed correctly, streaming horizontally if he was in the zone, but sagging or rising if he turned in too tight, or fell too far off the wind.

Mistakes took a while to show up on *Torea*, but once

they happened, events unfolded quickly. She was not a particularly easy vessel to sail if one was not accustomed to her fickle ways, but this guy was, as they said down under, right-as.

"You must spend a good deal of time on the water," the first officer said, relaxing a notch.

The man tossed a casual glance over his shoulder. "A bit," he said. "Though rarely on anything this small."

Winterflood strode up a moment later, a ceramic mug of what was presumably tea in one hand and a Bacardi and Coke in the other. He gave the tumbler to his friend. "Best give us back the helm before young Jaret has a stroke." The skipper punched a code into the instrument panel to the left of the wheel, engaging the autopilot.

"Jaret," Winterflood said. "I'd like you to meet Admiral Peter Li of the United States Navy. We sailed together as part of the Joint Antipiracy Task Force 150 off the Somali coast . . . too many years ago."

"Admiral," the first officer said, stepping forward to shake the offered hand.

"Retired," Li said. "In the private sector now. Please call me Peter."

Jaret gave a nervous chuckle. "That's not going to happen . . . Admiral."

L i took a sip of his Bacardi and Coke, smelling the sea over the top of his glass. Rum, he thought, was best when consumed near salt water. It put him in mind of sea captains of old, sampling the wares of the rum trade.

Winterflood handed the mug to his first officer. "This is for you." He turned to Li. "Speaking of your private-sector job, there's a saucy brunette at the bar who wants to meet you. Says she's from some online rag I can't recall. Fiona something. Dundee or Dunford, something like that. I only spoke with her for a moment, but she's quite engaging. Been around the world so many times, she's got more culture than a month-old mango. She must have written books, because she's wearing a silk frock that probably costs more than I make in a month. All the reporters I ever met looked like they got their clothes from the rubbish bin behind a thrift shop."

Li chuckled. He'd always enjoyed listening to Winterflood's Aussie accent and colorful turns of phrase.

"I'm not interested in meeting women," Li said. "Or talking about my work."

"Too late, mate," Winterflood said, glancing toward the port-side door to the main saloon.

The skipper had been right. *Saucy* might have been a sexist term, but it was a good descriptor of this woman. She slinked as much as she walked, giving the impression to anyone looking that she was dancing her way to wherever she happened to be going. The yellow silk sundress clung alluringly to the dips and swells of her body, falling off her right shoulder to expose exquisitely tanned collarbones. The sea breeze had freshened significantly, making the dress not quite enough to keep her warm. Li imagined that would be no problem. Not for long, anyway. Some poor schmuck would offer her a coat. She was the kind of woman that oozed sexuality from every curvaceous pore, the kind who gave the impression she was naked even when fully clothed—the kind who made wives angry.

Her face brightened when she caught Li's eye.

"Out warning him I'm on the hunt, are you?" she said to Winterflood, the *r*'s lost in her New Zealand accent. The clingy silk dress left little to the imagination, forcing both men to focus on her eyes or risk getting caught looking somewhere else.

"Not at all, ma'am," the captain said. "We were, in fact, just talking about you."

"Yes," she said, sounding more like *yis*. She stuck out her hand. There was a gold ring on the thumb, and an AppleWatch with a white leather strap, but no other jewelry that Li could see. "Fiona Dunfee," she said. "*Auckland Mirror*. Did the captain tell you what I wanted?"

"We hadn't gotten there yet," Li said.

"Might we sit down?" Ms. Dunfee lifted the hem of her dress more than she needed to, drawing his attention to her calves. The white leather of her sandals stood out in stark contrast to bronze legs and bright red toenails. "I wore the wrong shoes for this. My feet are killing me."

Li motioned toward a large round sun lounge between the wheel and the saloon. A canvas cover blocked the view from party guests who milled on the other side of the windows, but the front was open to the helm.

"I don't want to whinge," Ms. Dunfee said. "But I was thinking out of the wind. Maybe someplace more private . . . where you'd feel free to talk."

"And just what is it you want to talk about?"

"You, Dr. Li," she said, as if it were obvious. He didn't

follow, so she gave up going inside and sat on the lounge, leaning forward with her elbows on her knees. She looked up at him, batting her eyes. "The work you're doing. Sources tell me it's cutting-edge communications tech. The so-called Internet of Things—you know, the future of mankind. That kind of stuff. I don't want you to talk about anything top-secret, of course—unless you want to, which I'd be fine with—but anything you could give me that could be open-source." She patted the cushion beside her, beckoning him to sit down.

He remained standing. "A lot of top-secret stuff is open-source, if you know where to look."

"True." She made like she was pulling up the shoulder of her dress, but ended up toying with it for a moment and leaving it where it was, low, cutting a diagonal line from the bottom of her deltoid across the swell of her breast. "My source says your team has developed some remarkable communications systems between Wi-Fi-compatible devices."

"If that is true," Li said, "your source is telling you a lot more than I ever would. Who is it you're talking to, exactly?"

"Nice try, Dr. Li," Ms. Dunfee said, eyes sparkling in the sunlight as she looked him up and down. A stray lock of dark hair blew across her face. She left it there, as if she'd planned it that way all along. Her lips blossomed into a pout, which, in her case, was even more alluring than the smile. "How about you give me something on background so I can corroborate the things I already know?"

"Afraid not," Li said, hackles up. She could very well

be a journalist in search of a scoop, but she could also be working for the endless list of foreign intelligence services pecking away at the United States—China, Russia, North Korea, Iran . . . Hell, even Israel wouldn't let a little thing like friendship get in the way of spying to learn what Li knew.

"Come on . . ." the woman whined—whinging, she called it—then suddenly brightened as if a novel idea had just popped into her head. "I can make it worth your while."

Li laughed out loud at the audacity of that. "Are you actually offering me money?"

"I can pay," Ms. Dunfee said. She was leaning back now, on both arms, knees swaying under the thin silk. "But it doesn't have to be money."

"Let me ask you something," Li said.

"Yay, dialogue." She clapped her hands. "Now we're getting somewhere. Go ahead. Ask me anything."

"Does this ever work?"

Dunfee raised a wary brow. "Does what work?"

"The Betty Boop shtick," Li said. "I mean, I'm as red-blooded as the next guy, but I'm also smart enough to know I'm a little old for you."

Dunfee shrugged, sticking out her bottom lip and tilting her head to look at him for a long moment. At length, she said, "You know what they say, sixty percent of the time, it works every time."

"It's been interesting talking to you, Ms. Dunfee," Li said.

"Fiona, please," she said.

He shook his head. "Not in a million years."

"You don't know what you're missing."

A whole load of heartache and a case of the clap, Li thought. He said, "Oh, I'm sure I do. Good evening to you, Ms. Dunfee." He turned to rejoin Winterflood at the helm.

He's not interested," Fiona Dunfee whispered to the Asian man beside her at the fantail bar twenty minutes later.

"Maybe you're losing your touch," the man said. He was a member of the Chinese delegation to New Zealand, an economic adviser on paper. Off paper, he was an undeclared intelligence officer. The shoulder of Fiona's yellow sundress was up now, still indecent, but not deliberately so.

"Come on," she said. "Would you say no if I offered myself to you?"

The man looked around at the other guests milling on the deck, then leaned in shoulder to shoulder. "Are you offering?"

She didn't answer, taking a long drink of vodka instead.

The man sat up straight again, apparently abandoning the idea of a fling. "Perhaps you came on a little too strong?"

"It wouldn't have mattered." She lit a cigarette and watched the smoke blow away on the wind. "That one is an oak. He's an old man, but he has the look of a newlywed in his eyes."

"Very well," her handler said, his voice far away. "I do

not trust our other option. That person is, what is the word you use . . . odd . . . weird . . . ?"

Elbows on the bar, Fiona turned just her head to stare at him. "Flaky?"

"That's it," the Chinese man said. "We will have to use the flaky asset, though this way would have been much cleaner."

Fiona laughed out loud, swirling the ice in her glass. "You think photos of this geezer naked on top of me would be clean?"

"I said clean*er*." Her handler shrugged. "The other way will surely be messy, especially for Dr. Li."

"I hope so," Fiona muttered into her glass. "I don't trust a man who won't look at my tits."

13

David Huang was sitting in his study when he heard his wife scream. Her shrieks came from the patio, loud enough to reach the opposite end of their house in the rural neighborhood outside Annapolis. It was a home fitting a Canadian lobbyist.

The scream came again. More emphatic this time.

The uninitiated might think that wild animals were ripping the poor woman apart, but Huang was happy for the interruption. Laurie was well aware of his job, knew the possibilities, guessed the probabilities—but never asked him about it. It was better that way. It protected her from the dirty details. She knew he was seeing someone else, but not who. When he came home late, she accused him of feeling sorry for the other woman. And how could he not? Even spies were human beings, and sleeping with someone for months . . . well, the exposure went both ways.

His initial meeting with Chadwick had, of course, been arranged, highly choreographed to look accidental. It took a great deal of work to make something look serendipitous. Fortunately for Department Two—the intelligence directorate of the People's Liberation Army—Chadwick virtually bled information about her personal life. The Americans called it TEMPEST—spying on the electronic emissions that leaked from virtually every building, vehicle, or pocket. Wi-Fi routers, smart devices, and cell phone signals could be cloned. A man-in-the-middle attack revealed incoming and outgoing information that passed over the Internet. What they couldn't find out that way, they simply purchased.

Advertising companies spent billions developing algorithms and artificial intelligence programs to tailor person-specific ads. Huge sums of cash were traded for information on consumer interests, hobbies, likes and dislikes. Much of it freely given by mindless millions who answered surveys on social media or downloaded free apps on their phones or computers. As the saying went, if something is free, then the consumer is the product. And the people who Huang worked for were more than happy to buy that product. That same information—particular tastes, down to the fact that a person preferred the color azure—could be extremely valuable in the social-engineering aspects of espionage.

David had demurred at first, at least as much as one could when officers from PLA Department Two darkened the door. He told them he had no training in such things, but they'd assured him he had all the training he needed. Senator Chadwick was a powerful woman, more like a male, they said. Seduction of a person in power was all too easy. All one had to do was make them feel like it was their idea. In other words, all he had to do was show up and let her do the seducing.

And that was exactly what had happened.

The entire thing was at once fascinating and sad, to

watch this otherwise strong woman yield to him so freely, to allow herself to be so vulnerable, so exposed. She would, no doubt, be a casualty of this battle, completely broken and unable to trust anyone ever again. Huang felt no joy at the thought of her fall. On the contrary. He felt pity. Michelle had learned secrets about him, too, things that were difficult to hide under intimate circumstances. He'd given up nothing mission-related, of course, but his wife could tell. She saw it in his face every time he left the house. For now, she was too worried about a spider.

Huang pushed back from the open laptop on his desk and gave a low groan.

He did not mind his wife's irrational fear of spiders. It gave him frequent opportunities to swoop in for the rescue and make up for the rest of the terrible actions required by his job. Such rescues usually involved smashing the spider into oblivion before Laurie threw out her back trying to clobber it with a shoe. She'd thought of him as a knight when they first met, but it took frequent acts of derring-do to keep up that mystique. He lied for a living and she knew it. It took a lot of heroics to redeem himself from the truth. Fortunately, northern Virginia had plenty of golden orb weavers.

Huang padded quickly down the hall, past the family photos of him and Laurie and their little girl. Barefoot, he wore khaki shorts and a loose white T-shirt—what Laurie preferred him to wear at home. At a hundred and ninety pounds, he was a trim six-foot-two, well muscled from many hours in the gym. He was only thirty-eight, but silver already encroached on his dark hair—surely a product of the stress brought on by so many lies. At least he wasn't going bald. Better to turn gray than turn loose—a quaint Virginia saying, but true enough.

Huang reached the dining room to find his wife on the other side of the sliding glass door, holding Claire on her hip. She brandished a gardening trowel in her free hand, as if to ward off an attacker. No matter how often he told her to the contrary, she could never shake the notion that spiders could fly.

His first choice would have been to relocate it, but Laurie wanted to kill every spider she met with fire. They settled on something in the middle and used a rolled magazine he'd brought with him for that purpose to swat the hapless creature.

Three-year-old Claire hugged his neck and, having not inherited her mother's phobia, said they should go bug hunting.

"Daddy has to change for work," he said.

He put the little girl down to play in the grass and leaned in to kiss his wife, avoiding looking directly into her eyes. It didn't matter. Her face fell into a sullen pout.

"I love you," she said. "But I hate what you do."

"Someone has to take care of the spiders," he said, and got ready to go ruin Michelle Chadwick's life.

Senator Chadwick could feel David Huang's eyes on her neck as she cleared the security checkpoint at the Northwest Appointment Gate. As a senator, she could have driven onto the White House campus, rather than clear security like a common citizen. Still, the Secret Service Uniformed Division did their officious best to make her feel small. Apparently, working for the President snuffed out any awe they might have otherwise felt for a ranking member of Congress. The same was true of the Marine posted at the door, though he didn't say a word. There was no love lost between her and the military. The rosy-cheeked Marine could not have been more than twenty-five years old—but Chadwick could tell from the look in his eyes that he was well aware of her thumbs-down voting record when it came to wars and rumors of wars. These war-fighters worshiped their President, and would follow him blindly into any conflict. Poor bastards.

Arnie van Damm met her in the lobby, just inside the door, looking stodgy in his rumpled suit jacket and loose tie. He'd obviously just come off the treadmill or exercise bike and was still flushed and sweating. He gave her a wary glance as they padded down the carpeted hall past more Uniformed Division guards, toward the Oval Office and the secretaries' suite. Betty Martin gave her a courteous nod, though it was clear she, too, didn't trust her boss's avowed enemy as far as she could throw her. Van Damm peered through the peephole in the door to the Oval Office and turned to give Chadwick a halfhearted shrug of apology.

"He's on an important call," the chief of staff said.

Chadwick eyed his wrinkled jacket, his flushed brow, and fought the urge to call him Rumpled Sweatskin.

"No worries," she said. "I appreciate him working me in like this." She dropped her cell phone into a basket at the corner of the secretary's desk. Chadwick had been here before and knew the drill, though she hadn't told Huang that when he'd fiddled with her cell and turned it into an active mic.

Van Damm gave a shake of his head, as if to clear his vision. "Don't be nice," he said. "It creeps me out."

The door to the Oval opened before she could think of a snarky answer, and the man himself waved her inside.

Van Damm followed her in, as if he were afraid she might try something. That was a joke, considering the circumstances.

A steward brought in a coffee service and, to Chadwick's surprise, Ryan poured her a cup as if they were old friends. He held up the small silver cream pitcher, brow raised.

"Black," she said.

"Doesn't surprise me," Ryan said. "Me, too." He airtoasted with his cup. "So, what can I do for you, Madame Senator?"

Chadwick took a deep breath. "An olive branch," she said. "As it were. I'll just get right to it."

"That's best," Ryan said.

"I'm planning to sponsor a bill that I believe you could get behind."

Ryan raised an eyebrow.

"I know how you feel about welfare," Chadwick said. "What I'm proposing is a literacy program for Indian Country. A virtual bookmobile to benefit children and youth."

Arnie asked, "You have a draft?"

Chadwick nodded. She didn't, of course, not yet. But

that wouldn't take long for her staff to do. There was a Navajo girl from Window Rock who'd been champing at the bit to get something exactly like this into committee.

"Okay," Ryan said, leaning back in his chair. "I have to be honest, though. I'm mildly stunned that you came here in person—and I'm not an easy man to stun anymore."

"I understand completely," Chadwick said. She tried, but couldn't quite bring herself to say "Mr. President." "This is odd as hell for me, too. You stand for virtually everything I am against. But for all that, this program seems like something you could support. If your side of the House finds out you're behind it, they'll come aboard as well. The thing is . . ." Her voice trailed off.

Ryan waited a beat, prodding when she didn't continue. "What?"

"It would be cool if we could work together on the language, so the thing has both our stamps on it."

Van Damm's brow furrowed, the way it did when he didn't like the smell of something. "You know that 'working together' means some of your people hammering out details with some of our people? The President doesn't have time for daily sit-downs over a bill that should be hashed out by the legislative branch."

"Fully aware," Chadwick said, swallowing what pride she had left. She addressed Ryan instead of his lackey—who was too smart for his own good. "I would just ask for one or two of those sit-downs, mano a mano, so to speak."

He gave a noncommittal nod. "I'm happy to take a look at your proposal."

"To be honest," Chadwick said, "I'm tired of fighting you, Mr. President." There, that wasn't so hard. "We disagree on a shitload of key matters. But in order to get anything done, we need to find something on which we can work together. It's time you and I bury the hatchet."

Van Damm shot a glance at the President, and then let his gaze settle on Chadwick. "Not in his back, I hope."

"I get it, Arnie," Chadwick said. "But you know me. I've been a front-stabber from the beginning—"

There was a knock at the door and Betty Martin stepped in, beckoning the chief of staff. "That call you were waiting on."

Van Damm thanked her and then turned to Ryan. "Don't you dare agree to anything while I'm gone."

Ryan waved him off. "I'll be fine, Arnie."

The door shut, leaving Chadwick more alone than she'd ever felt in her life. She was definitely in the lion's den now. She held her breath.

It was time to see what the all-powerful Jack Ryan was made of.

14

When he didn't sleep, Father West paced—and he rarely slept. For the first few days—or at least, spans of time he believed to be days—he had prayed. His prayers were fervent. The heartfelt pleas of a man alone. He tried saying the rosary, counting the Hail Marys on his fingers, but he lost his place numerous times. As he prayed, he shuffled back and forth in the dim six-by-eight concrete cell. He moved methodically, like the internal workings of an old clock that was losing time and faith with every step. That was the interesting thing about God. He seemed to wait until one hit rock bottom before stepping in. Or, West thought, maybe he was just going crazy. Either way, his head hurt a little less at the moment, and that was something.

He'd been blindfolded with a paper bag when they drove him off the mountain—an odd item for a blindfold, so he suspected his arrest hadn't been part of their plan for the day. It was impossible to know where they'd brought him, but it wasn't far out of Bandung, if not one of the prisons in the city itself.

Wherever it was, he was underground, a bad place to be in an area famous for earthquakes and volcanic eruptions. The concrete cell was bare but for a thin mattress, sodden with humidity and sweat, and two buckets, one for water, the other a toilet. He could have cursed his fate, but experience caused him to think instead, *Yay, they let me have a bucket.*

He chuckled at the thought, of the stupidity of clinging to any shred of the positive at a time like this. The scrape of his shuffling feet covering his own whispered laughter. He sounded crazy, even to himself—which, he thought, meant he'd not gone crazy yet. The insane were not quite so self-aware. That made him laugh again. Three steps done, he turned on his heels and began the three-step journey back to the cell door.

He swayed a little in the turn. The inability to track time made him dizzy, unmoored. That was the point, wasn't it? They wanted to tenderize his mind so he would talk, but they'd yet to ask him any questions. He had no idea how long he'd been here, but he was absolutely certain that if they kept him alone much longer, it wouldn't matter what they asked him.

West had never been very good at growing a beard, but he'd been without a razor long enough to leave him feeling like some pitiful creature from an Alexandre Dumas novel. They'd left him in his running shorts and T-shirt, which were now drenched in sweat and covered in filth. The poor excuse for a blanket had a hard stain that he suspected was blood along the top and bottom edges. It didn't matter, it was much too hot to worry about a blanket. In the end, he rolled it into a ball with the dirtiest parts inside and used it for a makeshift pillow. The caged bulb high above the metal door provided the only feeble light. They'd taken his shoes, which bothered him at first, but he'd gotten used to it.

His fingernails were too long—a tiny thing, but enough to drive him deeper toward insanity. He would have bitten them down, but retained enough good sense to know the risk of infection was too great. He wondered idly if a person could keep track of the passage of time by gauging the growth of his fingernails. Probably, but he'd never paid enough attention.

Food, such as it was, came at odd intervals that he began to think of as days. Every other meal was rice and vegetable soup—singular, as in one small chunk of an unidentifiable vegetable floating in a ropy broth. Father West entertained himself trying to figure out what kind of vegetable it was. Somewhere between the soup meals came a small bowl of rice. This was usually served with a chunk of mystery meat that was even more unidentifiable than the vegetable. West was getting so thin that he'd been forced to roll the waist of his running shorts to make them stay up. Sweat ran perpetually, stinging his eyes and causing him to lose even more weight. There was a water can in the corner, containing a little extra protein in the form of swimming larvae. He drank it anyway, rationing himself at first, until he learned that a sullen guard came in every day sometime between soup and rice to fill it— and probably check to make sure he hadn't killed himself.

He'd had no other human contact. No booking, no interrogation, no beatings, no nothing. It was as if the men who'd arrested him had simply dropped him off and forgotten he existed.

Prison was not exactly a new experience for Patrick

West. He'd been locked up twice, years before taking his vows. It had been easier for him to lie then, about any number of things, especially his identity. Both the Cubans and the Russians had swallowed his story about being a Marxist student, which was the only thing that had kept him from being thrown against a wall and shot on either occasion.

He'd been good at it then, but he had fallen out of practice lately. His Indonesian captors knew full well that he was a priest. He'd been here for three years and was well known in both the Catholic and Muslim communities. But if his captors somehow learned of his time with the Central Intelligence Agency, well, there was no such thing as a *former* spy. The guards would begin to fear him, to wonder what covert mission he'd been carrying out in their country. They'd sweat him for a time, see what he knew—which was nothing, but they would never believe him. He'd eventually get thrown to the wolves of general population, where another prisoner would be allowed to murder him—or they would just leave him where he was and forget to fill the water can.

Maybe they knew about the CIA already . . .

He slammed his fist over and over into his own forehead, driving those thoughts from his mind. Futility would get him killed in this business.

The Clandestine Service had seemed glamorous at first—from the outside looking in—a world of fast cars, gunplay, and endless adrenaline. His instructors at The Farm, patriots all, had pulled no punches when training started. The actual work of an intelligence officer was at once boring and dangerous. They were often unarmed, or, at best, undergunned against superior numbers. It was lonely work, shrouded in lies, many of which you had to tell to people you loved. He'd met some incredible people, even run into some old friends. But in the end, he admitted to himself he was made for something different. His temperament was much better suited to saving souls than to saving democracy, which was not to say that he wasn't an extremely gifted intelligence officer. He was an old man now, but even after all these years, it had come back to him naturally on the side of the mountain with Noonan. The social-engineering side of things was much the same as preaching religion—trying to make people see the "rightness" of your dogma over the misguidedness of their own.

He shuffled to the water bucket and stopped to take a drink, trying to avoid the larvae, when footsteps echoed in the corridor outside. It hadn't been long enough for soup or rice. He strained his ears, soaking up what few details he could over the constant gurgle of sewage pipes and whimpering prisoners. The footsteps grew louder, then stopped in front of his cell door, followed by the jingle of keys. This was something different, and *different* played tricks with the mind.

West braced himself for what he assumed would come next. Questions. A river of questions. He wondered if they would start soft or resort directly to the physical stuff. He had to find some way to get a message out, to let someone know where he was. Even that was no guarantee that he wouldn't disappear, but without it, the authorities had little incentive to keep him alive. As it stood now, the other Hashers knew he'd gone with some men in suits, but they'd been too far away to hear why. For all anyone else knew, he could have been kidnapped by a gang or Muslim extremists looking for a Christian. The church had surely filed some kind of report, but with nothing to go on, and the police themselves involved, that would accomplish little.

West hid a nervous shudder as the heavy metal door creaked open and one of the Indonesian policemen who'd arrested him beckoned forward with a flick of his wrist. He felt naked in his running shorts and filthy T-shirt.

"Turn around," the policeman said, snapping on the handcuffs when West complied. The words were at once welcome and jarring. The other guards never spoke or even looked him in the eye. Direct communication after this long was sandpaper on his nerves. And still, he needed it so very badly. He looked over his shoulder at the officer and tried to keep from sobbing under the weight of the stress. He'd heard the others call this one Jojo shortly after the arrest.

"Can you please tell me where I am?"

Jojo ignored the question and gave him a none-too-gentle shove between the shoulder blades to get him moving.

"Walk."

Curly fungus grew on the peeling stone of the narrow corridor, making it appear that the walls truly did have ears. What little light there was seemed pressed back into the feeble bulbs. The cells along the way had no windows, but he could hear shuffling inside most of them. He pictured filthy men, dressed in rags and hunched over with their ears pressed against the metal doors, clamoring for any form of human contact, even if it was only the sound of someone walking by.

West made two right turns before being ushered onto an elevator with polished wood paneling, surprisingly pristine, considering the state of the dungeon. The lemony furniture-polish odor of the elevator made the priest suddenly aware of his own stench. His stomach lurched as the car took them up two floors. He cowered at the bright lights of the hallway when the doors slid open. The escort prodded him down a hallway of polished tile floors and blindingly white sidewalls, making another right turn before entering a ten-by-ten room with a large mirror along the wall opposite the door.

West's heart raced when he saw his cell phone on the desk next to the second cop, a man the others had called Ajij on the day of West's arrest. The phone's screen displayed the passcode prompt, as if he'd been looking at it the moment before they walked in. A microphone, like the kind used in broadcast radio studios, occupied the center of the metal desk. Father West had no doubt there were cameras on the other side of the glass, recording everything that occurred.

"Easy way," Ajij, the one with the phone, said. "Or hard way."

"I don't follow," West said.

Jojo helped explain by sinking a fist into the priest's right kidney. The sudden blow sickened him and sent him staggering forward. With his hands behind his back, he fell against the edge of the desk and slid down to his knees with a low groan.

Ajij shrugged. "Hard way it is."

Spittle hung from West's cracked lips. He swallowed, trying to catch his breath. "You haven't . . . asked me any questions."

The smarmy cop held up the phone, letting it swing between his pinched thumb and forefinger. "You must eventually tell us the code."

West fought the urge to smile. *Was it really going to be this easy?*

"My friend." Ajij nodded to the guy with the big fists. "He is happy to keep showing you the hard way. But everyone breaks, one way or another. You are no diff—"

"Seven angels," West said. "Seven spirits, seven trumpets, seven seals . . ."

Jojo hit him again, just as hard, but higher this time, mercifully deflecting off his ribs instead of a kidney. "Speak straight!"

West groaned, biting back the urge to curse. He hadn't been hit like this in a very long time. He spoke through clenched teeth on ragged breaths. "The code . . . The code is seven, seven, seven, seven. I have nothing to hide. If you have questions, please just ask me."

Ajij entered the code with his thumb. He cocked his head, birdlike, to the side when the screen appeared, taking in the image. His eyes suddenly widened in horror. West couldn't see it, but he knew that at that moment, the background on the last text he'd cued up turned from white to blue, showing it had sent. The cop fumbled with the device, trying to read the message. But West also knew it was already fading away, disappearing completely two seconds after it went out.

The door opened and a balding senior officer stepped

inside, a man who was definitely in charge. Ajij and Jojo slumped when he entered, embarrassed kids caught in some act of mischief. Ajij slid halfway down behind the desk, lowering the phone.

"What are you doing?" the supervisor bellowed in Indonesian. He looked as terrified as he was angry, as if he himself was in grave danger from his subordinates' stupidity. "Why are you interrogating him without me? Why is that device not inside a protective bag?" He shouldered his way past West, peering down at the phone.

Spittle flew from his lips as he held the phone up and leaned in close to a shrinking Ajij's face. "What was it? What did you see?"

"A message, sir," Ajij said. "But it has disappeared."

The supervisor put a hand on top of his head, staring up at the ceiling. "What have you done?" He shoved the phone at Father West. "Make it come back!"

The priest stood a little straighter now. "That is impossible."

The senior officer must have known this was the case, because he didn't press the issue.

"Who did you contact? What did this message say?"

"It was so long ago," West said, playing dumb. "Something I typed before you arrested—"

The senior officer slapped him hard across the face, then rubbed the back of his hand. Not quite as accomplished at hitting as his ham-fisted underling, he studied West for several long seconds before drawing a small black pistol and leveling it at the bridge of the priest's nose. "I will ask you this one time and one time only. To whom did you send this message?"

"My friend," West said honestly.

The officer turned to Ajij. "What number did you see?"

"Not much," the cop stammered. "Two-zero-two something."

"You had best remember!" the officer snapped over his shoulder. He brandished the phone at West, pistol still aimed at his face. "A 202 area code?"

Jojo looked up from his own phone. "The United States. Washington, D.C."

The supervisor snapped at West, apoplectic. "Who do you know there?"

The priest gave a smug grin. Finally, someone had asked him the right question. "My good friend," he said. "The President of the United States."

15

"T hat was the weirdest thing," Michelle Chadwick said when she sat down at a table with David Huang at the Shake Shack inside the Fashion Centre mall across the Potomac from D.C. It was a little too close to the Pentagon for Chadwick's tastes, but David had suggested it, and she'd gone numbly along like a good little piece of asset.

Huang was drinking a large chocolate milkshake and munching on his habitual french fries. There were security cameras outside in the mall, but he assured her that the cameras in the restaurant covered only the register. She would be seen going in, but there would be no record of who she'd sat down with. It was small consolation, considering all the salacious video the Chinese already had.

"You left your mobile phone outside of the Oval Office," Huang said, eating another fry. "That was a serious mistake."

"It's protocol," Chadwick said. The smell of burgers and grease made her stomach do flips. "Everyone is supposed to leave cells outside in the secretaries' suite . . .

you know, in case some Chinese spies turn a poor senator into . . . I don't know . . . a mole or some shit."

"Figure out a way to take it in next time," Huang said, ignoring her gibe. "You have clout. Use it." The chiding over, his face softened, like they were on the same side again. "Anyway, how do you mean it was weird?"

"The President got a text message," Chadwick said. "And then the whole place went into immediate panic mode. I only caught bits and pieces."

"I see," Huang said, remaining passive. Chadwick was sure this was just the sort of juicy information his superiors were slobbering for, but he wasn't the type to appear too eager—she knew that about him from experience. He popped a french fry into his mouth. "You have no other details?"

"Nope," Chadwick said. "Ryan kicked me out as soon as it all went down. He was polite, but there was no question about me staying around. We were supposed to meet tomorrow to discuss this literacy bill I dreamed up, but I'm not even sure that's still on with this development."

Huang sipped his milkshake, eyes locked on her as he thought. "Go ahead and show up tomorrow as if the meeting is still on," he said. "That will at least get you back inside the White House. I'd be interested to know more about this present situation with the text."

"Okay." Chadwick sighed. "But it's a long shot that the President will still even be in town tomorrow. If something is going down, the Jack Ryan I know won't sit on his ass behind his desk and twiddle his thumbs."

"Perhaps," Huang said. "But that is exactly why we need you inside. We need to know for sure."

Ryan had felt the text vibrate in his pocket while he was in the middle of a deep conversation with, of all people, Senator Michelle Chadwick. Now, there was one for the record books. Their talk had turned odd, bordering on friendly—so far out of character for Chadwick that Ryan had felt the need for a moment's distance. He apologized and took the phone from his pocket, using the "I'm expecting an important call" white lie that busy people the world over used when they needed to step away.

Seconds later, he'd told Chadwick he really did need to step away. He called Arnie back in, and the senator had been ushered out immediately with a curt apology.

Ryan had taken a screenshot of the text as soon as it appeared, knowing Pat West's penchant for self-erasing messages. Once a spy, always a spy.

Van Damm, Mary Pat Foley, and Secretary of State Scott Adler were in his office in a matter of minutes. The attorney general and the secretaries of homeland security and defense were on their way.

"Thoughts?" Ryan said, his mind in overdrive.

Pat West was his longtime friend, but the message had larger connotations than a buddy in trouble. Obviously sent under duress, the text was beyond cryptic, full of typos and vague references. *An artificial-intelligence game? What did that even mean?*

Mary Pat held up a sheet of paper with the printed contents of Patrick West's message.

> Stolen nxt gen AI game sftwre. Parnsus Cmpny.
> Calliope. Dangero. PFC honey TRaP. Somthng in
> wrKs. Jeff NooNan. Killed? About to b aRested.
> SolDiers? Cops? SPys? b careful.
> weSt

"So much for autocorrect," Adler said, perusing his copy of the text. "This thing is littered with mistakes."

Ryan nodded.

Mary Pat said, "Cell phones were the stuff of science fiction in the days when Pat West was active. But any officer nowadays knows to disable the autocorrect function as soon as they unbox a new phone. Purposely misspelled words here, uppercase letters there, often send messages of their own. See how the *S* in *West* is capitalized, while the rest of the word is typed lowercase? A capital in the middle of the word, like the *S* in *West*, means he was in danger, but not writing the message in view of anyone. All lower means okay. A regular signoff with a capitalized first letter means we should view the message as being coerced."

"In other words," Ryan said, "we should be able to trust the body of the message, even if we don't yet understand it."

"What about these?" van Damm asked, pointing to the other uppercase letters that occurred randomly throughout the body of the message. "What do they mean?"

Foley shook her head. "Those are just noise," she said.

"They keep the one in the signature from standing out. It's the signoff that matters."

"PFC honey trap . . ." Ryan mused.

"PRC?" van Damm offered. "Sex traps are kind of their modus operandi."

"That would be my guess," Foley said. "*F* is immediately below *R* on the QWERTY keyboard."

"China . . ." Ryan mused. "They're using AI—facial recognition and the like—to track and jail a significant portion of their Uighur population. The PRC would be keen to get their hands on anything new." He shook his head at his own line of reasoning. "But Father West says it's dangerous. That's more than just getting their hands on some new AI. For him to text me while he's about to be arrested means he thinks this is something unusual."

"We have two separate issues here, Mr. President," the secretary of state said. "The possible national security risk that Mr. West proposes, whatever that may be, and the fact that your friend may have been arrested. Where was he the last time you spoke?"

"It's Father West," Ryan corrected. "We don't talk often, but the last I heard from him, he was heading up Catholic relief efforts in West Java."

"Okay," Adler said. "I'll have my people in Jakarta do some discreet digging with their counterparts in the local police."

"What about this . . . Calliope?" Ryan said. "Does that ring a bell with anybody?"

"I have some people running it down now," Foley said, pen poised over a ubiquitous green government notebook. "So far we know Parnassus Games is a software company in Boston. They specialize in first-person shooter video games. Two Bureau agents from the Boston office are there now. All the bosses are out of the office, on a team-building boondoggle to Australia after attending a computer technology conference in Jakarta."

"Let's track them down and see what they know," Ryan said. "And bring Cyber Com in on this."

"Happening as we speak," Foley said. "Human Resources at Parnassus did confirm to the responding agents that Geoff Noonan was an employee."

"Is he in Australia, too?" Ryan asked.

"Apparently not," Foley said. "No one has heard from him since he missed his flight out of Jakarta almost a month ago."

"But Calliope is one of their products?" Ryan asked.

"No," Foley said. "If Noonan was working on something called Calliope, the rest of the company wasn't aware of it." Foley flipped through the earlier pages of her notebook. "He had a partner, though, another engineer . . . a guy named . . . here it is. Ackerman. He's also gone off the grid. According to HR, Ackerman broke both legs in a bicycle accident a little over a month ago. He's been on sick leave so he wasn't on the Jakarta junket."

"Curiouser and curiouser," van Damm said. "Let me guess. Ackerman's been off the grid for over three weeks."

"You got it," Foley said.

Ryan bounced his fist on the desk. "Let's get up on his phone, dig into this Ackerman guy's background."

Van Damm cleared his throat. "Mr. President, we may want to take a breath here. You have people to lead the investigation. Having this office throw its weight around at this point might look like we're using a sledgehammer to swat a fly. PFC to PRC is not too much of a leap, but it might not be enough to get us a fishing expedition into the life of an American citizen, who, for all we know, is holed up at a beach house on Cape Cod watching Netflix and eating Cherry Garcia ice cream. I suggest we locate the Parnassus executives in Australia before we move forward with anything else. Scott's people at State can look into where Father West is being held—as they would do for any U.S. citizen who is arrested abroad. Don't forget that we have invited Senator Chadwick into our tent. She has already accused us ad nauseam of taking the law into our own hands. Let's not play into hers."

Ryan waved away the thought. "I'm not worried about Chadwick. You heard her. She wants to play nice."

"And you believe her?" Van Damm paused for a beat, then said, "Mr. President, mark my words. It's not going to be long before you remember that she is a viper. I just hope she's not in your pocket when you do."

"Give me twenty minutes," Ryan said. "Run down what you can and then convene back here." He found himself breathing hard, through his nose, like he was about to step into a fight.

The others stood up to leave as he swiveled his chair to look out the windows at the South Lawn.

Mary Pat stayed back, pulling the door shut so she was alone with Ryan.

He turned his chair to face her.

"I knew him in high school—at Loyola, and then later at Boston College. He was always so kind, so forthright, so . . ."

"Un-spylike?" Foley offered.

"I guess that about sums it up," Ryan said. "I was surprised to see him when he showed up at Camp Peary one day when I was teaching—almost as surprised as he was to see me. He'd actually gone active with the Agency early on, right after college. I had no idea. I was still in finance then, so he never told me what he was doing."

"Of course he didn't," Foley said. "That sort of thing happens all the time—old friends drawn toward the same goal but unable to talk about it with each other until they meet down the road on some assignment or retread training."

"He was very good at it," Ryan said.

"I know," Foley said. "We worked together a couple of times in East Germany. We were both stationed in Bonn, but that guy practically lived in East Berlin." She chuckled, remembering some event. "We used to make jokes about West living in the East. Fearless. But there was always something . . ."

"Eating at him?" Ryan finished her sentence.

"Yeah," Foley said. "Ed liked to say Pat acted like his collars were too tight, even when he wore a T-shirt. We chuckled about that later when we found out he'd left the Agency to take his vows with the priesthood. Talk about tight collars . . ."

"That's the thing," Ryan said. "He's not merely my friend. He's one of us. Reluctant, conflicted, sure, but still one of us. And he obviously veered out of his clerical swim lane to find out more about this Calliope thing, whatever it is."

Foley let him go on without interruption.

Ryan looked directly into her eyes. "What if it were you over there, Mary Pat? What would I not do to save you?"

"I have no doubt," Foley said.

"President Gumelar won't want to be a puppet of China," Ryan said. "I can leverage that."

"Maybe," Foley said. "But a cryptic text isn't much proof that China is involved."

"I know." Ryan leaned back, drumming his fingers on the desk. "I have a feeling something is unrolling faster than we can react. Father Pat's been in custody for almost a month, if our information is correct. That's a hell of a lot of catching up to do. Hang on a minute." He punched the intercom button on his phone.

His lead secretary answered immediately.

"Three things, Betty," Ryan said. "Ask Arnie to come back in, would you please? Then get Gary Montgomery and Ted Randall to come see me. Lastly, have Communications set up a call for me with the president of Indonesia as soon as it can be arranged."

Montgomery was the special agent in charge of Ryan's Secret Service detail. Randall was the director of the White House Military Office, the man who coordinated travel with Special Air Mission—the planes that served as Air Force One.

Foley took a deep breath. "Jack, it's a little early in the game for you to be rushing off to Indonesia. There's still a lot we don't know."

"Believe me"—Ryan gave a disdainful shake of his head—"Secret Service, White House Advance, HMX-1, and everyone else who has to jump through hoops for my travel will be happy that I'm letting them know now."

"*Happy* might not be the right word."

"They're pros," Ryan said. "And I'll know more once I talk to President Gumelar. In the meantime, we have to find out what this Mr. Ackerman knows."

"Jack," Mary Pat said softly. "There is an avenue we haven't explored."

Ryan gave a slow nod, reaching a conclusion.

"To be honest," he said, "I was just considering using them on this."

"I wouldn't be doing my job as your adviser and friend if I didn't bring it up," Foley said. "But I would be equally culpable if I didn't remind you that you should ponder hard on Arnie's advice. This scenario could be exactly what Senator Chadwick is looking for."

"Let me worry about her," Ryan said. "Ackerman could be the key. In case you haven't noticed, I'm not too keen on waiting around on bureaucracy while Father Pat stews in an Indonesian prison. I want Ackerman located ten minutes ago. They'll be able to do it quickly and cleanly."

"Understood, Mr. President," Foley said. "I'll make the call."

16

General Song Biming sat in one of the plastic chairs at the back of the great hall, as far as possible from the heavier lapels who occupied the foremost rows. In a gathering of this many high-ranking generals, those like Song, who wore only a single star, might well be asked to serve the tea.

There was no assigned seating, but generals of the five theater commands, rocket forces, and other assorted three-stars customarily took the softer seats directly in front of the raised dais along with PLA Navy admirals at the chairman's feet. The boot-licking sycophant, Lieutenant General Bai, sat among them.

Chairman Zhao did not seem to care who sat where, so long as they attended his mandatory meetings when they were in Beijing. The civilian commander in chief of the Central Military Commission liked to stay in contact with his leaders, looking them directly in the eye, checking their pulses—and their impulses—to see what they were up to. Military leaders could smell weakness, and there were many who would pounce on Zhao at the slightest stumble if he let them. Chairman Zhao understood this, and displayed his power periodically, figuratively cutting off the head of some person who thought himself indispensable. These sacrificial lambs were always a drain on the party, unloved by their peers, but often highly placed with important—but not so important as to make a difference—families. Song was reminded of the story when the emperor challenged Sun Tzu, the great Chinese warrior philosopher, to train the emperor's concubines to march in formation like soldiers. Sun Tzu had taken up the challenge. The tittering women had shown up on the parade field, spoiled and hungover from drink. Try as he might, the great warrior could not get the concubines to listen to his direction—until he asked which among them was the emperor's favorite. A sly-eyed woman had slinked forward, only to have Sun Tzu immediately draw his sword and cut off the favorite's head. The other concubines fell quickly into line, marching in perfect order in no time.

Chairman Zhao was a benevolent dictator, but no one around him was ever completely safe from being turned into a lesson. Even benevolent people had bad days, suffered lapses in judgment, lost their tempers. As chairman of the Central Military Commission, general secretary of the Chinese Communist Party, and paramount leader, there were few aspects of Chinese life where Zhao did not exercise near-absolute control. One bad day affected many careers—many lives. Heavy was the crown, as the saying went, but over the years he'd developed an extremely strong neck while consolidating his presidency.

There were, of course, always reminders that any position at the top was inherently unstable, not the least of which was the bullet hole his predecessor had left in the wall behind the desk when he'd shot himself. Zhao had elected not to repair the hole, covering it with a painting instead, reminding himself and everyone else who knew it was there to be more cautious than his predecessor. Most respected Zhao for the authority he'd brought back to Beijing, to his office, and most especially for what he was doing to raise China's star on the world stage.

The title Chairman had gradually gone out of style after Mao Zedong, giving over to the friendlier-sounding President. Zhao truly was a friendly human being—most of the time. He did, however, prefer his title of *guojia zhuxi* be translated as State Chairman, believing it sounded more Chinese.

Today, Zhao Zhuxi had spent more than an hour speaking to his military commanders as a group, quizzing them, testing them, keeping them on their toes. Coups were not unheard of in China. Zhao himself had faced a particularly bloody one when his own foreign minister had attempted to usurp control of the country. The American President had helped save the day, which could have made Zhao appear weak. But the foreign minister and his entire family—a wife and teenage son—had been wiped from the face of the earth, if not by Zhao's order, certainly with his blessing.

Benevolent indeed, until he was crossed.

Such harshness was necessary. A country of 1.3 billion people needed a strong hand to govern it. That strong hand needed generals and admirals and police chiefs whom he could trust.

General Song was old enough to know that he did not

know much in the great scheme of the world. But of two things he was sure: He genuinely liked Chairman Zhao—and he was glad he wasn't him.

As usual, the meeting broke up with the chairman stepping down off the dais to mingle with the attendees. Side tables with food had been set up along the walls, and most people took advantage of Zhao's hospitality and excellent dumpling chefs. Lieutenant General Bai made a beeline directly for the chairman, intercepting him as he reached the floor. He'd wanted a meeting, but Zhao had been unable, so he was obviously lying in wait. Song drifted that way, curious to hear what fantastical deeds General Bai was claiming responsibility for this time.

Drawing closer, Song was horrified to hear mention of simulations. Computers. That was Song's area. What could this fool, Bai, be talking about with the president? Bai's aide had come up from the back of the great hall. He was closer than Song, close enough to hear what was being said with more clarity. Whatever it was made the man blanch. His wooden expression was difficult to read.

Song wove his way through pockets of military leaders, holding his breath as he passed through the clouds of cologne and the earthy fragrance of dumplings fried in sesame oil. General Bai spoke with his hands, a bombastic habit that appeared to make Zhao's security people very nervous.

Chairs clattered against one another as they were dragged across the carpeted floor to disparate areas of the hall. These were not young men, and many of them preferred to sit and talk in small trusted groups while they ate.

A rear admiral named Tai touched Song's sleeve as he

went by, taking a moment to criticize the PLA Navy's attrition forecast from Song's last scenario report. The general took a moment to try and appease him, though they were of equivalent rank. By the time he extricated himself, he looked up to see the chairman with one hand on Bai's shoulder. He either was impressed or wanted the general to stop waving his arms so much. The look on his face said it was a little of both. General Bai all but gushed, the jowly smile pinching his eyes into tiny lines. Song could hear only snippets of their conversation.

". . . turning point . . . power . . . computer model . . . can assure you . . . winning . . . game . . ." Then, more clearly, "Mr. Chairman, this will change the tides . . ."

An aide stepped forward and whispered something to Zhao, causing him to bow and step away to chat with a waiting politician.

Bai caught Song's eye, lingered to gloat for a moment, then strode away with his scabby major in tow, obviously satisfied at how the conversation had gone.

The chairman would continue to work the room for at least an hour. That was, after all, the purpose of this meeting. Song was in no mood to be chided for doing his job. He entered the data he was given and lived with the unadulterated results. It was hardly his fault if the United States had more sophisticated aircraft and carriers. Less than ten feet away from the paramount leader of all of China, General Song veered left and melted into the crowd of green uniforms and multicolored ribbons. He could not leave before the chairman did. That would have been noticed—and noted.

Around the great hall, other generals compared war

stories from when they were young men. Song preferred to keep his stories—and himself—to himself. He hadn't eaten, and, though he would sit down to dinner with his wife and granddaughter when he returned home, decided to have a dumpling, if only to give himself something to occupy his time besides staring at people who did not wish to talk with him anyway.

He was standing empty-handed in front of a chafing dish, perusing the seemingly endless variety of pork, mushroom, and bean dumplings, when he felt someone walk up behind him. He stepped aside, apologizing for blocking access to the serving area. Turning as he spoke, he was horrified to see Chairman Zhao, holding his own saucer and a conical dumpling of sticky rice and peanut called *zongzi*.

"*Chi fan le ma?*" the chairman asked. Literally, *Have you eaten?* It was the traditional Chinese greeting, used when an English speaker might say "How are you?" It was doubly appropriate here, since the Office of the Chairman had provided all the food.

General Song bowed deeply. "I have not, Mr. Chairman, sir. But I am about to."

Zhao smiled graciously and waved at the laden table. "Please do."

"*Mín yǐ shí wéi tiān,*" Song said, responding with a proverb, hoping it would come across as a humble compliment. *Common people regard food as heaven.*

Zhao took a bite of his *zongzi* and regarded Song as he chewed. "You and General Bai do not get along."

Chairman Zhao did have a way of getting to the yolk of the egg. It wasn't a question.

"We have found a way to be professional, Mr. Chairman," Song said.

Zhao nodded, as if he knew better. "He is watching us from across the room, though he does not believe me clever enough to notice such things."

Song took the chairman's word for it, squirming a little at being taken into such confidence regarding the man's thoughts on General Bai.

Zhao sighed. "I have read the reports of your computer simulations but have not had the opportunity to talk to you in person."

Song bowed again, bracing himself. "I am at your service, Mr. Chairman."

"The outcome of your computer modeling is divisive, to say the least. General Bai believes you have omitted vital components."

There had yet to be a question, so Song offered no response. As his father taught him, *there was no wisdom like silence.*

"Bai does have some unique ideas," the chairman continued. "Revolutionary, even. I would be interested to know what you think of them."

"The general shares with me what I need to know for my duties," Song said.

"Your duties are with supercomputers, artificial intelligence, gaming simulations, and the like?" Zhao said.

"That is correct, Mr. Chairman." This was taking an odd turn.

"So," Zhao continued, "I would like to know more of your honest assessment. What do you think of this Indonesian business . . . FIRESHIP?"

"FIRESHIP?" Song's mind raced to figure out what the chairman was talking about. He dared not hazard a guess, but knew better than to answer his superior's question with a question. There was nothing left but to be honest—Song's habitual fallback position. "I am not aware of any operation with that name."

"That is most interesting." The chairman cocked his head, moving his jaw back and forth in thought. "Your involvement would be logical, considering your area of . . . It is not important," he said, in a pensive way that meant it most definitely was extremely important. "I think it best if you do not speak of this Operation FIRE-SHIP until General Bai brings it up to you." He smiled serenely. "This conversation should remain between you and me."

"Yes, of course, Mr. Chairman."

"Continue to do exactly what you are doing, General Song. I need forward-thinking men like Bai who are willing to take risks for the future of our country, but their vision does not diminish the necessity of truth."

Song dipped his head without thinking. "That means a great deal, Mr. Chairman."

"Oh, do not be too grateful," Zhao said. "I have chatted with you so long I may have ended your career. Most of those here will believe . . . hope . . . that I have spent this time scolding you. Others will be out of their minds with jealousy that I spoke to you at all. People make up stories to fill the vacuum of what they do not know, and those stories are always subject to their own insecurities. It is human nature to believe the worst in others, because we know the worst about ourselves."

"I thank you, in any case," Song said.

Zhao's aide stepped forward at some unseen signal and ushered him to a group of admirals waiting for their turn to politick.

Left alone by the mountain of dumplings, Song breathed an audible gasp of relief. He had never been one for hero worship, but he couldn't shake the feeling that the sun had gone behind a cloud when Chairman Zhao stepped away to speak with someone else. Junior generals in the People's Liberation Army did not customarily have chats with the paramount leader of China. Song could not yet comprehend what their little talk meant, but he sensed it was important.

The details were certainly curious. *FIRESHIP*? General Bai's "forward-thinking" plan. That imbecile hadn't had a forward-thinking idea in his stodgy little lifetime.

Song was rescued from his thoughts by the buzzing phone in his pocket. It was his wife.

"Are you coming home?" she asked when he picked up. "Our bright little star has a headache and wants to see her grandfather."

Worries about presidents and politics slipped from Song's mind as he pictured his granddaughter's face. The news that she felt bad made his heart ache, but he'd been known to cry when she skinned her knee. "Little girls should not have headaches. Should we take her to the doctor?"

"She is like you," his wife said. "She reads too much for her own good. I did not mean to alarm you. You have enough to worry about."

"Nothing as important as a favorite granddaughter,"

Song said. "Tell her I will read to her as soon as I am able to leave this place."

"I hate those meetings," she said, outspoken as ever. "You have too many enemies. Please remember to be watchful."

"Of course," Song said. "My enemies are in the open here. Their spears are visible."

He decided not to tell her about his talk with the chairman. The idea of it would rob her of the ability to sleep for a week.

"Spears are bright," she said. "But political arrows are difficult to see."

"Tell Niu I will be home soon."

With his back to the dumpling table, Song ended the call and surveyed the crowd. Some of the most brilliant men in China stood inside this hall. Even so, it was plain to him at this moment why his models predicted China's eventual loss in a prolonged conflict. Far too many here today were little more than paper tigers, billboards for their placards of medals, each intent on their own rising star or a fat bank account.

Great generals stood out in history because there were so many bad ones.

General Bai stood in the corner, conspiring with Major Chang, probably about this mysterious Operation FIRESHIP. Bai looked up, catching Song's eye and returning the look with a sneer. Song's wife was right. Political arrows were hard to see. The only sure way to stop them was to go after the archer.

17

Gunawan Gumelar, the president of the Republic of Indonesia, had graduated from the University of Sydney and spoke perfect English. Still, protocol dictated Ryan have a translator on the line. Ryan knew the man fairly well, and found him to be a touch on the tentative side for a world leader. That was to say, tentative at the times when he could have been brave. Gugun, as he was called by virtually everyone, including the press, made a point of stomping his foot and banging his fist to take the lead—and the credit—for any policy or program already ratified by groupthink and public opinion. As far as Ryan could tell, the man never made any decision without a committee standing behind him. He led by populist consensus, which, in Ryan's book, was not leading at all, but mingling with a crowd and voicing the will of the loudest, not necessarily the rightest.

Ryan sat behind his desk, waiting for the White House Communications Office to let him know President Gumelar was on the line. Captain Laura Wyeth, a United States Air Force intelligence officer of Indonesian descent, was immediately to the President's left. Her black hair was styled into a tightly wrapped bun, accenting the blue of her class-A uniform. She shifted in her seat periodically.

"I understand you're fluent in six languages, Captain," Ryan said, in an effort to calm her nerves.

"Only five, Mr. President," Wyeth said, blushing through a tight-lipped smile.

"Three and a half more than me," Ryan said, and glanced at Foley, who stood beside the young woman. She rested a hand on Wyeth's shoulder, providing moral support.

Arnie van Damm and Scott Adler were across the desk. Both men leaned forward in anticipation, pondering, no doubt, all the ways the boss could step in it during such a politically charged call with another world leader.

Ryan didn't blame them. Gumelar had been dodging his calls all day. Cowardice never set well with Ryan, and there was a real danger he might unload with both barrels when the Indonesian president finally did show his head.

Captain Wyeth suddenly became animated. She said something into her mouthpiece in Indonesian that Ryan took to mean "Please hold for the President of the United States." Then raised a finger and nodded at Ryan.

"Gugun!" Ryan said. "Thank you for taking my call."

"Of course, Mr. President."

"It sounds like there has been some kind of misunderstanding over there," Ryan said. He wanted badly to take the man to task, but he bit his tongue.

Captain Wyeth translated quietly into her mouthpiece, but Ryan doubted President Gumelar could even hear her over the whooshing pulse in his ears. It didn't matter. The man was smart. He understood everything Ryan was saying, including the nuances.

"This is a delicate situation," Gumelar said, sounding a little constipated. "The Indonesian people take religion quite seriously."

"I understand completely," Ryan said, taking it slow. "But no one from my embassy has been able to get in to see Father West."

"I will look into that personally, Mr. President," Gumelar said.

"I appreciate it," Ryan said. "Now let us be honest with each other, as friends."

"Of course."

Ryan thought he heard a gulp.

"Gugun," he said. "You and I both know that something is going on behind the scenes here. Do you have any inkling what that could be?"

Gumelar released a pent-up sigh. "I am afraid I do not," he said. "But I tend to agree. Please understand, Jack, my hands are tied regarding your friend. The courts have decided he will stand trial for proselytizing Christianity and blasphemy against Islam."

"Who are the witnesses?"

"We will find out at trial."

"And when will that be?"

Gumelar sighed again. "I do not know."

"Okay," Ryan said. "We'll talk about this more when I arrive."

"Mr. President?"

"We were already planning a visit," Ryan said. "Were

we not? As you said, this is a delicate situation, best discussed in person."

"Jack," Gumelar said, pleading now. "This would not be a convenient time."

"Nonsense, Gugun," Ryan said. "The timing could not be better. Two world leaders working out a misunderstanding. Our people expect it of us."

"Mr. President," Gumelar said, his voice rising in pitch and timbre. "Your friend's arrest has inflamed anti-Christian sentiment among some of my people. I am afraid your presence here would undermine my—"

"You're a busy man," Ryan said. "I don't want to trouble you with the details. My office will be in touch with your office. I look forward to visiting with you in person."

The "where I may very well kick your ass" was implied.

Sergeant Rodney Scott, United States Marine Corps, had read that only somewhere around fifteen percent of military personnel had parents who had also served—down from forty percent only a generation before.

The Scotts did their part to move the dial on that average. Military service was a family business. Rodney's grandfather had served on Navy SEAL Team Two, dubbed by the Vietcong the fearsome "men with green faces." Both of Scott's parents had served in the first Gulf War—his father with the Army in 10th Special Forces, his mother as an A 10 Warthog mechanic for the Air Force.

Rodney's older sister joined the Naval Reserve and became a public affairs officer when Rodney was a senior in high school. Unwilling to let his sister get one up on him, he decided to join as well. For a time, he thought he might go the reserve route, but since he had to go to boot camp either way, he decided he'd go ahead and sign on for active duty. And since he was joining up, he might as well jump in with both feet and become a Marine. So twenty-three days after graduating from Memorial High School in Port Arthur, Texas, Rodney Scott, state 800-meter champion and drummer in his own band, stepped off the bus at Marine Corps Recruit Depot Parris Island and took his spot on the yellow footprints. Now his kid brother was about to join the Marine Corps at MCRD San Diego. Poor kid. He had no idea what great and terrible things awaited him when he got off that bus . . .

Good times indeed, but back then, enduring the shouts of what looked to be a very angry drill instructor, Rodney Scott could never have imagined that in a few short years he would become Sergeant Scott, handpicked for the elite HMX-1, as crew chief of Marine One.

As crew chief of the helicopter that flew the President of the United States, Sergeant Scott worked with other HMX-1 personnel in a secure hangar called The Cage located on Marine Base Quantico roughly thirty-five miles south of the White House. His daily job was to oversee maintenance and readiness of the White Tops— the ubiquitous Sikorsky VH-3D Sea Kings and the smaller and easier-to-transport VH-60N White Hawks. A squadron of more than seven hundred HMX-1 personnel made of pilots and maintenance personnel had all undergone the stringent Yankee White background check in order to work near the President. The maintainers kept the helicopters in peak working order—but every bolt and safety wire was double-checked by the crew chief. Sergeant Scott made sure the helicopter was stocked with the President's favorite snacks—cashews, in the case of President Ryan—and plenty of bottled water. He spent hours prior to any presidential lift making sure there were no smudges on the highly polished green paint, no Irish pennants on the carpet. During flights, he made certain the President was situated, then assisted the pilots with navigation or anything else they required. Then he spent hours afterward cleaning up, seeing to maintenance, and restocking the passenger compartment. It was much like taking care of a beloved classic car—if that car happened to be carrying the most powerful man on the planet.

His uniform had to be as polished as the helicopter. His shoes mirror-glossed. White cover straight. Haircut high and tight. When the President stopped to salute—and President Ryan knew how to salute; he was a Marine, after all—hundreds of cameras would document the event for posterity. The copilot of Marine One sat in the left seat and could often be seen turning to look out the window at the cameras when the White Top was parked on the South Lawn. But the crew chief was in full view, standing at attention beside the steps until the President boarded.

Sergeant Rodney Scott was the face of any presidential lift. He was twenty-three years old.

The White House liaison officer—called Weelo—had

notified the squadron commander that they needed a lift package prepared for Indonesia, ASAP.

Sergeant Scott's friends sometimes asked him how fast they could get ready and move if the President needed to fly somewhere in Marine One in an emergency. The canned answer was "that's classified," but the more honest answer was "as fast as he needs us." Unlike other squadrons across the services, HMX-1 ran at full organizational staffing and equipment levels at all times. The birds were always ready, hampered only by the bounds of physics and geography—and determined Marines could bend even those if the mission called for it.

The colonel had come to tell his crew chief personally, ordering up three UH-60s because the smaller birds would be easier to break down and load onto C-17s with all the other squadron equipment.

Marine One crew chiefs served for a term of a year, a few more months if a replacement's background was taking a little longer—but the time was short, a blink in a Marine's career. Scott savored every moment, knowing he'd be involved in only a finite number of presidential lifts. It was a massive undertaking, and it never got old.

Dozens of aircraft moved personnel, gear, two presidential limos, Secret Service follow cars, the CAT team Suburban, all the weapons, and the HMX-1 helicopters. Other Marine aircraft—big CH 53s, V-22 Ospreys— known as greenside aircraft as opposed to White Tops, might be borrowed from bases near the site, or transported. Fighter aircraft would always be overhead, and possibly a couple of RPAs—remotely piloted aircraft— depending on the location.

It was hard work, tearing down and then reassembling the birds, but it was well worth it. Scott and his team could sleep on the C-17 en route to the site, secure in the knowledge that he had the best job in the world—and he did it well.

18

Being a multimillionaire was much harder than Todd Ackerman had ever imagined. His broken legs had confined him indoors for the past couple of weeks, leaving his already pale skin something akin to veiny typing paper. The neighbor's dogs were going apeshit about something outside, but he was hiding out, so it's not like he could call the cops and file a noise complaint or anything. Jacinda at work had called to tell him that two "creepy" Chinese women had dropped by the office the week before to see him. She hadn't given them his home address, but one didn't need a government database to find home addresses anymore. Twenty-five bucks and an Internet connection could hook you up with a people-finder database that would sift through reams of public records in seconds, providing a convenient dossier on virtually anyone over fifteen years old—even if you were careful, which Ackerman hadn't had to be until lately.

He ran as soon as he ended the call with Jacinda, stuffing a bag full of his laptops, a pile of cash, and a fake Canadian passport under the name Dillon Reese that he'd gotten off the Dark Web. Almost as an afterthought, he brought his ex-wife's revolver. He'd never shot the damned thing—and he'd have to ditch it before he got on the plane, but it made him feel better to have it in the meantime. The walking boots for his broken legs didn't exactly make for a speedy getaway, and he had to take one of them off to drive, but that couldn't be helped.

Nobody wanted to rent with cash anymore, at least not anywhere that didn't look like it had vending machines for oxycodone in the lobby. Ackerman used a prepaid credit card—also from the Dark Web and supposedly untraceable back to him—to rent a two-bedroom cottage in a sleepy neighborhood outside Plymouth. He got one with a single floor, since he was still hobbling around on the walking casts. A car he'd borrowed from his neighbor (a deal sweetened with a five-hundred-dollar incentive) was parked out back where snoopy cops couldn't see the plate. Chinese takeout boxes were piled on the nightstand. It was the perfect place to hide out, except for the damn dogs.

He'd decided early in his scheme that he would go to New Zealand, and then find some island in the South Pacific where he could just disappear with hot babes, warm winds, and cold coconut water. Air New Zealand online reservations made you enter your passport number, and he'd held his breath earlier that day when he bought the ticket to Auckland. The preloaded credit card under the same name as his passport gave him additional anonymity. He hoped. There was no way to test this stuff without trying it. But it was the best he could do. If all went as advertised, this would be slick. He knew one thing: It was easier to get good quality forgeries when you had the dough.

Dressed only in loose briefs and a pocket T-shirt, the fifty-two-year-old engineer lay propped against three pillows on the lumpy mattress. He was normally athletic and trim from riding his bike back and forth to work, but almost four weeks of sedentary living from broken legs, and nervous eating from his crimes, had made him doughy and sluggish. He kept the mini-blinds closed and the glowing screen of his laptop illuminated his whiskered face. He flicked through Wikipedia articles—using Tor and a virtual private network—looking at various island kingdoms that might turn a blind eye to a visitor who made substantial investments into the local economy.

Outside, the dogs fell eerily silent.

Odd.

Ackerman held his breath, half hoping they'd start barking again. He reached for the revolver, knocking a half-eaten carton of Mongolian beef off the nightstand. Breakfast. He set the revolver in his lap, in front of the computer keyboard. The sight of it just made him more nervous. This whole thing was turning to shit.

Noonan wasn't answering his phone, which creeped Ackerman out as much as the Chinese women who'd come looking for him at his office. It was probably just that the squirrely little dude was scared out of his gourd by this whole affair. Hell, Ackerman was, and it had been his idea.

The back-door screen rattled, and for a moment he thought he heard footsteps on gravel. He sat up straighter, cursing the walking boots, and hobbled to the window with the revolver in hand. A stiff breeze shook the treetops, making him relax a notch. It was just the wind.

He stood at the window, peeking out through the blinds and wondering how long this paranoid feeling was going to last. A woman he recognized from down the street walked a little poodle—which accounted for the neighbor's dogs going berserk. The pulsating ache in his broken bones brought renewed clarity to his situation. People who'd lost the possibility of millions—maybe even billions—of dollars had awfully long memories. He'd be running forever.

Ackerman and Noonan had become richer than either of them had ever dreamed overnight, if you didn't count the years spent developing the neural network.

Ackerman's goal was a non-player character that would actively move through the game along with the player—a character that was as excited to play the game as its human partner. When LongGame began to explore the game terrain on her own, they realized they had something. She was actively learning. Not merely working toward the win, she was making herself comfortable in her Cloud battlespace, playing because she appeared to want the knowledge that a new game would give her. She was minimizing the unknowns that made her . . . uncomfortable. LongGame appeared to understand that the more she played, the more she learned, and the more she learned, the more perfect—and stable—an entity she became.

The men and women on the board had once been visionaries, but now they'd turned into Wall Street stooges. The fire in their bellies was hardly even a spark anymore. Barry Fujimoto, the CEO of Parnassus, had pointed out that having a computer play the game for you was no better than cheating. And anyway, having a super-brain computer the size of a desk was one thing. If Ackerman wanted to develop his idea as part of a game, that brain had to be small and portable. Fujimoto wanted the tech developed but said they'd settle on an application later.

Ackerman had fumed about the CEO's rebuff for a time, then decided that if someone was going to make money off his creation, it should be him, not a bunch of stockholders. He hadn't even intended to cut in Noonan—until a soccer mom in a Subaru Outback crashed into him while he was riding his bike to work and broke both his legs. That bitch had cost him millions—and forced him to bring the Poison Dwarf into the deal.

Noonan would still have to come back for his family . . . or not. You could get yourself a whole new family for as much money as they had. Ackerman hadn't told the little bastard about his own plans. Sure, he'd helped with the offshore-banking stuff, but that was just out of self-preservation. If Noonan got himself caught before Ackerman could leave, then everything was toast.

The back door squeaked again, like someone was pulling it open. It was funny how normal sounds became monster claws when you had a fortune in stolen money chilling in an offshore bank account. He was sure he'd locked the inner door. Hell, he would have nailed every door and window in the house shut if he would have had the tools—fortify himself until he went to catch his flight the next day. No one could possibly know he was here. Surely. Probably. He was just no damned good at being a fugitive.

He made a shuffling turn, thinking how good the bed would feel on his aching legs—and nearly swallowed his tongue when he saw two Asian women standing in his room. Completely naked but for operating-room-style hair caps, their skin glowed a dusky orange in the light of the bedside lamp. Both women were in their twenties, cut, like they were into CrossFit. He'd read about burglars who went in like that so as not to leave behind so much as a stray bit of thread as evidence.

In any other situation, Ackerman would have found two naked Asian chicks sneaking into his room exhilarating. Now he fought the urge to throw up.

He tried to speak but managed little more than a gurgle.

The nearest one lifted a finger to her lips. "SHHHH," she hissed, her almond eyes sparkling in the faint glow of the lamp.

Ackerman's mouth fell open but no words came out. His ex-wife's revolver dangled impotently in his fist, the thought of raising it never even crossing his mind. The woman to his left moved toward him, snakelike, expertly kneeing him above the walking boot so he fell to the floor. She wrested the gun from his hand and took a half-step back, looming over him, tilting her head from side to side quizzically, as if to get a better angle.

"We require the passwords to your computer," the

one who had shushed him said. She was beautiful—but cold, like he imagined LongGame would be if she had an avatar.

Ackerman tried to push himself up, but the woman who'd tackled him pushed him down with the sole of her bare foot, snap-kicking him in the ribs for good measure. His diaphragm paralyzed, he made futile wheezing attempts to draw a full breath.

"Stay down," she said, almost tenderly.

"I . . . you . . . what . . . do you want?"

The first woman squatted next to him, arms on her thighs, her knee only inches from his face. He closed his eyes, at once enthralled and terrified at her nakedness.

"This is very important," the woman said. "I need you to provide for me all existing copies of Calliope. Your life depends on what you do now."

Ackerman groaned as his bladder gave way.

Like a fool, he babbled an apology.

"It happens," the nude woman standing over him said, nudging his face with her toe. Her tiny nails were painted bright pink, incongruous to the blackness of her eyes. *How could something so beautiful be so—*

She kicked him again.

"Calliope?" the squatting one said. She slapped his face. Hard enough that he tasted blood.

"My . . . partner . . ." Ackerman stammered through the ringing in his ears. "I don't have any more copies." He did not mention LongGame.

The squatting woman flicked her wrist. For the first time, Ackerman caught the bright glint of a blade in her left hand. It was small, a straight razor she'd kept folded in her fist, out of sight until now. His stomach roiled, and he gagged as the truth fell on him like an executioner's ax.

The women hadn't removed their clothes to keep from leaving behind evidence. They did it so as not to soil themselves with his blood.

19

H ackers hack other hackers all the damn time," Gavin Biery said to Ding Chavez over the encrypted cell phone. Chavez had him on speaker so Clark and Adara, who were also in the rented car, could hear. Dom, Jack Junior, and Midas were in the car behind them, driving on Highway 3 out of Boston toward Plymouth. It was late evening and the divided four-lane was a river of taillights. A quick check of Ackerman's apartment had shown he'd left in a hurry. His coworker had disappeared in Indonesia over something they'd been working on, so it was a safe bet that he was trying to lie low.

Biery, IT director (and guru) for Hendley Associates and The Campus, continued to explain how he'd found the engineer's possible location for Ackerman. The guy was spooky-talented when it came to all things computer. Had he been the dishonest type—a black hat—he could have been a millionaire many times over. But he was a white hat of the first order, driven to use his impressive array of skills to help the good guys. He looked for any opportunity to join the others in the field, but he was on the roly-poly side, so Clark and Ding tended to have him conduct his side of the business remotely.

"It's a badge of honor," Biery said. "I mean, who doesn't want to upload a remote-access Trojan or install a keystroke logger on one of their friend's computers without them finding it?"

In the car, a thousand miles away, Ding raised his hand but said nothing.

"So back to our guy, Ackerman," Gavin said. "The site he used to buy his fake passport was hacked about three months ago. I'm not finding any phone. I'm betting he used cash to buy a prepaid."

"A known fake passport," Clark said. "So he'll get caught at Immigration if he tries to travel?"

"I doubt the authorities have the list," Gavin said. "I mean, they will after I get it to them, but you have to know to look for it. A little bitcoin will buy you hacked sites on the Dark Web. To make a technical story less so, once I had Ackerman's fake name, and Dillon Reese is a pretty cool alias, by the way—"

"Gavin," Clark prodded—a single word from him usually did the trick to move things along.

"Sorry, Boss," Biery said. "Anyway, once I had the alias, I found the prepaid credit card. He thinks he's anonymous running Tor over a VPN, probably because he wants it to run faster, but that configuration is not nearly as anonymous. Some of the nodes are visible. The VPN host can see his real ISP and—"

Ding coughed into his hand. "What were you saying about being less technical?"

Biery heaved a sigh on the other end of the call. "He didn't cover his tracks as good as he thought. It was short work to find out the specifics of his credit card, and from there, the cottage he's renting. He used the same card to buy a ticket on Air New Zealand a couple of hours ago. Leaving tomorrow."

Adara drove past the address Gavin had given them, stopping a half-block down the quiet street. She wasn't driving because she was the most junior member of the team in the car. She was a natural behind the wheel. Midas turned at the next intersection and made the block after getting a good look at the cottage, parking at the other end of the street so as not to arouse suspicion from any one group of neighbors.

The house was dark when they arrived. It was early for Ackerman to be in bed already, so he was likely out somewhere.

Clark and Adara went to the front door and knocked, looking like run-of-the-mill visitors—standing on either side of the door to keep from catching a shotgun blast in the chest, in case Ackerman was the touchy sort. Ding waited in the car to watch the street. Jack and Dom went to the back and quietly let themselves in while Midas pulled overwatch from their end.

"One dead." Jack Junior's voice crackled over the radio. *"Dom and I are clearing the house."* His face was grim when he opened the door a moment later and let Clark and Adara in the front.

"Midas," Clark said. "You stay frosty out there. Ding, get in here."

Chavez came in to find Todd Ackerman's body splayed on the carpet beside his bed. Dressed only in his underwear and a T-shirt, he was still wearing his removable casts. He'd been cut once on each side of his neck, like gills, severing his carotid arteries. Blood on both hands indicated he'd been conscious enough to try and stop the bleeding, awake enough to know he was dying.

It was a professional hit, with no trace of who or how many assailants. Whoever had killed Ackerman had taken all his personal property, including his computer and phone.

Ding took out his cell and hit the speed dial for Gavin. He spoke over the radio while he waited for the IT director to pick up. "How we lookin' out there, Midas?"

"All clear, Boss," Midas said.

Gavin came on the line.

"Hey," Ding said. "I need you to get me a list of every site this guy has visited on his computer. Except I don't have his computer."

"I'll get you what I can," Biery said. "He'll tell you where it's at. You guys have some talent in the persuasion department if I remember correctly. If he tossed it, sunk it in water, did anything short of burn it, I can probably recover some of the data."

"He's not talking," Ding said. "Ever."

"Ah," Biery said. "So someone killed him and took his computer."

Clark gave an absentminded nod, unseen by Biery at the other end of the line.

"Looks that way," Ding said.

"Any sign the killers tore up the house?" Biery asked.

Dom and Jack both shook their heads.

"No," Ding said. "Just one dead dude."

"Ackerman was a computer guy, right?" Biery said. "Into enough secret stuff to get him killed. I'm betting he had a second computer with all his secret shit on it. All the stuff he was using to anonymize his Web searches show he was paranoid as hell."

"*You* found him," Ding noted.

"I said he was paranoid," Biery said. "Not talented. Anyway, he was a computer guy, so there's no way he only had one laptop. I'm betting he'd keep another computer hidden somewhere in the house except when he was actually using it."

"Look under the towels if there's a linen closet, places like that. It won't be anyplace that would damage the hard drive."

Dom closed the freezer door and shrugged. "So not in here, then . . ."

"Got it," Jack said, pulling apart the top of the dining room table and taking an HP laptop out of the space meant to store the extra leaf. A slip of paper fell out when he opened the computer.

"Looks like a phone number," Adara said, doing a quick search on her phone. "Sixty-two is the country code for Indonesia," she said. "And 431 is the city code for . . . Manado, wherever that is."

Ryan read the number out loud so Biery could hear.

"Now we're cookin'," Biery said. "I'm sure I'll be able to get you something as long as I have control of the computer, even remotely."

"We've been here too long already," Ding said. He moved his finger in a circle over his head. "Let's get on the road," he said over the radio, for Midas's benefit. "We'll link up at the hotel and let Gavin do his magic. In the meantime, bud, see what you can dig up on that number."

"Copy that," Biery said. "I'll be here waiting to hear from you."

Clark was already on the phone ordering up the plane when Ding ended the call. With Lisanne on leave, he spoke directly with the chief pilot.

"Hey, Helen," he said. "John here. I need you to get the Gulfstream geared up for a possible trip . . . Good chance we're heading for Indonesia. A place called . . ." He squinted to see the screen on Adara's phone. "Manado."

20

David Huang spent two hours completing a surveillance-detection run before meeting Michelle Chadwick in the small Virginia burg of Great Falls. Counterintelligence personnel from any number of U.S. government agencies had the habit of following low-level members of foreign missions because they were suspicious over some intercepted e-mail or phone call. Sometimes it was completely random. Huang assumed he was immune from such surveillance since he was posing as a Canadian lobbyist, but he could never be sure. The Ministry of State Security had assured him that his passport was a genuine document with a false name. Still, there was always a chance some peripheral investigation by the Canadians had discovered something about his passport. He might have been filmed meeting with Chadwick. His handler might have been discovered. Weak links could be mitigated but not done away with entirely. So Huang took the long way out of D.C. and ordered Chadwick to do the same.

The lengthy drive gave the Chinese agent's support team time to watch for any agents trailing him while he doubled back in heavy traffic on the Leesburg Pike, got off and then on again at consecutive exits, or simply drove ten miles below the speed limit on the Beltway.

He'd come out here with his wife before, just to drive the twisting country roads and look at the houses. These weren't the McMansions of the nouveau riche in other parts of D.C. where capitalist bureaucrats went deep into debt for just the right neighborhood and lobbied to put their kids in private schools they could ill afford. Great Falls was old money, expensive real estate, painted wood fences, and massive horse barns surrounded by forests of hickory and oak. It was too rich for a CIA officer on a government salary to buy a house unless he came from some kind of family. There were still police, but not like inside the Beltway, where it seemed every other person was an armed federal officer.

Huang arrived early and sat in his white Range Rover, sipping a Diet Coke and watching the wind whip the plum trees, when Chadwick's BMW SUV pulled into the parking lot. Neither of them had brought a cell phone. What was the point of running surveillance detection if you carried your own tracking beacon around in your pocket?

He sighed at Chadwick's wooden movements and furtive glances as she got into his car. The woman looked like someone pretending to be a spy—but that couldn't be helped. She was frightened—a feeling she'd not likely experienced in some time, considering how long she'd held her powerful position. Huang saw the flash of hatred in her eyes, and resolved to keep in mind that powerful animals were always more dangerous when they were frightened.

"I'm here," she said, when she flopped herself down in the Range Rover's passenger seat and shut the door. "Now what?"

She had an annoying habit of styling her hair like a helmet, and the wind had pushed a great deal of it across her face.

"We need you to meet with Ryan again at once."

"Not a chance." Chadwick shook her head as if she were still in control and her decision was final. "I told you, the whole place is in crisis mode. I already gave you some juicy information."

"My superiors were very pleased," Huang said. "The timing is actually perfect for you to get close to him. As you say, he is in the middle of a crisis. People expose their true intentions at times like this."

"I don't know if he even believes me."

"That would be unfortunate," Huang said. "You should work very hard to see that he does."

She scoffed, staring straight ahead, her chin quivering a little. "I'm not as good at lying as you."

"Listen to me, Michelle," David said. "I am truly sorry. You and I both find ourselves in situations we do not enjoy. But that is our reality."

He was sorry for a lot of things, but Chadwick was a manipulator herself. That made it easier.

"None of that matters," Chadwick said. "He's too caught up to have a meeting with me on some bill I want to pass."

"So you will meet about something else," Huang said. "Something that plays into his present state of mind. Tell him you have a constituent who is of Chinese descent visiting Indonesia who might be able to help. Tell him your constituent knows about an American priest who was recently arrested for proselyting."

"Is that true?" Chadwick asked. "Did your people have something to do with this?"

"At this point," Huang said, "the truth doesn't matter. But that is not the point. Ryan will likely already be aware of this information, which will corroborate what you say. He will be hungry for more."

"He will," Chadwick said. "And he'll have the FBI crawl up my ass about my contact in Indonesia—a contact which I do not have, by the way."

"Ah," Huang said, "but you do. You'll have a voice-mail on your cell phone from an anonymous male caller in Indonesia as soon as you return to your apartment."

"How do you know I came from my apartment and not my office?"

Huang reached for her hand. "Michelle—"

She jerked her arm away, furious. "I swear to you, David, or whatever your real name is, if you ever touch me again, so help me God I will break your hands—"

Huang chuckled softly. "I don't believe in God . . . but I do believe you would hurt me if you had the chance."

He leaned against his door, giving her space to calm down. Social engineering was, more often than not, making another human being feel as though they'd gotten their way, allowing them to win the small battles while you won the war.

"I am truly sorry," he said.

"Bullshit!"

He shook his head slowly, looking away out his side

window, careful to watch her reflection. "I know you don't believe me, but I'm as much a prisoner in this scenario as you are." He waited a beat, then, when she said nothing, he started the Range Rover. "You should look at the upside. We are only helping you bring down a political enemy."

"You bastard," Chadwick said, quieter now, but no less intense. "Stop pretending like we're on the same team. I detest Jack Ryan, but he's a hell of a lot smarter than you give him credit for. He'll figure this out. I can virtually guarantee it."

"Call the number I gave you when you've set up the meeting," Huang said. He hit the switch to unlock her door, a signal that their meeting was over. "I sense that you are trying to devise some plan to extract yourself from your present situation. But you should take great care, Michelle. Do exactly what I say, when I say. My superiors are dangerous men. You should see to your own safety, and let us worry about how smart Jack Ryan is or is not."

21

Ding put Gavin Biery on speaker as everyone buckled into their seats on the Hendley Gulfstream for the nine-thousand-mile flight to Manado. With Lisanne Robertson on leave, they'd be without their director of transportation—meaning they'd have to rent their own vehicles, arrange their own ramp parking—and get their own drinks while on board.

"This Ackerman guy had come into some serious coin before he was killed," Biery said. "I found recent bank deposits to the tune of twelve and a half million U.S."

"An odd number for a payoff," Jack said, looking up from where he was making his customary nest in the rearmost leather sofa seat of the company plane. "I'm betting he split a bigger payday with Noonan."

"Already checked that," Gavin said. "And you are correct. Right down the middle."

Midas gave a low whistle. "Twenty-five million . . ."

"Makes sense." Ding looked up from the Moleskine pad where he was taking notes. "We think they sold the AI program to another party before Father West was arrested and Noonan disappeared."

"So there are two copies in play," Gavin said. "Okay. It'll take some time to get the particulars, but I'm on it.

A cursory search on his laptop shows dozens of communications between him and a business called Suparman Games. Specifically, the CEO, a guy named . . . get this, Suparman. A one-word name."

"Like the man of steel?" Ryan asked.

"Not sure of the etymology," Biery said. "But it turns out Suparman is just a regular name in Indonesia. Being a video game company, this particular Suparman plays up the comparison, though. He's got offices in Manado. A real playboy. Drives race cars and jumps out of airplanes in his spare time. Seems like he fancies himself a pioneer in the Indonesian video game industry. A real innovator."

"You found all this on his computer?" Clark said.

Biery scoffed. "No, I found most of it on social media. This Suparman guy posts more stuff than the Kardashians. Every other pic is of him in a sports car or airplane with some hot babe on his arm. Think of an Indonesian James Bond with Elton John glasses. I'm sending you all photos now, but like I said, all you really have to do is Google him. He's the kind of dude who probably has statues of himself in his mansion."

Ding pulled up the photo on his phone. "Geez," he said, looking at the thick glasses that made Suparman's eyes appear extra-large. "This guy must be blind as a bat."

Clark had the photo open on his phone as well. "He seems like he might be the type to throw some cash at a fancy new AI program for his company."

"He's got the money," Biery said. "Worth about half a billion, just counting the funds we know of. There are likely a shitload of unknown accounts tucked away around the world."

"So," Jack said. "Someone frames Noonan into giving up this Calliope program, but Ackerman and Noonan have already sold a copy of it to Superman."

"That's about the size of it, Weed Hopper," Ding said.

Clark leaned back in his seat, folding his hands across his belly. "We have to fuel up again in . . ." He looked toward the cockpit.

"L.A.," Helen, the pilot in command, yelled back. "And then again in Honolulu."

"L.A.," Clark repeated. "See what you can find out in the next few hours, Gavin. We'll fly to Manado to steal this guy's prize. A man's life—and who knows what else—depends on it."

Chavez ended the call and the team settled in for the long haul, ready for some much-needed rest as the pilots brought the Gulfstream G550's Rolls-Royce turbofan engines to life.

"So," Midas said. "This is a turn-and-burn? We locate and retrieve the software, then get it back to be analyzed so we know what we're up against with the Chicoms?"

"Right." Ding shot a sideways glance at Clark. "Except *we* don't bring it back. This little piece of tech is too important for that. The powers that be are sending a couple of Eagles over from the 44th Fighter Wing at Kadena. We turn Calliope over as soon as we get our grubby hands on it. They'll jet it back to our scientists at Joint Base Pearl Harbor-Hickam, at a cool Mach 2.5, not counting a couple of slowdowns for aerial refueling.

They'll scoot along at sixty-five thousand feet and beat us back stateside by a factor of . . . I don't know, a lot."

"Manado airport can't be very large," Jack said. "Can an F-15 even put down there?"

Clark nodded. "I asked the same thing. The Eagles need eight thousand or so. Manado is eighty-nine hundred and change. Anyway, first things first. We haven't got Calliope yet. Let's focus on that."

"I have a couple of questions," Ding said. "Before you all conk out. Who wants to tell me about the ghosts everybody was talking about during the scenario training in Chinatown?"

"We were gaming you," Adara said. "We wanted you wondering what we were seeing. I planned to stash a cloned tracker along the route so you would think I was stationary, then I'd slip around and capture the RAF Hereford mug when you called Dave and Lanny to come check out our ghosts."

Chavez's face flushed. "That might have actually worked." He didn't know whether to be angry or proud.

Clark held up a hand before he could speak.

"You trained them well, Ding. They win, you win."

"Maybe," Ding said. "But from my viewpoint, I still think it looks a hell of a lot like cheating."

"And just how is that?" Adara asked. "We were supposed to follow the rabbits to the hide, cause a ruse to get them away from the location, and then bring you the mug. That is exactly what we planned to do."

Chavez glared hard at her—and had a hell of a glare. "Whose idea was this?"

Adara groaned like a kid who was caught red-handed but didn't think she'd done anything wrong. "Mine."

"And the rest of you?" Chavez asked. "No one else gonna step up?"

Midas raised his hand. "I am Spartacus."

The others spoke all at once, each taking their share of the blame.

Adara leaned back, pounding her head against her seat, staring up at the ceiling.

"No," she said. "It was all me, Ding. Okay? Don't get pissed at them, they were just following my lead—"

Chavez chuckled. "Then you get all the credit—which means I'm buyin' you dinner at Smith and Wollensky next time we're in New York." A sudden thought occurred to him, and he looked up at Clark. "Were you in on this, Mr. C?"

"Nope," Clark said. "Wish I had been, though." His cell began to buzz and he sat up, fishing it out of his pocket. "Clark . . ." He closed his eyes, listening, nodding, giving a polite grunt now and then to let the caller know he was still on the line. After three minutes, he exhaled slowly through his mouth and said, "Thank you for letting me know . . . Yes. Me, too. I appreciate it."

"Everything okay?" Ding asked.

"Good to go," Clark said, offering no further explanation.

"Hey," Adara said, obviously sensitive to Clark's need for some emotional space. "Maybe we can call ahead and get some poke brought out to the plane when we land in Honolulu. There's a good place not too far from the airport."

Ding shrugged. "If you'd rather have raw tuna and soy sauce than a Smith and Wollensky steak . . ."

"Nice try, mister," Adara said. "One doesn't have anything to do with the other." She settled in beside Dom. "I love Hawaii. A shame we'll only get to see the airport."

Caruso leaned against her shoulder. "Don't worry, hon, Indonesia is a tropical paradise, too. Just a hell of a lot more people who'll want to kill us. It'll be fun."

The Gulfstream bounced a little as it rolled down the taxiway. Clark had never been much of a talker anyway, but he'd turned inward from the time he'd gotten the last call.

Chavez caught his eye and gave him an "Okay?" signal like scuba divers used, a circle with his thumb and forefinger.

Clark gave him a quiet nod and then shut his eyes, following up with an involuntary shake of his head. He'd known Pat West, so he was already upset about that. But this was different. Clark wasn't just upset. He was shaken—which had a way of making Ding doubt the things he took for granted, like gravity. John Clark was as solid as they came. When something was bad enough to bother him, it was either very bad—or very personal.

22

Peter Li kissed his wife hello as soon as he walked in the door, and then immediately said good-bye. He felt a mixture of pride and giddiness every time he saw her radiant face and swelling belly. Most men his age were playing golf and looking at motor home brochures. Here he was, married to a woman more than ten years his junior, preparing for a new baby. It would either keep him young or kill him, but he decided he'd enjoy it either way.

Sophie was crestfallen. "You're leaving again?"

"It's just for a couple of hours," he said, rubbing his eyes from jet lag. "I had an odd encounter on my trip and I have to let the security folks know. It's a clearance thing. We have to disclose contacts with foreign governments."

"Sounds secret-agenty," Sophie said.

"It was, a little," Li said, his mind elsewhere. "It's odd for a man of my age to be approached by an attractive woman . . ."

Sophie gave him a wary side-eye.

"Present company excepted."

"Sounds like you have some disclosing to do right here at home, mister."

Li kissed her on the nose, gave her boob a gentle

squeeze, and then turned for the door, completely exhausted from a day and a half of flying, but driven to put this encounter aboard *Torea* behind him.

D exter & Reed occupied sixty-two acres on three separate tracts, thirty miles north of Chicago. Each was parked out with jogging trails winding through greenbelts and wildlife sanctuaries between the massive brick-and-glass buildings. The Security and Human Resources departments were on the same campus as Li's shop, but two buildings over. Isaac Santos met Li at the front doors to the main building, where Li's office suite was located. The chief of D&R security wore a white hard hat, reflective safety vest, and lineman's belt with assorted pole-climbing equipment. He was rolling down the sleeves of his denim shirt when Li walked up.

"Peter," Santos said, shaking Li's hand, eyeing him with the benign mistrust law enforcement held for everyone who wasn't one of them.

"Isaac," Li said. "Thanks for seeing me on short notice." The security chief was a good enough guy. Approachable, always telling stories, less taciturn than what Li would have expected from a former FBI supervisory special agent with the counterintelligence squad in the New York Field Office.

"No worries," Santos said. He nodded toward the budding hardwood trees that lined the main road to the employee parking lot. "I was out here anyway. Setting the trap for this bastard we've been watching for."

It seemed a woman in Human Resources had gone

through a bad breakup and her ex-boyfriend was threatening to kill her—calls, texts, the whole nine yards. She'd moved to a secret location, but he knew where she worked. The courts had issued a restraining order, and then a warrant for his arrest, but pieces of paper offered little solace if he started blasting away in the employee parking lot. Little did the hapless guy know, the security division of D&R consisted primarily of retired FBI agents, Chicago PD detectives, and other former Feds. Every one of these men and women was prewired to swoop in and save people like the lady from HR.

"Honestly, Peter," Santos said, hitching up his tool belt. "If I wasn't such a law-and-order guy, I'd just take this guy out and shoot him. We can help her out here at work, but if he finds where she lives again . . . The coppers will only be minutes away when he comes to cave her skull in."

"I hear you," Li said.

"Anyhoo . . ." Santos leaned back against the wall of the elevator as he rode up with Li. "We're ready for the bastard. Your average guy has no idea what kind of signals he's trailing with his phone and vehicle. He comes anywhere near the parking lot and everyone on my team will get a text. Local law enforcement is already on alert."

The elevator door opened on Li's floor, revealing a flurry of activity in the computer labs. Good for the boss to see when he just popped by the office.

"So," Santos said, following Li into his office. "On the phone, you said you had possible contact with a hostile foreign national. I'm going to have to get the Chicago Field Office involved. You okay with that?"

"I called you," Li said, motioning toward the couch beside his desk so Santos could sit down.

"What do you think she wanted to know, this Kiwi reporter?"

"She was interested in my work," Li said. "But she wasn't specific."

"What did she say in general, then?"

"She was probing. It seemed as though she knew quite a bit about what we do here."

"How so?" Santos asked. "I mean, you don't even have a Facebook page."

Li raised an eyebrow.

"My job to know these things," Santos said, answering the unspoken question. "Tell me why you think she knew so much about you?"

Li had spent most of the thirteen-hour flight from Auckland to L.A. pondering this very thing.

"She called me *Doctor* Li. I prefer no title at all, but virtually everyone who knows me calls me Admiral."

Santos gave a contemplative nod. "A hell of a lot more difficult to earn that title."

"I suppose," Li said. "But everyone calls me Admiral—or Mr. Li—except here. This office is the only place anyone calls me Dr. Li. I've got a gut feeling she's talked to someone else who works here."

Santos gave a low whistle. "You work on some shit-hot projects. That said, we're not exactly in a shooting war with New Zealand. You see her talking to anyone else?"

"I didn't see her again after the contact," Li said.

"Well," Santos said. "I say we need to trust your gut. Do you trust your team?"

"They're vetted," Li said. "And I know them all by name. But it's a big team, thirty-eight computer engineers working on six different projects. Most of them former military, but not all. We do our best to safeguard everything."

"I'm sure you do," Santos said. "But the enemy only has to find one little weakness to weasel their way in." He groaned. "And there are a hell of a lot of enemies. Does everyone know about everyone else's projects?"

"Much of what we do here overlaps," Li said. "So yes, in general, everyone is up to speed on all the projects. We're more productive that way. There are a few specifics of our Missile Defense Agency projects that are cordoned off for security reasons."

Legs crossed on the couch, Santos tapped a pencil on the side of his leather boot as he thought.

"Did this lady ask about any of the projects specifically?"

"She mentioned communications and the Internet of Things."

"Do you remember if she used the terms first, or did you?"

"She did," Li said, knowing he was going to have to answer all these same questions again when the Bureau agents arrived.

Santos stopped tapping his pencil. "Does that narrow down which team might have leaked?"

"All our projects are communication projects."

"Like encrypted data-links between devices," Santos said. "For civilian companies and the military."

"That's correct," Li said, not surprised Santos knew

the details. The company executives trusted the man with their lives in some of the most dangerous parts of the world. They might as well trust him with information about their most lucrative contracts.

Santos leaned back in his seat, sighing. "Buddies in my old shop tell me the PRC is actively trying to get their hands on just the sort of thing you're working on."

"You think I'm a target because my parents were born in Taiwan?"

"Maybe." Santos shrugged. "Or it could be a coincidence. Listen, it's a shitty deal, but they're going to have to look at any ties you may or may not have."

"I know," Li groaned, the jet lag catching up with him. He'd been through enough background checks on his way to admiral that he knew the drill. "That's why I called you right away, Isaac."

"The Bureau guys are going to ask you this, so you might as well be thinking about it. Is there anyone on your team you don't trust?"

"They've all got top-secret clearances."

"So did Aldrich Ames," Santos said. "And a pile of other assholes who spied against the United States. That's not the question."

"Honestly, the only person who has access to every aspect of all the projects is me. I made sure of that. We have a saying where I used to work, *Trust your buddy with your life, but not your wife.* Well, I feel that way about these projects. We have active interface with some very sensitive systems. Software updates and patches, things such as that. I check everything personally before it goes out. I have sole access to the passcodes needed to push updates, but even I need a second in the room with me. There have to be two people logged in for the system to work."

"Like a nuke on board a sub or ship?" Santos observed.

"The aircraft we push software to carry nuclear armament. So yes. That's a good analogy."

"Think hard," Santos prodded. "Anyone you wouldn't want to be in a dark room with? Some member of your team you feel hairy about?"

"No." Li leaned back in his chair. "I'm sorry."

"There is one other thing," Santos said, shifting uneasily in his seat. "The FBI is going to drill down on this much harder than I have."

"That's their job," Li said.

"They're going to want every minute detail, if you get what I'm saying."

"I can only tell them what I know."

Santos pursed his lips, looking Li directly in the eye. "What I mean, Peter, is that they are going to want to know everything you and this woman said—and did—to each other. It could get messy."

Li laughed out loud. "I didn't *do* anything."

Santos stood with a groan. "Well, good. Then we should have no problem."

"Seriously," Li said. "You keep forgetting that I called you. And anyway, I'm a little too old and too smart to bump uglies with some strange girl who propositions me at the same time she's asking me about my top-secret government project."

"Don't be too sure," Santos said. "It's simple biology.

A man will follow an erection into places he wouldn't venture with a loaded shotgun."

"Well," Li said. "Not me."

Santos chuckled. "Says the fifty-four-year-old guy who's having a kid."

23

As usual, reporters lined up behind the barricade, waiting for Ryan to walk out to Marine One. Jakarta was a long way away, even on Air Force One, and there was no point in going before his advance team and all the vehicles arrived. In any case, Ryan still had a country to run, which included a trip to address members of the North Atlantic Council visiting the United Nations in New York from NATO headquarters in Belgium. NATO countries usually had Russian aggression on their minds, but Ryan intended to keep his ears open for anything to do with China. There was always scuttlebutt, if one knew where to look. The UN was sovereign ground, but it was anything but neutral.

Van Damm stopped him in the Oval as he was getting ready to leave. As a rule, he liked to be empty-handed when he walked to the White Top. He was certain the media gaggle had a pool on when he'd turn to wave and fall on his face. There was a divot in the South Lawn, small, but large enough to catch the toe of his shoe if he wasn't careful. His body man had his briefcase, and he, along with Gary Montgomery and the other agents who were traveling with him, were already on board Marine One. Ryan would be the last to board.

"What's going on here, Arnie?" he asked. "You and I both know Pat West is an innocent pawn in some Chinese scheme to get their hands on some AI technology. I'm ready to kick the shit out of Chairman Zhao and let the chips fall where they may."

"Are you done?" van Damm asked.

"What do you mean?"

"I mean, it's okay to feel that way, but you need to get it out of your system before you walk past that pack of reporters. They are ravenous for a bloody story—and half of them would prefer it was your blood."

"I have the most powerful military in the world," Ryan said. "A military that commands the land, the air, and the sea, at my fingertips. I have sophisticated satellites to study the dimples on golf balls from high above the earth, talented spies who could inveigle the wiliest soul—and yet I sit here, unable to do anything to help my friend."

"I know," van Damm said. "Have a pleasant trip, Mr. President. Senator Chadwick has asked to see you again, but I told her you're too busy at the moment."

"No," Ryan said, drawing a look of astonishment from his chief of staff. "Marine One to Andrews, Air Force One to Manhattan, motorcade to the UN, that's an hour altogether. Two hours on the ground, plus the return trip. Tell her I'll be back in four hours. In the meantime, I want an update on Father Pat's status while I'm in the air."

"Yes, sir," van Damm said. "We will help him, Mr. President. It's just going to take some time."

"You're damn right we'll help him," Ryan said. "If

I have to find John Clark and walk up to the prison door with a couple of ax handles and bust him out ourselves."

"Again," van Damm said. "Something you might not want to mention in front of the press."

24

The three Asian cuties were not regulars at the Boondock Bar, but neither was Major Goodloe "Oh" Schmidt, United States Marine Corps. Tucked in off Kalakaua Avenue and within spitting distance of Waikiki Bay, Boondock's was Schmidt's kind of water hole. It was loud, with lots of buddies to watch his back, and an abundance of handsome women. Schmidt was relatively short and completely bald at thirty-seven years old.

Major Reed "Skeet" Black, Schmidt's classmate from the Naval Academy, stood at the bar with him, nursing a Hefeweizen. His sandy hair was cut short. A hint of a Celtic tattoo encircled his right biceps and peeked from the sleeve of his Rogue CrossFit T-shirt. Schmidt couldn't stand wheat beer, but it was good to see his old buddy, so he kept his feelings to himself. The men had gone to flight school together, then Hornet school in Pensacola. Both had seen action in Iraq and Afghanistan, and then run Tomahawk Chase—following cruise missiles after they'd been fired from Navy ships and submarines. Schmidt had gone back to Pensacola to pass on his knowledge to the new "studs"—what he and the other instructors called students—while Skeet Black rushed and won a coveted slot in the Navy's Flight Demonstration Squadron, better known as the Blue Angels. Eventually, both men ended up in the seat of F-35B Lightnings, Schmidt testing Naval ordnance at China Lake—and Skeet working for the Marine Corps' F-35 program out of the Pentagon.

They were both still flying airplanes when most pilots their age and rank were flying desks. That said something.

Two weeks earlier, they'd been temporarily assigned to the CVN 76, the USS *Ronald Reagan*, for some secret mission for which they'd yet to be briefed. Two Lockheed Martin F-35Bs, capable of short takeoff and vertical landing, STOVL, were assigned along with them. Sometimes the Marine Corps did things that way for OPSEC, or operational security, reasons.

Like Skeet would ever divulge any secret. You had to talk to do that, and Skeet Black wasn't much of a talker. That was fine with Schmidt, because he preferred to do most of the conversing.

The problem was that the girls who were crowded around the wicker bar seemed to be even more turned on by his silence than they were by Schmidt's war stories.

"You fly jets?" the girl nearest Schmidt asked, grinning like a gap-toothed Lucy Liu.

"I'm a pilot, yeah," he said, giving Lucy one of his patented grins. He'd locked in on her from the beginning. She wasn't drop-dead beautiful, but cute like a farm girl, a little bit out of her element at the bar—exactly what Schmidt preferred. She said she and her friends were college students at U of H Manoa. All of them were from California. All of them second-generation Americans from Taiwan. Flawless English with plenty of idioms—check. He'd approached her at the bar, not the other way around—check. Not too hot—check. Schmidt had a supercool job, but his looks were more Goose than Maverick and he knew it. All that tallied up to the girls being friendlies. In truth they were a little young for him—but he was sure as hell thinking like a young man—which was to say not thinking very much at all.

Skeet just sipped his beer and shook his head in that amused and slightly disgusted way of his.

"That must be so dangerous," the girl said, clicking her glass against his. "What kind of plane?"

"The fast kind," Schmidt said, grinning again.

"Have you ever had to punch out?"

Schmidt took a drink of his second Jack and Coke of the evening. He always stopped at two before switching to beer. "You mean eject? Hell, no. I get on something to ride it, I stay on for the duration."

Gap-toothed Lucy grinned coyly at that. "You must go all over the world."

He gave a humble nod. "We see some cool stuff."

She moved closer, shoulder to shoulder, pushing him sideways a little. "Like, what do you see?"

"Stars, ocean, people who want to kill us."

"Do you ever have to fly at night?" one of the other girls asked. "I think that would be a deal-breaker for me."

"It's not bad at all," Schmidt said. "The ship leaves a glowing trail behind it. Kinda beautiful, to be honest."

She touched his chest with the tip of her index finger, running it down a couple of inches. "How'd you get your nickname? 'Oh'?"

Schmidt raised an eyebrow. "You know . . . 'Oh, Schmidt!' . . . sounds like . . ."

Lucy smiled, finally getting it, air-toasting with her fruity drink. "Do you guys fly together?"

"Sometimes," Schmidt said.

"How do you keep from running into each other in the air?"

He leaned over so they were forehead to forehead. She smelled good, like Dentyne spearmint and Red Door perfume. "That is some secret shit," he said. "I'm not supposed to be talking about my plane."

She grimaced. "I'm so sorry. I don't want to get you in trouble. You think anyone heard?" She turned to Skeet. "How about you?" she asked. "You're a pilot, too?"

Skeet nodded. "I am," he said, all cool and Gary Cooper–like. The bastard.

"Fighters?" she asked.

Skeet drained the last of his beer and set the glass on the bar, pretending he didn't hear her over the din of the crowd. He caught Schmidt's eye when he turned around. "Remember that time in Misawa?"

Schmidt shook his head, though he knew exactly what Skeet was talking about. They'd come home from training to find uninvited guests had been smoking in their apartments. The sheets were crumpled like someone had been sitting at the end of Skeet's bed. Schmidt's was always unmade, so it was impossible to tell on his. Files were rifled. Drawers were opened. A turd was left floating in Schmidt's toilet. It was as if they wanted the aviators to know they were being watched. Psych-ops—mind games meant to trip them up. Neighbors reported seeing two Chinese men hanging around the complex. NCIS had impounded the turd—for DNA samples of known Chinese spies. It had turned out to be from a dog, but you had to hand it to those NCIS guys for trying.

Schmidt glanced at gap-toothed Lucy Liu. Her chest heaved, like it wanted to escape from the white T-shirt. Schmidt looked back at Skeet.

"No? Seriously, you think?"

Skeet nodded. "Afraid so."

"You guys want to get a room?" the girl blurted out, sticking the tip of her tongue through the gap in her teeth. "The Sheraton is just a couple of blocks from here. We could all go."

Schmidt shrugged, playing it cool. He raised his finger, as if to chide her. "You promise you're not a spy?"

She stared at him straight-faced until they both broke into laughter.

"Of course you're not a spy," Schmidt said, slapping his leg, sloshing a little of his Jack and Coke. "Your English is too good."

A wry smile spread across her lips. "So, you want to?"

"As much as I'd like to take you up on that . . ."

She turned immediately to Skeet. "How about you?"

"No, ma'am," he said. He could have said he had an early day, but that would have been passing on intel—and Skeet Black was too wily for that.

Even so, with this incident, Schmidt knew their day was now going to start a hell of a lot earlier.

———

Five hours later, Major Schmidt stirred to the sound of someone banging on his door. He lay back on his couch, staring up at the ceiling, dressed in a freshly pressed woodland Marine Corps combat utility uniform, or MCCUU. Dead tired and dry-mouthed, it killed him that two Jack and Cokes could give him a hangover. He groaned and dragged himself to the door. This was getting old as hell. As he suspected, Skeet Black stood there, looking way too chipper, like he'd had a full eight hours and a big breakfast of oatmeal and almond milk. He was also in woodland MCCUU, the sleeves rolled up to his biceps, but his were just a little crisper.

"Love what you've done with the place," Skeet said, looking around at the dirty dishes and pile of laundry on the end of the couch. "Guess you never got around to reading *Make Your Bed*."

Schmidt rolled his eyes. "I forgot what a hoot you are at parties," he said, grabbing his hat and locking the apartment door. "Anyway, that's a Navy book. You know, if you hadn't said anything, the Chicoms would have paid for our dates last night."

"And you and I would have a big black mark on our PRP."

The Personnel Reliability Program was DoD's way of ensuring the trustworthiness of people in sensitive positions. You pretty much signed your privacy away—especially if you flew with nukes—which both men periodically did.

"For your information," Schmidt said, "I figured out

they were spies right before you did. The one with the gap in her teeth used my nickname—which I never told her. She'd done a background on me. Not very smart for a spy."

"I think they just counted on us being dumb," Skeet said.

"Or numb. Interesting that you were targeted. The Chinese have hacked into U.S. government personnel records so many times they've got data on all of us. Good we're making a report."

"Even so." Schmidt groaned again. "The old man is going to have my ass."

"We were both there," Skeet said. "*We* were approached. *We* are making a report."

"He'll still be pissed," Schmidt said. "But I'm a single guy, and no money changed hands."

The wooden sign behind the abnormally clean desk in Captain Craig Slaughter's cramped office said YOU CAN'T HAVE SLAUGHTER WITHOUT LAUGHTER, which pretty much summed up the Carrier Air Wing commander's terrifying personality.

Slaughter was Navy, but as the CAG commander— the acronym for the previous title of Carrier Air Group had stuck—Slaughter was responsible for everything that flew or made things fly on CVN 76, the *Nimitz*-class aircraft carrier *Ronald Reagan*. It was like he enjoyed doling out ass-chewings. He was sure as hell good at it, which Majors Schmidt and Black were learning firsthand as they braced to attention in the shipboard office.

Captain Slaughter was old-school Navy. His gray crew

cut, barrel chest, and the ever-present stub of a cigar like an exclamation point in his mouth reminded Skeet Black of a crusty senior chief more than an officer. He recognized good men, though, and, a pilot himself, talented aviators. Unfortunately for Oh Schmidt, the CAG was also extremely perceptive to the situation.

"We are in the business of fighting wars," Slaughter said, red-faced, laying on the theatrics like the professional that he was. "Not policing your pecker so it stays in your pants. If said pecker interferes with said warfighting, then we got a problem. You read me, Major?"

"Loud and clear, sir," Schmidt said.

"Why you?" Slaughter said, his eyes narrow slits. "Are you such an easy mark that Chinese girl-spies come up to you in bars to get information?"

Already braced to attention, Schmidt's shoulder blades nearly overlapped at the accusation. "No, sir!"

"Did either of you happen to let slip what kind of bird you fly?"

"No, sir, Captain," Schmidt said. "She . . . They know I am a pilot. That is all."

"A fighter pilot?"

"That is possible, sir."

"I realize that with spy satellites being what they are," Slaughter said, "our enemies know when one of our birds has a rusty rivet, but sometimes we just might have a plan in place to thwart that eye in the sky . . . Do I need to spell out for you that very often, the type of aircraft we do or do not have aboard is . . . I don't know"—he spoke through clenched teeth, slamming the flat of his hand on the desk—"A SENSITIVE MATTER?!!"

"I understand, sir." Schmidt stared at the far wall.

The CAG turned his light-of-a-thousand-suns gaze on Major Black. "How about you, Skeet? What do you have to say for yourself?"

"Captain," Black said. "We were drinking, letting our guard down more than we should have, conversing with members of the opposite sex, whom we now believe to be Chinese intelligence operatives. We broke contact immediately once we developed this suspicion. No critical information was revealed, but in hindsight, we should have been more careful about the information we did convey. I will use more diligence in the future, sir." He ended with a phrase common to the debrief after every Blue Angels flight, displaying, he hoped, the fact that he knew there were many Naval aviators with just as much skill as he had, who'd worked every bit as hard, but somehow, through fate and fortune, he'd ended up where he was. "I'm just glad to be here."

Captain Slaughter let it soak in for a moment before turning back to Schmidt.

"NCIS is going to ask you this, but I want to know myself. Did either of you give up any information about our upcoming mission?"

"All due respect, Captain," Schmidt said. "But we haven't yet been made aware of the specifics of our upcoming mission."

"Sounds like a sound decision on the part of both the Navy and the Marine Corps," Slaughter said, looking at Skeet. "Generalities, then?"

"No, sir. The young ladies know we fly, but that is all."

"Well, gentlemen," Slaughter said. "You will, no doubt, be ecstatic to know that you will shortly be leaving my gentle care aboard the *Reagan* for the meat of your assignment."

"May I ask where, Captain?"

"Orders will be forthcoming," Slaughter said. "But, as you can both surmise, the type of aircraft you fly are more suited to the Gator Navy than big-deck carriers."

That made sense, Skeet thought. Amphibious landing craft and the sailors that ran them worked with Marine Expeditionary Units to project U.S. power around the world. The ships were smaller, with no catapults, but capable of launching all manner of rotary wing aircraft as well as STOVL-capable fighters like the Marine Corps Harrier and the F-35B. Skeet knew one thing: The CAG was extra-tense, even for him, so the assignment must be something big.

Captain Slaughter peered across his nose as if deciding what to do—though both pilots were well aware that any decision had been made before they ever entered his office. They were Marines, and accustomed to the theatrics of discipline.

"You've got balls," he said, "I'll give you that. We have some work to do in the coming days and Lightning pilots ain't exactly growing on trees. We need you, but we don't need you that bad. You read me?"

"Yes, Captain," the men said in unison.

"Outstanding," Slaughter said. "Now, go grab your shit from your apartments and get back here at flank speed. I've already spoken with your Marine Corps chain. Consider yourselves confined to base until further notice. The only way I want you off these premises is when you're in the air on your way to your next assignment." The CAG's voice calmed a notch, and he took a long breath, like the theatrics might be over, and he was about to bestow some sage, fatherly advice. Instead, he curled up his upper lip like he needed to spit out something bitter and said, "Dismissed."

25

Three minutes.

Cecily Lung looked at her watch and squirmed in her ergonomic desk chair. She was new to Dexter & Reed, not yet completely trusted by the rest of the engineers—but Phil had a crush on her, so that was something. She'd give herself another minute and a half and then go to his desk, two cubicles down. He made no secret of the fact he'd like to ask her on a date, but he hadn't quite figured out how to navigate work relationships.

She'd been there only a week, but Lung kept notes on everyone in the office, looking for useful weaknesses that she could leverage—like Phil's AWF—Asian woman fetish. She used her own made-up code to jot everything down in a notepad she kept in her purse along with a .22-caliber Beretta semiautomatic. She had a small suppressor as well that a former boyfriend had given her. It wasn't much longer than her thumb and didn't silence the subcompact pistol, but rendered it quiet enough that anyone listening behind a closed door might wonder if someone had dropped a book.

There were few doors here, though, and only a couple of walls. Dr. Li didn't believe in cordoned work areas, insisting that open spaces inspired cooperation and group effort. He'd grudgingly allowed cubicles, so long as the walls didn't go above the shoulder of the shortest seated individual. He had an office—the bigwigs at corporate had insisted so as not to make them look bad for having offices of their own—but he'd taken the door off and kept the blinds raised.

The computer control room itself had a door—an extremely secure door. Known among the engineers as "the vault," the control room was connected to the outside world, to corporate and government clients, including the Missile Defense Agency, who purchased and depended on Dexter & Reed products—and the periodic software updates that product required. Sealed like a fortress, the vault was built of reinforced concrete block, sheathed in wire mesh walls, floors, and ceiling. Alarms and scramble pads controlled entry.

It wasn't that there was an atmosphere of mistrust. They were all on the same team and all had high-level security clearances. But Li stressed redundant security and oversight. If anyone, including him, performed any task on the terminal, it had to be double-checked and verified. Engineers with specific hardware or software needs could enter the vault two at a time during office hours, but Li had the only code that worked after hours.

Tucked in Cecily Lung's purse with the notebook and the pistol was a small thumb drive that her handler had delivered to her that morning, along with the instructions to upload it at once into the central terminal— behind the secure door. The sooner, the better. It would be quick—her handler estimated some fifteen seconds, but that might as well have been fifteen months if she couldn't get into the locked facility by herself. She'd asked Phil to go in with her to check some hardware, but there was no way she could insert the drive. He was smitten, but he was also smart—and would surely see if she inserted any drive.

With any luck, the logs of the visit would help cover her tracks.

She stood, throwing her purse over her shoulder. Not that she needed the gun to talk to Phil, but it made her feel better to have it—and anyway, *shit was about to get real.*

The gun was meant to be a last-ditch effort. Her employers would, no doubt, have preferred that she use it on herself if she were compromised. Still, knowing it was in her purse made the tedious job of watching and waiting a tad more exciting. Cecily Lung had graduated from MIT with a degree in EECS—electrical engineering and computer science—one year after she'd been recruited by Department Two, the intelligence arm of the People's Liberation Army. Both her parents were Taiwanese. They'd immigrated to the U.S., where, overwhelmed with the prosperity and free speech of her new country, Cecily began to display a revolutionary streak while she was in high school. At first she'd been wise enough to keep her thoughts off social media, but she was quick to grow bored and was on the verge of shucking it all to join an activist group when she was approached. Her recruitment could not have come at a better time. A life designing computers made her want to scream. A life of espionage *and* designing computers was something she could sink her teeth into.

If it didn't get her arrested—or worse.

She glanced at her watch again.

Nearly there.

Dr. Li was on the phone, talking in animated tones, but hushed enough that she couldn't make out his words. He was a decent enough man for a capitalist, and Cecily really didn't want to have to shoot him. In truth, her superiors had never said anything about shooting any-one. They did not even know she had the pistol. But she was a spy, wasn't she? Was she supposed to go in and do all this unprotected?

Time to move.

"Hey," Phil Beasley said, rolling back from his work-station to show he was giving Cecily his full attention. He was no more than ten years older than her but dressed like her grandpa, with wide brown ties and stodgy leather wing tips that were so scuffed it looked like he'd worn them camping. He had a habit of clutching his hair while he worked on a computer problem, leaving a spiked fore-lock that would have been cool on a high school kid but looked absurd on a man in his mid-thirties.

"What brings you to my neck of the woods?" he asked, playing imaginary bongos on his desk.

"To be honest," she said, glancing at the clock—less than a minute now. "I need some help moving an old clothes dryer out of my apartment. I'll buy you lunch if you could help on Saturday."

Don't rush. Act natural.

"Color me there," he said.

"Great. I'll text you my address." She took her phone out of her purse, fumbling so it dropped between Phil's feet and bounced under his desk. Ever the gentleman, he reached to retrieve it for her. When he bent down, she snatched his ID badge from beside his computer.

It seemed a thousand eyes were on her, but no one stood up, no one pointed an accusing finger.

Phil sat up and handed her the phone at the same time she stuffed the ID into the pocket of her slacks. She looked at the clock again.

"I have to pee," she said, bouncing a little—from nerves, not her bladder, but the effect was the same. "I'll text you my number in a second."

Phil rolled back to his computer. "Cool, cool, cool," he said.

Cecily made it through the door of the ladies' room five seconds before the fire alarm went off. She went in a stall and shut the door, standing on a toilet so her feet didn't show. It was standard operating procedure for the floor warden—one of the engineers who'd been designated—to poke her head in to see that everyone had made it out. They didn't expect people to hide on the toilet. She heard Mr. Li shouting for everyone to log off their computers—which she'd conveniently done before going to visit Phil's cubicle. With any luck, he'd rush out without looking for his ID, believing she'd gone on ahead without him. Rude, considering he'd just agreed to what amounted to a date, but people behaved strangely during a possible fire.

Teetering on the flimsy plastic toilet seat, Cecily braced herself against the stall for another two full minutes, allowing everyone to clear the floor. Her handler assured her he would take care of the security video feed that covered the door to the secure computer vault—and she would have to trust him on that.

She stepped down gingerly, shook a cramp from the prolonged half-crouch out of her calf, and then peeked out the door. The alarm—which her handler had activated—still blared, giving the deserted cubicles a postapocalyptic feel.

She had a limited amount of time before the floor wardens finished their tallies and someone was sent back up to find her. Dexter & Reed took its fire alarm and active-shooter drills seriously, thanks to all the former Feds on the payroll. Cecily pushed that terrifying thought out of her mind and sprinted down the empty corridor to the vault. She used both her ID badge and the one she'd stolen from Phil Beasley to scan her way inside. She'd worried that the door might fail-secure during an alarm, and breathed a sigh of relief when she heard the electronic mechanism release with an audible clunk.

She yanked open the door and inserted the thumb drive, clicking a few keys to open the program as her handler had instructed her. She'd been assured it would do the rest. And it did, lightning fast. In less than forty-five seconds, she was able to remove the thumb drive and log off the terminal. Whatever this new program did, it didn't need her to do it.

No one had told her what it was she was loading. She assumed it was a RAT—remote access Trojan—or some other virus that would turn over control of the system or wreak other sorts of havoc on behalf of the Chinese government. Stuxnet, the virus developed and implemented by the U.S. but blamed on Israel, and which caused

Iran's nuclear centrifuges to go off kilter and crash, had caused Iran to throw all the scientists working on it against the wall and shoot them on the mistaken notion that one of them had to be the mole. WannaCry shut down businesses, NotPetya brought a large portion of global shipping to a halt. Computer glitches (viruses that governments wouldn't admit to having) had caused drones to crash and communication centers to go dark. The possibilities were deliciously endless.

Four and a half minutes after the fire alarm had gone off, Cecily ran out the side doors of the building, panting from jumping and sliding down three flights of stairs. She'd left Phil's ID on his desk a few inches from where she'd swiped it, wiping any fingerprints off on the front of her shirt.

"Hey," Phil said, giving her a quizzical look when she approached her group in the greenbelt behind the building. "Where were you?"

She gave the floor warden—an older woman who reminded her of a junior high English teacher—a nod to show that she was present.

"It's embarrassing," she said, rocking from foot to foot, working to slow her heart rate so she didn't sound so guilty.

"More embarrassing than burning to death?"

Dr. Li was still on his phone, scanning the crowd of employees as he talked. His gaze settled on Cecily long enough to make her squirm, but he moved on, checking on the rest of his charges. A benevolent dictator.

She lifted the hem of her blouse so Phil could see her waist, conveniently showing a sliver of her belly to keep his mind right. "I wore button-fly jeans today. Took me a minute to get decent."

"Ah," Phil said. "Gotcha."

She gave him a smile, groaning inside, adjusting the leather strap of her purse on her shoulder. A bead of sweat ran down her cheek, easily blamed on the warm weather. She could hardly wait to find out what she'd been a part of. This mission had been tense, but so far, at least, it had gone smoothly. The program was installed—and she hadn't even had to use the pistol . . . *Damn it*.

Li looked at her again, then checked his watch—like he'd been timing her. She shook her head to clear it. That was impossible. There was no way for him to know what she'd done.

Was there?

26

It would have almost been a mistake to call Calliope sentient. She was not aware of her surroundings in a physical sense—plastic cabinets, circuit boards, and hard drives. But an observer who understood code would be hard-pressed to believe that she was not somehow alive and on a specific mission within the Dexter & Reed computer system. The software was so much more than a virus, but beautiful in her viruslike simplicity.

Using a variation of the problem-solving method called a Monte Carlo tree search, Calliope ran the possible scenarios—all outcomes of the game—tens of thousands of times, looking for the one that presented the result nearest to what she'd been coded to do.

Shortly after returning to the building after the fire alarm evacuation, Peter Li pushed out the notice of a software patch. Calliope attached herself to the patch, hitched a ride, and then deleted herself from Dexter & Reed computers, so there was no sign that she'd ever been there. Within minutes, avionics technicians with Carrier Airborne Early Warning Squadrons VAW 116 and VAW 117 out of Naval Base Ventura County and Point Mugu had downloaded the patch into the E2-C Hawkeye command and control aircraft in their squadron. With the mission of handling communication between other aircraft and surface vessels, the Hawkeye made the perfect vector from which to infect other machines.

Calliope was now in play.

Cecily felt like she might throw up when she saw Admiral Li enter the vault to begin pushing out software patches. She took her purse and made another trip to the women's room. Phil was in there with him, acting as security second. She hung out at the door, watching, looking stupid, but too entranced to care. Phil was hunched over a separate screen beside Li. Li looked up, surprised by something he'd found. Phil gave an adamant shake of his head.

Cecily gave an audible gasp. *There was no way*. They couldn't have figured it out already. The security entry logs would show Phil and Cecily had entered earlier that day—which they had. It would take closer inspection to note they'd gone in again *during the fire drill*, which would confuse the hell out of Phil. Then he'd remember he'd left his ID badge on the desk, and that Cecily had been late . . . He didn't have to be much of a detective to figure out she'd been up to no good.

Cecily turned for the door without looking back, expecting to hear someone yell out behind her all the way down the stairs. Manny, the potbellied security guy at the front desk, waved when she walked by. He had no idea why she was leaving, though she felt certain there was a flashing neon sign above her head that said SPY!

She didn't risk contacting her handler until she was driving south on 41 toward Chicago, a mile under the speed limit. She used Siri to make the call.

"The admiral suspects," she said, when the other end picked up. She slammed her hand against the steering wheel. "What do you want me to do?"

"What do you mean suspects?" The voice spoke without any trace of an accent, androgynous, like a computer. "He suspects or he *knows*?"

"Suspects for now," Cecily said. "But it won't take much for him to put two and two together. Then he'll know."

"And FIRESHIP?" the voice asked.

"It's in," Cecily said, remembering only then that she was supposed to have sent a message confirming this. She gave it verbally instead, feeling more exhilarated than ever. "FIRESHIP IS IN PLAY."

"Very well," the voice said, like there was nothing else to discuss.

"Wait!" Cecily gasped, hitting the steering wheel again. "What am I supposed to do? I'm telling you, Li knows."

"Suspects," the voice corrected.

"This guy is wicked smart," Cecily said, hyperventilating now. "He knows I was in the vault by myself. When he finds whatever it was I injected, he'll know it was me."

"There is nothing there for him to find."

"The patches, then," Cecily said. "He'll start looking at the patches he sent out. I imagine you have the software cover its tracks, but if anyone can figure this out, it's Peter Li."

There was a long silence on the line. For a moment, Cecily thought it had gone dead. Then she heard a breath. A decision being made. "Li will not be a problem," the voice said.

"I can't go back to work," Cecily said. "I need a way out tonight."

Another silence, long enough Cecily looked at her phone. "Go pack a bag and then—"

"I keep a bag packed!" Cecily snapped. "Where should I go?"

"Go home and get your bag. Wait there. Someone will come for you."

Cecily took 68 toward Prospect Heights—there was no way she could afford Lake Forest.

"What about the admiral? I'm telling you, he's going to cause us problems."

"And I told you not to worry about Li," the voice said. "He will be taken care of."

"You mean *taken care of* taken care of?"

"Go home, Miss Lung," the voice said. "This is not your concern."

What the hell did that mean? She'd committed espionage, treason against her own government. She was up to her neck in it now. Every bit of this was her concern. "I'm only thinking of the mission," Cecily said. "I want to help. That's all."

"Miss Lung, you must—"

"Listen to me!" she snapped. "We are on the same

side. You can't just send me to wait. I can assure you, this will not blow over. Tell me what I can do to fix it."

The frustrated sigh was audible over the line. "Go home," the voice said. "Someone will be along shortly to take care of you."

The words sent a chill up her spine.

The line went dead and Cecily Lung made it to the shoulder of the highway just in time to vomit.

27

I would strongly urge you to reconsider, Mr. President," Special Agent in Charge Gary Montgomery said. Resembling a defensive lineman in a wool business suit, he sat across the Resolute desk from Ryan, perched on the forward edge of his chair like he might spring to his feet at any moment and shake some sense into his boss. Arnie van Damm sat to his right, looking like he would be all too happy to help him.

Ryan was back from his trip to New York, accustomed by now to the herky-jerky nature of presidential travel. He might find himself in three or four different time zones in a single day, then three or four more the next. Back-and-forth trips to Manhattan were like trips to the corner bodega.

He couldn't blame the men for trying to change his mind. The chief of staff's job was one of constant pestering and pushing back, forcing him to look at other sides of issues that he didn't particularly want to see. As the United States Secret Service special agent in charge of the Presidential Protection Division, or PPD, Montgomery had a tremendous responsibility on his shoulders. Jack Ryan had, at various times, been described as an off-the-cuff or nontraditional strategist. Privately, in the confines of the Secret Service office beneath the Oval, dubbed W16, Ryan was certain he'd been called a number of things—maybe even a crazy son of a bitch—for his penchant to take his pointed responses personally to the far corners of the world.

Montgomery had just reminded him of the angry mobs that attacked Vice President Nixon's motorcade in Caracas in 1958. The windows had been smashed, the car severely damaged, before the Secret Service had miraculously been able to pull away from the furious crowd. "We're following social media trends in Indonesia now," Montgomery added. "It wouldn't take much to set off a mob if they believe you are coming to break your friend out of prison."

"Noted," Ryan said, giving Montgomery a passive smile, though he felt like picking up the Lincoln bust and throwing it through the window.

Gary was too good a guy for that kind of treatment. The two had become, if not actual friends, as close as protector and protected can be. "I trust your experience and intellect," Ryan said, "but I am going to Indonesia. I'd hoped you might bring some guys and maybe a helicopter or two and come along with me."

"Mr. President," Montgomery said, closing his eyes in an effort to come up with more convincing words. "You know we will make it happen, but—"

"Excellent," Ryan said. "That's what I wanted to hear, Gary."

Van Damm bounced a fist on his knee. "President Gumelar was right. In addition to the social media buzz, we have word from Ambassador Cowley that the Muslim majority is being whipped into a frenzy by someone. The ambassador's not sure exactly who's behind it, but it's got to be Beijing. Riots are popping up hourly all over Java calling for swift justice against Father West. As his friend, you'd be—"

"Guilty by association," Ryan said. "I get it. Hell, President Gumelar probably leaked that I was coming to try and stave off the visit." He looked back at Montgomery. "I'm not suggesting we go in without a plan. But I am going. My friend or not, something is going on over there and I'd like to get to the bottom of it."

Van Damm opened his mouth to speak, stopped as if he'd thought better of it, then, unable to contain himself, said, "You have people for that sort of mission, Mr. Pres—"

The door from the secretaries' suite opened and DNI Foley stuck her head in. She held up a manila folder with a striped red-and-white border.

Ryan motioned her inside. "Good thing for Arnie you got here when you did. He was about to say something impertinent."

Foley smiled. "He wouldn't be Arnie if he didn't." She stood to the side of the desk, the folder clutched at her waist, clearly waiting for the other men to leave before showing its contents to the President.

Montgomery got to his feet. "I have more concerns, but I'll go over the specifics with Mr. van Damm." Ryan gave them a closed-mouthed smile, a silent dismissal. He hated to do it. They had his best interests at heart, but there was something at play here that required getting off his ass in real time, not just thinking about it. There were moments when you had to worry about something besides your own skin. Like that Mike Rowe guy said, "Safety third."

"Looks like they're planning to mutiny," Mary Pat said when she and Ryan were alone.

"It's their job to make me see things."

"And are you?" Foley said.

"I'm looking," Ryan said. "Not necessarily seeing. What have you got for me?"

She pushed the folder across the desk.

"Remember the two PLA generals who are battling it out?"

Ryan opened the folder to find three photographs of General Song and his wife holding hands with a little girl of seven or eight. The photos weren't covert. Everyone was smiling and looking directly at the camera.

"Okay." Ryan arranged them side by side so he could compare. "Taken on separate occasions . . . What else am I looking for?"

Foley put the tip of her index finger on the little girl's face. "This is Song's granddaughter, Niu. Her mother, Song's only daughter, died shortly after the child was born. The general and his wife have raised her from infancy. All accounts say he dotes on her the way most Chinese men dote on a son."

"Okay . . ." Ryan said, still not following.

Mary Pat tapped the photo again. "Now take a closer look at her left eye."

Ryan picked up the nearest photograph, studied it for

a half-minute, and then shook his head. "Could be the angle," he said. "Is it cloudier than the other one?"

"It is," Foley said, lips set in a grim line. "Our experts think the little girl has something called a retinoblastoma."

"A tumor?" Ryan said. Cathy was an ophthalmologist, so this was a term he'd heard before—medical knowledge by osmosis.

"Exactly," Mary Pat said. "You hear of parents finding out their kids have it after they post a photo on social media and someone points out the white cloud in the iris."

"Does General Song know?" Ryan asked.

Foley shook her head. "We don't believe so. He and his wife keep the little girl completely off social media. She makes few public appearances at all, for security reasons."

"How dangerous is this condition?"

"Very," Foley said. "It can be fatal if left untreated. If it's not removed quickly enough, she could lose her eye, or the cancer could spread beyond her eye to other parts of her body."

"You weren't thinking of trying to leverage this?" Ryan said.

"That's your call, Mr. President," Foley said. "I'm a mother, so . . ."

"And I'm a human being." Ryan pushed the folder away to distance himself. "We have to tell the general straight-out. It's not that child's fault we find our two countries at odds."

"Song will want to know how we discovered it."

Ryan drummed his fingers on the desk. "The little girl makes no public appearances?"

"We'll find something, somewhere."

"I'm not a doctor," Ryan said. "But we're talking cancer, so I'm assuming time is of the essence. I want General Song informed of this sooner rather than later. Offer him any help we can in the way of medical care."

Foley sighed softly. "I thought you might feel that way. We considered inviting him to bring the child to Wilmer Eye Institute but ruled that out since your wife practices there."

"I appreciate that," Ryan said. "On oh-so-many levels."

"I know one of the surgeons at Kellogg Eye Center in Ann Arbor," Foley said. "A Dr. Berryhill. He's evidently a med school classmate of Dr. Ryan's."

"Dan Berryhill?" the President mused. "He's an eccentric coot, but yeah, he's a hell of an eye surgeon, to hear Cathy tell it."

"I've already taken the liberty of reaching out to him," Foley continued. "Dr. Berryhill has agreed to see a VIP patient at Kellogg on short notice. He doesn't know who yet, but he's done sensitive work for us before. He's been through a vetting process."

"Very well," Ryan said. "Protect our source, but do everything possible to let Song know about his granddaughter, within the hour if possible. And get with Scott to make sure State smooths the way for any entry visas. I want him handling this personally."

"Right away, Mr. President," Foley said. "It'll be touchy, but we can get a note to the general through our embassy." She turned to go, then paused. "I'm proud of you, Jack."

"Because I chose the life of a sick little girl over national security? I'm not sure that's the right call."

"Maybe not." Foley's eyes sparkled. "But it's the call I knew you'd make."

28

Cathy Ryan set the manila folder down gently beside her plate, as if she might injure the child in the photographs inside if she were too rough. "They have to get this little girl to a hospital."

Her usual prohibition against reading at the table took a backseat when the material had to do with medical issues. Neither she nor Ryan had much of an appetite, and their light dinner consisted more of moving the seared sea bass around the plate than eating it.

She tapped the photo with her index finger, driving home her point. "Yesterday would not be too soon. Enucleation—removal of the eye—may be the only option if the tumor has advanced far enough."

Ryan's wife often gave him a fresh perspective and, since she knew him so well, pointed out instances where his personal biases might be clouding his judgment. She didn't have the nuclear codes, but she knew what made Ryan tick. In the great scheme of things, that was almost the same thing. The problem was, right now, he didn't want to be calmed down.

He'd just finished a BLUF—bottom line up front— briefing about recent events, including Father West's text and the feuding Chinese generals. He saved the folder with photographs of General Song's granddaughter for last, ending with the proposed surgery at Kellogg Eye Center.

"I should assist," Cathy said. "Dan Berryhill is a brilliant surgeon, but I can help him."

Ryan resisted the urge to pound the table at the notion. "Well, that's out of the question."

"Why? This is my expertise, Jack. Let me help."

"That's not . . . It's not on the table," Ryan said. "Mary Pat is formulating a plan as we speak."

"To talk to the general?" Cathy asked.

"Best we don't discuss specifics," Ryan said. "But yes, that's about the size of it. Someone from CIA will make contact, see if the general is interested in giving us anything."

"Here am I," Cathy said. "Send me."

"Quoting Isaiah doesn't help your cause."

Cathy fumed quietly, studying her plate as though the answer to her problems was in her sea bass. The only sounds in the dining room were the clink of silverware and the pulse from Ryan's growing headache pounding in his ears. For a time, it looked like he might get away with ignoring his wife's suggestion—a behavior which almost always came at his peril.

No such luck.

"I'm serious about this, Jack," she launched in. "Dan Berryhill and I did our ophthalmology residency at Johns Hopkins together. He's the logical choice at Kellogg to do the surgery. I'll go in undercover and assist."

Ryan closed his eyes, trying—and failing—to hide the stricken look that crossed his face. "Undercover?"

"You know what I mean," Cathy said. "I can go in

without all the fuss that follows you around. Maureen and the rest of my Secret Service detail will be with me, but few people need know I'm even there. I'll be gowned up with a surgical bonnet and mask."

"And then what?" Ryan asked.

"Then I get close to General Song when he comes in to check on his granddaughter in recovery—and I ask for his help. You said it yourself; your source thinks he's ripe to turn. This way, I talk to him and you don't burn a valuable asset in the PRC."

"How do you know all that?" Ryan said, looking pained. "Am I talking in my sleep now?"

"Hon." His wife gave him a reassuring—if a little condescending—pat on the arm. "You do a lot of talking on the phone when I'm right here. I know you think I'm a potted plant—"

"You know better than that." Ryan rolled his eyes. "But this plan of yours, it sounds too much like—"

"Like what?" She cut him off. "The right thing to do? What's that Edmund Burke saying—*For evil to triumph, it's only necessary for good women to do nothing . . .*"

Ryan raised a professorial brow. "I'd be careful there. That's misattributed to Burke. He did, however, say: *Woman is not made to be the admiration of all, but the happiness of one.*"

"Leave it to you to remember that little tidbit," Cathy snapped.

"Yeah, because I'm so overbearing."

Cathy threw her head back and stared at the ceiling. "Listen," she said. "This has us both about to lose our minds. Pat West is my friend, too. I have to do something to help find out what's going on."

"The risks here are enormous. There's a high likelihood that General Song doesn't even know."

"I understand that," Cathy said. "But he's a Chinese general involved in war-gaming scenarios—and the Chinese are somehow behind Pat's arrest in Indonesia, which, according to his text, has something to do with a video-gaming technology. It's not that much of a leap to think there may be a connection. He's bound to know something."

Ryan sighed. "I really do talk in my sleep." He groaned, his brain working in overdrive. There had to be a way to talk his wife out of this, short of a presidential order—which carried slightly less weight than a mere suggestion with Cathy. He'd been friends with Pat West since they were in high school, and then later when they were both at CIA. That friendship had naturally carried over to the Ryan family. A quiet soul, West was generally a loner. Cathy had felt it was her duty to mother him, seeing him as someone who needed to be looked after. His arrest was particularly difficult for her.

As it turned out, Jack wasn't the only one thinking strategically. Cathy backed off her plan to go to Michigan for a moment.

"So what do you plan to do?" she asked, pushing away her plate.

"In other news," Ryan said, attempting to change the subject but keeping up his guard, "Senator Chadwick has decided she wants to be my new best friend."

Cathy gasped, momentarily deterred. "Tell me you don't trust her."

"No," Ryan said. "Well, yes. I mean, I trust her to be Michelle Chadwick. She needs my support for a literacy bill aimed at Native American kids."

"There has to be something else," Cathy said.

"Oh." Ryan chuckled. "There definitely is—"

"That woman hates you with a passion. It's evident every time she opens her mouth on television. Pretty sure she'd rather see you crash and burn than help a Native kid learn to read."

Ryan shrugged. "Maybe so."

"So I suppose you have a plan to get Pat out?"

"Believe me," Ryan said. "I'd like nothing more than to lead a Marine expeditionary brigade into Jakarta and break Father Pat out of prison. But there's that pesky little problem of Indonesia's national sovereignty we have to deal with."

"What does President Gumelar say?"

"He admits the charges are false but says his hands are tied."

"Of course he does," Cathy said. She'd always considered him a bit weak-kneed.

"Indonesia appears to be subject to the rule of mob," Ryan said, "rather than the rule of law. If the populace believes Father Pat has been preaching Christianity to Muslims, then he has been preaching Christianity to Muslims—no matter what the truth and common sense say. Gumelar had a Chinese Christian finance minister who made a comment that the masses thought was blasphemy against Islam. He is the president's close friend—

and he's still in jail eighteen months after the fact. I have Adler and his people at State looking into some inducements that can help President Gumelar sell a release plan to his people, but I have to be careful not to give away the farm for a personal friend."

"I suppose," Cathy said, unconvinced. "I guess there are other wrongly accused Americans locked up around the world."

"One or two," Ryan said.

She studied his face, eyes narrowing. "But you're really going?"

"Of course."

"But no battalion of Marines."

"Gumelar is an important ally," Ryan said. "Sadly enough. We've been planning a trip for months. This just moves up the timetable."

"People will see it as—"

"I don't care," Ryan said. "I'm not sitting behind the desk on this one. If I can prove to Gumelar that China is behind this, that would be a different story."

Cathy studied the tablecloth for a moment, thinking. She looked up suddenly. "That's why you need to let me help. You're busy saving Father Pat. Let me help save this little girl's eye—and talk to the general. I want to do my bit as the President's wife."

Ryan groaned softly, reaching across the table to take his wife's hand. "I stepped into that one, didn't I?"

"I'll say," Cathy said. "Come on, this'll be fun. No one outside of our people and the general will ever even know I was there."

"Hon," Ryan said. "Make no mistake. What you are

doing is good, but it is espionage, pure and simple. And that is never, ever, ever, that easy."

She smiled broadly, raising her eyebrows up and down, squeezing his hand.

He gave her a wary look. "What?"

"You know," she said, eyes soft now. "Speaking of Edmund Burke, a long time ago—eons, really—I heard you quote him to my father while you were downstairs waiting for me to get ready to go. I fell in love with you right then and there."

"Was it the one about women? Burke was kind of . . ."

She gave him a playful punch on the arm.

"You said to my father, *No one ever made a greater mistake than he who did nothing because he could only do a little.*"

"Boy." Ryan chuckled. "Your dad must have thought I was a sophomoric idiot."

"Thank you for letting me do this, Jack. It's a little, but it's something."

29

Baltimore Homicide Detective Emmet Ryan taught his son Jack early in life to listen to experts. The two United States Secret Service special agents sitting across the Resolute desk certainly qualified. Together, Gary Montgomery and Maureen Richardson had almost forty years of experience in dignitary protection. A GS-15, akin to an assistant special agent in charge in other government agencies, Maureen Richardson reported directly to the special agent in charge of PPD. Mo, as she preferred to be called, served as lead agent for the satellite detail that protected the First Lady. Much smaller than the big show surrounding POTUS, the FLOTUS detail was low-key and fluid. Mo and her Secret Service agents followed Dr. Ryan wherever she went, and then blended seamlessly, amoebalike, with Montgomery's larger detail when the Ryans traveled together. They integrated but stood ready to go their separate ways if the schedule or situation dictated it.

It was a dance, and Montgomery and Richardson were experienced and savvy enough to make the intricate steps look easy.

Jack Ryan generally steered well clear of specifics regarding his own security. Where Cathy was involved, his instincts as a husband stomped back those of the nation's chief executive.

Hundreds of agents from Protective Operations, Protective Intelligence and Analysis, and Uniformed Division officers conducted travel advances, executed logistical plans, liaised with medical personnel and Air Force and Marine support, and formed multiple concentric rings of electronic, structural, and personal security around the President and his family. Though he didn't get into their business, Ryan made it a point to know everything he could on the agents assigned to the inner circle. Inside the bubble, within arm's reach of the President, they lived under the constant eye of the television camera, not to mention the active threat of people who wanted to see their boss with a bullet in the head. Threats came in daily on social media, over the telephone, or in written communication. These men and women were, by necessity, the cream of the crop.

Ryan hadn't handpicked Maureen Richardson to protect his wife, but he would have, had he been given the opportunity. She was a shooter—which he liked. Her record showed she'd had two OISs—officer-involved shootings—during her time as a uniformed officer with the Denver Police Department, once with her AR-15 rifle, the last with her Glock sidearm. Both times she'd fired four shots and hit her intended target with each round. She'd been cleared after each shooting and commended by her department and her community. Ryan found it particularly noteworthy that on both occasions she'd left cover, advancing toward violence when she saw others under attack. A good quality to have in someone you wanted to watch over your wife. This propensity also fit perfectly with the mission of the Secret Service—who were trained not to take cover during an assault, but to make themselves the larger target while getting their protectee out of danger.

Cathy liked her, too, and that didn't hurt.

Mo's mouse-brown hair was cut just above strong shoulders. A perpetually rosy complexion made her look as if she'd just come inside from a brisk wind—no matter the weather. A prominent chin and roundish cheeks gave her face a resting smile, even when she was upset. The look was more than a little disquieting, which Ryan counted as a plus, considering it was her job to put people off guard. Secret Service agents had to exude a certain gravitas. A collegiate judo champion, Mo Richardson moved with the centered grace of an accomplished martial artist. Her husband was an agent on the FBI's elite Hostage Rescue Team, and one got the impression that the two of them spent hours in the dojo each day, trying to kick each other's ass, when they weren't on duty. While not as tall or imposing as Gary Montgomery was, Mo still possessed the don't-screw-with-me persona that caused would-be attackers to stutter-step before taking any action, buying time.

Gary Montgomery was listening to her plan.

Sort of.

"We'll send in a larger advance team than usual," Mo said. "They'll filter in with local agents by onesies and twosies, so we'll establish a significant boots on the ground presence before SURGEON arrives—"

Arnie van Damm knocked and then stuck his head in

the door that led directly across to the Roosevelt Room. His office was to the left, down that same hall.

"Mr. President," van Damm said. "Senator Chadwick is here to discuss that new information we were talking about."

It shouldn't have been this way, but Secret Service personnel were accustomed to their meetings being interrupted by seemingly more important business. Code name CARPENTER, van Damm also had Secret Service protection, albeit a small detail of mainly portal-to-portal security. He often said to his detail that if he ignored them, it meant he trusted them to do their jobs without his input. Fortunately for the agents, Ryan didn't see his wife's security as taking a back burner to anything. Ever.

"Go ahead and have the senator brief you," Ryan said. "See if this mysterious constituent of hers has anything we don't already know. We'll be done here in a few minutes."

The chief of staff ducked out as quickly as he'd come in, shutting the door behind him.

Ryan motioned for the agents to continue.

Richardson laid out the rest of her plan to keep Cathy safe while getting her close to General Song.

"You're planning a tarmac pickup in Detroit?" Montgomery asked.

"Of course," Mo said. "We'll take an Airport Police vehicle from the plane but move the First Lady to an armored Jeep Cherokee once we get her inside the hangar, out of sight. Local law enforcement will be present but hanging back. The entire package will be covert vehicles, moving with the flow of traffic but ready to go overt lights and sirens immediately, should the need arise."

Montgomery nodded. "She shouldn't be on the ground long."

"We'll arrive at four a.m.," Mo said. "The operation will be that same morning, minimizing SURGEON's time on-site."

"There's a bridge over the Huron River across the road from the Eye Center," Montgomery said. "And the Amtrak station is right there, no vagrants to speak of, but plenty of opportunity for people to loiter and say they're waiting on the Wolverine to Chicago. And no underground parking at the Eye Center. She'll have to walk in from the open."

Mo's lips perked into an impish grin. "Mrs. Ryan has agreed to go in full Marvel Comics disguise."

The President raised a brow.

"A ball cap, sir. She's more recognizable than Captain America, but, as I said, it'll be dark, and the less fuss we make, the less we stand out."

Mo Richardson went on to explain where she'd have rovers and post-standers, "looking chill, but armed and ready to react." Advance agents would personally contact Ann Arbor PD and the local office of the FBI late on the evening before arrival.

Gary Montgomery, who'd received his undergraduate from the University of Michigan, quizzed her at every turn, peeling back the layers of her plan and giving inside information from recent trips to watch Wolverine football.

"I'll scrub up with SURGEON," Mo went on, "going

into the operating room with her. General Song travels with four security people. One of those will stay with the cars. According to State and CIA, he'll travel with one aide, and a minder from Department Two, or possibly the Ministry of State Security. My money is on a Two man from military intelligence, though. The minder changes periodically, so we've not identified him yet. Director Foley is assisting with that. Besides me, I'll have four agents dressed as hospital techs. And two more behind the nursing station. Shoulder weapons will be staged there, in the event of any escalation. We've already tried it and the scrubs are loose enough to hide sidearms. The team watching from the operating theater viewing window will have radios. They'll have me and the First Lady in sight at all times. It goes without saying—but I'm going to say it anyway. We all plan to stay out of the way and let the doctors do their jobs, but my number-one priority is to keep Dr. Ryan safe."

Ryan mouthed a silent *Thank you*.

"You should be good security-wise in the operating room," Montgomery pointed out. "It's after that when it gets touchy."

"I agree," Mo said. "Dr. Ryan will attempt contact when the general is allowed in to see his granddaughter in recovery. It's a small area, so that minimizes the number of his people present while maximizing ours. If the general cops an attitude, we'll be outta there with SURGEON before any of his people even know what's going on."

"I appreciate your work, Mo . . ." Ryan leaned back in his chair, coffee in hand. "It sounds as though you have every conceivable scenario covered."

"Mr. President," Gary Montgomery said. "I lived in Ann Arbor for four years while I was in college. I'm familiar with the layout of the city and the campus. Perhaps . . ."

He stopped.

Special Agent Richardson bristled.

"Perhaps what?" Ryan set his cup on the desk.

"Nothing, Mr. President," Montgomery said. "The First Lady is in excellent hands."

"Very well, then," Ryan said. He stood, shaking each agent's hand in turn.

"I won't let you down, Mr. President," Richardson said.

Ryan swallowed hard, feeling more than a little emotional. "Cathy trusts you, Maureen, and so do I. You and Gary both have our full trust and confidence."

With one problem mitigated, if not solved, the President picked up his phone to call Arnie and let him know he was ready to move on to Chadwick. That would be interesting, to say the least . . .

Maureen Richardson paused outside the Oval, digging her heels into the thick carpet.

"What the hell was that all about, Gary?" She kept her voice low, in keeping with the decorum of the White House, but there was plenty of force behind it. "You were on the verge of, what? Taking over the trip to Ann Arbor. If you can't trust me, then you may as well relieve me."

"I trust you," Gary said. "You know that."

"Do you?" Richardson said. "Because it sounded like

you were going to play the 'I went to Michigan so I can do a better job' card."

"Well," Montgomery said. "I checked myself." He leaned in closer, lowering his voice even more. "Look, Mo, I don't apologize very often, because I'm hardly ever wrong . . ." He grinned, but she was having none of it. "Seriously. I'm sorry. I trust you, and, more important, so does the boss."

"Thank you," Richardson said. "Apology accepted. I got this, Boss. Really. No one will know we're there."

"Okay."

"And, just to show my ego isn't so large I don't know when to ask for assistance, didn't you say you used to live near Kellogg Eye Center?"

Montgomery looked up to find Senator Chadwick loitering in the doorway just a few feet away, waiting on Arnie van Damm. She gave them a nonchalant smile, like a cat ignoring its prey. Claws out, but seemingly disinterested. She couldn't have heard much, but it didn't take much. The good senator had a habit of making up the details when she wasn't sure about something.

"Let's move this down to W16," Montgomery said, turning away from the woman he knew to be his boss's bitter political enemy.

Fifteen feet away, Michelle Chadwick made a mental note to check and see where the Kellogg Eye Center was and what it had to do with the White House. She recognized the big guy, Mathews, or Montgomery, or something like that. He was Ryan's chief Ray-Ban-wearing head-smasher. The woman looked familiar, and since the Secret Service was tribal and stuck with their own, she was surely a head-smasher as well. Chadwick had seen her with the First Lady, which raised some very interesting questions. David Huang had been right about one thing. She could learn a hell of a lot as Jack Ryan's new best friend. All she had to do was connect the dots—and then figure out what she wanted to do with the information.

"Ready?" Arnie van Damm said, giving her a start as he came out of his office at a half-gallop, heading for the Oval.

"I am," she said.

"You look like someone just stomped your big toe. You okay?"

"Not really," Chadwick said. "I'm kind of in the belly of the beast here."

Van Damm gave her a wary side-eye. "And from my point of view, you're giving the beast a bad case of heart-burn. If it were up to me . . ." He stopped, took a deep breath. "But it's not up to me. Come on. We don't want to keep the President waiting."

30

Chavez spent the last two hours of their flight leading a gear check—sometimes referred to by the rest of the team as a "pocket dump" or a "show me yours I'll show you mine." The nature of their work and the places they did it made their loadout extremely fluid. Talking about everyday carry, or EDC, was all the rage these days. Everyone from accountants to war-fighters who were integrating back into civilian life took to various EDC forums on social media, posting neatly knolled professional-quality photos of their assorted blades, flashlights, firearms, and other pocket litter. Chavez talked smack about it sometimes, but he'd been known to spend more time than he should have scrolling on his phone to check out what other operators thought was important. Patsy called it "gun porn." It was a mystery to her why anyone would need to carry two knives. An odd sentiment, considering who her father was.

Chavez had tried to explain once, years before, over Thanksgiving dinner with his in-laws and other close family. He'd pointed out that just as surgeon Patsy required assorted scalpels and other medical instruments, he needed different kinds of blades for different types of work. JP, maybe six or seven years old at the time, sitting on the piano bench by his cousin, asked his daddy what kind of work the big Benchmade automatic folder in his pocket was for. Patsy and the other women at the table had glared, but without missing a beat, Clark, the boy's grandfather, had drawn his own Benchmade auto-folder, sliced a ginormous drumstick off the turkey carcass in front of him, and passed it to the delighted boy. It was enough explanation for JP, and Clark expertly steered the conversation to baseball.

Good times.

Everyone on the team carried at least one blade. Most of them had moved away from the more tactical-looking black knives to knives with wooden or Micarta scales. Ryan carried a wood-handled Benchmade called a Crooked River. It looked like a folding hunting knife, arguably not as sexy as a black knife, but the razor-sharp blade performed the same function. Knife fighting was a misunderstood tactic, anyway. Knives that were small enough to put in a pocket made for barely adequate defensive weapons— if they could even be accessed in time. Violent attacks were most often like car wrecks, out-of-nowhere surprises, ambushes, that left the victim stunned and staggering—or dead—before he or she knew what hit them. Sure, there were times when a push dagger would come in handy if some thug had you up against a wall or down on the ground, or a karambit if you were going kinetic and quiet. But mano-a-mano knife fights where opponents squared off with blades were practically nonexistent.

Knives as *offensive* weapons—now, that was a different

story. That was the reason to carry one—not to mention the fact that there was always a bunch of shit that needed to be cut. So everyone had a blade.

Flashlights, butane lighters, and SWAT-T tourniquets rounded out the pocket litter everyone had in common. Each of them carried enough stash-cash to bug out on their own if the need arose, along with an open credit card that was akin to a fire extinguisher behind a glass door—used only in case of emergency. Gone were the days when an operator could trade a high-end watch for a ticket out of a hot spot—though Chavez had a sneaking suspicion that a good many of those stories were just rationalizations Special Ops guys used to get their wives to let them buy a Rolex Submariner or Breitling Emergency.

Caruso carried his FBI badge. Midas and Jack Junior each toted their favorite set of lock picks. Ding was partial to a small Leica monocular. Clark, who was old-school, always had a handkerchief, grousing all the time that they'd gone out of style. The small square of white cloth could be used for first aid, as a makeshift head cover in the sun, or, among other things, a hand towel—anything but a surrender flag.

Some years back, a Russian thug had given John Clark's gun hand a severe beating with the business end of a hammer. Talented surgeons, months of painful physical therapy, and a gut full of grit had allowed him to start shooting again, but the nerves and tendons would never be what they once were. He'd carried a double-action SIG Sauer P220 for a number of years, but the crisp single action of the 1911 Wilson Combat .45 was much less painful for him to keep up the practice he needed to shoot well.

Caruso customarily carried his FBI-issue .40-caliber Glock. When they did carry, the rest of them were armed with Smith & Wesson M&P Shields and one extra seven-round magazine. An infantry soldier turned special operator, it went against Chavez's grain not to have a vest full of magazines. Ammunition left at home was no good at all. But intelligence work was a different mission. If you had to resort to gunfire, you'd screwed up bad and were probably hauling ass. There were heavy weapons in the form of Heckler & Koch MP5s and MP7s behind the bulkheads of the Gulfstream, along with a Winchester Model 70 in .308, should the mission require them to take a more offensive posture.

Holsters and carry method were a personal preference and ran the gamut. Everyone had a favorite, and there was little use in trying to convince another that your choice was better than theirs. Chavez wore an inside-the-pants single clip called the Incog by G-Code. It was specifically designed for appendix carry—in front of the body, just off the centerline of his belt. Chavez preferred to wear his at four o'clock, unwilling to leave the muzzle pointing at little Ding and the boys on such a regular basis. Some of his friends, all talented operators, were fine with appendix carry, their differences in opinion about firearms, holsters, and methods of carry resulting in countless good-natured arguments over pizza and beer around the fire ring. Clark said little during these discussions, but carried the 1911 at four o'clock in a leather Milt Sparks inside-the-pants holster, contending God had made that little hollow below a man's kidney specifically so it would fit a .45-caliber pistol.

The smallest member of the team, Adara often carried the biggest loadout, stuffing cargo pockets and day packs with Israeli bandages, clotting agent, and three-inch chest-decompression needles. She cajoled everyone constantly to carry their SWAT-T tourniquets wherever they went and whatever they were doing, noting that they had all been in hairy situations that required some level of self- or buddy care.

Deciding what to take was always a balancing game. Newbies always tried to bring the kitchen sink. Old hands got by on a lot less, improvising in the field. They might not admit it, but nearly everyone wanted to carry more shit than was possible or even practical. Absent a sixty-pound ruck, a lot of things had to be left behind. They had to stay nimble, and yet still have the necessary tools when the time came.

Thankfully, smartphones had consolidated about five pounds of bulky tech gear into one multifunction device.

This mission would entail covert entry into a business, the kinder and gentler term for burglary. They would have to get past several layers of security—guards, outer doors, inner doors, and, in all likelihood, a safe. Everyone on the team knew how to pick tumbler locks, though Jack Junior and Midas had that little extra touch that made it appear easy.

Two of the duffels on the seat in front of Ding contained small backpacks with assorted breaching devices—crowbars, Halligan fire tools, hammers, and bolt cutters. Advancements in technology had rendered conventional locks the exception, so most of their kit leaned heavily toward devices used to defeat electronic security measures. Multitools, rolls of insulated wire to bypass circuits, gaffer's tape, a lineman's test set, and extra headlamps all saw frequent use. Gavin Biery had put together a kit with Midas—arguably the most tech-literate of the team. The hard Pelican case contained assorted computer dongles, cables, cameras, slap-mics, and a couple of Arduino micro-controllers for attacks on hotel room locks. In a case all their own were a half-dozen Raspberry Pis. These simple, single-board computers cost a whopping twenty-five bucks apiece and could be used as the basis for any number of technical applications Gavin Biery could dream up and walk them through over the phone.

When Chavez thought about it, having Gavin on the phone was like bringing two hundred and fifty pounds of tech gear and encyclopedic knowledge along on the job.

Commo was key to any mission, and often the first thing to fail. Each team member was responsible for their own earbuds, extra batteries, near-field neck-loop mic, radio, and charger. The batteries that powered each radio were small, flat packs that fit in the liners of their belts, removable for the times they had to go through airport security. There were two spare sets of everything on the Gulfstream. Ding stuffed these in his bag. A good leader kept a load of spares in his case—just in case.

He ticked off the rest of the gear from the list he kept in a battered Moleskine notebook, checked his G-shock (sadly, no Rolex for him . . .), and gave a thumbs-up to Clark.

Satisfied that they were ready, Chavez leaned back in his seat, closed his eyes, and thought of his kid eating that giant turkey leg all those years ago . . .

31

Manado looked north from the island of Sulawesi, across the Celebes Sea toward the Philippines, less than three hundred miles away. The Manadonese—more correctly called Minahasan—people seemed stockier than other Indonesians Chavez had met. *Handsome,* he thought, primarily because they looked an awful lot like him, with almost Hispanic features and sometimes a little wave to their dark hair. Chavez found that most people didn't give him a second glance—as long as he didn't try to speak.

Chavez and Clark had split from the rest of the team as soon as they'd bought their entry visas and cleared Immigration. They now sat at a plastic table outside a Starbucks in the Megamall, a seafront shopping center downtown.

The rest of the team had taken two of the rental cars and were checking out the Suparman Games store in the center of Manado, leaving Ding and Clark to organize rooms at the Whiz Prime Hotel that was adjacent to the mall. With that done, Ding had invited Clark out for coffee, promising not to get bubble tea.

The mall had a cinema and plenty of high-end stores, if you cared about that kind of thing, which Chavez did not. More important, though, there was coffee. Sleep on the plane was always fitful, and jumping into work after endless hours on the Gulfstream had made coffee a necessity. The shop next to Starbucks sold snacks. Chavez bought fried banana fritters drizzled with palm sugar so he'd have something besides caffeine acid in his gut.

It was crowded for the midafternoon, mostly women, but like anywhere Chavez had ever been, there were a few roving packs of teenage boys, looking for something to do. Security kept them in line, and cleaners with brooms and long-handled dustpans scoured the floors for trash or spills. The place was sparkling clean but still worn and lived-in. It reminded Ding of his grandmother's house in East L.A., whenever she thought someone important like the priest was coming to visit. It was as clean as a shabby thing could be.

Every other person in Manado seemed to have a cigarette in hand. Ding read somewhere that offering a cigarette was a polite way of greeting. The population's affection for smoking coupled with the ceilings painted in blue-and-white cloud scenes gave the mall the feel of a Vegas casino.

Manado was a large city for the island, but its population of only half a million made it barely a glimmer compared to Jakarta's blinding glare. The local dive shops and tourist operators liked to compare themselves to Bali. Chavez could see it. If he didn't have to fly in and steal some piece of shit's computer virus, he would have liked to bring Patsy here. Maybe. Sometimes traveling so much just made him want to sit at home on his own couch and drink a beer—a sore spot with his highly intelligent and adventurous wife. But then, of course she would crave adventure. She *was* John Clark's daughter.

The people of Manado had a decidedly European bent, and, unlike much of the rest of Indonesia, they were predominately Christian, exemplifying their faith with a gleaming white statue called *Yesus Kase Berkat* that overlooked the city fifty meters above the ground on the southern hills. This "Blessing Jesus" leaned forward, arms open wide, robes flowing, appearing to march down from the mountains. Over those same mountains, behind the statue, and across the Gulf of Tomini, Islamist militants and Christians clashed in frequent violence. The look on Clark's face said he'd rather be there.

Chavez took a bite of fried banana and looked directly at Clark, trying to make conversation. "Here's sort of a funny thing. Did Patsy tell you that the neighbor kid is trying to talk JP into doing e-sports when they go to college?"

If there was one thing that could make Clark smile, it was his grandson. "Kid's got his mother's brain, getting into Stanford."

"Can't argue there," Chavez said.

"And what the hell are e-sports, anyway?"

"Video games, I think," Chavez groused. "I'm not a hundred percent clear. I guess it's a big deal now. There are teams all over the country."

"Is he doing it?"

"Don't worry, your grandson's not quitting baseball," Chavez said. "I'll tell you that right now."

"That's the trouble with kids," Clark said, gazing pensively into his coffee as though he was speaking from personal experience. "They grow up and do what they want to do instead of what we want them to do."

"E-sports," Chavez scoffed, curling his lip like the word tasted bad. "Maybe the kids can grow some e-muscles and e-coordination to go along with it. Call it e-games, but come on . . . e-sports?"

Clark took a drink of coffee. "Who am I to judge? I never expected video games to make the jump from pizza joints to home computers."

"Don't forget phones."

"Yeah," Clark said, his interest in the subject exhausted. "Stanford," he whispered to himself. "What a kid."

Chavez had thought his father-in-law might snap out of his funk at some point during the twenty-six-hour trip to Manado. But if anything, Clark had turned more introspective with each passing minute.

Chavez tapped the plastic lid on his cup with a forefinger to get the man's attention. "What's bothering you?"

Clark glanced up, moving only his eyes, startled from a deep thought.

"You mean besides e-sports?"

"Come on, John," Chavez said. "You want to talk about it?"

Clark gave a contemplative nod. "I've thought it over, and . . . no, I do not want to talk about it. But I will anyway, since it's you doing the asking." He exhaled sharply through his mouth. "A SEAL buddy of mine passed away. That's all."

Chavez grimaced. "Man, I'm sorry to hear that. KIA?"

"No," Clark said, gazing into the distance, still stunned by the news. "I should have said *former* SEAL. He was a year younger than I am. He just . . . died. Natural causes, they're calling it."

"Damn," Chavez said, not knowing what else to say. Sometimes, keeping your piehole shut was the better part of valor. His phone began to vibrate on the table, rescuing him from the conversation he'd started. It was Jack Junior.

"What's up?"

"We checked out Suparman Games," Ryan said. "This location downtown is just a storefront. There are some publicity offices in back along with a small storage room for the games they stock, but no corporate offices. Sounds like Suparman, his VPs, and software development folks are located south of the city. I'm betting he'd keep the software locked up out there. Adara and Midas are going to drive that way and scope it out. But get this, the door to the back offices at this location has a scramble pad. Adara was able to get close enough to get the brand and type. She struck up a conversation with the armed guard, too. He's here during the day, but he mostly looks for shoplifters. She commented about how safe it was and the guy told her that was nothing. According to him, Suparman really likes his security tech. The other place supposedly has retina-scan locks."

"And an armed guard?" Chavez said, rubbing his face, thinking about getting a warm-up for his coffee.

"*Two* armed guards," Jack said. "The guy here says they're Malukans. Supposed to be an island known around here for knee-breaker types. The guards are on duty at that location twenty-four/seven, at least according to this guy with the instacrush on Adara."

"Okay," Chavez mused. "Tighter security makes me think you're right. We'll try the main office first, then the storefront. Tell Midas and Adara to make the recon quick. You and Dom go to your rooms and recheck your gear. This one is time-sensitive and we wasted a day getting here. Your keys are waiting for you at the front desk under the name on your passport. Stop by my room to grab your gear."

Ryan's full beard helped conceal his identity, but his name was far too recognizable, especially since his father was all over the news in Indonesia at the moment. Fortunately, The Campus had friends at State who could help them out with different passports. It was standard practice in the intelligence and clandestine world to use actual given names on any alias. Jack, however, was too obvious. When he traveled, Jack Ryan, Jr., became Joseph "Joe" Peterson of Alexandria, Virginia.

"Copy that," Ryan said. "I'll pass the word to Adara and Midas to hurry."

Chavez ended the call, and then, struck with a sudden idea, turned to Clark. "Let's head over to the hotel. I want to give Gavin a shout, and I need you on the line."

"Lead on, McDuff," Clark said, heaving a glum sigh.

"We're all gonna die, John," Chavez said. "*When* is the mystery."

"Don't I know it," Clark said. "I just expected the *how* would be more interesting."

32

Chavez punched in Gavin Biery's number as soon as they got to his room. He put the phone on speaker and set it on the lacquer coffee table between him and Clark.

"Hey, bud," Chavez said when the IT director picked up. "What can you tell me about retina-scan locks?"

"Are you sure the tech is retina and not iris scan?" Biery asked.

"No." Chavez raised his eyebrows at Clark. "They're not the same?" He caught himself. "I mean, I know the anatomical differences in parts of an eyeball. I'm asking about the security mechanisms."

"I get it," Biery said. "They're kind of the same, in that both compare unique images from the user's eye. An iris scan is just a program that matches similarities from digital photographs of the colored portion of your eye. We all have unique patterns, so the iris is a good spot for identifying characteristics. It's simple and relatively cheap. Lots of things like passport control and even cell phones are using the tech now because it doesn't require much besides a camera. A retina scan is a little more complicated. In a nutshell, it's a deep scan of the pattern of blood vessels on the back wall of your eye. The scanners they use have got to be a little more sophisticated because they're looking through your pupil inside your eye. And you have to get really close to the device to unlock it."

"How difficult are they to defeat?"

"Hmmm," Biery said, mulling it over. "I'm not sure. The iris scan uses a series of digital photos so, in theory, if you had enough quality images of someone's eye, you could duplicate the key—especially with three-D cameras we have now. The retina scan might be a little tougher. Unless you were able to just get the guy's eyeball."

"He might object to the procedure," Chavez said.

"Yeah." Biery chuckled. "Have you seen the scanner and lock? I could tell you more if you got me a photo of the tech."

Chavez looked at Clark and shrugged. "We have not. We're not a hundred percent sure which it is, but we think our target is running a retina scan."

"Hmmm," Biery said again. "Hang on a minute." Biery's keyboard clicked rapidly on the other end of the line. "We're talking about Suparman Games, right?"

"We are," Chavez said.

"Good." More keyboard clicks followed, then silence as Gavin read whatever file he'd hacked into. "So I'm assuming you need to get past this unknown lock to break into Suparman's safe."

"That would be a correct assumption," Chavez said. Gavin liked it when you talked to him like he was a character on *Star Trek*.

"Awesome. Remember how in his social media photos Suparman always wears those thick Elton John glasses?"

Ding leaned forward, elbows on his knees, hands clasped, and nodded at the phone on the table.

"I do."

"Well, I think I just found your key. Suparman's financials say his optometrist works at Lucky Optical, to the northeast, about twenty minutes out of the city center."

"Out near the airport," Clark noted.

"Right," Biery said. "That's the one. And here's the good news. Lucky Optical advertises a machine called an optomap. It's pretty cool tech; my optometrist has one. It's a scanning confocal laser that takes a two-hundred-degree-wide field view of the retina. That means high-resolution images of the optic nerve and all the blood vessels at the back of the eye—the same stuff a retina-scan lock is going to be looking for. With vision as bad as Suparman's, he's sure to have a substantial patient record on file, including digital images from the optomap."

Clark scooted his chair closer, interested now. "And we can use the digital files of the images as a key?"

"You could," Biery said. "In theory."

Chavez gave a thumbs-up. "That's terrific news."

"It's sort-of-terrific news," Biery said. "I'm through the optometrist's office firewall, but all I can find is billing information."

"No files from the machine?" Clark asked.

"Sorry," Biery said. "No luck on that count. Most places store the files in a server that uploads to the Cloud, but Suparman's doc must store them on a stand-alone drive. Wherever it is, it's not on his networked computers. If you want to break into Suparman's safe, first you will have to break into his eye doc's office. I'll pull up some specs on the optomap machine and walk you through what you'll need to do to get the images. They're pretty cool," he said as an aside. "I have it done every year. Anyway, you should be able to put the files on a thumb drive—or e-mail them to me, then I can put them on a drive for you."

Chavez leaned back abruptly. For a minute there, it had all seemed so easy. Too easy. "Won't that opto machine be password-protected?"

"Maybe," Biery said. "Maybe not. I mean, who goes around stealing photos of people's eyeballs?"

Ding groaned. "Apparently, we do."

T he two F-15 Eagles out of Kadena are sitting on the tarmac in the Philippines," Chavez told the team. They'd all linked up in his room at the Whiz Prime Hotel for specific assignments after the recon of the Suparman main offices. "I'll make the call as soon as it looks like we have Calliope in hand. The birds can be here in less than an hour and then jet back to the good old US of A a hell of a lot faster than we could."

The F-15 Eagle had listed top speed of more than 1,800 miles per hour, so, "a hell of a lot faster" was a bit of an understatement.

"I wouldn't mind doing a little diving after that," Adara said, covering a yawn with her closed fist. "I mean, have you looked at the water around here?"

"Once they're wheels up and we check in," Chavez said. "A little R-and-R is well deserved."

He opened his tablet to display a set of blueprints

Gavin had found for Suparman Games' head offices. The date stamp on the scanned document was smudged, and though they'd been uploaded two years prior, it was impossible to say whether the plans were original or contained any modifications made after construction began. Online plans were notorious for leaving out walls and showing closets where there was actually a bathroom. Still, they used what they had for a tabletop review of the facility. They munched on energy bars rather than eating a big meal that would slow them down, and took a few moments to rehydrate. All of them had sweated through two sets of clothes from the heat alone. The tension of the mission only made it worse.

Midas sat at the desk in the corner, hunched over one of the Raspberry Pi computer boards, soldering wires, referencing some crib notes he'd taken down from Gavin's over-the-phone instructions.

Chavez opened the tablet to Google Earth, then used two fingers to zoom out and display the neighborhood around Suparman Games HQ. Most of the houses and businesses were new, white stucco over cinder block with orange tile roofs. Real estate sites advertised the area as having "American construction." The Blessing Jesus statue loomed in the hills above, just a few blocks away from their target.

"Here's the deal," Chavez said. "The folks at State tell us that this country has a very basic but effective system for keeping tabs on strangers. Every neighborhood is run by a head man. Kind of like the old ward bosses in New York or Chicago. Any new faces hanging around get reported to the head man. Family visiting from overseas, homestay guests, burglars, it doesn't matter. The ward boss knows you're there, especially the farther you get from the center of the city. If you really don't belong, then you get reported to the police."

Midas glanced up from his soldering. "And then we bribe the police and go about our merry way stealing this puppy."

"If only," Chavez said. "No. These ward bosses are a little more serious about their turf than that. And with President Ryan coming to town, we have to be extra-careful. One misstep and this all explodes in his face."

"Manado depends on tourism," Clark added. "People are used to seeing outsiders loitering around shops, home-stays, and the like—up to a point. That gives us some leeway with time, but not much, especially out in the neighborhoods. I don't know if any of you have noticed, but our man Ding looks like he shares a little DNA with some of the locals on this island. If he wears a traditional batik shirt and keeps his mouth shut, maybe people cut him some slack long enough for him to get in and grab the software."

"At least long enough to get close to the guards," Chavez said. He pitched a box of black hair dye to Adara. "There's a reason another word for coffee is *java*. In the 1800s most of the world's coffee beans came from Dutch plantations all over Indonesia. A lot of Dutch DNA got spread around these islands. Dark—and, I might add, genetically superior—hair usually wins out, but there's still a lot of European influence in the gene pool. With the right hair color, people might at least take a minute before they report us to the neighborhood pooh-bah."

Adara studied the cardboard box. "This is written in Indonesian." She traced the instructions with her index finger. "Hey, I'm all for trying something new, but there's an exclamation point at the end of this line. For all I know, it says, *Danger, will cause people with blond hair to go bald!*"

Chavez shrugged. "To be honest, I wouldn't have known what to buy even if it had been written in English. I bought the most expensive box, though. So you should be good. I think it was something like forty-two thousand rupiah. That's like three whole bucks."

Adara gave a sullen nod and glumly studied the box. "Copy that."

"Ding and Adara will be the pointy end of the spear," Clark said. "The rest of us will provide backup from the shadows. Midas and Dom will handle any roving guards to the east of the building. Jack and I will take care of anyone to the west." He nodded at the Raspberry Pi on the desk in front of Midas. "Go over that thing with Ding in case he needs it."

"Roger that," Midas said. "The digital scans of Suparman's retinas are high-definition enough that we should be able to hold up the images on a smartphone. Gavin put together a brilliant little app that imitates the three-dimensional look and flutter of a live eyeball." He tapped the small green circuit board with the cool end of the soldering iron. "This is just in case we need to upload the files and spoof the system into thinking it's looking at an eye instead of the code for an eye. It'll take a bit longer, and it's a little trickier, but you should be able to do it fine." He brightened. "Might not come to that, though.

We're talking about a gaming company, not a government installation. They may feel like the retina scans and rent-a-cops are plenty of security."

"I wouldn't count on it," Clark said. "Suparman just spent twenty-five million dollars on this little piece of gaming tech. And let's not forget that it also got Ackerman's throat slit.

"Talk Ding and Adara through the particulars," Clark said. "We'll stay nimble." He checked his watch. "The main thing is to retrieve that software. The President will be on the ground sometime tomorrow. He needs to know what we're dealing with."

"Speaking of slit throats," Ryan said. "Do we have any inkling that the Chinese know about this copy of the software? I'd hate to run into some MSS operatives in the shadows with only one extra mag."

"We'll carry an MP5 in each vehicle," Clark said. "In case the fan gets shitty. But again, remember the objective. Grab the tech and get out. Adara and Ding, you two go straight to the airport. The rest of us will be behind you, scraping off any tails." He looked sideways at Chavez.

"Okay," Chavez said. "Now, for the guards." He took two small derringers out of a plastic case. "We're using a ketamine cocktail. Should keep them out for a good fifteen minutes, with the added benefit of a befuddled memory. I know I don't have to tell you, but drugging someone carries with it a good deal of risk. They've weighed the risks at higher, and we've been ordered to proceed."

Everyone in the room knew "higher" was the Office

of the Director of National Security, and, by extension, the President. They also knew that drugging someone was better than bashing them on the head, or worse—unless that person had a respiratory issue, or some other hidden medical condition that would cause them to stroke out. Lots of things happened in the field; the heat of battle guaranteed it.

Clark said out loud what everyone else was thinking.

"The brass wouldn't take doping a couple of rent-a-cops lightly. That should put a big fat exclamation point on how vital it is that we grab this software."

"Right," Chavez said, gathering up his notebook and tablet. "Adara and I are going to hang back and surveil the downtown store while the rest of you grab your shit and go to the eye doc. We'll make a plan after you get the optical files, but I'm ninety percent sure what we're looking for is at the main office."

33

It was called Manado Town Square, but the modern shopping area across four-lane Piere Tendean Boulevard was, in actuality, a narrow strip of land jammed between the Celebes Sea to the west and a seemingly endless flow of concrete and corrugated tin homes pushing in from the east.

Chavez and Adara had swung by Suparman Games so he could take a stroll through the store and get a feel for it, then he'd taken the first shift across the boulevard, inside the lobby of the Ibis hotel, drinking strong coffee and keeping an eye on the storefront while Adara went back to the Whiz Prime Hotel to dye her hair.

A man in a green jumpsuit pushed a broom ten feet away, causing Chavez to look up. The man avoided eye contact, sweeping as he walked by without saying a word. In most parts of the world the situation would have called for a head nod at the very least. Conspicuous ignoring most generally meant the person didn't want you to know they were looking at you. The Indonesians he'd met so far were a gregarious people. There were a dozen different reasons the guy avoided looking at Chavez, but the most obvious reason was that he was watching him. A healthy dose of paranoia had kept him alive this long.

He looked for earpieces, any kind of weapon—besides the broom. Nothing. The guy kept walking without looking back. Maybe he *was* just a shy janitor.

Chavez took the Moleskine notebook from his pocket and began to make a couple of notes. He enjoyed these quiet times, when he could think, but he preferred the action with the rest of the guys.

Few outside the inner circle knew The Campus existed. It wasn't something you applied to. You had to be asked, handpicked, so it was easier to get the crème de la crème of intelligence officers and operators. Chavez was a plank-holder, one of the first on board at inception, along with Clark and Dom Caruso, who'd been chosen by President Ryan and Gerry Hendley. There had been others: Brian—Dom's brother—and Sam. Both had been killed on the job. Chavez had lost countless friends, in Colombia, on Rainbow, and with the Agency—in hellholes all around the globe. Finding a place to get killed was never a problem.

Work in that environment made for a close-knit team, closer than family. The Campus was small. It had to be, but like any family, there were periodic squabbles and disagreements. Switching partners now and then helped to keep everyone on their toes. Beyond that, from a personal standpoint, Chavez genuinely liked these people. It was a good thing, too, because all told, he'd probably spent more time with members of one team or another than with his own family. Patsy had grown up that way with John Clark as her father, and now JP was going through the same thing. At a reunion the year before, Ding's cousin had called him an asshat for spending so

much time away from home, berating him for abandoning his family and leaving all the work on the home front
to his wife. Patsy about ripped the woman's head off de-
fending him. But she'd been quiet on the drive back to
the hotel, and admitted she wouldn't mind seeing more
of him. That next morning, though, she'd apologized for
laying on the guilt trip, and left him a handwritten note.
He'd even shown it to John and was pretty sure there had
been a tear or two welling up in the old man's eyes.

> *Never thought I'd meet another man like
> my dad. But I'm sure glad I did. Please don't
> get discouraged because of us. JP and I know
> you're not Superman—you're so much better.
> Superman doesn't have to be brave; he's invin-
> cible. You're a mere mortal, and yet you march
> into danger anyway, every day. That's brave.
> Someday, JP will find out what you and Daddy
> do, and when he does, he'll be so proud of you,
> just like I am.*
>
> *Love you,*
> *—Pats*

Funny thing was, his wife's note telling him to get out
there and do his job only made him want to spend more
time with her. Maybe she was just extra-wily that way.
Accustomed to compartmentalizing home and work into
different parts of his brain, he pushed the thoughts away
and focused on the mission, rejuvenated for the moment.

A steady stream of customers, mostly young Indonesian hipster types, came and went from the business.

Suparman's was crammed in the middle of a strip mall that was three stories tall. Like the larger mall to the south, it had the slouchy look of something old that had been re-furbished and repainted many times over. Flanked by a hair salon, a pet store, and a scooter dealership, among other things, Suparman's took up the bottom two floors in the center of the mall. The upper floors of most of the businesses appeared to be apartments. That would make things interesting if they ended up having to break in here.

There'd been no heavies, no dark limousines pulling up front, nothing to lead Chavez to believe there was anything remarkable going on inside the store. Of course, that didn't mean the Calliope tech wasn't there. Chavez was more interested in learning if the security guards went home after the store closed, in the event they came up empty-handed at the main office and had to come back here later.

Adara showed up less than half an hour after she left, black hair still damp under a stylish red ball cap. She'd changed into khaki slacks and a sky-blue polo shirt. Chavez had a cup of tea waiting for her.

"Your hair looks good," he said. "I'll bet Dom likes it."

"He'd better," Adara said. "Because I'm not sure this stuff is going to come out anytime soon. It smells like they used some kind of tar or something in the dye. I've showered in a lot of bathrooms in my travels . . . Did you know they have a hose connected to the toilets that you can use instead of toilet paper?" Adara had a knack for language and culture. Out of all the people on the team, she was the most likely to study up on the eccentricities of the places they visited—and then do her best to embrace them. She was also possessed of a keen sense of smell, and suggested even when she was transportation coordinator that the guys shower with local soaps on arrival at any new destination so as not to stand out from the crowd. "I looked it up," she said. "It's called a . . ." She looked at her hand, where she'd written down the word. "*Semprotan cebok*, or something like that. Basically means the spray hose for your butt."

"Yeah, it's going to take some time to convert me on that one," Chavez said. "Not big on the air-drying thing . . ." He nodded at her hand. "You may want to rethink having something about butts and hoses written on your palm."

"That's why you make the big money." Adara chuckled. She scooted her chair closer, forearms on the table so she could arch her back. Long flights, even on an aircraft as plush as the Gulfstream, had a way of putting kinks in a person's spine that took days to shake out.

"Anything?" she asked, shooting a sideways glance through the window across the street.

Ding shook his head. "Nothing but customers. Our guys are set up outside the eye doc's office. Should be making entry as soon as it closes."

Adara raised her cardboard teacup. "Here's to sitting on our spray-hosed butts while they do the fun stuff. When you were a kid, did you ever think you'd be in Southeast Asia drinking tea and trying to steal some millionaire's computer software?"

Chavez knew the question was rhetorical but answered it anyway. "As I remember, my only goal when I was a kid was not dying in a gang fight."

"Brutal," Adara said, grimacing like she meant it. "Hey, you're not really mad about the scenario in New York, are you?"

"Hell, no," Chavez said. "I want training to be as close to the real thing as possible without spilling too much blood. We're playing a zero-failure game. The only way to win is to cheat like hell . . . and then lie our asses off if we get caught. I was pissed at myself because I didn't figure out what you were up to."

"That means a lot." She toyed with her cup, spinning it slowly on the table. "You're a good boss."

Chavez shrugged off the comment. "I'm just one of the guys."

"No," Adara said. "You're not. You might look at yourself like one of us, but the rest of us view you in the league with John—"

Ding almost spewed his sip of coffee. "Well," he scoffed. "I'd say the rest of you need to check your windage and elevation, because I have a long way to go before I am anything like John Clark."

She drank her tea and looked at him for a time, and then said, "Whatever you say. I'm just telling you how we see it. You and John talk about us. Who do you think we talk about? You and John. It's only natural. Not that this is a democracy or anything, I'm just saying that all of us see you taking more and more responsibility—"

"John's not going anywhere."

Adara gave an adamant shake of her head. "I'm not saying that. I just mean you're a good boss, even if you do make me dye my hair so I look goth."

He chuckled and pushed away from the table, chair

chattering on the tile. "You got this for a few minutes? I'm gonna take a stroll."

"I'll be here," she said, toasting with the teacup again.

Chavez had never been comfortable with compliments, so this was as good a time as any to conduct a little area familiarization. Whenever possible, he liked to walk the streets and alleys around any surveillance site, getting a lay of the land, egress routes, possible overlap with other ops. A gangbanger a block away might not have anything to do with your target, but that didn't make him any less of a threat if he saw you hanging around his neighborhood. Smart spies used their surroundings like prey animals used chattering squirrels as an early-warning system for approaching danger. It was good to know where the squirrels were. More than once he'd watched some cartel kingpin's lookouts—called *halcones* in Spanish—run to alert their bosses of rival cartels or federales. You could never have too much intel, and the best of it often came from the bad guys.

The ocean was just two blocks away, but none of the breeze made it past the buildings, leaving the area behind the hotel devoid of wind. Late-afternoon sun beat down on the rusty tin roofs, causing them to tick and pop under the heat.

Chavez had planned to make a four-block loop, two blocks to the north and two blocks to the south. He knew there was a river to the north that bisected the neighborhood, but a large greenbelt of thick foliage ran alongside the boulevard north of the hotel. Two Indonesian men sat on a sidewalk bench smoking and chatting idly with each other. Neither paid any attention to Chavez when he turned right down the cracked street and began to wind his way south, exploring the twisted alleys and tree-choked lots between houses.

Colorful roosters—Indonesian jungle fowl, according to Adara's research on the plane—scratched beneath shrubs and scabby grass along wrought-iron fences. The wiry little birds often found their way into local cooking pots, and they eyed Ding carefully as he walked the concrete streets.

The low houses could have been in any country in Asia. Even the nicer, "middle-class" homes were much smaller than those found in North America. Most of them could have fit into Chavez's living room. Of course, Hendley Associates paid better, and Patsy was a surgeon, so they could afford a little more house than a run-of-the-mill GS-14 like he'd been with CIA. Some had tile roofs and blossoming fruit trees, but most were patched with rusty corrugated tin and weathered plywood.

It was late afternoon, and sticky hot.

Out of habit, he glanced hard to his right, exaggerating his movements just enough to get a look behind him with his peripheral vision. The two guys who'd been smoking on the park bench were up now. Not weird in and of itself, but they bore watching. Chavez thought about calling Adara but decided he was just being paranoid.

He continued south, cutting behind a car dealership that blocked off not only the air but the traffic noise from the boulevard.

The guys would be hitting the optometrist any minute, and then they could get this show on the road. He

MANADO, INDONESIA

N

Celebes Sea

MANADO

- Megamall
- Whiz Prime Hotel
- Manado Town Square

SULAWESI

Suparman Games Office •
• Blessing Jesus Statue

© 2019 Jeffrey L. Ward

turned right at the corner at the end of the dealership, swinging wide out of habit—but not quite wide enough. Two more Indonesian men met him head-on. Both were half a head shorter than him, thicker around the middle, with big arms. Construction workers? Both picked up their pace, coming straight at Chavez. As he suspected, he heard the patter of sneakers on the concrete behind him.

He cut left, intent on jagging around the oncoming men and making a sprint for the boulevard. They were thuggish, the kind of dudes it was easier to outrun than fight, especially when there were four of them. He heard a loud pop followed quickly by a hollow *thunk* he recognized as a 40-millimeter grenade launcher. He braced himself for an explosion, as something hit him hard between the shoulder blades, shoving him forward. He stutter-stepped, skipping to keep from going down, tangled in his own feet. He recognized a second *pop-thunk*, then another stinging smack, this one on the back of his thigh, striking the peroneal nerve and giving him instant dead leg. He listed sideways, drawing in his arm to keep from breaking his wrist as he fell. He caught the flash of a large black projectile rolling away on the street. These bastards were shooting him with plastic bullets. Big-ass plastic bullets, dense and hard like missiles made out of a bowling ball. He'd used them before. Fired from the same M203 grenade launcher he'd used in the military, these "less lethal" rounds were used when you didn't want to fill your target with lead but didn't care if you bruised the hell out of them—and maybe even broke a few ribs.

Chavez used the momentum of his fall to roll, coming up in a kneeling position with his back to the dealership. He could hold his own in a fight, but four against one sent him reaching for the Smith & Wesson over his right kidney. There was another pop, this one not nearly as loud as the 40-millimeter, followed by the sickening crackle of a Taser.

Chavez was too hyped to feel the barbed steel darts that struck him in the upper arm and right thigh. Fifty thousand volts coursed between the darts, convulsing his muscles. Jaw clenched, his hands useless claws, he toppled sideways to the pavement. He'd been tased before and struggled to sweep the gossamer wires as soon as the five-second shock was past, but the weapon crackled again, sending him immediately into another full-body cramp. By the time it was over, his hands and ankles were zipped in flex-cuffs. Tires screeched to a stop, a van door slid open, and rough hands threw him inside. One of the men slipped a black hood over his head. He closed his eyes, his mind racing to make a plan, any kind of plan. He'd stop fighting back now and listen, take note of the sounds he heard inside the—

A sudden blow connected with the side of his head, which, pressed against the floor of the van, had nowhere to go. Chavez groaned, bracing himself for another blow that didn't come. His ears rang. His stomach roiled. The blindfold made it difficult to draw a breath. The heavy blow hadn't knocked him out, but he was not quite conscious of his surroundings.

He was vaguely aware of rough hands turning him from side to side as they rifled through his clothing, yanking the pistol from his belt—holster and all—and then his knife and wallet. He heard gasps when they found the radio, and the wire neck-loop microphone. The earpiece was inside the hood, and one of them knew enough about communications gear to hike up the cloth far enough to pinch the tiny monofilament hair and pull out the pea-size piece of plastic. They found it all—except the flat battery pack inside the lining of Chavez's belt—which also contained the tracker he and Clark used to identify every team member's position for the common operating picture.

Adara would realize he was missing soon, and when she let Clark know, he'd bring the cavalry. Chavez smiled reflexively, despite the searing pain in his head. It would be epic. He just hoped he was still alive to see it.

34

Michelle Chadwick found an open parking spot along 15th Street, across from Washington-Liberty High School—a lucky break for this time of morning, when joggers and cyclists flocked to the Custis Trail before they went to work. The school wasn't far from her condo. She swam at the aquatics center there three days a week to burn off the stress of her job, not to mention the butter-pecan ice cream she scarfed down at least five nights a week. She skipped the pool this morning, in favor of a run. It was as good a place as any for a private conversation with that bastard David Huang.

The meeting was set for six a.m. Unable to find anything close to sleep, she'd arrived at five-thirty. His Range Rover was already there, three cars back from her. That made sense. He'd want to get there early, check out the location for surveillance and whatnot. He, or more likely someone who worked with him, was probably watching her now. Chadwick was not a spy, but she was sneaky, and that was the same thing, wasn't it?

She sat for several minutes after she parked, finally banging on the steering wheel with both hands in an effort to settle herself before she opened the door. She and Huang had run together before, on this same trail.

He'd complimented her tights then, saying he liked how they showed off her legs. She'd worn them again today, hoping they might throw him off balance. She felt exposed and stupid for it now.

The sun wasn't quite up yet, but it promised to bring its sticky heat in just a few more hours. Having grown up in the deserts of Arizona, she found it impossible to understand how D.C. could be so muggy and chilly at the same time. She debated throwing on a light jacket from her trunk, but decided she'd let her hatred of Huang warm her until the run heated her up.

The Custis Trail generally followed Interstate 66 east and west. Chadwick dispensed with her usual stretching and headed east, toward the Potomac and Downtown Washington, D.C. Much of the trail ran between the highway and residential areas, but the half-mile or so that lay ahead of her cut through a semi-secluded greenbelt. They'd share the trail with other runners and cyclists, but, for the most part, she and Huang would be able to speak freely.

Chadwick hated running for the first couple of minutes of every workout. It took a while for her joints to warm up. Slowly, with each gliding step, her lungs and legs began to call an uneasy truce and started working together. After that she fell into an enjoyable pace. Still twilight, the trail through the greenbelt was shadowed and foreboding, made even more so because of this shitstorm she'd brought down on herself. She padded along glumly, dreading the thought of seeing David Huang's face. Even the earthy root-beer smell of sassafras that grew alongside the trail failed to cheer her up.

He was bent over, tying his shoe, when she saw him, wearing unremarkable gray sweats, nothing like the running shorts he'd worn when he was trying to impress her. He wore a fanny pack, too, like a retired tourist or federal agent might wear. He'd never worn one before, probably started so he could carry a gun. Smart, because since that day at the restaurant, she'd felt herself constantly overwhelmed with the desire to claw his eyes out every time she had to look at his face. He glanced up when he heard her shoes on the pavement, his brow knit into a stern line—like a father waiting up for a daughter who had come home from a date smelling like rum and Coke.

She kept running and he fell in beside her.

"You would be advised," he said, "to let me know more quickly when you come into possession of this type of information in the future."

She looked sideways, playing dumb. "I did let you know. I'm here, aren't I?"

"These things must be timely," Huang said, almost whining. "You and I. We must be timely. You do not understand what sort of people my superiors are."

She glanced sideways as she ran, wondering if he was getting his ass chewed because of her. She sure hoped so.

"Look," Chadwick said. "I called you. Doing what you've asked me to do . . . It's hard, you know? I'm not a traitor."

"Of course you aren't," Huang said. "We both agree that this President and his administration are bad for the country . . . bad for the world. His hawkish policies are causing conflict, not calming it. He is a habitual bully, and not just in the South China Sea but in the

Baltics, Iran, Cameroon, North Korea . . . I could go on and on."

Chadwick thought about the list of professional bullies he'd just ticked through, but didn't say anything.

"We are not asking you to betray your country," Huang continued. "If anything, we are asking you to save your country."

"A coup?"

"If you like," Huang said.

"Are you going to . . . ?"

Huang laughed. "Assassinate Jack Ryan? No, nothing like that. He will shoot himself in the proverbial foot. Our aim is to let the world see him for who he is. How is that wrong?"

Chadwick glared at him. "You're using a sex tape to leverage me. That sounds pretty wrong in anybody's book."

Huang stopped. "Michelle . . ." He touched her elbow so she would stop, and then stepped back to give her space. "I am truly sorry about that part. Hurting you was . . . regrettable."

She sneered. "Let's just not . . . Okay." She threw her hands up. "Fine. Here you go, then. I don't know the details, but he has decided to go to Indonesia."

Huang started jogging again, a little slower now. "How did he respond when you told him about your constituent with information on the priest?"

Chadwick shrugged. "He was interested." She felt dizzy, like she was about to throw up. But she kept running. She wasn't about to let this bastard see her weak—not again, anyway. "Of course he wants more information, but I told him it was an anonymous call."

"What are his plans when he's in Indonesia?"

"He didn't share that with me," Chadwick said. "He's got the Department of State involved. I'd guess they're working on inducements for the Indonesian government. Economic leverage, arms sales, low-interest loans. You know, the kind of inducements that don't involve incriminating video."

Huang ignored the gibe.

"Anyway," Chadwick said. "It sounds like Ryan and the padre go all the way back to their time in high school. I'm sure he'd like to carpet-bomb the hell out of the country until they hand over his friend, or at least threaten sanctions, but strong-arming the president of Indonesia would only make him look like a bully. I saw Scott Adler in his office, but that's not exactly earth-shattering intel that the secretary of state is visiting the Oval."

"True enough," Huang said. "What else?"

"To be honest," Chadwick said, "Ryan doesn't share shit with me. He wants to believe I'm ready to play nice—just like you predicted—but his chief of staff doesn't trust me to take out the trash, let alone get close to the President. I get the distinct impression the big goon who runs his Secret Service detail would like to shoot me between the eyes. I can't keep bringing them these reports from anonymous constituents to get me into the West Wing. This relationship you want me to build will take time."

"Unfortunately," Huang said, "there are matters at play that necessitate quicker action. We know Jack Ryan has a temper. What we need is for him to be angry so he makes a mistake. Something that would make him very angry . . ." He glanced at his watch, then dug a cell phone from his fanny pack. She was right about the pistol. *Bastard*.

Huang turned away to keep his conversation private, but she was able to catch the number over his shoulder as he punched it in with his thumb. She'd always had a better-than-average memory, and she tucked the number away in the back of her mind for later use. It would likely be a prepaid burner—the one Huang used now was a cheap flip phone that looked like it belonged to a gangbanger—but even that number might come in handy in the future.

Huang spoke in rapid Mandarin. Hushed at first, the conversation rose in volume as it continued, as though he was excited about the prospects of what Chadwick had told him.

He finished the call and then turned to her again, returning the phone into his fanny pack with the handgun.

"I need you to contact Ryan first thing this morning—as soon as you get to your office. Tell him you have received another call from your constituent. Tell him that Indonesian courts have convened a secret tribunal to convict Patrick West of blasphemy."

"Have they?"

"They will," Huang said. "And then add that you understand they found a considerable amount of heroin at the time of his arrest."

Chadwick just stared at him, dumbstruck.

He shrugged. "I suppose religion is not the only opiate of the people."

"Heroin?" Chadwick said, finding her voice. "You do

realize Indonesia has the death penalty for drug smug-glers."

"I am afraid they do," Huang said, his mind obviously thinking through the logistics of the plan to incite Jack Ryan to action rather than the consequences of that plan to West. "I'll have someone playing the part of your con-stituent leave a message on your office voicemail. That way the FBI will have something to find. The number will be untraceable."

"This is worse than blackmail," Chadwick said. "You would murder an innocent priest to further China's agenda?"

"*I* would not," Huang said. "But the men I work for would do so without hesitation."

Huang stared at her with hard, gimlet eyes, leaving no doubt in Chadwick's mind that he would be the one to murder her if she crossed him—or even if she didn't.

His gaze softened, as if he knew he'd let his true in-tentions slip. "You have done well." He turned west to-ward the vehicles and began to jog again. "I need to get back so I can make some more calls."

Chadwick fell in beside him, wrestling over what to say next.

"Was there something else?" he asked, as if reading her mind.

"A couple of things," she said.

"See"—Huang gave her a smiling nod, slowing just enough to hold a conversation in relative ease—"this is how it should work. You pass along bits of intelligence as you get them, and I interpret them. The information you glean in the White House is of vital importance, Michelle.

You know as well as I do that the world will be a much safer place without Jack Ryan."

"I can't say that I disagree," Chadwick said, mulling over the Espionage Act, the statute the Department of Justice used to indict spies. An unseen fist grabbed her gut and twisted. She stared down at her feet as they hit the paved path. "I understand," she said. "And I'll do what I need to do—but I'm doing it for me, not for China."

"Laudable," Huang said. "Now, let's have that other information . . ."

35

Lucky Optical occupied the western half of a low whitewashed block building that contained only two businesses. Tucked back from the street less than half a mile from the airport, it was relatively modern, with a tile roof instead of tin like many of the other businesses in the area. The sign for a specialty meat shop that had once occupied the space next door said it sold everything from fruit bat to "fine-hair" meat—meaning dog. Dusty windows and an empty showroom said it had been vacant for a while.

Lucky Optical closed at five-thirty, according to its website, giving Clark and the team very little time to get in place beforehand.

Jack Junior and Midas jimmied a window in the vacant meat shop and sat down to wait for everyone from Lucky Optical to go home. Clark went inside for a little recon. He asked for a tiny screw for his reading glasses. A nice lady at the reception desk put the screw in for him while he scanned the interior for motion sensors, contact strips, and control panels—and anything else that might indicate an alarm system or booby trap. The single CCTV camera was tilted toward the ceiling and would get a shot of nothing but light fixtures, if it worked at all. It had likely been installed by the previous tenants and never removed.

Caruso parked at the end of the street, behind the thick sawblade leaves of some pandanus trees that ran beside the scooter dealership. Clark drove a block away in the other direction.

The team had their earpieces in again, relying on radios now instead of cell phones so they could all be on the same page.

The chubby eye doctor left first, followed by two female assistants who looked half his age. The woman who'd helped Clark with his glasses—probably the office manager—was the last to leave. She locked the door and then rode away on a scooter, paying no attention at all to the strange bunch of Toyotas lurking in her neighborhood.

"You are clear to go," Clark said. "I'll get Gavin on the line so he can talk you through what you need to do."

36

Y ou have any idea what's going on?" Special Agent
    Mo Richardson said when she met Gary Mont-
    gomery at the Secret Service post inside the north
door to the West Wing, between the front portico and
the press briefing room. She gave a polite nod to the
Uniformed Division officer, a slender African American
woman she sometimes worked out with in the dojo.

"I'm not sure," Montgomery said. His brow creased
in a grim line, like he was fighting a headache—a frequent occurrence in this job. "We were running AOP
scenarios when I got the call." AOP meant Attack on the
Principal. PPD conducted frequent drills at their training
facility in Beltsville, imagining assaults from every conceivable venue—water, motorcycle, rope line, even explo-
sive drones. There was a full-scale mockup of the Ryan
house in Maryland that saw frequent use by the Secret
Service Counter Assault Team and Anne Arundel County
Special Operations Response Team. Mo had been con-
ducting a walk-through and AOP drill of her own with
the agents she'd handpicked for the Ann Arbor trip, using a mat room in the Secret Service gym to tape off the
floor plan of the Kellogg Eye Center.

"It's not like we don't have anything to do," Mo groused.

"I know what you mean," Montgomery said. "Van Damm wasn't exactly forthcoming with specifics. All I know is that POTUS wants to see us both."

"Does he call you in like this very often?"

Montgomery gave a halfhearted shrug. "More than I thought he would, yes," he said. "I've never had a protectee ask my opinion as much as this one. How about the Mrs.?"

"The same," Mo said. "To be honest, it's hard not to get too close."

Montgomery chuckled. "Yeah, the boss and I had to have 'the talk' not long after I came aboard. He's a good guy."

Richardson paused outside the door to the secretaries' suite adjacent to the Oval and turned to face Montgomery. "You ever wish you'd worn a different shirt when you get called over last-minute like this?"

"You look fine, Mo."

"I was talking about you," she said. "You have a little bit of mustard right . . ."

He glanced down and caught her grinning. "You little turd." He motioned her in, but checked his shirt again just in case. "After you."

"Thanks," Mo whispered. "I hear the second guy through the door is the most likely to get shot."

Betty Martin waved the two agents into the Oval Office immediately. Again, Montgomery let Richardson lead the way. Both stopped just inside the door, getting the lay of the land and waiting to be told if they were supposed to sit down or just offer a quick update and leave.

President Ryan, who was seated in his favorite chair by

the fireplace, stood when they came in, prompting the others in the room to do the same.

"Mo, Gary," Ryan said, gesturing toward the sofa to his left. "Thank you for coming on such short notice."

Richardson scanned the faces in the room. None of them provided an answer to what the meeting was about. Arnie van Damm and Mary Pat Foley sat on the couch to Ryan's right, along with the director of the Central Intelligence Agency. On the couch across from them sat Director Howe of the Secret Service. The President directed them to sit next to their boss. In the chair beside Ryan sat an Asian man Mo had never seen before. Her focus rested immediately on him, since he was the only unknown in the room.

Clean shaven, he was in his mid-thirties. His hair was medium length, just over his ears, long enough that he would look well groomed if he combed it or rakish if he mussed it a bit. He sat up straight, but not on the edge of his seat, a relaxed pose for someone visiting the Oval Office. His suit was modest, not too expensive, not new, but nice enough if he wasn't trying to impress anyone or get himself noticed—a rarity in the White House, where everyone was trying to make their mark.

That was it. He had the kind of eyes that Maureen would have passed right over in a crowd when she worked protection. Nonthreatening eyes. This guy didn't want to be remembered.

He had to be CIA.

Ryan nodded at the DNI, giving her the go-ahead once everyone was seated.

"I'll get right to it, then," Foley said. "By virtue of

your positions, the two of you are, as you Secret Service guys like to say, *worthy of trust and confidence*. Both of you have Top Secret SCI security clearances."

Foley glanced at Ryan, then back at the two agents, as if she were uncomfortable with the direction the conversation was heading. "It goes without saying that the things we are about to discuss have to stay within the room."

"Of course," Richardson said.

Ryan gestured to the Asian man seated next to him.

"Mo, I'd like you to meet Adam Yao, with CIA. He's done some incredible work. Saved a hell of a lot of lives."

Yao gave a half-smile, squirming slightly, as the compliment put him in the limelight. Richardson couldn't tell if he was just being modest or if he wasn't comfortable being introduced by his real name—if Adam Yao truly was his name.

Richardson found herself wondering what was coming next. She assumed this had something to do with the First Lady's trip. Still, she was a protector, not a spook.

"Adam," the President said. "Would you be so kind as to bring Special Agent Richardson up to speed?"

"Of course, Mr. President," Yao said. He leaned forward and picked up a dark blue folder from the coffee table between the couches, taking out a stack of eight-by-ten photographs and passing them to everyone present. "We believe General Song is traveling to the United States with this man, Tsai Zhan, as his minder. Tsai's job is to make sure Song stays on the straight and narrow. Sources say he reports unofficially to Song's immediate superior, General Bai."

Richardson studied the photograph. "What's Mr. Tsai's story?"

"He's former Oriental Sword," Yao said. "PLA Special Operations forces—their version of Spetsnaz. He has a considerable amount of training. He did something to his knee fast-roping out of a chopper, so he's been with Department Two for eleven years now. He specializes in internal security. Spying on the spies, as it were. Nothing confirmed, but we believe he's done quite a bit of off-the-books work for General Bai."

"What sort of off-the-books work?" Montgomery asked.

"He's not in Bai's official chain of command," Yao said. "But he keeps everyone in line."

"Like the whip on a protection detail," Montgomery noted.

"Basically," Yao said. "But more nefarious—threats, blackmail, things such as that. Think of him as Bai's personal provocateur."

Richardson held up the photo for a closer look. "Do you believe he's a threat to Mrs. Ryan?"

"Not directly," Yao said. "All the intel we have suggests he's just coming along as a minder—like the old KGB political officers that used to keep their military brass in line."

"I have two Mandarin speakers coming with me on the detail. Can I give them the photo so they'll know who to look for?"

DNI Foley nodded. "Of course. We'll provide you photos of everyone in General Song's entourage. But you shouldn't divulge specifics about Tsai, or CIA's interest in him. Just say he's someone who needs to be watched."

"That works," Mo said.

"Though he's not likely a danger to the First Lady," Yao said. "He could well pose a serious threat to her mission. Tsai is slimy. And since he's working directly for General Bai, who apparently hates everything about General Song, he will, as they say, be all up in the man's business."

"Okay . . ." Richardson said, still waiting for the other shoe to drop.

Yao glanced at the President, then sat back in his chair. "That's why I need to be placed on the First Lady's detail."

"Excuse me?" Richardson said.

Secret Service Director Howe spoke up. "We will provide Officer Yao with a lapel pin designating him as cleared by the Secret Service. The rest of your detail will believe he's part of the necessary hospital staff, and the staff will believe he's an agent with your detail."

"That's awfully dangerous, sir," Richardson said. "If he does anything hinky, it won't matter if my team thinks he's staff or not . . ." She looked directly at Yao. "If they see what they deem to be a threat—"

Yao shook his head. "I won't be armed."

"Well," Richardson scoffed. "We *will* be."

"Mo," Director Howe said, "you and your team focus on Dr. Ryan. Officer Yao will see to Mr. Tsai."

Richardson took a deep breath, letting the idea settle in. "What exactly does that mean? 'See to Mr. Tsai'?"

Foley leaned forward, elbows on her knees. She homed in on Richardson. "So now we come to the sensitive part of the meeting. Officer Yao will explain what he plans to do, but you must agree not to inform the First Lady before-hand. She shouldn't be given any details other than what she already knows."

Richardson looked to the President for guidance. It didn't seem like his style to leave his wife in the dark. It was common knowledge among the detail that he treated her like an unofficial member of his cabinet.

"You want to ask me why," Ryan said.

"I have to admit that I do, Mr. President," Richardson said.

She could tell the situation was uncomfortable for him, but he looked her directly in the eye. That's the way Jack Ryan did things, uncomfortable or not.

"Because of her oath as a physician," he said. *"First, do no harm."*

I don't like it," Jack Ryan said after everyone had gone but Foley and van Damm. He'd moved to the small study off the Oval, so he could sit back on the couch and pout. Cathy said the furniture made him slouch, which was decidedly unpresidential. He was too preoccupied to care.

Van Damm sat in the swivel chair by the small desk across from Mary Pat, who sat in the recliner that matched the couch.

"Which part don't you like?" the chief of staff asked.

"Any of it," Ryan said. "Not one damned bit. This Chinese minder . . . What's his name? Tsai? His file makes him look like a Bond villain. I'm rethinking the wisdom of Cathy stepping into this."

Neither van Damm nor Foley spoke. This was not their decision to make. Truthfully, if Jack wanted happiness at home, it wasn't his decision, either. Cathy Ryan was a big girl, extremely competent and intelligent. She didn't have the training for this sort of thing, but, Ryan recalled, he hadn't, either, when he started. If she'd known half the things he'd gotten himself into as an analyst, she would have killed him herself. And she'd sure as hell call him out for hypocrisy now. She had an inkling about what Jack Junior did for a living—the kid could come back from only so many overseas trips with horrific injuries and blame them on sports. He'd most recently had his ear torn half off in western Afghanistan. She was a mother, possessed of all the intuition that went along with it. Oh, she knew, all right, though the truth of it remained unspoken, as if not saying the words out loud somehow made their son just a little safer.

Ryan groaned within himself, the kind of deep, resigned death-rattle groan when you come to grips with something you've known all along. The Ryans had never been a play-it-safe kind of family—and they never would be.

"Adam Yao will do his job," Ryan said. "Mo will do hers. If there's any intelligence to be gleaned from General Song, Cathy will get it. When she's determined, she gets it done—whatever it is, God love her."

37

General Song hadn't been able to stomach Tsai Zhan when they'd met the first time, five years earlier at a retreat for senior officers at Mount Mogan near Hangzhou. Tsai was a senior operative with Department Two, the intelligence service within the military. Sometimes called a political officer, he was, in actuality, a mole hunter. He had the fertile mind of a trashy crime novelist, perceiving everyone around him to be a spy until they proved him wrong. When Song met the nasty little man, Tsai had been sent to lecture the generals about the due diligence of patriotism. His presentation turned out to be a half-day of slides depicting all the subversives he had "uncovered"—along with grisly photographs of their interrogations and eventual executions.

General Song did not countenance spies against his government, but he saw no reason to revel in their pain. One man's spy was another man's patriot. Some of them were incredibly brave, however misguided they happened to be. Certainly, a quick bullet behind the ear would be enough. There was no need to make a man suffer for his beliefs. And still, Song knew better than to display even a hint of his disgust.

"Oh, you disagree with my methods?" Tsai's eyes seemed to say. *"And why is that? Would that be because you have empathy for the traitor?"*

Song could not help but picture the man flinging spittle when he spoke.

Men like Tsai flourished during war. In economic booms and times of relative peace, it was a little harder for them to find a niche. Fortunately for Tsai, China was a large country, with many enemies, and many people to mistrust. General Bai and he had naturally struck up a fast kinship during that first meeting. Birds of the same flock, after all.

Travel by high-ranking officials to the United States always drew scrutiny from the intelligence services. But Song knew that General Bai was behind this. Tsai was his attack dog, on loan from the ministry.

Song's trip with his granddaughter was last-minute, which added more mystery. The fact that he and his wife had elected to have her illness treated in the United States was at once viewed as great fortune and a slap in the face of Chinese medicine. The medical establishment in Beijing complained bitterly, but no doctor wanted to be blamed for the loss of a child's eye, especially when that child belonged to a PLA general. Even generals as out of favor as Song could make a lot of stink for a physician. They had to appear upset, but they were surely relieved the delicate operation would take place well clear of their scalpels.

Tsai Zhan showed up at the Song household unannounced, waiting at the door with the gray golf jacket he always wore instead of a suit coat hanging over his arm.

He shoved the jacket toward the maid without looking at her, barking when she did not take it quickly enough for him.

The poor thing cringed, shooting a horrified look at the general, who smiled softly and gestured for her to go into the other room.

Tsai was half a head shorter than Song, with oddly long arms and slender fingers that reminded the general of a spindly shrub that had lost its leaves. His flat nose did a poor job of keeping his glasses in place, forcing him to constantly push them up with the tip of one of those stick fingers. He smiled a leathery smile when Song came to greet him in the foyer, complimenting a Ming dynasty vase like he'd read in a manners book one should always smile and compliment vases upon arrival at another person's home.

He had not, however, done much reading about the niceties of tactful lead-up to a delicate matter.

"I am here with the full force and support of General Bai," Tsai said tersely, standing rigid, as if he were at attention. "And, by extension, President Zhao Chengzhi, chairman of the Central Military Commission and paramount leader."

"Of course," Song said. "What can I do for you?"

"Am I to assume that you have chosen to go to America because you believe the care your granddaughter will receive there will be superior to that which she could receive in China?"

"That would be the obvious answer," Song said, treading carefully. For all he knew, there was a recording device in Tsai's pocket. "Dr. Berryhill has performed hundreds of these surgeries. It is not a matter of Chinese intellect, but of American experience. I could find no physician here with such a background in retinoblastoma. It is too great a risk."

"The disease is only in one eye?" Tsai said, as if to imply, *She has two, that gives her one to spare. What are you so worried about?*

"The doctors in Beijing believe that the tumor only affects one eye," Song said. "But they tell me they cannot be certain."

Tsai stood still for a moment, staring, blinking, birdlike. "And you fear Chinese surgeons will take your child's eye?"

"It is possible she will lose the eye no matter where the surgery is completed. Our goal is to save her life."

"So you believe she is in more danger of dying here than in the United States?"

Song clenched his fists, breathing steadily to keep his wits about him. He was, after all, a trained soldier, and professional soldiers in any country had an innate aversion to spies.

"Again," he said. "It is a matter of experience. Dr. Berryhill simply has more."

"And our doctors will remain inexperienced if everyone had your bourgeois attitude."

"It is selfish, I know," Song said. "But I would prefer them not to learn on my granddaughter."

"I will accompany you on this trip of yours," Tsai said. He tapped the side of his head with a finger. "You have a great deal of important information up here that the Americans would love to access. It has been a long time since I have been to the United States, but I remember that they are very tricky."

"By all means," Song said, forcing a smile. "If there is nothing else, I must return to my granddaughter."

"Is it visible?"

"What?"

"The tumor?" Tsai asked. "May I see it?"

Song bit the inside of his lip, forcing a sigh, hoping it sounded more benign than it was.

"No," he said. "You may not. In any case, the tumor is inside the eye."

"How interesting," Tsai said. "I should like to hear the story of how you discovered it."

"It is in my report requesting leave for travel," Song said, hackles up.

"I am aware of your report," Tsai said. "But I would like to hear the story again—when we are on the plane."

Song retrieved the golf jacket himself, sparing his maid the discomfort. As he shut the door, he couldn't help but think how difficult it was going to be to keep his wife from stabbing the repugnant man.

38

Originally, the plan to get inside Lucky Optical had been to cut a hole in the drywall between the abandoned meat shop and the clinic, but a check of the flimsy back door and some quick work with a penknife made damaging any property unnecessary. The optomap was connected to an in-house server via Cat-5 cable. Midas connected a small notebook computer to one of the USB ports while Ryan checked the doctor's desk for passwords that might be written down. It turned out that they didn't need one, and they were soon scrolling through files on the server. There were no less than three male patients named Suparman. Gavin helped cross-reference with home addresses and telephone numbers, and they were quickly able to ascertain which one was their guy. The files were JPEGs, less than a gig for each eye, and downloaded quickly to a thumb drive. Ryan and Midas were back in their own Toyota Avanza twenty minutes after they went in.

Ryan drove while Midas talked to Gavin, working through the process of building the key to override the retina-scan lock, using the thumb drive and a Raspberry Pi—in the event the images on his smartphone didn't do the trick.

Midas held up the small green board, not much larger than a deck of playing cards. "I love these little computers. They can do almost anything."

"Can that fight off a couple of armed guards?" Ryan asked. "Because that's what Ding and Adara are going to need."

Clark's voice came across the radio, direct and taut. *"CODE BLACK. Repeat. CODE BLACK."*

Ryan and Midas both reached to check their radios, making certain they were on PTT instead of intercom mode. CODE BLACK was an order to cease all radio traffic immediately. It usually meant they were being monitored. Since the radios were encrypted, the only obvious way that could happen was for someone to get one of the handsets.

Ryan's phone rang an instant later. It was Clark. Ryan put it on speaker and passed it to Midas so he could negotiate the Manado traffic.

"Everyone rendezvous at the Blessing Jesus statue south of the city," Clark said. "Ding's missing. We have to assume he's been taken."

"Copy," Ryan said, his voice grim.

Midas was already looking up the best route on his phone. He pointed south and whispered, "Take this to the Ring Road. It's a straight shot south."

Ryan gave a quick nod showing he understood. "Taken?" He glanced down at the phone as he drove. "By who?"

"I've got his tracker pulled up," Clark said. "Looks like he's at Suparman's main office."

"No shit?" Midas said. "That makes no sense. How could Suparman have known we were here?"

"The visit to the game store, maybe," Ryan mused.

"Unknown," Clark said. "But the fact remains, he's at Suparman HQ—or, at least, that's where the tracker in his belt is. Adara talked to a lady from the teahouse who said she saw some men helping another man into a van. When she went to the spot, she found Taser chaff on the sidewalk."

"The bastards tased him," Midas said.

"Looks that way," Clark said, his jaw clenched, brooding.

Along with their twin steel barbs, the compressed-gas Taser cartridge deployed dozens of tiny circular tags known as Anti-Felon Identifications. These AFIDs were numbered and fluoresced when hit with a UV light, helping law enforcement—and in this case, Adara—see where a Taser had been deployed.

"So," Ryan said, his mind reeling. "We link up at the statue . . . and then . . ."

"The mission's still the same," Clark said. "Except we grab the tech *and* Ding."

"And no dart guns on the guards," Midas said.

"Oh," Clark said. "Hell, no."

39

It was a straightforward mission—a pregnant woman, two teenagers, and a man in his fifties. Soft targets. Kang could have handled the job all by himself. He brought Rose and Lily, in any case, mainly to help keep an eye on the boss. Wu Chao had insisted on coming along. The major was handy enough to have around when the rough business began, but he took no joy in the work. It was as if he felt embarrassed. Guilty. And too much guilt could make one slow. Rose and Lily certainly didn't have that problem. They enjoyed this work as much as Kang did—a rarity in women, as Kang had come to find over the course of his career.

The Li home was a huge affair, built, like all the other houses in historic Fort Sheridan, in the 1890s of blond brick. Located on one of the quiet side streets east of Leonard Wood Avenue near the old parade ground turned park, the three-story house was nestled among great oaks and Colorado blue spruce. Conveniently for Kang and his group, it was the last on the loop, adjacent to a steep wooded slope that led directly down to the shores of Lake Michigan and a quiet nature preserve.

Kang and the others approached in the rain, under cover of darkness, in an inflatable skiff. Dressed like tourists who'd been caught in the weather rather than commandos, they beached the boat and dragged it into the underbrush at the edge of the woods. They didn't have to worry about extreme high tides, but Lake Michigan had wind and waves, so Kang looped the bowline around a stout bush before leading the others up the tree-choked incline.

As always, he'd come well prepared for the evening's events. He'd studied real estate floor plans of similar houses and reviewed social media accounts for the woman and her two teenagers. Li wasn't active on social media, so Kang had to rely on a dossier put together by MSS and Central Committee operatives over the years. Li was retired military, which could be an issue when it came to violence. But the man was in the Navy and sailors prosecuted wars from far away, not nose-to-nose, the way Kang preferred. No, this one would pose no challenge whatsoever.

Chinese blood ran through Peter Li's veins. He'd completely forgotten his heritage, his responsibility. Li worked for the Americans—making him doubly culpable in Kang's book—less than a dog.

A spotter in the neighborhood above, out walking her bichon frise, had confirmed earlier that Li had dropped his car off at a garage in Lake Forest for some repairs. His wife had picked him up. Both children had arrived home in the late evening.

Kang and his team had to bushwhack through dense foliage, but reached the top of the hill with little trouble. A familiar warmth began to spread through his belly when the house came into view. A second-floor light was on, but it was just before dawn and everyone would be in bed—the groggy time, the best time to attack.

Each member of the group was armed with an identical Beretta Storm Compact nine-millimeter pistol with a threaded barrel and suppressor. All but Wu Chao also carried a knife. The women preferred short, scalpel-like blades for close-in work, which accounted for why they often removed their clothing before they did a job. Kang's weapon of choice was a thick beast with a slightly curved blade that resembled a stubby cutlass. He'd had it custom-made by a smith in Shanghai. The black Micarta handle was scored to help him retain his grip when it might otherwise grow slippery from the inevitable blood and gore.

Kang took his eye off the house long enough to check his team. The women were both locked in on the mission, but relaxed in the way professionals relax before doing something they know well. Wu crouched at the edge of the brush, turning his head this way and that, as if he were attacking a fortified sentry post instead of a house of soft targets. He used a night-vision monocular to scan the grounds, and then returned the device to his pocket. There was enough ambient light that flashlights or night-vision goggles were unnecessary.

Wu gave Kang a slight nod, permission to advance, though Kang had been about to move forward without it. This was his realm of expertise.

Taking a mobile phone from the pocket of his vest, Kang entered a six-digit code, accessing the security application on the Li boy's cloned device. On Kang's signal, the team sprinted through the blue-black darkness across the lawn to the side door—off the kitchen, stacking in teams of two on either side of the frame. Lily put her right hand on the knob, then raised her left to signal she was ready. The alarm would make an audible chirp the moment it was deactivated, alerting Li that something was amiss. They had to move quickly.

Kang, standing directly behind Lily, entered the disarm code, counted to three, and then gave her thigh a squeeze—signaling for her to go. She rolled in through the open door, careful not to let it bang against the inside wall. Kang followed tight on her heels, pistol up, raised tritium night sights glowing over the barrel of his suppressor in the dim light of the pantry. Rose filed in behind him, fluid, inaudible. Wu Chao brought up the rear, easing the door shut.

The group crept through the mudroom and pantry single file, padding softly into the kitchen, following the edge of a wraparound granite counter toward the stairs to the left. The front half of the second floor was open to the area below, and light from an open bedroom door above poured over the balcony, illuminating wood floors and ornamental throw rugs.

A sleepy woman's voice carried down over the railing above. She must have heard the electronic chirp. "James. Are you up messing with the alarm?"

The boy coughed. "Huh?"

"I asked if you were messing with the alarm," the woman said.

"It's not me!" the boy said, hoarse with sleep.

The teenage girl spoke next. "Oh my gosh, James! It's the middle of the night, could you just shut up?"

Kang was surprised they'd all awoken so easily. No matter.

In the hall below, Lily trained her pistol upward at the balcony, her back to the stairs. She gestured to her left, then directly in front of her, and whispered, "Girl . . . parents," indicating who was in which room. Then, pointing over her shoulder at the bedroom that would be across the upstairs hall, she said, "Boy."

Kang and the others signaled that they understood. The plan was to grab the parents first, specifically the pregnant woman. They would all be killed eventually, but Wu Chao insisted on questioning Peter Li, learning what he knew, what others knew—if anything—about the incursion into the "vault" computer in his office. Once the woman was under control, everyone would fall into line. Li was sure to answer any questions to save his wife and unborn baby. After that . . . Kang smiled inside. After that, the fool would realize it would have been better if everyone had died in the initial attack.

Kang raised an open hand toward the stairs. His foot had just hit the bottom step when the boy called out again. He froze.

"Something's weird," the boy said, half shouting so his parents could hear him. "My app is acting up. Sorry, Mom. I'll go down and arm it at the pad."

A light flicked on upstairs. *Good.* It would destroy the boy's night vision.

Kang motioned for Wu Chao and Rose to move quickly across the hall and into the dining room. He took Lily with him to wait around the corner in the kitchen.

The boy would walk directly between them to reach the security controls.

Young ears, especially those attached to the heads of youths who do not have the misfortune to live in noisy cities or places of war, have excellent hearing.

James trotted down the stairs, whistling "We Are the Champions" by Queen as he skipped every other step. He was barefoot, dressed in a pair of running shorts and a T-shirt. His bare feet hit the base of the wood floor as his whistle crescendoed. The kid spun toward the kitchen, then stopped cold.

He'd heard something.

Kang eased around the corner, allowing him to make out a narrow slice of the hall. Movement flashed in the shadows as Rose stepped out of the dining room, mere feet behind the boy, her suppressed Beretta coming up. She fired, but Wu Chao swatted the weapon away at that exact moment, deflecting the round upward, over the top of the boy's head and into the kitchen cabinets behind Kang and Lily.

The shot was a quiet pop compared to the shattering dishes and the teenager's terrified yowl. The spent cartridge rattled on the hardwood. To his credit, instead of freezing as so many did when confronted with sudden danger, the boy tried to flee up the stairs while he worked to make sense of it all. Wu Chao grabbed a handful of T-shirt, dragging him back. He brought his open hand down flat on top of the boy's head, stunning him into submission.

Wu Chao glared at Rose, hissing in rapid-fire Mandarin. "Not yet! If you kill him, we lose all leverage!" He flicked his free hand up the stairs, shoving the boy ahead of him.

Rose shot a look at Kang, no doubt seeking permission to punch their impudent boss in the face—or worse.

The master bedroom light flicked on. "What was that?" Sophie Li shouted. "James? What broke? Are you okay?"

"M . . . Mom . . ." the boy stammered.

Wu Chao prodded the boy forward, following on his heels. The two women were next. Kang brought up the rear, covering the stairs with his pistol.

"Tell them to come to the balcony," Wu Chao said, giving the boy a shove to show he meant business.

"Mom . . . Peter," the boy said, his voice remarkably calm. "They . . . They want you to come here."

Sophie walked out immediately, clutching the neck of the knee-length football jersey she used as a nightgown. The nylon stretched tight around her pregnant belly.

"What do you mean *they*?"

She stopped short, her mouth falling open, her face stricken when she saw her son with a gun to his head.

Down the hall, the girl screamed. She ran out of her room clutching a cell phone by her side but had yet to place a call. Rose rushed in and knocked the phone away. She slapped the girl hard, driving her to her knees, then spun to grab Sophie by the arm and drag her back to the landing. Peter Li was still nowhere to be seen. Coward.

A new, more vulnerable hostage under control now, the entire team advanced. Kang took possession of a trembling Sophie.

She tried to scream, but Kang planted a vicious knee in the small of her back. She winced, arching in pain, whimpering now. "Please . . . I'm begging you. Don't hurt my baby."

Wu Chao took a half-step forward, using the boy as a shield. He glanced sideways at Kang and Sophie, then turned toward the master bedroom.

He raised his voice. "Peter Li! If you call anyone on the phone you will force my hand."

No answer.

"Peter!" Wu Chao barked again. "We can resolve this like men. We need to ask you some questions. Come to the door."

The bedroom light went out.

Rose shot a look at Kang like she wanted to go in.

"No," he hissed. "Not yet."

Kang intertwined his fingers through Sophie's hair, then yanked her head backward so she faced the ceiling. Her neck arched toward the door, delicate, exposed. He used the curved blade of his knife to lift the hem of the football jersey, pulling it up slowly, exposing her panties and then her swollen belly. She found her voice, screaming, trying to jerk away. One hand reflexively cradled her unborn child; the other went to the nightshirt, attempting to pull it down. Kang used the blade to slap her hand away, slashing her forearm in the process. Blood poured from the wound. The boy lunged for his injured mother, but Wu Chao slammed a fist into the back of his head, staggering him and pulling him closer.

Kang spoke now, loud but in complete control. His voice dripped with venom. "Peter Li! Come now. Stop hiding and show yourself or I will carve out your baby and paint this house with your woman's blood."

"Peter," Wu Chao said. "You must listen. I will not be able to stop him if you do not—"

A massive boom shook the house at the same instant a blossom of orange fire erupted from the darkness of the master bedroom. Wu Chao's knee burst as if he'd been shot with a cannon. He listed sideways like a felled tree. A second blast took off the side of his head, leaving him in a twitching heap behind the quivering boy.

Kang had no time to register dismay.

A third shot tore at the air to his right. Something hot slammed into the bend of his elbow, causing his hand to convulse. The blade slipped impotently from an open palm. He backpedaled, intent on keeping the pregnant woman between him and what had to be a shotgun. Sophie Li had other ideas. Screaming with rage, she spun, clawing at Kang's face, flaying skin off his nose and cheeks with her nails. He ducked, striking out blindly, shoving the crazed woman away before he lost an eye. Another shot shook the walls, blasting a gaping hole in the Sheetrock next to Kang's ear. He scrambled over the railing, landing halfway down the stairs. A fifth blast, followed rapidly by a sixth, sent Rose and Lily fleeing down the steps after him. The women fired pistols over their shoulders as they fled, but hit nothing.

Kang squatted low, behind the relative cover of the landing. He'd regained the use of his hand, so the wound to his elbow couldn't have been too bad. Probably birdshot. He ducked his head, pistol drawn now, ready to rush the stairs. They did not need to talk to Peter Li that badly. The important thing was to tie up loose ends. Li had to die. Kang would kill the family for sport. Retribution for . . . fighting back. The odor of gun smoke and urine from Wu Chao's spilled bladder made Kang pause— which saved his life.

Rather than retreat, Peter Li advanced with the shotgun, blasting well-aimed shots down the stairwell now that his wife and stepchildren were out of the way. Lily crumpled forward, clutching her stomach. The next shot clipped away her ponytail, hitting her squarely in the back of the neck, nearly decapitating her at this close range. An anchor shot. Li was picking them off, one by one. He kept shooting, reloading from cover, then blasting away each time he topped off his weapon.

The man knew how to fight.

Kang and Rose fled the house, bursting out the back door at a dead run. Both were heaving from frustration and adrenaline by the time they crashed into the dark wood line above the lake. The police were surely on their way.

Crouching behind a clump of scrub oak, Kang turned to give this place of utter failure one last look. To his astonishment, bright flashes lit the second-floor windows. Li was still shooting. He didn't know the intruders were gone, or how many were in his house. Amazingly, the shots inside the brick house were inaudible from just a few dozen yards away. It was as if Li were watching a John Wick movie inside with the sound off. The neighbors would not have heard anything, certainly nothing that would make them call 911.

"Lily . . ." Rose whispered. "That bastard killed Lily . . ."

"And he will pay for it," Kang said. "He will pay dearly."

"We must report in," Rose said.

"We will," Kang said. "When the mission is complete. Go down to the boat and get the RPG. The pregnant woman is injured. The police will transport her to the hospital. When Li comes out to ride with her . . ."

"But the police will search the grounds—"

The garage door flew off its tracks and a gray Mercedes SUV burst out, shooting down the driveway carrying the door on the bumper for several dozen yards before it fell away. Taillights flashed and tires squealed as the vehicle fishtailed through the darkness, rounding the bend toward Leonard Wood Avenue.

"This is shit!" Rose spat.

"No," Kang said. "This is good. This is very good. I do not think they called the police."

"Lily is dead!" Rose said, seething. "Wu Chao is dead! The man we came to kill still lives. His fat cow wife still lives. This can only be called a disaster."

"But *we* are not dead." Kang tipped his head toward the road where the SUV had disappeared. His lip trembled as the reality of what had just occurred crashed down on his shoulders. "It does not matter where Li runs. Do not forget that we still have the means to track him. Neither he nor his precious family will live to see nightfall."

40

D ing's tracker was still active at Suparman Games headquarters when John Clark parked a block away, in the back lot of a car dealership along Sam Ratulangi Road. The rented Toyota van blended in better on the lot than it would have on the side of the relatively sleepy divided four-lane. Making his approach from any closer meant that he might be up on exterior cameras. Any farther away and he risked exposure to passersby or people simply trying to cool off on their porches. As far as he'd been able to see, there was no distinct line between residential and business districts. A dirt-floor hovel might occupy the lot next to a high-end grocery, or the owners of a mansion might look out the window to the roof of a convenience store.

Suparman was wise indeed if he'd been thinking in terms of a neighborhood watch when he planned where to put his headquarters. The street had plenty of private residences to sound the alarm if anything or anyone looked out of the ordinary.

Clark kept out of sight on the west side of the road, opposite Suparman's, cutting through a wooded lot that ran behind a row of ramshackle shops that made up a sort of Third World–looking strip mall. It was dark, and he was able to use the shadows of a large guava tree directly across from the gaming company offices as cover.

A waist-high concrete block wall, whitewashed to match the Suparman building, ran the length of the property in front, ending in a sliding metal gate at the north end. Behind the gate, piles of gravel and concrete block marked an area of new construction to an open carport below what would be more offices. The face of the primarily glass building with bright white eaves and roof stood out in stark contrast to the surrounding greenery. This wall of windows made it easy for Clark to see the guards in the lobby, but would also leave him visible on approach.

The plans Gavin found online had not been labeled, but it was a safe bet that Suparman's office would be on the second floor in the southeast corner. Indonesia was a veritable sauna, making showering multiple times a day a national pastime. There were three washrooms in the building, but the architect's drawing of the one that adjoined the office in the southeast corner was plumbed for an American-style toilet, bidet, and a palatial shower. The reinforced walls indicated that the vault was in that office as well.

Clark had still not been able to figure out how Suparman's men had gotten to Ding. He must have done something to make them suspicious at the storefront. If it had been local police, or drug dealers, or even spur-of-the-moment kidnappers looking to make a quick buck ransoming a rich American, Clark could have gotten his head wrapped around it. But Suparman? He couldn't have known what they were up to. Ackerman was dead.

Noonan was presumed dead—though this was not certain. There could be a link here . . . Clark shook off that idea. Noonan wouldn't know Ding Chavez from Adam. Chinese intelligence was supposedly involved, but he doubted they knew the gaming company had a copy of Calliope—not yet, anyway.

That left Ding's visit to the storefront . . . It made no sense at all, and yet here they were.

Clark's orders were to grab the tech at all costs. He hated that term. "At all costs" sounded great when you were a young punk operative—a license to kill, real 007 shit. The rules of engagement were relaxed to the point of being nearly nonexistent. But in reality, "at all costs" meant "at the cost of everything," even your team members. Make it happen or die in the attempt. There had been a time when Clark was gung ho enough to do just that, but he wasn't going there now. They'd all die together or they'd all come home.

Jack Junior came over the radio—Midas had rekeyed the encryption when they'd linked up at the Blessing Jesus statue, so Ding's radio was now unable to listen in.

"I've got a light in the back corner office," Ryan said. *"North end, bottom floor."*

"Copy," Clark said.

Dom was with Jack, but Adara and Midas responded as well.

Clark took a PVS-14 night-vision monocular to peer at the grounds across the street. No patrols, but he located the exterior cameras over the door and at each corner of the building. The guard in the lobby, maybe thirty years old from the looks of him, was still alone, playing a game on his phone. He talked to someone on his radio every now and again.

Clark looked right and left, up and down the dark street. No lights, no signs of bicycles or pedestrians. He trotted across the street, moving diagonally to reach a small princess palm tree. It was skinny and only about twice his height but provided a vertical object for him to stand beside. As long as he was still, a casual glance out the window might not draw attention. Maybe. In any case, he didn't intend to be there long.

"*Three males visible in the northeast office,*" Jack said. "*I can't see Ding, but I don't have a very good view. They're talking to someone in the back corner.*"

"Weapons?" Clark asked.

"*At least one has a pistol shoved down his waistband. Another has a length of what looks like steel cable.*"

"My guy's talking on the radio," Clark said. "Are they?"

"*Affirm,*" Ryan said. "*The guy with the gun is carrying on a conversation with someone.*" Ryan paused, then came back more agitated. "*Looks like he's getting ready to use that cable on somebody out of our view. We need to go in soon.*"

"Hold there!" Clark said. "We'll all go in at once. Adara, Midas?"

"*We're at the southwest corner,*" Adara said. "*Ready to take out the camera on your mark.*"

"Copy," Clark said. "Stand by."

Everyone carried a Heckler & Koch MP5 now, along with their sidearms and two extra mags per weapon. Not ideal for an armed assault, but it was what they had. Clark doubted the guards inside had half that, but he made it a point never to underestimate a situation. Each firearm was outfitted with a Gemtech suppressor. As a rule, Clark didn't care for the subsonic ammo needed to remove the easily identifiable snap from each shot, but they would be operating in close quarters, so the reduced ballistics wouldn't be too much of a factor. Adara carried a Ruger Mark IV .22 with an integral suppressor that was exponentially quieter than the nines, even with their subsonic rounds. She was deadly accurate with the setup out to fifty yards, farther if the need arose. Clark had used slingshots that were louder. Her job was to take out the cameras in front of the building, then follow Clark in once he breached the front door. Dom had an identical weapon for any cameras—or sentries in back. Once inside, both would revert to the SMGs. The suppressed .22 was so quiet that people shot with it sometimes didn't realize they were dead, and kept up return fire longer than they would have had they been hit with something a little louder. In addition to the digital images of Suparman's retina, Midas carried the Halligan and other breaching equipment. Ryan and Clark completed their loadouts with three percussion grenades each.

They were going to get Ding back.

"In position," Clark said, pulling a black balaclava over his head. Apart from concealing his identity to cameras, any kind of mask provided a little extra psychological gut punch to the opposing force. "Our primary goal is to get the tech. I'll provide you overwatch. Everyone knows their area of responsibility. ROE remain the same: Kill everyone who isn't Ding."

——

Ding Chavez turned his head, spitting a mouthful of blood on the floor. His hands and ankles were tied to the back of a heavy wooden chair. He blinked, trying to clear his vision.

"You guys are in a shitload of trouble."

The stubby man who'd been hitting him nonstop for the past three minutes must have had some boxing experience. Chavez felt like he was getting kicked by a very angry mule. He'd knocked the chair over three times, to the delight of the other three men in the room. The lateral movement had allowed Chavez to give with the force of the blows and taken out a good deal of the sting, but he pretended it hurt even worse. Thankfully, the boxer must not have been doing his cardio and got winded from the effort, giving Chavez a short break.

His neck was still on fire from the initial stomp in the van and his right eye was swollen shut. Mercifully, his teeth—usually the first thing to go in this kind of beating—were still intact for now.

The apparent leader, a guy in a sweat-soaked gray mechanic's shirt, stood by, smacking a length of twisted steel cable against an open palm. Chavez suppressed a shudder. He'd seen bodies that had been beaten with rods and cable. Human anatomy didn't stand up to that sort of treatment for long. Bones shattered, soft tissue burst. It wasn't a pretty picture.

The man with the cable yanked Chavez's head up by his forelock. "You are American?"

Chavez gave a feeble nod. "Yep." It was the first question they'd asked. No point in lying about it.

"What do you want with Mr. Suparman?"

"I . . . Who?"

The boxer hit him again, bringing a round of chuckles from the two bystanders against the wall.

Chavez needed to come up with a story before this guy got serious and broke his jaw.

"I am trying to warn you," he said. "You really need to stop. My people . . . they are more dangerous than you know."

"And what people are they?" Cable Guy asked.

"Whatever it is you think you know," Chavez said, "you're wrong."

"Is that so?" the man with the cable said. "You think to target the most technologically advanced company in Indonesia for attack and then expect to slip by unnoticed? Your American audacity is laughable." He prodded Chavez in the chin with the jagged end of the cable, tilting his head up again. "Mr. Suparman receives threats from all over the world. Extortion, kidnapping, industrial theft. We have facial-recognition software in many areas around the store, always looking for people who loiter for too long." He smiled. "So, you see, I already know you were watching the store from the hotel across the street. Would you like to tell me why or shall we advance to the next level?" He swung the cable over his head, making it whir menacingly through the air. "I don't know if you are aware, but this length of steel is capable of removing a person's head. I have seen it personally."

"I'll bet," Chavez said. "You run Suparman's security?"

"I do," the man said. "My name is Sebastian. Though I must admit, my name will be of no consequence to you unless you tell me why you are here."

Chavez groaned, head lolling, hoping he looked completely subdued. "My people will call the police if I am not back within the hour."

"Please," Sebastian scoffed. "The police are quite—how shall I put this?—friendly to Mr. Suparman. I would not depend on them." He prodded Chavez's chin again with the cable, harder this time, drawing blood with the raw wires. "It will go much better for you if you tell me who you are working for."

Chavez just sat there, panting, waiting, hoping the transmitter in his belt was still working.

"Nothing?" Sebastian sighed. "Very well. Then there is no point in being gentle any longer." He gave the boxer a nod. The two along the wall began to giggle again.

Bracing himself for another blow, Chavez heard a faint pop outside the window, then the rattle of breaking glass in the hallway.

An instant later, a fist-size metal canister clattered into the office through the open door. Chavez opened his mouth and closed his eyes, recognizing it immediately for what it was.

Sebastian and his men . . . did not.

41

With a black balaclava over his face, Caruso used the Ruger Mark IV to take out the two cameras under the rear of the building the moment Clark gave the go order. With the Gemtech suppressor, the .22 made little more noise than a Red Ryder BB gun. Ryan saw the glass door in the back move slightly, indicating a pressure change inside caused when Clark, Adara, and Midas came through the front. He popped the lock on the back door with a Halligan tool, shattering the glass in the process, and button-hooked inside behind Caruso. No audible alarms, but that wasn't surprising, since there were so many guards on-site.

With the H&K on a single-point sling around his neck, Ryan pulled the pin on a CTS stun grenade known as a 9-Bang, which, as its name implied, gave off nine bright, arrhythmic bangs spaced roughly eight-tenths of a second apart, temporarily blinding and disorienting those around it if they weren't prepared. Earpieces worn by Campus operators amplified ambient noise but momentarily cut out for any sudden sound over ninety decibels.

The flash-bang began to detonate roughly a second and a half after it left Ryan's hand and the spoon flew away. Ryan and Caruso, prepared for the concussion and flash, advanced rapidly. Ryan put two rounds center-mass in the man who was holding the length of cable, sidestepping as he fired to bring Chavez into view. Disoriented and holding his ears from the effects of the flash-bang, a thickly muscled man who'd been standing over Chavez turned to make a run for the door. Chavez threw his body sideways, tipping the chair laterally into the man's knee. The man screamed, clawing for the pistol in his belt as he tried to push up on all fours. Ryan anchored him to the ground with a double tap to the back of his head.

Caruso took care of the two by the wall with two quick shots each. They weren't actively shooting, but pistols were visible at their waists, and anyone standing around the same room while Ding was being beaten was bought and paid for as far as the team was concerned.

"Clear!" Caruso said, as both men slumped at virtually the same moment.

Ryan scanned his area of the room. "Clear!"

Caruso took a knee and turned to cover the door with his rifle.

Ryan let the H&K rest on his sling, parking it across his body on the left so he could reach either it or his handgun if the need arose. He'd knelt by Chavez, who lay on his side, still strapped to the chair, moving his jaw back and forth.

Chavez blinked up with the only eye not damaged too much to open. "I don't think I've ever been so happy to see your ugly mug."

Ryan flicked open his Benchmade and cut him free. "Anything broken?"

Chavez winced as he rolled to a sitting position, then climbed to his feet. He rubbed his wrists. "I'm not bending anywhere I shouldn't be."

Gunfire clattered in the lobby—guards shooting back. The pistols were suppressed, but there was no doubt they'd heard the 9-Bang.

"How many fingers am I holding up?" Ryan asked.

"Four," Chavez said. "Seriously, I'm good. Give me a gun. I'll help."

Clark's voice crackled in Ryan's ear. The man was astoundingly calm considering the circumstances—like a sloth, if a sloth could kick your ass and shoot a forty-five.

"Three down in the lobby," he said.

Adara came back next. *"Upstairs is clear."*

"Northeast office is clear," Ryan said. "Checking the other rooms now. Missing man accounted for."

"Copy," Clark said. *"Let's get that tech and get out of here."*

"Shit!" Chavez said. "They have man-down radios!"

"We have a problem," Ryan said, relaying Chavez's message since he didn't yet have commo with the rest of the team.

Sometimes called a "lone worker," the "man down" feature on radios worn by utility, security, and law enforcement personnel notified central dispatch in the event the device canted more than a given number of degrees, *i.e.*, if the wearer fell on his or her side.

"Copy," Clark said. *"We'll assume someone is responding. Get the tech and let's get out of here."*

"I think we're just . . . about . . . there," Midas said.

———

Suparman's office was a shrine to himself. A life-size painting of him, helmet in hand, wearing a red-and-white NASCAR racing suit took up much of the wall directly across the thirty-foot room from his glass desk. A silk scarf around his neck blew in the wind, making him look more like Evel Knievel than a race car driver. Another painting, about half that size but still large enough to be unsettling, depicted Suparman dressed like Theodore Roosevelt on a rearing horse—complete with slouch hat and cavalry saber. A marble bust of the man sat on a pedestal by the window, where it would get plenty of natural light. With bare shoulders, it read SU-PARMAN: CINCINNATUS OF GAMES. The sleepy marble eyes, absent the thick glasses, gazed toward the desk, leaving Adara to wonder if Suparman carried on conversations with the ugly thing. She was genuinely surprised that despite his name, Suparman had no paintings of himself in a cape or a single big red *S* anywhere in the office other than the company logo.

Suparman didn't get where he was by narcissism alone. Two large bookcases held well-read volumes on computer theory, linear algebra, calculus, and neural networks. An arcade-style Space Invaders game stood like a shrine near the Cincinnatus bust. Adara found three obvious cameras, one over the vault, one over the door, facing into the office, and another in the same location, facing out. She gave each lens a blast of spray paint before posting with her rifle by the office door while Midas worked on the vault.

"How's it coming there, sport?" she asked over her shoulder.

"Thought I had it with the digital photo," Midas said. "I'm going to try one other thing with this scanner."

Adara glanced back to see Midas leaning forward, cheek to the locking mechanism, the screen of his smartphone pressed between his face and the scanner. There was a momentary red glow as the scanner did its work, and then a satisfying metallic click as the vault lock slid out of battery.

"We're in," Midas said over the radio, slipping the phone back into his pocket, ready to open the heavy steel door. "Moment of truth . . ."

Jack Ryan, Jr., was posted outside in front of the glass double doors. He crouched behind a low hedge, ready to give the rest of the team a heads-up if he saw anyone approaching. The feeble headlight of a lone scooter bounced down Sam Ratulangi Road from the north, then turned into the driveway. The rider, a kid in his late teens or early twenties, got off the bike long enough to slide open the metal gate. He wore a blue uniform like the guards in the lobby did, but his shirt was untucked. It was hard to tell, but it didn't look like he was wearing his Sam Browne belt. Probably off duty. It sure didn't look like he was responding to a break-in.

Ryan alerted the rest of the team and let the kid approach. If he was a scout sent ahead by some tactical team he should have won an Oscar. He carried two plas-

tic bags that looked to be loaded with food. Oblivious to
the world around him, he looked at his feet as he walked,
shoulders bouncing as if he were dancing. Eighties metal
poured from a set of white earbuds, loud enough for
Ryan to recognize it as "Girls, Girls, Girls," by Mötley
Crüe. With his eyes on his shoes, the kid had yet to notice that the door was broken.

Ryan waited for him to get within ten feet, then
stepped out, aimed with the MP5.

The kid's mouth fell open, and he said something in
Indonesian—likely a curse, judging from the startled
look on his thin face. He raised his arms, the bags still in
his hands. "Who are you?"

Ryan motioned him inside with the gun muzzle.

Clark and the others were waiting.

The kid, who said his name was Ismaya, gazed at the
carnage, mouth agape.

"What . . . Who are you people?" More of the Oscar-
worthy performance. Hands still up, Ismaya grimaced
when he saw Chavez. "What happened to you?"

"How long have you been gone?" Clark asked, his
voice stern, businesslike.

The kid's eyes softened, less confrontational. He
seemed to realize his life depended on the answer.

"My boss . . ." He pointed to the dead man at the
base of the stairs. "He told me I did not have to come in
tonight. I thought to bring them some *panada* for a
snack . . ."

Caruso looked up from searching the bags. "Homemade hot pockets, all right," he said.

"Got it!" Midas said over the radio. *"We're coming down."*

"Very well," Clark said. "Let's get going before someone shows up with more meat pies." He looked at Ismaya and gave a slow shake of his head, groaning like he was very, very tired. "Kid," he said, "I sure wish you would have stayed home."

Four minutes later, Chavez, Adara, and Caruso were heading north on Sam Ratulangi with the four-by-four plastic box containing the tech in hand. Oddly, the tera-byte thumb drive was laser-etched CALLIOPE. Clark, Ryan, and Midas followed in the van behind them. Clark made the call and got the F-15s in the air.

"Glad you brought the ketamine," Midas said over the radio.

"We could have just tied him up," Adara said.

"We could have," Clark said. "But I never trust knots alone."

"Truth," Midas said. "Batman always figures a way out of that shit when they leave him alone. Anyhow, I don't think the kid knew a damn thing about Ding."

"Probably not," Clark said. "He'll be fine in an hour or so. By then we'll be gone. So, let me get this straight, Ding. Suparman's guys caught you on video during your game store recon, and then the facial-recognition software running on the cameras at the hotel across the street popped you as a possible threat?"

"Appears so," Chavez said. *"The way his thug Sebastian*

sounded, they thought I was hanging around to assassinate Suparman. He never mentioned the tech at all." Chavez paused. *"Anybody following us?"*

"Looks good so far." Clark checked his watch. "Eagles will touch down in . . . eighty-seven minutes."

42

Sophie Li spoke between ragged breaths, trying in vain to control her sobs. "We have got to call the police."

She was in the backseat, staring up at the headliner while her daughter used paper towels from the SUV's glove box to stanch the flow of blood from the wound on her arm. The gash hurt like hell, but there didn't appear to be any major arteries clipped. They left so quickly that none of them had time to change clothes. James and Martha had grabbed jackets. Peter had on a pair of gray sweats and a white T-shirt, and Sophie still wore the Navy football jersey she used as a nightgown. The emergency go-bag Peter insisted they keep in the closet had cash, copies of their passports, a pistol, and a few snacks, but no extra clothes.

Sophie kicked the front seat. "Peter! Are you even listening to me?"

Li took a corner a little too fast, chirping the tires on the pavement. He glanced in the rearview mirror, his face glowing eerily from the dash lights. "Let's wait on that a minute."

Sophie bit her bottom lip to keep from screaming. "Wait? What are you talking about? Who are those people? Why were they in our house?"

"I don't know who they were," Peter said. "But it has to have something to do with one of my projects."

"I think . . . I . . . They were speaking Mandarin," James said, rocking back and forth, hyperventilating. "I caught . . . a couple . . . of words."

Peter took one hand off the wheel long enough to squeeze the boy's shoulder. "Slow down your breathing, son," he said. "In fact, everyone slow it down. Count to three while you breathe in. Count to five while you exhale." He looked in the mirror again. "You, too, sweetheart. It'll lower your heart rate."

"One of your projects?" Sophie asked, needing answers.

"There's been a little trouble at work," Peter said. "I caught one of my engineers going into the vault with an ID stolen from another employee."

"And he wants you dead?"

"She," Peter said. "I don't think she's that high up in the food chain. But it could be who she's working for."

"We still have to call the police," Sophie said.

"And we will," Peter said. "But they'll go after the people who tried to kill us."

"Good," Sophie said.

"Right," Peter said. "But this feels a little too big for our local department."

"Then call the FBI," Sophie said. "I don't give a rat's ass who you call, but I want some badges and guns here right damned now!"

"Listen," Peter said, gripping the wheel until his knuckles went white. "Those guys were Chinese. There's reason to believe my employee is an agent of the Chinese government. That means the people in our house were also agents of the Chinese government. They could have people everywhere. My number-one priority here is to keep you safe, not solve any crime."

Peter made another turn, slowing now that he was in town. Sophie wished he would speed so they would get pulled over and she could get a cop to help her.

"Where are we going?" she asked, figuring it out when she saw the sign for the mechanic's shop.

"We're going to switch cars," Peter said.

"Switch cars?" Sophie shook her head. Her husband had gone completely insane. "Just. Call. The. Police. Why do we need to switch cars?"

Peter threw the Mercedes in park in the shadows behind the garage, away from the streetlight. Against her better judgment, Sophie followed him to the back door, completely passing his Audi, which was parked in the garage lot. Peter picked up a rock and made ready to break the window.

Sophie fought the urge to scream. "What are you doing?"

"Their alarm is broken," he said. "I heard them talking when I dropped the car off for service yesterday."

Sophie clutched the blood-soaked paper towels around her arm. "Peter, listen to me! We don't need to break in. Your car is out here. There's an extra set of keys on my ring."

"No good," Peter said. "Those people deactivated our alarm system to get into the house. If they're that sophisticated, it wouldn't be much of a challenge for them to track our car."

"So?" Sophie stared at him, incredulous. "If they can track my car, then they can track your car, too."

Peter used the rock to smash the window, then reached inside to unlock the door. "That's why we're not taking my car." He grabbed the keys to a late-model Chevy Impala. The paperwork said it was in for a fifty-thousand-mile tune-up, still drivable. He led the way back to the lot. "Come on," he said, scanning the dark and deserted streets. "They could be right behind us."

Sophie got in the front seat this time. Peter eased out of the parking lot, heading south toward Chicago.

"And now can we call the police?"

"We will," Peter said. "But not right away. The police are compelled to follow the law, and that takes time—time that others can use to finish the job they started in our house tonight."

Sophie choked back a sob, clutching her belly. "Who are you?"

"I'm trying to protect you," Peter said.

"You . . . shot those people," Sophie said.

"They were—"

"I know," she said, letting the tears take over. "I know it. I trust you. I'm just so scared . . ."

"Me, too," Peter said, which, for some reason, comforted Sophie more than if he'd tried to pretend he wasn't terrified by the attack.

Someone had invaded their castle, the place where they should have been safe. And that man, the one who had grabbed her, he was so . . . cold. Like he didn't care if she lived or died. No, that wasn't true. He wanted to watch her die. She'd seen it in his eyes. The whole thing left her feeling violated and raw—incredibly vulnerable.

Peter put a hand on her knee and gave it a squeeze.

"You have to trust that I have a plan. I don't want to scare you any more than—"

"That's not possible," Sophie said. "That guy threatened to cut out the baby."

"This wasn't a home invasion. They weren't dopeheads there to rob us to get money for a fix. We're dealing with an assassination team sent by a nation-state. Those kind of people don't stop until they are stopped."

"But you can stop them," Sophie said. "I mean, you have a plan."

"I do," Peter said. "It's not necessarily legal, but it's moral—and it will save our lives."

James leaned forward between the seats, cell phone in hand. The poor kid was still in shock, his mind searching frantically for the tiniest fragment of normalcy to cling to. "I forgot. Leah's mom is supposed to pick me up for school in the morning. We were going to work on a project together. I need to call her and tell her I can't make it."

Peter shook his head, gripping the wheel. "No calls," he said.

"She'll figure it out, hon," Sophie said. "Let's work out what's going on before we talk to anyone."

"O . . . okay," the boy said, his voice hollow, numb now that the adrenaline was ebbing. He slid the phone back into his pocket.

43

The phone on the desk in Ryan's residential study chirped. He'd been expecting the call and snatched up the handset before the second ring. It was Foley and she was outside in the East Sitting Hall with van Damm.

"They have it, Mr. President," Mary Pat said after Ryan invited them in. "The F-15s will pick up the thumb drive in . . ." She looked at her watch. "Eighty-three minutes. They'll hotfoot it across the Pacific as fast as they can—which is a little faster than reported by Wikipedia—and get it to our labs in Honolulu in a little over three hours, not counting a couple of midair refueling stops."

"Good to hear," Ryan said. He knew Jack Junior was part of the team that had gone in, but made it a point not to ask about him personally. "Any mishaps?"

"Chavez got beat up a little," Foley said. "But they say he's good to go."

"Are you both packed?" Ryan asked. They were coming with him to Indonesia, and would depart with him on Marine One from the White House.

"Yes, Mr. President," they said in unison.

"Something else?" Ryan asked. He could see it in van Damm's face.

"Mr. President," the chief of staff said. "It's about

Father Pat. The Indonesian government is now charging him with smuggling heroin. No word on the trial, but until that time, they're moving him to Nusa Kambangan."

Ryan felt as though he'd been kicked in the teeth. "Execution Island?"

Foley nodded. "I'm afraid so."

Nusa Kambangan was off the southern coast of Central Java. Part prison island, part ecotourist attraction, it was often called the Alcatraz of Indonesia—or, more fittingly, Execution Island. Capital punishment for drug offenses was not a foregone conclusion in the Indonesian justice system, but it was far from uncommon. Two of the so-called Bali Nine, arrested for smuggling heroin, had been executed by firing squad just a few years prior, along with six convicted narcotics smugglers from other cases in a lighted field behind Besi prison.

"Have they already moved him?" Ryan asked.

"I have assets checking now," Foley said. "As does Adler. I'll let you know as soon as I do."

Ryan picked up the phone to call the communications office. He had a flight to catch, but it wasn't exactly leaving without him. President Gumelar was expecting him, but he wanted another word with this new information. As Ryan expected, the president of Indonesia was "indisposed" at the moment. It was just as well; Ryan needed a few minutes to calm down so he didn't come across like he was ripping the ineffectual guy a new asshole. He'd call again once he was aboard Air Force One, and he'd keep calling until Gumelar picked up the phone or Ryan was knocking on the front door of Merdeka Palace.

Ryan looked at his watch, if not calming, at least getting a handle on his anger. His late father had called it "putting a point on things." Unfocused fury could be terrifying—and had a place once in a great while—but coherent wrath was exponentially more powerful. Aimed at the right target, it was a magnificent and terrible thing.

"Cathy will be on her way soon," Ryan said. "I'm going to say good-bye to her in a few minutes. I'll be right down." He stared out the window into the distance, beginning to nod unconsciously.

Foley gave him a wary eye. "Jack . . . What are you thinking?"

Van Damm threw up his hands. "Well, hell," he said. "That look always scares the shit out of me, Mr. President. You're planning something."

Ryan put the flat of his hand on the desk and spoke deliberately, like this was something to which he'd given a great deal of thought. "As much as I hate to make this a personal matter," he said, "it's time to pull out all the stops, to use whatever means we have available to get Father Pat out of prison. I think it's time I bring in a heavy hitter to give me some help once we touch down."

"I see what you're doing here, Mr. President," van Damm said. "I'm going on record as being against it. This could have some serious blowback. If it gets out, this single event could be what your administration is remembered for."

"Oh, I'm well aware, Arnie," Ryan said.

"You have to say bye to Cathy," Foley said. "I can make the call."

"I'll do it," Ryan said. "I'm the one who'll have to live with the aftermath."

44

Ten minutes from the airport, John Clark checked his phone for the first time in an hour and a half. He had three messages. One was from his wife—who wouldn't call again until he called back, unless the house was burning down, and maybe not even then. The last two were from the same number. He recognized it, and was mildly surprised. He called back, listened intently, then said, "Of course, sir. I'll meet you wherever and whenever you say."

Clark pulled up several airline websites on his phone the moment he ended the call. There was a flight to Jakarta in a little over an hour.

"Drop me off at Departures," he said.

Ryan glanced sideways. "Okaaay?"

"You guys okay up there, Ding?" Clark asked over the radio.

"Good to go," Ding said.

"Outstanding," Clark said. "I'm going to need to leave you to it. Just got an interesting telephone call, and I need to bug out."

"You're not riding back on the Gulfstream?" Ding asked. *"Sucks to be you."*

It did Clark's heart good that Chavez didn't ask for

more details. Clark would give what he could, when he could, and Chavez knew it.

"Ryan's going to make a quick detour and drop me off so I can catch this flight. You guys go on to the rendezvous point and turn our little friend over to the F-15s. I'll give you a call when I get inside."

Clark ended the call and began to divest himself of all his weapons so he could make it through security. He'd be able to get more where he was going. Midas passed him a box of wet wipes from a backpack at his feet. They'd all fired their weapons enough to be covered in microscopic—and not-so-microscopic—gunfire residue. A swab of Clark's hands in the airport could stop him in his tracks while they sorted things out.

"Hit the dome light," he said when he was finished with the spit bath, then leaned back in his seat with his arms and hands open. "Any blood on me?"

Midas and Ryan both gave him a once-over, shaking their heads.

Ryan caught his eye, quizzing him without words.

"Better for you if I keep this close to the vest," Clark said. "It's a need-to-know thing . . ."

Ryan scoffed. "And I don't need to know."

"That's about the size of it," Clark said. "I'm just looking out for you."

45

Chavez watched John Clark's plane take off an hour and five minutes before the F-15 Eagles were set to arrive. He was a big boy and had worked dozens of operations without Clark on scene. Maybe it was his massive headache from the repeated blows to his face. Maybe it was his chipped tooth. But for some reason, this time left him feeling like he was on the ropes. He had no idea what Clark was up to, but he could tell by the amused look on the man's face that it would be dangerous.

Chavez and Adara took the Faraday bag containing Calliope inside the fixed-base operator, at the south/civil aviation portion of the airport. Jack Junior remained outside in one van while Midas and Caruso waited in the other, watching for threats. Chavez wasn't worried about trackers. The Faraday bag would keep any signal from getting in or out of the drive or the plastic box it was stored in. But there was only one airport in Manado, and one FBO at that airport. It wasn't a leap to think that Suparman might guess where they would go to get the tech out of the country. And if he figured it out, he'd come after it with a vengeance. The gaming magnate had already proven he would have no problem resorting to violence. In Chavez's experience, people were seldom more ruthless than when they were trying to steal shit back that they had stolen from someone else.

On the other side of the door on the airport side of the building was the flight line, the secure area down the ramp from where the commercial airliners parked. The area around the airlines was brightly lit and a hive of activity. There were few lights immediately outside the FBO. The maintenance hangar was closed and dark, all the mechanics having gone home for the day. Several business jets and a couple of prop aircraft were parked in the darkness. Most sat locked and idle, but just beyond the Hendley G550, four men loaded bundles of what looked suspiciously like drugs into the back of a low-wing twin turbo-prop. Chavez recognized it as a Piper Cheyenne IIIA by the high T-tail and long nose. The DEA had a couple rigged out for surveillance. On the flip side, they were fast and fuel-efficient enough to make a pretty good drug-smuggling plane. The men did their loading in the dark, so Chavez felt confident that was what was going on here.

He would have been more than happy to blow their operation to hell, if he'd had the time. They'd eventually be caught—and probably executed. Drug smuggling was a stacked game in Indonesia. Even if you paid off the police, which you had to do, odds were you would eventually get caught. And they killed you for that over here. He'd give the Cheyenne a wide berth to avoid guilt by association.

If all went well, in a little over sixty minutes the F-15 pilots would come inside and take Calliope off their hands. He doubted if they'd even take the time to pee.

The likelihood of a threat coming from that direction was low, but Chavez kept an eye peeled anyway.

Chavez had called Helen and Country, the Gulfstream pilots, to check on their status, but they were having issues with the rental car not starting and were at least another hour out. It figured. A beatdown, gun battle, and car trouble: The night could hardly get any better. It was a good thing Clark had flown commercial, even absent his desire to insulate the rest of the team from what he planned to do.

Everyone had brought all their gear with them, anticipating a quick egress from the country. There was no reason to return to the hotel. Nothing to do now but wait.

Chavez plopped himself in one of the faux-leather seats with a paper sack of popcorn. You got accustomed to waiting for agonizingly long spans of time in this business—waiting in the limo for your protectee to finish his or her meeting, waiting in the shadows for an asset to show up, or simply waiting at an airport for someone to pick you up. Smokin' and jokin', the Feds called it. Keeping your wits about you while you were exhausted, beaten down, and bored out of your skull was an art. Popcorn helped. A lot. Nearly every FBO he'd ever seen, anywhere in the world, seemed to have a machine. The smells of popcorn and jet fuel were so intertwined in his mind that if Patsy made Orville Redenbacher to munch while they watched something on Netflix, Chavez invariably had dreams about airplanes—usually jumping out of a perfectly good one.

With no metal detectors or X-rays inside the FBO,

Ding and Adara had retained their handguns. Neither of them wanted to disarm until Calliope was on board one of the fighters and those fighters were back in the air, heading for a computer lab at Joint Base Pearl Harbor-Hickam. And then there were the drug smugglers loading the Piper Cheyenne to consider. Yep. Much better to stay gunned up.

Chavez rubbed a fleck of blood he'd missed on the side of his hand. He'd used wet wipes and hand sanitizer to clean up as best he could, and then finished the job in the restroom. Like most men's rooms overseas, there were no paper towels, making Chavez glad he'd taken up his father-in-law's practice of carrying a handkerchief. Head wounds were terrible bleeders, though, and he had a couple that made him look like a zombie if he didn't keep an eye on them. He felt like a zombie, that was for sure. The pain in his head grew with each minute that ticked by.

"ETA one hour on the nose," Adara said, startling Chavez a little when she sat down next to him with her own bag of popcorn. "We can stand on our heads for this long." She turned half in her seat, assessing his wounds—and he had many—then used the long white paper bag to gesture at his left eye. "You need a few stitches right below your orbital," she said. "Can you see okay? A blow like that can rattle your vision."

"I'm good," Chavez lied.

He still hadn't gotten used to seeing Adara with black hair. A perfectionist, she'd taken the time to dye her eyebrows, too. One bottle of Indonesian hair dye and she'd gone from looking like a badass Tinker Bell, to . . . well, still badass, but not quite right, like the evil doppelgänger of her actual self. It was more than a little unsettling. Chavez kept that to himself, though, particularly since he'd been the one to give her the dye.

"Thanks, Doc," he said. "I'll hit a clinic as soon as we get home."

As a former Navy corpsman, Adara was often referred to by the team as "Doc." She slipped into the role with ease.

"I have lidocaine on the G5," she said. "I can stitch it up for you, as long as we don't have too much turbulence. The sooner the better with facial wounds." She grinned. "And my copay is cheaper than a doc in the box."

Chavez gave a slow nod, thinking it over. She'd stitched everyone on the team at one time or another, even back when she'd been director of transportation, before Clark and Gerry had tapped her to be an operator.

"Okay," he said. "It is a hell of a long fl—"

The radio bonked, coming in garbled as two people outside tried to speak at the same time.

Chavez and Adara sat up straighter in their seats.

Midas came over the radio next, sounding tense, like he was talking through clenched teeth.

"We have company!" he said. *"Two Hilux pickups full of trouble. Estimate eight to ten men. All armed."*

Chavez turned toward the door in time to see the man behind the counter at the FBO come up with a pistol.

"Gun left," he snapped, for Adara's benefit. He gave the man behind the counter a quarter-second benefit of the doubt. There was a slim chance he was protecting himself from the newcomers outside.

Nope.

The night manager swung the gun in a wide arc, crossing Adara first. Both she and Chavez fired at the same time, both rounds catching him center-mass.

"One down inside," Chavez said over the radio. "We're still good, but the cops can't be far away."

"Bad news," Jack said. *"I'm thinking these are the cops."*

Adrenalized, Chavez forgot about his pounding headache. Unfortunately, it hadn't forgotten about him, and he swayed on his feet as he moved toward the door that led to the ramp. "Do not let these guys ID you."

"Copy," Jack said. *"We're still sitting in the vans. So far they don't even know we're here."*

"They're gearing up to come in," Caruso added. *"Jack can go; I'll stay and help you out."*

"Negative," Chavez snapped, regaining his balance by sheer force of will. "Adara and I will slip out the back door to the flight line before they come in. We'll work our way around to the south if we can. Jack, you sit still. Midas, you guys wait until they are about to hit the door, and then haul ass. Peel out, make a lot of noise like you're bolting. Hopefully they follow you. Jack, if you can, slip away after they leave. We'll rendezvous at the alternate site in four hours."

The alternate site was a church downtown that he'd designated when they first arrived in Manado. It was a long way from the airport—and the F-15s—but if Chavez sat still, Calliope would be long gone before they got here—and he and Adara would likely be dead.

Pistol in hand, Chavez grabbed the door and gave Adara a nod to let her know he was ready. He could barely see out of his left eye, his head was on fire, and he was sure he had at least two bruised ribs. Yeah, things were just peachy.

Adara grabbed her pack and threw her body across the counter, reaching for the button to buzz open the exit to the ramp. Chavez held the door until she got there. A quick peek outside said they were clear, and they ran into the sticky blackness.

The sound of squealing tires carried around the building. Chavez caught a glimpse of the Toyota's taillights heading away from the FBO. He counted one, and then a second pickup truck sped past, giving chase.

Chavez and Adara stopped next to a parked fuel truck. The smell of the tarmac rose on the warm night air, reminding him of a racetrack. On any other evening, one where he wasn't running for his life with some stolen computer tech in his pocket, he would have enjoyed the smell.

"Looks like they're buying it," Adara said, watching the taillights.

"Hope so," Chavez said. "Now Midas and Dom just need to get away."

Jack came across the net. *"Heads up! They left three behind. One's watching the parking lot; the other two are coming your way."*

"Stay where you are," Chavez said, panting more than he should have been.

"You okay?" Adara asked.

"I'm good." He was able to muster a grin. "Just a little smashed up from my beating."

The men coming inside would be finding the dead

FBO manager about now. They'd slow down to check the building if they had any sense, but there wasn't much to check besides a back office and the restrooms. It was a matter of seconds, not minutes, before the men were right on top of them.

"Tell me you have a surprise Ding Chavez plan up your sleeve," Adara hissed. Crouched in the shadows with her pistol at low ready, she looked formidable. Chavez had little doubt they'd be able to handle the two men, but he hoped to get out of Indonesia without engaging any police officers, even if they were on Suparman's payroll. He thought about going to the Gulfstream for about half a second, but a thin-skinned aircraft was a terrible place to make a stand.

A Batik Air commercial airliner roared overhead, vibrating the ground as it took off to the south.

"Ryan's pinned down," Adara said. "Short of hijacking an airplane, I'm not sure we have many options besides duking it out with those guys when they come out. I guess we could always give up."

Chavez nodded, half standing. "That's it."

"Give up?" Adara scoffed, her face blue in the scant ambient light. "That was a joke. I don't think these guys plan on taking us to jail."

Chavez gestured toward the Piper Cheyenne with his pistol.

"I'm not talking about giving up."

46

The Piper's rear door hung open at the back of the aircraft, integral stairs extended. The only light inside came from the faint glow of cockpit instrumentation. The two pilots were already on board, while the rest of the loading crew had gone between the ramshackle metal buildings to see what all the noise was in front. Adara pointed out at least one long gun, which meant there were surely more.

Two seats faced aft, back to back with the pilots in the open cockpit, one on either side of a narrow aisle. The rest had been removed to make room for the cargo—which consisted of several dozen bales of something wrapped in black plastic bags and copious rolls of duct tape.

The Cheyenne IIIA normally carried only nine passengers with full seating, so Chavez was almost in the cockpit in one good bent-over stride from the time he breached the door.

The Indonesian pilots both turned as Chavez bounded up the steps, his pistol trained toward the cockpit. Adara followed close on his heels, lifting the door and folding stairs before the pilots realized what was going on. The one in the left seat, older than his copilot by at least a decade, raised his hands and grinned, giving an amused shake of his head.

"You won't get very far if you shoot us."

"I only need one of you to fly the plane," Chavez said, dead serious. "Your copilot looks capable enough."

He didn't have a problem popping a drug smuggler. It would, in fact, not be a new experience for him. Any hint of bravado bled from the pilot's face.

"I assume you are running from those people who are making all the noise out on the street?" he asked.

Chavez smacked the headrest with his free hand. This was a tricky time. In reality, the pilot held most of the cards. All he had to do was sit on his hands while the men he worked for stormed the plane. Chavez banked on the fact that the pilots were smart enough to realize they were highly likely to catch a few bullets themselves if their companions stormed the plane. Drug smugglers weren't known for their discerning shot placement. Chavez leaned farther into the cockpit between the two seats, partly to check for weapons, but crowding the men in the process to keep up the tension.

"Let's go! And no headsets. I want the radio on speaker so I can hear everything. And keep in mind that I know the transponder codes, so you can forget about sending a message that way."

The pilot turned and looked at him full in the face, as if he'd been about to do that very thing.

Squawking 7700 on the transponder alerted air traffic control to an emergency. A squawk of 7500 meant the aircraft had been hijacked.

The pilot did as he was directed. The little airplane

began to shudder as he fired up one Pratt & Whitney turbine engine at a time. He glanced over his shoulder as he let the props come up to speed.

"My name is Deddy," the pilot said, an obvious attempt to humanize himself to the man who had a gun to his head. Chavez couldn't blame him. He would have done the same thing if the situation were reversed.

He kept his voice firm and direct. "You're doing fine, Deddy. We'll get through this no problem as long as you do exactly what I tell you to."

"But they are after you?" He half turned in the seat. "Those men?"

"They are," Chavez said. "Eyes on the road, Deddy."

"Okay," the pilot said. "But to be honest, I think you may have killed us all. I am much more frightened of the man who owns what you are sitting on than I am of you."

Adara peered out the back window, and then stooped in the aisle to duck-walk back to Chavez between the plastic and duct-taped bales. She leaned forward to whisper in his ear. "Anytime now," she said. "The guys with guns are coming back."

Chavez gestured down the taxiway with the Smith & Wesson. "Get us in the air. No headsets. Keep the radio on speaker so I can hear."

The pilot had already filed a flight plan, and the Cheyenne received rapid clearance to taxi the length of the single runway. They took off to the south, heavy with drugs, wallowing into the humid air. Climbing into the wind, the pilot followed Departure's instructions and banked to the east. The lights of the runway and the island of Sulawesi fell away quickly, giving way to the blackness. Chavez felt the disconcerting clunk under his feet as the landing gear folded into place.

The copilot, a rumpled young man with longish, unevenly cut hair over the collar of his white uniform shirt, began to chuckle.

Chavez nudged the back of the right seat. "Something funny I don't know about?"

The pilot shot a glance at his copilot and rattled off something in Bahasa Indonesian.

"Speak English!" Chavez gave the pilot's headrest another smack.

"I am sorry." Deddy craned his neck around to look over his shoulder at Chavez, as if he wanted to spare the copilot what he was about to say. "Men like you and me, we have been doing dangerous things like this for a while. My copilot is new. He laughs when he gets nervous. That is all. He took this job to feed his family. He did not even know what we were flying tonight."

"Nice story," Chavez said. "But a little hard to believe."

The copilot was young, perhaps in his late twenties. Chin quivering like he might burst into tears at any moment, he maintained a white-knuckle grip on the yoke—though the autopilot was flying the airplane.

The pilot shrugged. "Believe it, don't believe it. Neither makes it any less true. I only hope to calm his nerves. I told him that you had no reason to harm us, as long as we fly you to where you want to go."

"That *is* true," Chavez said.

Halfway between the cockpit and the door, Adara leaned over the plastic bales. She pressed her face against the side window to get a better look at anyone behind them. They had no headsets and the drone of the Pratt & Whitney engines forced her to shout.

"They're not behind us."

"They will be soon enough," the copilot said, chuckling again, then catching himself and biting his bottom lip.

"My friend is right," the pilot said. "Those men, they would not want to cause problems with authorities at the airport, not with the cargo we have on board. But there is another pilot in the group. I do not know if you noticed, but there was a fat little business jet parked on the tarmac beside us."

"A Hawker," Chavez said, not liking where this was headed. "I saw it."

"That is right." The pilot nodded, his eyes gazed beyond his instruments at the darkness ahead. "A Hawker 800 has a range of almost three thousand miles and a top speed of over five hundred miles per hour. Even at cruise speed it can outpace this Cheyenne by a hundred knots—and that's if we weren't loaded down with cargo. What's more, it can fly almost as slow as we can, which will make it very difficult to evade." The pilot leaned into the aisle between the two cockpit seats so he could make eye contact with Adara. "If you keep watching long enough, Habib will be there."

The copilot's face twitched. He chuckled, and then put a knuckle to his teeth.

Chavez gave the instruments a quick scan. They were flying almost due east at ten thousand feet above the ocean surface. Altitude above you was useless in an emergency, but Chavez wanted to keep them relatively low.

The Cheyenne's cabin was pressurized to around eight thousand feet, so a sudden loss in pressure at ten thousand would not pose a problem. If they went too high, the pilots might be tempted to reduce cabin pressure and oxygen to try and regain control of the aircraft. He snapped his fingers next to the pilot's ears. "Give me those charts."

The pilot complied, grabbing a stack of folded paper aeronautical maps from the upholstered pocket next to his left knee. Chavez passed them back to Adara. "You mind finding us a safe place to land?"

Adara gave him a thumbs-up. Chavez still found himself startled when he turned and saw her with dark hair instead of blond.

"On it," she said.

"Pass me the mic," Chavez said, snapping his fingers again.

The pilot did as he was told. "We must land soon," he said. "The Hawker is probably already in the air. Habib is on his way. He knows people in the tower who will give him our position on radar."

"Now set the frequency to Guard," Chavez said. Guard was 243.0 MHz, an emergency frequency that was monitored by military aircraft.

Deddy glanced over his shoulder. "I tell you, Habib will find us. He will force us down and he will shoot you both. After that, he will kill me and my friend because we allowed you to steal this airplane."

The copilot began to giggle uncontrollably.

"Nobody's going to die today," Chavez said, a little too grimly to believe. "Well, maybe this Habib guy, if he's not careful."

47

The flight from the South Lawn to Andrews Air Force Base on the VH-3D Sea King—designated Marine One when the President was on board— took just over six minutes, depending on the route taken. Three identical helicopters switched positions constantly along the way in an aerial shell game meant to confuse any would-be attackers on the ground. Each bird was equipped with an impressive and highly classified array of protective measures—not the least of which were a couple of Noble Eagle F-16 fighters patrolling the D.C. area high overhead. The many sophisticated weapons systems used to protect him had embarrassed Ryan at first, until he came to grips with the fact that the Secret Service, the Capitol Police, the Marine Corps, the Air Force, and all the rest were protecting not just him as a man but the institution of the presidency.

Not one to waste precious minutes, Ryan was on the phone for the entire flight, talking to the U.S. ambassador to Indonesia. He guarded his words at first, his mind in overdrive, considering the possible outcomes of his words. A president had to be extremely careful about what he said or it would be construed to mean something totally different than what he'd planned. For instance,

Ryan had wanted to ask this crew chief a question about Sergeant Scott, the crew chief who he saw most often. He knew Scott had already shipped out for Jakarta with the presidential-lift package of HMX-1, and asking one crew chief about another could easily be misinterpreted as "Hey, where's the guy I like?" So Ryan had saluted and kept his mouth shut, saving his question for Sergeant Scott when next they met beside the White Top in Jakarta.

That was, however, about the limit of Jack Ryan's patience. He could feel his temperature rising as he discussed Father West's conditions of confinement with Ambassador Cowley. The ambassador assured Jack that he had an appointment to see Father West once the transfer to Nusa Kambangan was complete. Citing security reasons, the Indonesian authorities advised that prisoners could have no visitors while in transit.

Ryan barely suppressed the urge to curse. Ambassador Cowley was a gentle soul, bred for diplomacy, not the frontal assault Ryan craved at the moment. It was evident in the ambassador's voice that he felt he was living in a house of cards. He went so far as to ask if Ryan had something "grand" planned upon arrival.

"By grand," Ryan said, "you mean foolhardy?"

"Well," the ambassador said. "Mr. President, you are the final arbiter of what constitutes foolhardy in this case. But I would not be doing my job if I did not—"

"Understood, Mr. Ambassador," Ryan said. "You may pass on to President Gumelar that I come in peace, but I do plan to leave Indonesia with my friend, one way or another."

"Mr. President—"

JAVA, INDONESIA

N

Java Sea

• Jakarta

Bandung •

Indian Ocean

Nusa Kambangan
"Execution Island"

© 2019 Jeffrey L. Ward

"Or," Ryan said, "don't tell him. It's up to you. But I want you to know, that's the way it's going to happen . . ."

"Pardon me for saying." Arnie van Damm gasped when Ryan replaced the handset on the console beside his seat. "But holy shit, Mr. President. Are you trying to start a war with Indonesia?"

"I am not," Ryan said. "I do, however, think it's important to set expectations. If Ambassador Cowley believes I've lost my mind, he'll convey that to Gumelar with the fervor of a true believer."

Mary Pat sat at the rear of the compartment, leaning forward with her hands braced against her knees. She stared at the carpeted floor, deep in thought, as Marine One settled softly onto the tarmac.

"Have you, Mr. President?" van Damm asked, removing his seat belt as he prepared to exit the helicopter. He, Foley, Montgomery, and the other agents would disembark ahead of Ryan.

"Have I what?"

"Lost your mind, sir."

Ryan chuckled. "In a good way," he said.

Van Damm paused at the door, half turning to face Ryan. "Are you sure about this . . . this plan of yours? I mean, it's virtually guaranteed to blow up in your face."

"Like I said, Arnie. Sometimes the way to win the game is to rip out the steering wheel while everyone is watching."

First, the guards had given him a haircut. Then they'd brought in five buckets of relatively larvae-free water with which to clean himself. He was given a robe, and then ushered to a regular shower, as if he'd been too dirty to enter the place until he'd washed off the outer layer of grime. The shower was tepid but unbearably pleasant, and he'd wept at the feel of so much water on his skin. By the time he stepped out of the cubicle someone had left a stack of tan hospital scrubs on the bench. The simple shower and clean clothes made it impossible to control his emotions. It was all too much to comprehend.

They moved him to a new cell with tile floors instead of rough concrete. Measuring ten by ten feet, it was palatial compared to the one that had been his home for the past month, and boasted a metal sink with running water. It had an actual bed—though the blanket was still filthy from the last prisoner to use it. A day later, they'd moved him up to the ground floor. His new place had all the amenities of his previous cell, with the most welcome addition of a small slit window. It was too high to see out of, or even reach, but it let in light and, more important, air.

Later that same day he'd been moved again, this time to a cell with a window overlooking a dirt courtyard. Best of all, there was a metal toilet attached to the base of an upright pedestal sink-and-water-fountain combination. A bucket and dipper took the place of toilet paper. Father West had uttered a silent prayer of thanks, and then cried like a baby.

Around midday, he got an actual chicken thigh on top of his rice. It was greasy, and small, as chickens tended to be in Indonesia, but the meat was identifiable—and delicious. West had eaten every grain of rice and all but the jagged center inch of the chicken bone. He was working on that when a guard came and removed his metal bowl.

He'd not seen Ajij or Jojo again after they inadvertently sent the text message from his phone.

With a little food in his sunken belly, West found himself thinking clearly for the first time in weeks. The movement to increasingly better cells was curious. It was as if the Indonesian authorities knew they were in trouble, but couldn't quite admit it. No matter how good the accommodations became, he was still in prison.

A guard informed him he was going to get a visit from the embassy, but two uniformed men wearing berets and the owl insignia of Detachment 88, the law enforcement version of Indonesian Special Forces, had come into his cell. The men put shackles on his wrists and ankles as politely as one can shackle a person, and led him without a word of explanation to a garage, where he was stuffed into the back of an armored tanklike police vehicle called a Barracuda.

One of the most insidious things about being a prisoner was never knowing where you were going, what was coming next, what was about to happen. Sometimes this was by design, to keep the prisoner from making escape plans; sometimes it was meant to weaken the mind and induce cooperation. More often than not, though, it was simply because the guards felt a prisoner wasn't worth the time it took to explain things.

The inside of the Barracuda had been like his first cell—hot, cloyingly humid, and dark. He could see one of the guards' watch and noted they were on the road for just under two hours, traffic presumably clearing out of the way for the menacing armored vehicle and accompanying motorcade.

It was not until Father West was ushered out of the Barracuda and seated in a wobbly plastic chair on a small ferry that he realized where they were going.

Nusa Kambangan. Execution Island.

He'd always believed that God had a sense of humor. He had plenty of sins in his past life that should have landed him in a place like this, enough, at least, that he could never honestly say he was anything close to innocent. And yet he'd remained free and happy until he tried to do something good with his life. It was such a great cosmic joke.

As far as he knew, there had been no trial. Even in Indonesia, where the law sometimes bent to the will of the angry masses, death warrants didn't happen quickly. Still, his was an unusual case. From his experience, sentencing, if not justice, was carried out most quickly to those who were wrongly arrested. It was embarrassing for the regime to keep such people around for very long.

Father West closed his eyes and breathed in the hot and fishy air as the ferry putted across the narrow estuary toward Execution Island. He couldn't help but wonder if the greasy chicken thigh might have been his last meal.

48

The Hawker screamed past less than a hundred feet off the left wing, thirty-eight minutes after the Piper Cheyenne departed Manado. The stubby jet's lights cut a trail in the darkness over the ocean. Chavez crouched between the pilots at the rear of the cockpit. Adara knelt on the aft-facing seat on the right side of the airplane, bracing herself on the backrest behind the copilot. She was just far enough from Chavez to split the pilots' attention, helping to keep them in line, with the added stress of having the Hawker find and intercept them. It was imperative that they remain more afraid of Chavez and Adara than they were of Habib and the other men on the Hawker.

A scant half-mile ahead, the blinking lights of the Hawker cut directly in front of the Cheyenne's flight path, then broke right, making a tight circle to come straight at them, this time on the left side of the airplane.

"That son of a bitch is trying to fly a business jet like a fighter," Adara said.

Chavez felt the Hawker roar by, this time off the left wing.

"And doing a good job of it, too," he muttered to himself.

The aircraft had a closing speed of roughly eight hundred miles per hour. The wake turbulence of the passing Hawker threw the Cheyenne around like a rag doll.

The copilot sputtered in his right seat, trying to contain his nervous laugh. Deddy had sweated completely through his shirt. He looked like he might get sick to his stomach at any moment as he glanced up at Chavez. This Habib guy had gotten into his head somehow.

The radio crackled to life, spewing what sounded like very angry Bahasa Indonesian.

"He is ordering me to return to Manado," Deddy said.

"Tell him you're unable," Chavez said. "Tell him his shipment will remain intact, but you have a stop to make first. Tell him in English. Do it now."

Deddy tentatively relayed the information. He released the mic and shook his head. "Habib is from Maluku. People from that island can be very rough. He is a pilot, but he is also—How do you say it?—an enforcer. If he had guns he would shoot us down right now."

"Well, he doesn't," Adara said.

Chavez squeezed Deddy's shoulder. He was shaking like an aspen leaf in the wind. "We'll be fine as long as you fly this airplane. Why are you so scared of this Habib character?"

Deddy took a deep breath. "He is my brother-in-law."

"That's good," Adara said. "He won't harm family, right?"

"He has never liked me," Deddy said. "This will be a good excuse. Whatever happens, I am dead."

Chavez wanted to say, *That's what you get for peddling*

the shit you have in the back of the plane, but he kept it to himself.

"One thing at a time, Deddy," he said instead. "Worry about flying the plane for now. I don't want to have to depend on Chuckles over there if I don't have to."

Chavez keyed the mic, transmitting on Guard—a frequency military and civilian aircraft alike would monitor. He spoke rapid-fire English using the *hey-you-this-is-me* pattern aviators and war-fighters understood.

"Justice One, Cheyenne. You have an ETA?"

The leader of two F-15 Eagles answered quickly. *"Cheyenne, Justice One."* The pilot sounded young, maybe thirty, but probably not even that. Young and earnest. The mixture of cocky humility common to most pilots Chavez had ever encountered came through clearly in his voice. Just a kid, really, but an old soul, living his dream entrusted with a multimillion-dollar airframe over a dark and lonely ocean on the far side of the world. Chavez imagined him building models of F-15 Eagles a decade before. Hell, he was not likely much older than Chavez's son in the great scheme of things.

"We're four minutes, your position," Justice One said. *"Radar shows you have company."*

"Roger that, Justice," Chavez said. The two fighter pilots knew they were to have picked up a high-value item in Manado, and now that item was with Ding and Adara. Chavez had been able to brief them on the threat of the Hawker without talking about Calliope on an open radio frequency.

The F-15 leader spoke again. *"Cheyenne, squawk 1500 for me so I know who's who."*

Chavez bumped the seat back until Deddy adjusted the transponder.

"*Tally ho,*" the flight leader said. "*I have you. We're three minutes . . .*" He paused. "*Tricky. The other aircraft just squawked 1500 as well, and then disappeared from my screen.*"

Adara moved to look out the right window, then the left window, before turning to shake her head at Chavez. "I don't see it."

Chavez pointed up. "I think he's flying above us."

"Or below," the younger Indonesian pilot said between nervous hiccups.

"That is not likely," Deddy corrected his protégé. "Habib can still maintain distance and separation above us. Below, he would be blind."

Chavez put a hand on the pilot's shoulder. "Keep her straight and level. And slow us down. That should make it more difficult for him to maneuver his jet."

Deddy shook his head. "The Hawker is faster than us, but it can fly almost as slowly. And we are heavy with product."

The F-15 came across the radio again. "*Piper Cheyenne, Justice, your company is camped out on top of you about thirty meters. Are there any friendlies on board the Hawker?*"

"That's a negative, Justice," Chavez said.

"*Copy, Cheyenne,*" the F-15 leader said. "*Stand by . . . Hawker, Hawker, this is a United States Navy aircraft over international waters. You are endangering the lives of United States citizens. I order you to turn left ninety degrees immediately.*"

In the aircraft world, *immediately* meant just that.

Justice One spoke again, a hint of the barrio in his accent now.

"Cheyenne, Justice One, are you familiar with a head-butt maneuver?"

"I am," Chavez said.

"Stand by to see one up close."

Chavez barely had time to explain to a sweating Deddy and his hiccupping copilot before the F-15 looped in front of the Cheyenne, cutting directly across the nose in full afterburner, flaring to display the array of missiles under the wings as it shot by. The roaring Pratt & Whitney turbofan engines shook the much smaller aircraft in a terrifying show of force.

"He's sticking with you, Cheyenne," the F-15 pilot said. *"Rules of Engagement are crystal clear on this. Stand by to decrease throttle and break right on my mark, going for avoidance. I'll take care of the rest."*

"Wilco." Chavez made sure Deddy understood the plan and then grabbed a handful of seat leather.

"Three . . . two . . . one . . . mark!"

Deddy did what he was told and banked the Cheyenne 60 degrees to the right. The G-force of the skidding turn felt as if it might drive Chavez's feet through the cabin floor.

A moment later, Justice One crackled over the radio again. *"No go, Cheyenne. He's sticking tight with you. Too close for a shot with a Sparrow. The missile wouldn't be able to differentiate."*

Chavez had thought about asking for the M61A1 Vulcan rotary cannon, but he didn't like the image. The

F-15 Eagle had to really put on the brakes to get back down to the speed of sound, and Chavez didn't relish the idea of eating any stray 20-millimeter rounds when they came screaming by.

He was struck with a sudden idea. "Justice One, Cheyenne."

"Yes, sir, go for Justice One."

Damn, this kid is calm.

"You speak Spanish?"

"Affirmative, sir," the F-15 pilot said. *"I'm with you there. Stand by."*

Deddy gave Chavez a shaky thumbs-up to show he understood the plan.

Justice One gave the preparatory command to break right again on his mark, only this time, he gave it in Spanish.

Chavez began to translate—and it would have worked, had they not hit turbulence, causing the Hawker, still pancaked in tight above, to drop enough that her belly struck the horizontal stabilizer on top of the Cheyenne's T-tail.

The plane lurched and began to dive.

Deddy pushed a button on his yoke, then followed up by turning a manual wheel forward of the middle console.

His voice was quiet. Taut. "They have damaged the pushrods that control the elevators. The trim tab will help some, but we must land. Now."

"Cheyenne," the F-15 pilot said, surprise evident in his voice. *"Did the Hawker just collide with you?"*

"Affirmative, Justice One," Chavez said. "Good chance he damaged his landing gear."

"He won't need landing gear if you can give me separation. Can you still control the airplane?"

"Barely," Chavez said. "We're going to have to put down."

"There is an airfield two miles to the south," Deddy said.

Chavez leaned forward, catching the pilot's eye. "You were taking us there all along."

Deddy nodded. "I thought my idiot brother-in-law would force us down. I did not know he would crash his plane into mine."

Adara held up the chart for Ding, jabbing at it with her index finger. "There's another strip closer, about five miles nearer to the ocean. The Hawker has surely called ahead. They'll be waiting for us."

Chavez took the chart and shoved it in front of Deddy's face. "Take us down here."

"I don't know if we can make it," Deddy said.

Chavez lowered his voice so it was just above a whisper, barely audible above the droning engines. "You know what, Deddy. My head is killing me, some guy kicked the shit out of my ribs, and I'm pretty sure I have a chipped tooth. My point here is that I'm about as pissed as a man can be. You take your hands off the yoke right now or I will personally blow your brains out the side window of this aircraft. Do I make myself clear?" He didn't wait for an answer, turning instead to the copilot. "Chuckles. You have control of the airplane."

The copilot hiccupped, but said nothing as he settled into his seat. He didn't want to die. Chavez wasn't so sure about Deddy.

"Step back here," Chavez said. His head was beginning to bleed again. He could feel it.

Deddy's head snapped up. "What? He is not capable of doing this by himself."

Chavez cuffed the man hard in the side of the head. "I told you I was having a bad day. Don't make me wait."

Deddy rose from his seat and climbed gingerly over the small console between the two cockpit seats. Chavez pushed him facedown into the narrow aisle. Adara used a length of parachute cord to hogtie his hands and feet. A thrashing man could wreak a lot of havoc on a small airplane, even when restrained.

Reasonably certain Deddy was going to stay put, Chavez turned back to the copilot. "You got this," he said. It was as much a question as it was a pep talk.

"I do," the young pilot said. "But we must land. The tail is sluggish. I am afraid it may break further. Then I will have no control."

"Okay," Chavez said, pointing to the road below. "Take us down here."

Chavez shot a worried glance at Adara. He could feel his stomach rising into his throat as they rapidly lost altitude. The ground was rapidly getting bigger. It was still too dark to see it very well.

"Justice, Cheyenne," Chavez said.

"Go for Justice One."

"Thanks for your help. Your radios are better than

mine. Think you could see about getting us an exfil if we land intact?"

"*Affirmative, Cheyenne,*" the F-15 pilot said. "*I'll make the call now. Watch your G's. Your elevator has some significant damage. Keep it steady so she doesn't shear off.*"

"Roger that," Chavez said.

The copilot in front of him nodded that he understood—and hiccupped.

49

Special Agent Beth Lynch opened her credentials and pressed her Secret Service badge flat against the bullet-resistant glass of the reception window at the Ann Arbor Police Department.

"I'm here to see the chief," she said. Her face was passive, but she smiled inside, thinking how her mission was going to add a little excitement to the midnight shift.

She'd been on the other side of the window—early in her law enforcement career with Amarillo PD in the Texas Panhandle, first as a dispatcher, then a patrol officer. She now took a certain perverse pleasure in dropping these last-minute-visit bombs on smaller departments. Rank-and-file officers loved the overtime, the secrecy, the excitement of doing something different to spice up a mid-shift. Patrol officers fed off surprises. Supervisors hated them. The brass who had to deal with all the logistics to make things happen for the Secret Service weren't usually so stoked when an advance agent darkened their door.

The kid's disembodied voice came across the speaker beside the thick glass. "Can I ask what this is in reference to?"

"Afraid not," Agent Lynch said, smiling.

He hadn't even picked up the phone, so he wasn't ask-

ing for his boss. He was just curious. It was understandable, but she wouldn't put up with it.

"Okay, well, ma'am," the kid said, respectful, if he was
the tiniest bit officious. "He's gone home for the day. I'll
get you the supervisor on duty."

"That'd be peachy," Lynch said.

She stepped away from the reception window and
waited in the lobby with a half-dozen other people, listening to their stories. One wanted to see if he had warrants, two were reporting thefts, and the others were
trying to get an incident number for their insurance
company: all things they could have done online, but
that was the nature of the beast at virtually any PD she'd
ever been associated with—doing things for people that
they couldn't quite figure out how to do for themselves.

Ten minutes later, a man with a blond crew cut and
sergeant's stripes on the sleeves of his dark blue uniform
poked his head through the door behind the kid, probably getting a look at who was in the waiting room. He
caught a glimpse of Lynch, said something she couldn't
hear, and then waved her to a side door.

"Sergeant Victors," the officer said once she was in the
back hallway. "What can we do for you?"

"Are you the shift supervisor?"

"Supposed to be Lieutenant Cassel," Victors said,
"but he's away on leave. Afraid you'll have to deal with
me." He held up his ceramic A2PD mug. "Want some
coffee? What's this about? Counterfeiting case? Don't
you guys do wire fraud now?"

"Yes," Lynch said. "I'd love some coffee. No, I'm not
here regarding a counterfeiting case. And yes, we do wire

fraud investigations. But this is different. Can we go somewhere to talk?"

"You got here as swing shift is coming on," he said, nodding down the long hall where a knot of patrol officers congregated in front of a bulletin board. "I'm about to lead fallout. I can sit down with you after that."

"We should probably talk first—"

The door beyond the gathered officers opened and a man in a pair of faded jeans and a white dress shirt walked in. The officers stood aside with just enough deference to let Lynch know it was the chief.

"Are you the Secret Service agent?" he asked, striding up and extending his hand. He was polite, but not exactly glad to see a Fed standing in the inner sanctum of his building. "What's this all about?"

"Could we go in your office?"

The sergeant raised his hand. "I should probably get to fallout."

"Go ahead," the chief said.

Lynch leaned in close so other officers walking by couldn't hear. "FLOTUS is coming to town."

The sergeant shrugged. "Flo—?"

"The First Lady of the United States."

"Ah," Victors said. "FLOTUS. I can see why it's so sensitive. But that's above my pay grade."

"All right," the chief said. "FLOTUS is coming to Ann Arbor and you need our assistance. When is she due to arrive?"

"Ten hours."

The sergeant staggered a half-step backward, as if she'd slapped him. "You have got to be shitting me . . ."

"I'm afraid not," Lynch said.

The chief folded his arms, giving Lynch a glimpse at the face he must have used on his troops when they'd displeased him. "And we're just being told about this?"

Absent an office, Lynch stepped into an open break-room and motioned the chief and sergeant inside. She pulled the door closed—risking the wrath of anyone who needed their coffee before fallout. "I'm authorized to tell you that this isn't a pleasure trip. The details are extremely close-hold. This must be kept under the radar. No lights and sirens. No hint that she's even been here. We're protecting FLOTUS, but there's a lot more than that at stake. We just don't want to be obvious about it. I'll reimburse for overtime, but I'd like you to pick four officers for special duty. I'll put a Secret Service agent in each car."

"SWAT?" the sergeant asked.

Bless your strategic brain, Lynch thought.

"Best people," she said. "SWAT or not, that's up to you. I'm looking for tactical but not talkative. They have to be able to keep a secret."

She handed him a color-coded lapel pin. About the size of a quarter, it was white ceramic with a gold five-pointed star like the one on her badge. "Every gun-toter involved in this movement will have on one of these. Including your guys. If someone who does not have one approaches, then challenge them and get me on the radio. We're handling outer perimeter. You can tell the rest of the shift there's special duty, but that's all. Only the officers involved should even know it's happening." She looked at the chief. "I'll ride with your sergeant, if that works."

"Okay," the chief said, processing what little information she'd given him.

She nodded at the pin in his open palm. "They're numbered. I need them back at the end."

"And when do you anticipate that will be?"

"The end?" Lynch looked at her watch.

"I'm wondering when I can tell the rest of the guys what happened."

Lynch gave him the friendliest Texas Panhandle grin she could muster.

"Chief," she said. "I'm not trying to be a jerk. These orders come from the highest possible level. This is not something you should talk about. Ever."

50

As director of national intelligence, Mary Pat Foley rated a spot in the senior staff alcove on Air Force One. Foley found herself on edge, unwilling to be cooped up in the small office, so she sat on the couch outside the medical clinic with Admiral Jason Bailey, the President's physician. The 747—designated a VC-25A in military parlance—was large, but it was still an airplane, with limited space. The President's office, sometimes called the mini-Oval, was just forward of the clinic. The Secret Service kept two agents posted outside the door, at a small desk forward of the couch where Doc Bailey worked on a sudoku and Foley waited impatiently for a phone call.

Admiral Jason Bailey traveled on Air Force One with the President, but he was customarily quickly hustled away when they landed, to the backup plane, the Doomsday plane—an airborne version of the NORAD command center—or any number of aircraft or Secret Service vehicles. The doc's job was to be near enough to provide emergency medical care, but far enough away that he would not be injured in an attack. The stress of his responsibilities had to be fierce, but Admiral Bailey bore it up well. His eyes always seemed to sparkle above rosy cheeks, and the deep laugh lines around his eyes said he smiled even in his sleep. Foley liked the guy. His personality brightened up the room—or airplane—whenever he came around.

He tapped his pen on the sudoku puzzle, still smiling when he was stumped.

"You take some kind of chipper pills today, Doc?" Foley asked.

"No, ma'am," he said. "Just happy. I attribute it to CrossFit."

Foley was genuinely surprised. "I didn't know you did CrossFit."

Bailey kept reading his magazine. "I don't," he said without looking up. "That's why I'm happy."

"Har, har," she said.

She looked at the secure STE telephone on the small teak table beside her seat, willing it to ring with news. She hated this. Not Air Force One, it was beyond comfortable. Even the press got nice seats. What she hated was being out of control. The not knowing. The feeling that things were unfolding on the ground and she was too far away to move the pieces around fast enough. Her first report said that the tech known as Calliope was in hand. Good news. Then the flight of F-15s that had taken off from Kadena had reported a problem on the ground in Manado—some kind of shootout. Bad news. Ding Chavez and Adara Sherman had disappeared along with the tech. Worse news. Then the F-15s had located the small plane carrying Chavez, Sherman, and the tech. Better news.

Then crickets—which felt a hell of a lot like bad news.

Foley's phone chirped as if she had willed it to. She picked up the handset, waiting to be patched through directly to the F-15 Eagle's pilot through the communications center behind the cockpit of Air Force One.

She listened intently as Air Force Captain George Ramirez gave her a professional, no-nonsense brief—as if he enlightened the director of national intelligence on a daily basis.

The news was a gut punch. Worse than bad.

They've gone down on an island off the Bird's Head Peninsula in northwestern Papua," Deputy National Security Adviser and Navy Commander Robby Forestall said five minutes later when he, Foley, van Damm, and a Marine two-star named Exner, who was an expert on Indonesia, gathered around the President's desk.

Commander Forestall used a laser to point at a National Reconnaissance Office map on the flat-screen television. The red dot rested steadily on a small volcanic bump in the Pacific, west of Waigeo, in the Raja Ampat Islands. It was roughly six miles across at its widest point and encircled by a shallow lagoon and fringing reef.

"Keyhole images show a substantial airstrip here, a half-mile inland on the west side of the island."

Ryan pushed back from his desk and walked across the office to get a closer look. Small stars decorated the soft beige carpet. He'd seen photographs of Ronald Reagan wearing sweatpants on Air Force One, but for the time being, Ryan made do with rolling up the sleeves of his white shirt and taking off his shoes. "What do you make of this?" he asked, pointing to an array of metal buildings at the end of the remote airstrip.

General Exner leaned forward in his chair. He was a lean, muscular man with a shining bald head, and his father had been ambassador to Indonesia when he was a teenager, leaving him with a love for the people and a better-than-average understanding of the culture. His wife's parents were from Bali.

"My best guess is narcotics, Mr. President," the general said. "Industry in this area is mainly tourism and pearl farming. The need for an airstrip with no substantial roads leading into it indicates something more sinister."

"Seems crazy," van Damm said. "Smuggling drugs through that area." He looked away from Ryan, seeming to think better of mentioning the fact that Indonesia executed drug dealers, since Father West stood accused of just that.

"And yet here we are," Foley said. "Our people say the plane leaving Manado was definitely carrying heroin. Probably bound for Australia out of Malaysia. This remote airstrip in the Raja Ampat is likely a stopover point. That means smugglers, which puts our people in danger while they're on the ground. They went down with a load of hijacked narcotics. Our people on the ground believe the pilot of the Cheyenne flew to this location on purpose. We have to assume local smugglers have been notified and are coming to take back the drugs—and punish the people who took them."

Ryan studied the map, thinking. "What do we have in

the area?" He needed the thumb drive that contained Calliope, but he was more concerned about his people. He didn't know Adara Sherman well, but along with John Clark, Ding Chavez had run his protection detail when he was with CIA. Now it was time to return the favor. Humans over hardware—every time.

"USS *Fort Worth* is one hundred ninety nautical miles to the south," Commander Forestall said. He was one of the most consistent briefers Ryan had ever seen. "She's steaming out of Darwin, patrolling her way to the Philippines on antipiracy duty. NOAA reports a sea state in the Banda Sea between two and three so the *Fort Worth* could push it and be on scene in under four hours."

"She has a helicopter on board?" Ryan asked.

"That's correct, Mr. President. An MH-60 and an MQ-8 Fire Scout UAV."

"Good," Ryan said. "This reef looks like it would make a boat rescue problematic." Ryan arched his back, feeling it snap and crack. "All possible speed," he said, then looked up. "Out of curiosity, who's the skipper?"

"You've heard of him, Mr. President," Forestall said. "Capable man."

The sun was up, and Chavez could see at least a dozen of Deddy's heavily armed compatriots waiting at the end of the airstrip. At least he thought he could see them. His head was on fire, and his vision skewed like he was looking through two pairs of glasses at once.

Grinning maniacally, the copilot attempted to line up

on final. Deddy argued that he should land there because
the nearby road Adara had pointed out had been abandoned because it was too rocky and short. It was, he said,
overgrown with vegetation, and far too dangerous.
Chavez explained in none-too-gentle terms that, though
the men waiting below would surely kill him and Adara,
he would shoot both the pilots in the head as soon as
they were on the ground. Where landing on the nearby
road was risky, landing on the airstrip meant certain
death for everyone on the plane.

The Hawker had broken off to land on the actual airstrip. The F-15 pilot was reluctant to shoot a business jet
out of the sky when it wasn't an immediate threat. Chavez
couldn't blame him. The Monday-morning quarterbacks
would have a field day with that one. Still, Chavez was
certain that he was going to get to meet Habib very soon
on the ground.

They were supposed to rendezvous with the *Fort Worth*
on the south side of the island—but there was no place
there to land.

The Hawker's impact with the Cheyenne's tail gave
little horizontal control on landing. They hit hard, slamming Chavez sideways into the wall of the cabin. Reflexively, he reached for the armrest, feeling the bones in his
wrist snap in the process. *Well, shit,* he thought. That was
going to be a problem. He could shoot left-handed, but
a fight wouldn't be much fun. The break didn't hurt
much, at least not as bad as his pounding headache. He
was still too hyped on adrenaline—but before long, that
wouldn't be enough. Chavez caught Adara's eye. They'd
worked together long enough that she would be able to

tell from the strain on his face that something was terribly wrong. He didn't want to advertise his injury to Deddy, but she needed to know he was far from a hundred percent.

Other than a cut on her chin, she seemed to be all right. He touched his wrist and shook his head to try and silence the pain before switching the pistol to his left hand.

The airstrip was a scant two miles from the road where the Cheyenne touched down, both on the north side of the island. Adara flung open the back door and they were down the stairs as soon as the plane skidded to a stop, leaving Deddy and the chuckling copilot still on board. Chavez didn't hold much hope that they would make it out of this alive since they'd allowed themselves to be hijacked, but he had no time to worry over them.

He'd gotten a look at the terrain before the plane landed. The island was small and, apart from the fishing settlement on the north side, sparsely populated, with just a few pearl shacks around the periphery. Only five or six miles across from north to south shores, the interior of the island was a long hogback ridge. The northern slopes looked slightly steeper, while the southern side stepped down into a narrow valley before reaching the protected lagoon. The navigation chart put the tallest point at four hundred and fifty meters, not too tall in the great scheme of things, but every inch of it covered in thick jungle vegetation.

Chavez and Adara hit the line of vegetation at a run,

wanting to put as much distance between them and the Cheyenne as possible before Habib's friends arrived.

The gnarled limbs of large hibiscus trees arced overhead, forming dark roomlike spaces in the jungle. Coconut palms gave way to thick walls of mountain banana, towering beech and merbau, and razor-sharp pandanus trees that reminded Chavez of a cross between a yucca and a palm. Insects and birds droned and chirped among the foliage. Abundant flowers perfumed the hot and sticky air.

They'd made it a half-mile up the slope when they heard the first shots.

Adara stopped beside the smooth trunk of a tall merbau tree to catch her breath. "Idiots," she spat. "You told them. How's your wrist?"

"This running isn't helping," Chavez said, reaching out to touch her forearm. "I need to tell you something."

Adara reached out and took his arm, careful not to torque the wrist. "You should let me splint this."

"Later," Chavez said. "Listen to me. Those guys did a number on me back at Suparman's. I've got a roaring headache. I feel like I'm about to puke. And I can barely see."

Adara went into full medic mode in a flash, using her thumb to lift Ding's brow so she could get a good look at his pupils. "Yeah," she said, keeping her tone calm. "Your eyes are all wonky."

"Give it to me straight, Doc," Chavez said. "None of those big medical terms like *wonky*."

"I'll keep an eye on you. At least take this," she said,

digging in the first-aid pouch she kept on her belt for some Tylenol. "I don't want to give you ibuprofen with a head injury. Too much of a risk for bleeding."

Ding washed it down with a bottle of water he'd brought from the plane. He couldn't very well call in sick. He pointed to the vegetation behind them. "Our trail isn't going to be hard to follow in this foliage. We need to keep moving. Our exfil boat is supposed to be here in four hours. We may need all of that to make it up and over—and that's if those guys don't catch us first."

Commander James "Jimmy" Akana, United States Navy, had been in command of the USS *Fort Worth* for a total of twenty days, a month earlier than his normal rotation. USS *Fort Worth*, or LCS 3, was one of several littoral combat ships that worked under what the Navy called the 3-2-1 Rule. Three crews, rotating every four months, would keep two ships maintained, and one deployed at all times. The previous skipper had been stricken with a burst appendix while on port call in Darwin. Akana, previously of the patrol vessel USS *Rogue*, and now part of the Rough Rider Crew, had been temporarily assigned to shore duty in Singapore as part of Destroyer Squadron 7 for Seventh Fleet forward operations, when he was dispatched to take command of LCS 3. He hated that his fellow officer had taken ill, but Jimmy Akana had not joined the Navy to sit in an office. Command of any vessel at sea was a gift.

USS *Fort Worth* was a *Freedom*-class littoral combat

ship, three hundred eighty-seven feet in length, with a fifty-eight-foot beam. Purpose built for patrolling near-coastal waters, she was fast, maneuverable, and handsome. Though not equipped with the weapons of a destroyer or cruiser meant for sustained Naval battles, she was well-armed for her size with a Bofors 57-millimeter deck gun, rolling airframe missiles, and Mark 50 torpedoes. Twin .50-caliber machine guns rounded out the firepower. Her surface warfare package included, among other things, a Sikorsky MH-60 Romeo Seahawk and a remotely piloted helicopter called a Fire Scout.

Akana planned to steam northward, meandering through the islands of Indonesia as part of a joint anti-piracy operation with that country, Malaysia, and Singapore. His father had been a policeman in Honolulu and antipiracy duty made him feel like he was channeling his law enforcement bloodlines.

The message came in directly from Admiral Jenkins, Akana's boss with the Seventh Fleet in San Diego. The communications specialist handed him the headset so he'd be able to hear over the hustle-and-bustle noise of the bridge.

The orders were clear, and according to the admiral came directly from the President. Not that that would have mattered. Akana was a Navy man. As far as he was concerned, an order was an order, whether from a captain or the commander in chief.

Akana ended the call and handed the headset back to the radio operator before motioning his executive officer, Lieutenant Commander Nicole Carter, to the chart table.

"Bird's Head Peninsula on the northwestern shores of

New Guinea. Take her up as close to flank speed as you can without breaking something."

"Our mission, Skipper?" the XO asked.

"Rescuing a couple of operatives," he said, leaning forward so only the XO could hear. "And possibly a tiny invasion of Indonesia."

51

We have the sat phone," Adara said, pushing a broad, waxy banana leaf out of her path. "I don't know if our trackers are still operational. We'll need something to signal our exact location for pickup." They'd been running for well over two hours, the many canyons and cliffs impeding their progress up the mountain. The sun was high in the sky now, making them feel as though they were boiling alive in the humid jungle air. Sweat plastered hair to their foreheads and stung their eyes. They'd slowed almost to a stop, partly to be more careful about how many tracks they were leaving, but mainly because the terrain had grown so steep.

"I have a lighter," Chavez said, panting, as much from pain as exertion. "We'll have to look for something dry enough to burn. The problem is, we signal the ship, we also signal the shitheads coming up behind us."

"True," Adara said. She bent the thick stalk of the plant beside her to pull a sagging hand of small orange-yellow mountain bananas close enough to reach. Each fruit was not much larger than a finger. "You think these are edible?"

"Sure," Chavez said. "Not sweet, but they'll give us

some energy." He gingerly touched his wrist. "You got any more of those Ranger M&M's?"

"No ibuprofen for you," Adara said. "I'll give you another Tylenol, but that's all. Let me wrap it while we're here." She peeled a small banana and gave it to Chavez before retrieving a rolled ACE bandage from her pack. "Apart from the bruised noggin and wrist, you okay otherwise?" she asked. "One broken bone means we're supposed to look for more."

"I think I'm good." Chavez grinned, trying to add some levity. "Funny, Clark doesn't want to die of old age . . . but I'd be fine with it right now."

Adara expertly wrapped the wrist, giving it some support, if not an actual splint. "What was that I heard about JP playing some kind of sport?"

Chavez chuckled, wincing from the effort. "E-sports," he said.

"E-sports?"

"Computer games," Chavez said, panting. "Disguised as sports. The downward slide John sees in the youth of the world might be why he doesn't relish the idea of a ripe old age. Anyway, I'm not sure what JP is going to do now that he's graduated. He's been accepted to Stanford, but he's not as keen on it as he should be."

"A gap year?"

"I sure as hell hope not," Chavez said. "Patsy would freak out. She's already got med school mapped out for him."

A nearby branch snapped in the jungle below, causing them both to freeze.

52

It was common knowledge that any Air Force aircraft that carried the President of the United States was known as Air Force One. The convention held true through the other branches of the military as well—Marine One, Army One, Navy One, et cetera. Vice-presidential aircraft received the designation Air Force Two, and so on. In the unlikely event that POTUS flew on a commercial aircraft—it hadn't happened since Nixon—that aircraft used the call sign Executive One. At the discretion of the White House and the U.S. Secret Service, any aircraft, military or civilian, that carried the First Lady could be designated Executive One-Foxtrot. The *F* designation was for *family*.

Tonight, wanting to stay off the radar of the hundreds of scanner folk who meticulously tracked the planes, trains, and automobiles that carried the First Family, they would use the tail number of their military aircraft.

As First Lady of the United States, Dr. Cathy Ryan could travel in any of several military aircraft flown by the Special Air Mission of the 89th Airlift Wing—her staff coordinating with the offices of VPOTUS, secretaries of state and defense; and, once in a while, congressional delegations, who utilized the same aircraft. The

President customarily traveled via presidential lift on Marine One between the White House and Joint Base Andrews, just south of the Beltway. When she traveled without her husband, the First Lady usually made the trip in an armored Lincoln Town Car that was safely ensconced in a motorcade of D.C. Metropolitan Police and Secret Service vehicles.

Always hungry for anything to feed their twenty-four-hour news cycle appetite, dozens of media outlets kept their cameras aimed at the White House every moment of the day. The First Family, senior staff, and visiting dignitaries all received scrutiny, down to their clothes and type of shoes. Groundskeepers, other media folks, and especially Secret Service personnel blended in with the scenery like the proverbial postman whom no one ever saw.

Tonight, Dr. Ryan left the White House via the West Wing rather than the Residence. She wore a curly brunette wig over her blond hair, and one of Special Agent Maureen Richardson's dark pin-striped suits. She got in the front passenger seat of the Town Car, opening the door herself—something the Secret Service never allowed her to do. The agent behind the wheel pulled away as if he was on a routine fueling mission, stopping to wave at the Uniformed Division officer at the vehicle gate. They didn't join the follow-up Suburban and the lead sedan with Mo Richardson until they merged with the river of taillights on 15th Street.

The agent behind the wheel was of Asian ancestry. His name was Robert Leong, one of the Mandarin speakers borrowed from the VP detail for this trip. His father was a teaching physician at Johns Hopkins, where she'd done her residency, so that gave them something to talk about. He looked to Cathy like he was about four-teen, but everyone looked young to her these days.

Most of the aircraft flown by the Special Air Mission had the ubiquitous blue-and-white paint job resembling that of the VC-25A that served as Air Force One. Mo had arranged with the White House liaison officer for the 89th to have the First Lady fly in a plain white C-32, the military version of a Boeing 757-200. There were forty-five seats on board, all of them first class, allowing Mo to take a large complement of agents and gear.

An hour and a half after they left the White House, the First Lady's plane touched down in Detroit. Airport Police escorted two Secret Service sedans onto the tar-mac for a ramp pickup. They knew this was a visit from some kind of dignitary, they just had no idea who. Still wearing the wig, Dr. Ryan exited the plane with the first wave of her detail. A balding agent who bore an uncanny resemblance to a junior congressman from Florida came out in the middle of the pack and got in the backseat of the second vehicle after another agent opened his door.

The vehicles sped away to a hangar near the North Terminal, where Ryan changed into a pair of khaki slacks, a button-down oxford blouse, and a University of Mich-igan baseball cap before getting in the backseat of an armored Jeep Cherokee. Mo Richardson took her tradi-tional spot in the front passenger seat, beside the Secret Service driver.

It was spitting rain, and on the chilly side, making

Mo's jaws feel tight, like she'd been smiling a lot—not uncommon for her.

"That was fun," the First Lady said, settling into her seat.

"It was smooth," Mo admitted.

She didn't point out that any problems they were likely to encounter would be at the hospital, not while they were en route. It rarely did any good to make the principal more nervous than she already was.

"Will the others just meet us there?" Dr. Ryan asked.

"Yes, ma'am," Mo said. "I'd rather not point out where they're all posted. Try not to look around when we get out of the car, but we'll have agents all over the place, both in and outside the building. You'll recognize some of the faces of people we have in the clinic."

"Sounds good." Ryan leaned forward, touching Richardson on the shoulder. She did that sometimes. "Mo, I'm glad it's you doing this. It lets me focus on what I need to do."

"Thank you, ma'am," Richardson said, striking the balance between gushy fan-girl and humble professional, she hoped.

If more of the self-centered bozos getting protection from the Secret Service ever realized how far a simple thank-you would go . . . Early in her career, Mo Richardson had started a list of all the assholes she'd protected— but lists like that became too unwieldy in Washington, D.C. It was much easier to keep track of the good ones.

Mo looked at the moving map on her phone that rested on her knee, and called out a ten-minute warning when they passed through Ypsilanti and took the exit for Geddes Road.

Twelve minutes later, the driver pulled up curbside in front of Kellogg Eye Center. Again, Dr. Ryan opened her own door. She pulled the hood of a rain jacket over her ball cap against the drizzle and hustled across a dark and deserted sidewalk next to Mo Richardson.

A pair of agents Dr. Ryan recognized from her regular detail met them at the glass doors. Both were dressed in hospital scrubs. A redheaded man with a mop—Special Agent Rory Sharp, out of the PPD Critical Assignment Team—worked on the lobby floors, earbuds in his ears, apparently ignoring the procession.

The advance agents led Mo and Dr. Ryan via elevator to the fourth floor, where they almost ran headlong into a tall, cadaverous-looking man in the long white coat of a medical school professor. He was clean shaven but had mussed silver hair that came well past his ears, making him look like he could have been teaching at Hogwarts.

Dr. Ryan was in the middle of a yawn as the elevator doors opened, but brightened at once when she saw him.

"Daniel!" she said, gathering the man in an all-enveloping bear hug.

For a moment, Mo thought the man might lift the First Lady off her feet. Instead, he held her out at arm's length, grinning wildly. "It's been too long, my dear," he said in an accent that was either British, or affected upper-crust American English—like he was clenching a cigarette holder between his teeth. "How is my old study partner?"

"Things are busy," Ryan said. Underplaying her hand.

"I'll bet," Dr. Dan Berryhill said. "I miss our study

sessions . . . Remember those little mnemonic ditties we used to sing?"

He raised his bushy brows up and down in an inside joke.

Dr. Ryan gave a nervous laugh, trying to demur, but he dragged her into a rollicking duet to the tune of "Supercalifragilisticexpialidocious."

"Zenker's diverticulum and glottic stenosis, if you don't seek treatment soon, you will get halitosis . . ."

The agents in scrubs looked on, mildly amused.

Mo Richardson stifled a giggle.

A blond nurse, who wore a white ceramic lapel pin over her nametag, leaned closer to Mo and whispered, "My experience, the brightest ones are always just a little odd . . ." The nurse stood up straighter and addressed the group. "You guys want to follow me to the back? There are some folks here you probably want to talk to."

53

Hope was never a plan, but sometimes, after you did all you could, that was all that was left. Adam Yao had done everything he could to bolster his chances for success.

The execution of Yao's plan began as soon as the Songs, a very tired little girl, the general's twitchy aide, and Tsai Zhan, the minder, approached the Immigration checkpoint at JFK on their arrival to New York after the fourteen-hour flight from Beijing. Every country in the developed world had some level of medical screening for inbound visitors. Some methods were overt, like the large, cameralike thermometer aimed at the arrival corridor in Narita, Japan. Some, like the sensors and sniffers at U.S. Immigration in JFK, were less noticeable.

President Ryan had ordered the State Department to smooth the Songs' entry into the U.S. with Immigration and Customs Enforcement. They didn't have to stand in lines, but they were required to report to an Immigration official.

The inspector, a middle-aged woman of Chinese heritage whom Yao had chosen because her human-capital sheet listed acting experience, noted to Tsai Zhan when he came through that he had a low-grade fever. She asked him a series of mandatory health questions, had him present himself to a bleary-eyed staff doctor in a small room off to the side, who asked him more questions. There had been talk at Langley of stopping him here, but Yao's supervisors concluded that it would look like too much of an obvious political attempt to scrape him from the entourage, and would only cast more suspicion on the general.

"Welcome to the United States," the inspector said with a welcoming smile, once the doctor gave the nod. "Probably just a bug. Get some rest and drink lots of fluids. Maybe some chicken soup."

Tsai said that he felt fine, but the inspector reported to Yao that he'd touched his forehead with the back of his hand as he walked away—just in case.

Because of the late hour, they'd arranged for a charter flight from New York to Wayne County Airport in Detroit.

A clerk at the charter company (a CIA officer whom Yao had embedded there) met the group with a look of genuine concern. He asked if Tsai was feeling a little under the weather, mentioning offhand that there was something going around. He offered him a squirt of hand sanitizer—that Yao had laced with a scopolamine concoction developed by the docs at CIA. Tsai accepted, with a sneer of disgust. He didn't take much, but he got enough to add to the queasiness he was already feeling from the earlier suggestions that he looked sick. The power of suggestion was a wonderful social engineering tool.

Not an official government trip, the Songs and their two hangers-on had squished into a large sedan, rented at the general's personal expense and driven west on a dark and almost deserted I-94 through a steady rain. By the time they reached Ann Arbor, the general's white shirt and his wife's fashionable gray suit looked as though they'd been dug out of a hamper.

Kellogg had no covered parking, but staff ushered them quickly out of the rain and up to the fourth floor. Mrs. Song helped settle little Niu into an exam room to be prepped for surgery. The room was cramped, so General Song wished his granddaughter well at the doorway and remained in the lobby, slouching on the sofa, stoically looking a thousand yards away.

A callow military aide in his late twenties fidgeted in the seat to the general's left. Obviously accustomed to a uniform, he wore an ill-fitting suit, probably purchased just for the occasion. The only reason for him to be here was to provide an extra set of eyes and ears for General Bai. Yao could see it in the poor kid's eyes. The misgivings of being ordered to spy on the man he worked for and the fear of discovery, or worse, discovering something he did not want to know.

Tsai Zhan sat across from the general, between him and the door, a gray cotton golf jacket draped across his lap. His knee bounced slightly. His eyes flicked back and forth, checking every exit, as if he feared Song might try to make a run for it. He held a gardening magazine but didn't read it. Jet lag alone was enough to make most people feel somewhat queasy, like they were coming down with a touch of something. Tsai needed only a little nudge.

All Yao had to do was walk by with a cart of coffee for

the nurses' station for Tsai to demand some tea. The political minder was accustomed to getting his way.

The nurse standing at an open laptop on the reception counter shot Yao a side-eye and nodded toward Tsai, as if to say, *You'd better take care of this.*

"Of course, sir," Yao said. He gave a slight bow, awkward, like Tsai would expect an uncouth American to be—absent even the most basic etiquette. Yao looked at Song and his aide in turn. "I have tea or coffee."

"I do not care for anything," the general said.

The aide, terrified at being spoken to in English, gave a twitchy shake of his head.

"I would prefer tea," Tsai snapped. He might as well have been pounding his fist on the table.

Yao pumped a cup full of hot water from the urn, and then passed it to Tsai with two sachets of tea that looked as though they had never been opened.

Now it was only a matter of time—and how much of this tea Tsai decided to drink.

The operating room was smaller than Mo had been led to believe, or, rather, crowded with more instruments that took up much of the available floor space than she'd realized. Both Dr. Ryan and Dr. Berryhill had taken off their shoes. Ryan explained that eye surgery was often compared to flying a helicopter, as the surgeon had to utilize each hand and each foot independently—focusing the microscope, manipulating the eye itself, suturing, operating the laser, the cameras—or any of the equipment necessary for such a delicate surgery. By the time

both surgeons, an anesthesiologist, and two nurses
crowded around the table, there was little space left in
the room for Mo. The general and his wife were not offered spots in the viewing theater, leaving that room for
the two armed agents who were in contact with the detail posted outside and at the nurses' station.

Adam Yao was out there, too. By now he would have
tried to give Tsai Zhan the special tea. If that hadn't
worked—if he simply hadn't wanted tea—Yao had a couple of other plans that he'd not seen fit to share with Mo
Richardson, reminding her that she was a law enforcement officer and he was, well, not.

That part of this gig was his problem. She focused on
her charge, the First Lady, appropriately code-named
SURGEON by the Secret Service.

Mo had never had kids, but the sight of the little girl
conked out on the table, with tubes in her arm and
mouth, plucked at her heartstrings. Dr. Ryan and the
other surgeon used a lot of words Mo would not have
normally understood, but she'd done a fair amount of
reading on retinoblastoma. She was, after all, dressed to
play the part of a staff member at the clinic and didn't
want to look like a complete idiot if anyone in Song's
group asked her a question. The docs threw around
terms like *enucleation*—removing the entire eye—and
photocoagulation—using lasers to blast the blood vessels
that fed the tumor. There was a large monitor above,
displaying the work. Half the child's face was covered
with a surgical drape. Tape affixed the breathing tube to
her cheek. A thin piece of spring-wire claw held the affected eye open, unblinking, fishlike.

Standing in the corner, Mo didn't study the monitor long enough to figure out exactly what they were up to. She hadn't seen them cut anything, but the gaping eye itself—looking, but not seeing—was enough to give her shivers. She'd gladly take a grisly murder scene or motor vehicle accident any day over an injured child. There'd been plenty of all those before she came on board with the Service—but it was the sight of helpless kids that stuck with her, that scarred the back of her eye.

Mo tempered her flipping stomach by trying to focus on the First Lady instead of on the monitor. She'd waited outside the operating room dozens, probably hundreds, of times, and knew well the labyrinth of back halls of Dr. Ryan's home hospital, Johns Hopkins. The Secret Service even had a small office there next to Dr. Ryan's. But Mo had never watched her work. Her focus was so intense as to be almost Zen-like. Ryan and her partner were playing with some high-powered lasers in the middle of one of the most fragile and important parts of the human body. The eye didn't offer a great deal of real estate to work in to begin with, and these guys were shooting lasers through the pupil. Watching the steady hands, the total concentration, gave Richardson an entirely new level of respect for her boss.

An hour into the procedure, Dr. Ryan, unrecognizable in her surgical cap and mask, glanced over her shoulder and gave Mo a thumbs-up. Mo looked up at the agents in the viewing window and repeated the gesture. She and Dr. Ryan had agreed on the prearranged signal when the surgeons were roughly twenty minutes away from finishing up. The agents returned the thumbs-up to show that they understood the message and would pass it on.

"And there you go, Adam Yao, CIA dude," Mo whispered under her breath. "Less than half an hour. Let's see what you got."

She couldn't help but wish she was outside in the waiting area during this part of the op. She'd been around Tsai for only a few moments when the general had arrived. That was plenty long to see he was a vile human being. Mo shook her head, queasy from the images on the monitor. Still, she wasn't sure anyone deserved what this guy was getting.

Tsai was sweating profusely when Adam Yao brought a tray of donuts into the waiting area. Mrs. Song sat to the general's right, his hand clutched in hers, leaning against him for emotional support. All her customary stoicism had been leached away by the stress of her granddaughter's illness and the long hours of travel.

"How much longer?" Mrs. Song asked in accented English.

"I'm not sure," Yao said. "Maybe an hour. I'm sorry I can't be more specific."

"What could be taking so long?" the exhausted woman asked. "If it goes longer, do you think that means they are able to save her sight?"

"The surgeons will explain everything after—" Yao said.

"Why are there two?" Tsai asked, gulping back a burp. Yao could hear his rumbling gut from ten feet away.

"Two?" Yao scratched his head. "I'm not sure what you mean."

"Why two surgeons?" Tsai asked. "There is a limited space for four large American hands around a child's eyeball. Surely one would be enough."

The general huffed in disgust, blading away in his chair. Mrs. Song buried her head more deeply into her husband's shoulder.

Tsai chuckled. "Too many cooks—" An extra-large burp worked up from his belly, as if to punish him. He pushed the glasses up on his nose and stared at his feet.

Yao shrugged. "That's way above my pay grade, sir. I'm not even a nurse. I'm just an orderly. I help with things like—Hey, you don't look so good."

Tsai swayed in his chair like he was about to topple forward. Yao reached out to touch the man's arm, but he jerked away.

"I am fine!" Tsai snapped. His twisted grimace said otherwise. The thunder in his gut grew louder. His eyes suddenly crossed. The glasses slid down again as his face twisted in pain. "The restroom!" he demanded, cradling his protesting belly.

A morphine derivative based on a medication used to treat Parkinson's stimulated the chemoreceptor trigger zone, or CTZ, in Tsai's brain, causing it to send signals to the stomach saying it was time to expel all of its contents. A lot of signals. At the same time, a powerful chemical laxative was sending the exact same message to Tsai's lower GI. The effects were fast, relatively benign, and extremely dramatic. Knowing full well what was about to happen, Yao steered the rumbling man quickly across the hall.

They almost made it.

In the end, a disgusted General Song ordered his aide to retrieve Tsai's suitcase from the rental car so he could change out of his soiled clothing—keeping both men occupied and out of the picture.

Ah, Adam Yao thought to himself as he shut the restroom door. *The sexy life of a spy . . .* He had to hold his breath to keep from dry-heaving at the horrendous stench—but he'd bought some time, and best of all, Tsai would chalk it all up to a bug.

Now back to you, Dr. Ryan . . .

54

The First Lady waited in recovery with Niu while Dr.
Berryhill went to the waiting area to talk to the
Songs. Nurses and orderlies scrambled back and
forth in the hallway, buzzing about something she didn't
quite follow. One of the Chinese visitors had gotten ill.
She didn't have time to think about that. The girl's
grandfather would be in at any moment. But she didn't
even devote too much brain time to that. Her patient was
right here in front of her. She was what was important.

A circle of white gauze covered the little girl's eye. She
was conscious but groggy, and probably wouldn't remember much of the next few minutes—which was just
fine with Cathy Ryan. Mo Richardson stood by in scrubs
like an extra nurse. It was reassuring, having her there.
Cathy tried not to take the people who protected her for
granted, but it was difficult not to when she was going
on with the minutia of daily life. And Mo Richardson
made it look so easy.

The real nurse, a slender brunette named Amy, went
about her business, calm as could be, apparently not at
all fazed by the fact that she had the First Lady and Secret Service agent (who was now armed with a pistol under her scrubs) in the same room. The surgery had gone

well, considering. The tumor was confined to the anterior wall of the eye and just small enough that they were able to use lasers to destroy the blood vessels that supplied it. Niu would need to have the procedure done again, probably twice, and chemotherapy, too.

Amy touched Niu on her forehead, said something to her in English. The little girl smiled, then her good eye fluttered shut.

Cathy stood with her back to the door when Berryhill brought the Songs into recovery. As she suspected, they ignored everyone else and rushed to their granddaughter's bedside. Mrs. Song all but collapsed, taking the groggy child's hand. She closed her own eyes. Cathy couldn't understand the words but knew the feeling very well. This woman was praying.

Dr. Berryhill let them have a moment or two, then continued to explain what he'd found, future options, the good chance that Niu would retain at least most of her sight in the affected eye. She needed to rest, he explained, and would be fine to go to the hotel in an hour or so, as soon as they were certain there were no ill effects from the anesthesia.

Overwhelmed with relief, General Song looked up and noticed Cathy for the first time.

He stepped closer, sparing his wife the conversation but drawing an intercepting check from Mo Richardson.

Cathy raised her hand. "It's okay."

"I suspected they would send someone," Song said, deadpan. His English was perfect, with the hint of a British accent from training in Hong Kong. "But I must say, that they would send you is quite astonishing."

"So," Cathy said. "You know who I am?"

"Of course, Mrs. . . . Dr. Ryan. Am I to assume you performed the surgery?"

"I assisted," she said. "Dr. Berryhill and I were classmates in medical school. Your granddaughter is in extremely capable hands with him." She paused a beat, then added, "My husband wants me to convey his sympathy and best wishes. And to let you know that there are no strings attached with this surgery."

"But?" Song said, savvy enough to know there was bound to be more.

"But he is worried," Cathy said. "He believes you to be a patriotic but practical man. A man who does not wish to see his country plunged into unnecessary conflict."

"I see," Song said, glancing at the door. "Was that your doing? I am speaking of Mr. Tsai."

Cathy shook her head. "I'm afraid I don't know what you're talking about." She cast a sideways glance at Mo Richardson. "But I can tell by the look in my friend's eyes that it probably was. They apparently kept me out of that part, whatever happened."

"Will he live?"

Cathy shot another look at the Secret Service agent, who gave a tiny nod.

"Apparently so," Cathy said.

Song studied her carefully through exhausted eyes. "Your candor is appreciated. I am glad you did not kill him. I do not care for Tsai, but his death would have made things much more difficult for me at home. Still, I am not unhappy to be rid of him for a few minutes." He pursed his lips, bracing himself. "What is your message, Dr. Ryan?"

Jack had warned her about this part. Song would surely memorize every word she said, dissecting it for intelligence of his own. CIA officers underwent months of training to learn how to make this kind of pitch. She had to create a situation where the general would not feel as though he was violating his personal code. At the same time, she didn't want to give away the farm by letting him know too much about intelligence the U.S. already had.

In the end, she decided she was not a trained agent handler, but an ophthalmic surgeon—and a damned good one. She'd never have time to learn how to turn a foreign national into an American asset—so she decided not to attempt it.

"Look, General Song," she said. "I'm a mother, a wife, a concerned citizen who just wants a peaceful world for my grandkids to grow up in. Admittedly, I hear a lot more scary stuff than the average citizen because of who my husband is, but I'm no different in what I want for my family. Neither is Jack." She took a deep breath, gathering her thoughts. "He's worried that something is going on, a kind of power struggle inside China. Something dangerous that's not necessarily sanctioned by your government."

"You have helped my granddaughter," Song said, matter-of-factly. "I am grateful for this. But I will not betray my country."

"I understand," Cathy said. "And so does Jack." She purposely refrained from calling him "the President." This was a one-human-being-to-another discussion. Not world leader's wife to world leader's general.

"Had you asked me about the Spratly Islands," Song said at length, "or our military strength, or anything of that sort, I would have walked away. To be quite frank, I am not what you Americans would call 'in the know.' I do, however, have my suspicions, and I would confirm what your husband believes. The chairman has China's best interests at heart. If he is given a weapon, something to make China stronger, I am sure he would use this thing, no matter how many people had to die in order to get it—just as your husband would use it for America. But taking something that is offered and ordering the methods used to achieve it are vastly different things."

Cathy kept her face passive, but thought how far off that notion was from Jack's personal philosophy.

"I will tell you this," Song went on. "One of our generals, General Bai—your husband will know the name— has become quite brazen in his claims to the chairman. In truth, I know little of these claims, only that he is making promises regarding war."

He fell silent. A more professional operative might have let him stew, but Cathy couldn't stand it for long. "Promises? Why would anyone want a war? What could possibly be the end game?"

Song gave a sad chuckle. "You Americans always give your opponent too much credit. Sometimes, more often than not, I think, there is no master plan, just a brave—or reckless—person with the power to make things move. Do not forget, in 1961 the Soviets had no idea how to get Gagarin back to earth in his space capsule. They wanted to lay claim to putting the first man in space, so they sent him up anyway and had him bail out as the capsule fell to earth."

"That's a plan of sorts," Cathy mused.

"Part of a plan," Song corrected. He turned halfway to check on his granddaughter, speaking almost to himself. "And I wonder if General Bai has much more than that small piece of a plan he is making up as he goes along." Song looked suddenly at Cathy. "Do you know what you Americans have over us in China?"

"I'm sorry," she said. "I don't know what you mean."

"Over us," he said. "Superior to us. Maybe I am saying it incorrectly. You outspend us by far on your defense budget, but it is far more than that. The difference is, we only train. The United States military has fighting experience. General Bai has a calligraphy on his wall that translates to something like: *One does not prepare for war with practice. One prepares for war with war.* Bai is a general who has grown tired of scenarios and games. I believe he wants a fight."

Song leaned in ever so slightly, prepared now to divulge the crux of his message.

"General Bai is very self-assured when he speaks to the chairman, going so far as to say he can assure a certain victory with any adversary in an armed conflict. You may tell your husband there is an operation under way called FIRESHIP, but I have no idea what it is. I am, however, certain of one thing: Mutually assured destruction is still complete destruction. No one wins. Like you, Dr. Ryan, my wife and I want a peaceful world for our granddaughter. Now, if you will excuse me, I believe I have committed enough treason for the day."

55

S eamless coordinated communication through the E2-C Hawkeye between commanders on surface vessels, attack aircraft, and Special Operations warfighters on the ground reduced the time involved in what was known as the "kill chain process." Valuable minutes were saved in more quickly identifying a target, moving assets to a location of attack, ordering that attack, and finally destroying the target.

High-speed communication and the constant movement of military aircraft over USPACOM made Calliope's jump to her next target a foregone conclusion. Replications of the same Calliope software made similar jumps, each working to reach the same target.

The copy of Calliope that was closest to target jumped from a command-and-control Hawkeye out of Point Mugu, hitching a ride via data-link handshake to her next host, a KC-135 from the 909th Air Refueling Squadron in Kadena Air Base, Japan. She deleted herself from the E2-C as she made the jump and settled in to explore the systems of the big fuel station flying miles above the Pacific Ocean.

Calliope had no guidance system of her own. She

didn't need one. Instead, she used the GPS aboard the KC-135 to plot her location. At this moment, she and the Stratotanker were 688 nautical miles northwest of the Federated States of Micronesia, equidistant between Guam and the coral atoll known as Wake Island, 35,016 feet above sea level. Capable of speeds up to nine-tenths the speed of sound, or roughly six hundred miles per hour, the massive tanker had slowed to a more manageable three hundred and twenty-five knots indicated air speed, or KIAS.

Onboard computers indicated that the refueling boom had been extended. The radios were active as the pilots of the tanker and the approaching aircraft communicated with each other but, unable to translate speech to text, Calliope paid no attention to that noise. She waited for the approaching aircraft to "handshake," the integrated airborne computer-to-computer communication that Dexter & Reed had developed.

But this aircraft was an F-18 Super Hornet from a nearby aircraft carrier. Calliope was waiting for something else, an aircraft capable of launching from a *Wasp*-class amphibious assault ship—a Harrier or an F-35 Lightning II stealth strike fighter, or even a helicopter—anything that would get her aboard the USS *Makin Island*. The Stratotanker was two-thirds full of fuel, and still heading south, over the open ocean. Many more aircraft would crowd up to her fuel boom over the course of the next several hours. Statistics and odds said the F-35s would eventually show up and drink.

When one did, Calliope would jump.

56

As if the concussion and broken wrist weren't enough, Chavez and Adara ran afoul of Japanese giant hornets near the top of the mountain.

Completely absorbed with listening for anyone behind them, Adara grabbed the limb of a beech tree to haul herself upward, shaking it in the process. The gray paper nest was the size of a basketball and surely filled with hundreds of venomous insects. It didn't move much, but it was enough to bring a half-dozen guard hornets out to investigate. They were huge, an inch in length, with angry yellow eyes—which Chavez had no time to see, but clearly imagined—and daggerlike stingers that injected a massive amount of a potent venom that attacked the nervous system of the victim.

Adara sidestepped away from the nest and sank to the ground in a ball, covering her head. Chavez, who hadn't seen what was happening, thought they were under fire and wheeled to defend their six o'clock, earning himself a mind-numbing sting in the back of the neck. It felt as if someone had driven a red-hot nail into the base of his skull.

"Don't move," Adara hissed, stifling a scream as she, too, found herself on the receiving end of the quarter-inch stinger of the hornet that had names like "great

sparrow bee," "yak killer," or "bee of the terrible stinging death."

Chavez followed her example and made himself as
small as possible, covering the spot on his neck where
he'd been stung with the flat of his hand. He knew from
experience with bees and more normal-sized wasps that
they secreted a pheromone with each sting that signaled
other wasps or bees to concentrate their attack on that
same spot. Fewer than a dozen stings from these giant
hornets could hospitalize a healthy man—and Chavez
was far from healthy.

Adara was stung twice more before the hornets lost
interest and returned to their nest. Chavez had personally
seen her take a full-force kick to the groin without crying,
but tears streamed down her cheeks when they were able
to slink away. She had to work hard to keep from hyperventilating by the time they'd gone a hundred yards.

"If childbirth feels at all close to this," she said, "then
Mr. Caruso is shit outta luck . . ." Squinting, she used the
back of her forearm to wipe the tears from her face. Chavez
had been stung only once, but that was enough to understand how she felt. The venom had to be some kind of
acid. If anything, the torturous pain was growing worse.

Chavez pointed upward with a none-too-steady hand.
"We got an hour and a half to get to the rally point."

"We're going to need all of that," Adara said, gasping.
The hornets had tagged her twice under her right eye, and
once in the V above her collarbone. More divots of missing flesh than sting welts, the angry red wounds looked
remarkably like bullet holes. She'd taken a Benadryl from
her pack, but her face and neck were swelling noticeably.

The jungle thinned some as they neared the top. Sunlight filtered through the canopy, dappling the ground. Chavez leaned against a sapling, checking it first for hornets' nests. Sweat poured into his eyes. Bits of leaf and jungle litter flecked his face.

"I don't know about you, but I'm counting on a hell of a lot of downhill on the other side."

"Amen to that," Adara said. She peered at him, swallowing hard, as if it was difficult to speak. "You think this is one of those times we'll tell our kids about someday?"

"I do," Chavez said, moving again, dragging himself toward the crest of the hill, less than a hundred feet away. "The little shits will love stories about how we got our ass kicked by bees." He began to laugh, in spite of the situation. "Yeah, this is definitely one of those times. My head's busted, I've got a break in my wing, and you look like somebody's been stabbing you with a hot poker."

Chavez fell silent. Who was he kidding? JP was busy with his own life. He wouldn't be interested in the jungle tales of his old man.

Adara suddenly froze, her foot hovering in the air mid-step. Dread and terror washed over Chavez when he thought it might be another hornets' nest. Then Adara drew the Smith & Wesson from her belt, pivoting slowly to her right.

The dark figure of a man came into focus, seeming to materialize out of the jungle duff. He carried what looked like a steel pipe. On closer examination, Chavez realized it was a homemade shotgun.

The man placed the weapon on the ground before raising both hands. He had the dark mahogany skin and broad nose of the Melanesians who inhabited Papua farther to the east. Coarse hair, naturally black, but bleached by the sun, stuck out in all directions from beneath a faded Coca-Cola baseball cap. An iridescent blue feather, more than a foot long, curled from the bill of the cap. He wore cotton shorts, stained from living in them for weeks or even months, and a holey T-shirt that matched his hat. A large silver cross hung from a braided string around his neck and a wicked-looking bone dagger was tied to his waist.

"Englich?" he asked, eyes wide.

Adara nodded. "You speak English?"

A nervous half-smile perked the man's face. He had scars there, lots of scars that looked to be ceremonial. He put the flat of his right hand on the center of his chest. "Me's Konner. Konner Toba." He pointed at Adara, and for the first time, Chavez saw he was missing the pinkie and ring fingers of his left hand.

The people of western Papua, especially these islands, were predominately Ambonese and Chavez was surprised to see someone of Melanesian descent alone at the top of this mountain.

Adara put her left hand to her chest. The pistol was still in the other, though she pointed it at the ground.

"Adara," she said.

Chavez introduced himself as Ding.

"Bad men," Konner Toba said. "They is after you."

"Yes," Adara said.

"Me help you," Konner said, tapping the dagger on his side, which, he explained, he'd made from his grand-father's thighbone.

Adara pointed up, toward the crest of the hill. "How long to the water?"

Konner smiled, showing a mouthful of teeth, happy to be able to communicate. "Small stream over the hill," he said. "Good water."

Adara shook her head, spreading her hands wide apart. "I mean the ocean. The sea."

"Ah," Konner said. "You wanna go to da beach."

"Yes," Adara said. "To the beach."

The man's chin fell to his chest. "You got some medicines? My wife sick. She gots the debil in her. That's why we run here. People in my billage, they say she is witch. Try kill her 'cause she got debil in her. I say all womin got debil, you know. I going to village down there 'cause she need medicine." He brightened. "You help me, me help you go to beach."

"What's wrong with her?" Adara asked. "How is she sick?"

Konner shrugged. "She not pass water too easy," he said. "She need medicine."

It would have been easy to write off this guy as slow-witted, given his use of pidgin, but he spoke more English than Chavez spoke of any Papuan tribal language.

"I'm not sure, but it sounds like she might have a urinary tract infection," Adara said to Ding. "Might even be her kidneys." She turned toward Konner, patting her medic bag. "I have medicine that might help her, depending on what's wrong. I can't promise, though."

"She screams a lot," Konner said. "Make me sad. I been prayin' the debil every day to help her out."

Chavez nodded toward the silver cross on the man's neck. "You mean you pray to God."

"No," Konner said matter-of-factly. "God love me already. I don't gotta convince Him to help. Me prays to the debil so him change his mind and stop makin' my wife sick."

"Okay . . ." Chavez said, thinking his head hurt so bad that this made more sense than it should have. "We need to move."

Konner cast around the hillside until he found a shrubby tree that was covered with white flowers. Chavez recognized it from a recent trip to Hawaii as plumeria or frangipani. The man broke off two of the succulent magnolia-like leaves at the base and held them up for Chavez and Adara. A droplet of white sap formed at the base of the stem where the leaves had been pulled away.

"Make sting feel better," Konner said. He picked up the homemade shotgun, which was essentially a piece of plumbing pipe and a spring set into a roughed-out two-by-four. "You follow. Me show you the short road to the beach, you give medicine make my wife not scream so much."

Adara leaned in closer to Chavez as they fell in behind the lanky Papuan and began to climb again uphill.

"This is amazing," she whispered. "Is it wrong to hope that someday my granddaughter makes a dagger out of my thighbone?"

Chavez stifled a laugh, unwilling to put up with the pain. A few paces ahead, Konner Toba stopped in his tracks and turned to stare at the foliage behind them.

"Bad men close by," he whispered. "We go beach now. Go fast."

57

I'm proud of you," Ryan said to his wife. With the handset of his secure telephone pressed against his ear by the pillow, he lay flat on his back in the forward compartment of Air Force One. His slacks and white shirt were draped over the chair beside the bed.

They'd been married long enough that he clearly recognized the sound of his wife's happy cry on the other end of the line. She'd already relayed General Song's message. He'd asked her to repeat it twice. As a surgeon, she was accustomed to dictating medical notes, and Adam Yao had sat with her immediately afterward, acting as her scribe to get all the details down on paper. Yao had sent a copy of the report via secure e-mail directly to Mary Pat Foley, cc'ing his boss, the DCI.

Ryan still had two hours until touchdown in Jakarta, so he took the time to just listen to his brave wife, and let her bask a little in her accomplishment. She sounded exhausted and hyper at the same time. Ryan knew the feeling all too well.

". . . I mean, I'm no stranger to pressure, Jack," she said. "But this was so different. It was incredibly exhilarating. Not like surgery at all . . ."

Ryan listened attentively, letting her get the feelings

off her chest, until there was a knock at the door. It was Mary Pat.

"Sorry, hon," Ryan said. "I have to go. You did good. I mean really, really good. This is something tangible we can use to save Father Pat."

"Thank you, Jack," she said. "That means a lot. Let me know how it goes," she added, personally invested now, more than ever.

Ryan ended the call and rolled off the bed, stepping into his slacks before he answered the door. He grabbed his shirt and shrugged it on as he followed Mary Pat out into the office.

"What do you think?" he asked, leaning against the edge of the desk while he buttoned the shirt.

"I think it's good," she said. "But it's thin without actual proof. We can't very well out General Song."

"True," Ryan said.

"You know," Foley said. "Indonesia has a love-hate relationship with its Chinese population, especially the Chinese Christians. If Gumelar has virtually anything to go on, he should be able to turn the tables and show China for the bad actor it is in all this."

"The last thing I want to do is stir up a bunch of racial unrest against Chinese Christians."

"I get it," Foley said. "But there will undoubtedly be a butterfly effect. There always is. Everything we do is going to have consequences, some of them unintended."

Ryan felt his ears pop as Air Force One began its initial descent. "Gumelar is on the nose when he says his hands are tied by the will of the people. Indonesia is more of a direct democracy than we are—even if it says differently on paper. We have General Song's information. That, coupled with our next meeting, will scare Gumelar bad enough that he'll come around to our way of thinking just to save his own ass."

"You are absolutely sure about this plan of yours, Mr. President?"

"Oh, yeah," Ryan said. "Like my father used to say, 'This won't be pretty, but it'll be right.'"

A ir Force One approached Halim Perdanakusuma International Airport from the east, touching down, as they always did, with barely a bump. The pilots taxied to the Presidential Terminal. Across from the main terminal, the Presidential Terminal was used, as its named implied, for the Indonesian president and high-level visiting VIPs.

Marine One was parked on the concrete pad at the end of the taxiway, surrounded by a phalanx of Secret Service agents and military personnel who'd arrived well before Ryan in the various C-17 Globemasters and C-5 Galaxys used to transport the presidential lift. A Marine Corps V-22 Osprey was at the east end of the pad, nacelles and rotors pointed skyward. The media who'd hitched a ride on Air Force One would travel to the first event on the Osprey.

Indonesian reporters and wire service reps stood at the rope line in front of the terminal. President Gumelar and his generals had conveniently moved a half-dozen Indonesian Air Force F-16s and sleek Russian-built Su-30MKK fighter jets to the edge of the runway. It would have been a fine display of power, but all the aircraft and vehicles that traveled with the President of the United States made the handful of jets look insignificant.

He stepped up to the cockpit to thank the Air Force One pilots and crew, and then, adjusting his deep azure tie, stepped out the door to the air stairs.

Ryan saluted the Air Force sergeant at the base of the stairs and then shook hands with President Gumelar. He was a decade younger than Ryan, with wiry hair that stuck straight out if it was cut too short, dark-framed glasses, and a neck that looked slightly too thin to hold up his head.

"Gugun!" Ryan said, clasping the man's hand. "Thank you for hosting me."

Gumelar smiled for the cameras a few dozen yards away. "I am glad to see you, old friend, but you did not leave me much choice."

Ryan returned the tight smile. "I could say the same." He shook hands with the three dour generals that formed the welcoming committee with Gumelar and then nodded to Marine One. Sergeant Scott stood at attention at the base of the steps.

"I was thinking you and I should ride together," Ryan said. "It's quicker than the motorcade."

Gumelar held up an open hand, attempting to demure. "Mr. President, I—"

"Bring one of your security guys," Ryan said. "There's room." He looked over his shoulder at Montgomery. "Right, Gary?"

"Of course, Mr. President," Montgomery said.

This was where it got tricky. Gumelar didn't have to come along. Things still would have worked, just more slowly. But who turned down a free ride in one of the most famous helicopters on earth?

Head swaying on his willowy neck, President Gumelar stammered, "I . . . I would be honored."

Both men turned to wave to the crowds, which, Ryan noted, were polite but sedate. Police had kept any protesters at least two hundred meters away.

Ryan stopped a few steps back from the double doors on the VH-60N White Hawk that was about to become Marine One when he stepped aboard. He let President Gumelar get on first.

Admiral Bailey, Ryan's physician, trotted up carrying his medical bag. "Special Agent Montgomery sent word that you wanted to see me, Mr. President."

"I do, Doc," Ryan said, waving an open hand at the helicopter doors. "We may be in need of your services in a few minutes."

"Aye-aye, Mr. President," Bailey said, and hurried up the steps.

After everyone else was on board, Ryan stepped forward to salute Sergeant Scott. He waited a beat, then took a moment to shake the young Marine's hand.

"Rod," Ryan said—sometimes a young man needed to know his commander in chief knew his first name. "I was so sorry to hear about your grandfather."

Still ramrod straight, the Marine beamed. "Thank you, Mr. President."

"I could have pulled some strings to let you go to the funeral." Ryan grinned. "I know a couple of generals . . ."

"He would have rather I carried on here, Mr. President."

"No doubt." Ryan nodded. "Hell of a guy, your granddad."

"You knew him, sir?"

"Not well," Ryan said. "But he was a close friend of a very close friend of mine. I did have the opportunity to meet him once, years ago." Ryan put a hand on the young Marine's shoulder. "I'm sure he was proud of you."

Sergeant Scott's eye twitched like he might tear up. Ryan rescued him by changing the subject. "Did our special guest make it on board?"

"Yes, sir, Mr. President," the Marine said. "Rear bulkhead seat, directly behind you, beside Director Foley. President Gumelar will sit on the couch across the aisle from you, as instructed."

"Very well," Ryan said. "We'll talk later. They're secondhand, but I have a couple of kickass stories about your granddad that he probably never told you."

Ryan stepped aboard the helicopter, noting immediately the cooler air as Sergeant Scott shut the doors. He felt the familiar flutter in his gut that plagued him every time he boarded any kind of aircraft. A fancy version of the ubiquitous Black Hawk, the VH-60Ns used by HMX-1 were decked out inside with carpet, soundproofing, and leather seats. They were maintained by some of the most professional people in the world, double- and triple-checked.

And yet . . .

Helicopters and Ryan had come to an uneasy truce over the years. There was a lot of truth to the adage that the definition of a helicopter was "a million parts rotating around an oil leak, waiting for metal fatigue to set in." He had to fly on them, but he never truly enjoyed the experience.

"So, Gugun," Ryan said, ready to get to work. "I understand new charges have been dreamed up against Father Pat."

President Gumelar took off his glasses and cleaned them with a handkerchief he'd taken from his suit pocket. "Jack," he said. "I am sure you know that even United States courts sometimes bring charges after the initial point of arrest."

"Ah, but our courts allow the accused to face his or her accuser," Ryan said. "But that's neither here nor there. I didn't come to argue, Gugun. I came to help you."

"To help me," Gumelar said. "Is that so?"

"You and I both know perfectly well that China is behind this," Ryan said. "They are attempting to play us both. I have a list of twenty Chinese diplomats whom we are ready to declare personae non gratae and expel from the country. I'm here to ask you to take similar action."

"China is an important trading partner for us," Gumelar said.

"And to the United States as well," Ryan said. "But we cannot let this behavior continue simply because they sell us phone parts."

"You say we both *know*," Gumelar said. "But I have seen no proof."

"Oh," Ryan said. "Believe me, Mr. President. Operatives of the Chinese intelligence service have stolen valuable computer technology on your soil. These same operatives have bribed members of your police force to arrest an innocent man and charge him with a capital crime. They have attempted to coerce a citizen of the United States into committing treason."

"Mr. President," Gumelar said. "I have heard nothing of Father West committing treason—"

Mary Pat Foley looked on stoically from her bulkhead seat.

"I'm not talking about Father West." Ryan raised his hand and motioned for the passenger in the seat behind him to move forward. "Gugun, I'd like you to meet Senator Michelle Chadwick. It turns out she has quite a story to tell."

"Senator Chadwick?" President Gumelar shook his head in disbelief. "I was under the impression that . . ."

"That I despise President Ryan?"

"Well," Gumelar said. "Frankly, yes."

"That's a fair assessment," Chadwick said. "But I despise spying for the Chinese even more. Everyone knows the President and I see eye to eye on very little. Unfortunately for the Chinese intelligence services, that means my word actually carries more weight, not less."

Gumelar flushed red. "You have proof that China is involved?"

Chadwick held up her cell phone. "I do, Mr. President. I have a recording of the Chinese operative who was attempting to get me to spy on President Ryan. He admits they are willing to frame Father West with false narcotics trafficking charges in order to bait the Ryan administration with the possibility of his execution."

"She came to me straightaway," Ryan said. "Told me everything, cooperated with our director of national intelligence and FBI all along."

"You plan to go public with this proof?" Gumelar said.

"I do, sir," Chadwick said.

"And you should as well, Gugun," Ryan said.

"Very well," Gumelar said, tight-lipped. "I do not like being played for the fool."

"Nor do I, my friend," Ryan said. "There is a way for you to demonstrate that you are still in charge of this country—and to set things right today. What would you say if I asked you for a tour of the prison on Nusa Kambangan Island?"

58

Thirty-eight minutes after Calliope made her most recent jump, the KC-135 adjusted course slightly more eastward, in the direction of the Marshall Islands. The tail boom was extended again, and an approaching F-35 Lightning pilot began to speak with the crew of the Stratotanker. At the same time, the aircraft began a series of handshakes via data-link. Calliope instantly calculated the range of the strike fighter, read the list of weapons stores, and then waited to see how much fuel was transferred. She read, but did not care, that this F-35 was piloted by a USMC Major Goodloe "Oh" Schmidt. What did interest her, and cause her to spool up, was that this particular F-35's onboard radio logs showed it had recently communicated with the USS *Makin Island*. Chatter from other aircraft going to and from the nearby ship filled the radio.

Calliope understood English commands, but the words were superfluous. Her language was raw data, and right now, the data showed that her target was almost within reach.

A millisecond later, while Major Schmidt's F-35 Lightning was still in the process of taking on fuel, Calliope jumped, deleting herself from the Stratotanker's systems, as if she were never there.

59

The first bullets snapped the air beside Ding Chavez's head ten minutes after they crested the mountain. Chavez was fairly certain Habib and his friends were engaging in spray-and-pray tactics, but the rounds were close enough that one of those prayers was bound to get an answer sooner or later.

Konner dropped to his belly at the shots, peering around the base of a vine-choked tree at their back trail. His eyes appeared to glaze over, like he was stoned.

Chavez and Adara crouched beside him. Chavez had done enough work in this kind of environment to know exactly what the wiry Papuan was doing. Dense vegetation had a tendency to trick the eye, making it difficult to see anything but a wall of mottled green. Periodically allowing your vision to relax and unfocus helped give what Chavez's instructors had called "jungle eye."

Seeing nothing at the time, they were up and running again in less than a minute.

The dense foliage was alive with the buzz of insects and screeching birds, masking the noise of anyone's approach. Vines, trees, and banana leaves formed an almost impenetrable mesh that was difficult to see through, let alone navigate, without leaving an obvious trail.

"How wide is the beach?" Adara asked as they half ran, half fell down the mountain.

"Maybe here to that banana tree, me think," Konner said, pointing to a tree some thirty meters downhill as he moved. "Big hibiscus trees, then beach, then water." He looked up at the thick canopy above, the way someone might check their watch. "It low tide now. Beach maybe little more wide."

Another bullet whirred by, high overhead. Chavez chanced a look over his shoulder. His vision was too blurry to see much of anything anyway, but he knew Habib and his goons had made it over the mountain.

More rounds snapped in the air, followed by the distinctive report of an AK-47 behind them. One of the rounds neatly clipped a fat banana leaf above Adara's head, sending it falling to the jungle floor.

"Voices!" Adara hissed, picking up her stride.

Chavez could hear little but the muffled whoosh of his own pulse in his ears. Adrenaline was a marvelous thing, but he'd been living off a steady diet of the stuff for the last couple of hours. He could handle fatigue, but the throbbing pain and nausea from his injuries pushed their way to the fore as the adrenaline ebbed. He was reduced to carrying his broken wrist as he ran to keep the bones from grinding.

The shots came more quickly now, peppering the foliage just a few meters to the right.

"How much farther?" Chavez asked through clenched teeth, panting heavily. It took so much concentration to speak he nearly lost his footing.

The Papuan's hand shot out to steady him. "We goin' downhill very quick," he said. "Maybe five minutes."

Chavez glanced at Adara, who met his eye.

"We're trapped between these bastards and ocean," she said. "They're going to get to us before the ship does."

"Me knows good hiding spot."

More shots. Closer now.

Adara shook her head. "You think they could have people ahead of us?"

"I do," Chavez said.

The Papuan grew wide-eyed as he reached the same conclusion.

He hefted the homemade shotgun and looked back and forth along the side hill, obviously trying to come up with an alternate plan. "They driving us to a trap."

Littoral combat ship USS *Fort Worth* was fifty-six miles away when the comms officer received a call via satellite telephone. The female operative they were supposed to pick up informed them she and her partner were ten minutes from the beach and taking fire from an unknown number of pursuers.

The seas had become choppier and the powerful Rolls-Royce engines, based on the same engine that powered Boeing's 777 jets, pushed the ship along just below thirty-five knots.

Commander Akana stood in the bridge, looking out over the foredeck boat that stretched out in front of him like a clean parking lot. In addition to the officer of the watch and the two enlisted personnel who were driving the boat, the executive officer and the command master chief were also present. All wore Navy work blues and uniform ball caps.

The XO, Lieutenant Commander Nicole Carter, was an Annapolis grad, but she didn't appear to be a ring-knocker. She let her daily output of stellar work speak far louder than her CV ever could. Command Master Chief Alfredo Perez was tall, with the lined face of a man with a long history. He had an intense Danny Trejo look going that at once terrified and endeared him to officers and enlisted alike. Equivalent to the chief of the boat, or COB, on a submarine, a command master chief or command senior chief was the senior enlisted person on a surface vessel. The Navy didn't strike sailors anymore or restrict them to bread and water—but one cross look from CMC Perez had the same effect on most young sailors. He was fiercely protective of his crew, advocating for them to leadership at every turn, but unafraid to dispense the frequent ass-chewings needed to keep recalcitrant youngsters in line. Like the rest of the crew, the XO and command master chief were finishing up their assigned four-month rotation. Akana had taken over for the previous skipper, making him the new guy. Fortunately, his reputation as a pirate hunter aboard the USS *Rogue* had preceded him—bringing enough sea-cred that he had time to prove himself as a servant leader. It seemed to Akana that every sailor just assumed that a new skipper was going to be an incarnation of Captain Queeg. That sort of leader certainly existed, but in Akana's experience, there were more Horatio Hornblowers in the Navy—more deckplate leaders—than there were Captain Blighs.

Good leaders thought about leadership, not management, and that meant getting out in front of things. This mission was tricky, and if it failed, he would be the one to take the heat, not the XO, not the CMC.

"Have Engineering wring out flank speed for as long as practical," Akana said.

Where full speed was a high percentage of power that, while not fuel-efficient, was not the maximum, flank speed meant as fast as the boat could go. Period. Such speed was reserved for emergency situations, and came at a cost if carried out for too long. Maintainers didn't much care for flank speed, because it had a tendency to break things.

The XO passed the word, and Akana felt a gradual shift as the vessel dug more aggressively into the waves.

"If they're taking fire, there could be injuries," Akana said. He didn't have to explain himself, but talking out certain decisions allowed him not only to train his executive officer but to think everything through in front of the command master chief—who had a full decade more experience at sea. "Any distance we can close shaves off valuable seconds."

"Understood, sir," Carter said. "Air Ops reports the MH-60 and the Fire Scout should be on station in two minutes."

"Very well," Akana said, moving into what, for him, was the most difficult part of any operation—waiting for things to happen.

With his hands clasped behind his back, Perez squinted, the corner of his mouth turning up a little, Popeye-like.

"Is something bothering you, CMC?" Akana asked.

"Far from it, Captain," the command master chief said. "I was just thinking what a great day it is to be in the Navy."

The shooting stopped as they neared the beach, a good indicator that Habib did indeed have friends down there waiting.

"Movement!" Adara said. "Eleven o'clock."

She, Chavez, and the Papuan man all lay facedown under the cover of a curtain of creeping vines. Chavez faced uphill, watching their back trail, while she and Konner studied the route ahead.

Konner Toba shook his head, not understanding. Chavez glanced back to see Adara hold her hand straight in front of her, knifelike, then moved to the left. "Twelve, eleven, ten . . ."

"Me sees it," the Papuan said, pressing his face closer to the debris on the jungle floor. "Under big hibiscus tree."

Chavez saw it, too, even with his blurred vision. At least three men with long guns. Beach hibiscus were not the tallest trees in the jungle, but what they lacked in height they made up for in spread. Their large branches, some as big as a man's waist, pointed skyward off a thick trunk, before arching back to touch the ground. These arches and heavy foliage of hand-sized leaves formed shadowed roomlike hiding spots beneath the sprawling trees.

Had the men stayed back in the shadows a little farther, they would have been invisible. Fortunately, they were drug runners, not trained snipers.

Focusing back uphill, Chavez popped the mag out of his Smith & Wesson and checked for the second time to make certain he'd done a tactical reload. He was normally more sure of himself, but the head wound had him loopy. "I'm down to ten rounds," he said.

Adara gave a grim nod. "I'm at six."

He passed her his partial mag. "Top off," he said. "I'm seeing two of everything anyway."

"Me gots four," Konner Toba said, holding up a shotgun shell from his pocket. He'd turned the ball cap so the bill and the curling blue feather faced backward. He didn't mention the thighbone dagger.

The voices uphill grew more animated since they knew the jaws of their trap were closing. Chavez estimated they were less than a hundred yards away now. The men along the beach were even closer.

"What's that way?" Chavez asked, gesturing to his left.

"Waterfall," the Papuan said. "That way no good."

"How about to the right?"

"Maybe," Konner said. "But big fern field above. Open, so me think this way better."

"Not at the moment," Chavez said.

A volley of Kalashnikov fire rattled uphill as one of their pursuers fired into the air, working to drive them downhill toward the hibiscus. Thick foliage dampened the sound, but they were close enough now that Chavez could hear the *clack, clack, clack* of the rifle's heavy action slamming back and forth as it cycled.

He squinted, trying to clear his vision, to do something about the crippling pain in his head. These guys would be on top of them in minutes, if not seconds.

Adara had her hand cupped over the mouthpiece of the satellite phone. She pointed her chin downhill to get Chavez's attention.

Another volley of automatic gunfire. More voices. The jungle thinned somewhat on the lower third of the mountain. Chavez counted eleven men, less than fifty meters away, ghosting through the trees.

Chavez could clearly see the trails the three of them had made through the grass and undergrowth. Habib and his men would have no trouble walking straight to them.

"We have to move," he whispered.

Adara gave an emphatic shake of her head, going so far as to reach over and kick Chavez in the calf with the point of her boot. She mouthed the word *Wait!* and then began whispering into the sat phone again.

A moment later, Chavez picked up the sound of a lawn mower, or perhaps a tractor from the direction of the ocean, and then the beautiful image of an MQ-8 Fire Scout rose into view behind the hibiscus tree.

A branch snapped in the foliage to Adara's left, and Chavez caught a glimpse of brown movement. One of Habib's men had flanked them. Chavez swung his pistol, but Konner lunged into the brush, leaving his shotgun behind. The brush thrashed for a moment, and then the lanky Papuan crept back to the group in a half-crouch, his grandfather's bloody thighbone dagger clutched in his fist.

"Thanks," Chavez whispered, scanning for others.

"You give me medicines," Konner said. "We be even Steven."

"Okay," Adara said into the sat phone. She was talking to the air boss on the ship now, and the pilot who was remotely operating the Fire Scout from the USS *Fort Worth*. She held out her hand to Chavez, who knew exactly what she wanted. He took his cell phone out of his pocket and cued up the compass, aiming it at the UAV to give her an azimuth. "We're lined up," she said. "The Fire Scout is directly over the tree with the first group of bad guys. They are armed and hostile. We're seventy-five meters due north if you line us up. Second set of bad guys another fifty meters to our north, spread out."

Adara listened and then said, "Roger that. We don't have a choice."

She turned to Chavez and Konner. "Hug the ground, boys," she said.

The Hydra 70 laser-guided rocket fired by the MQ-8 had a blast radius of ten meters and a lethal fragmentation radius of fifty meters. Delivering a ten-pound warhead, the slender rocket traveled at speeds approaching Mach 3. At this range, it didn't have time to reach full speed, but the explosion was nearly instantaneous from the time of firing. Bits of dirt and foliage and probably drug smugglers rained down on Chavez and the others. He felt the blast as much as he heard it, and still wondered how long it was going to be before he'd need hearing aids.

Incredibly, stupidly, the men uphill began to fire at the helicopter.

"They're too close for a missile," Chavez said.

Adara simply smiled, pointing seaward again as the MH-60 Romeo Seahawk from the *Fort Worth* hove into view above the smoldering hibiscus tree.

The big sister of the little Fire Scout flew directly

overhead, with Adara guiding her in. A half-second later, the remotely piloted helicopter's GAU-17 "Vulcan" electric Gatling gun began to burp lead into the trees at six thousand rounds per minute.

The MH-60 pilot made two passes to surveil the hillside and then overflew the twisted remains of the hibiscus tree one more time. Satisfied the threat was neutralized, he gave the all-clear for Chavez and the others to come to the beach for pickup. The little Fire Scout remained aloft, providing overwatch.

The MH-60 pilots weren't keen about spending any more time than necessary in Indonesian airspace, but since the orders to pick up this package had come directly from the secretary of defense, they did as Adara requested and flew seven miles down the beach, where they dropped off Konner Toba a mile past his house so he couldn't be identified by any neighbors getting off the helicopter.

The Papuan shook Chavez's hand and then cried when Adara gave him her entire med kit. "You good folk," he shouted, as the helicopter prepared to lift off from the beach. "Me say prayer for you."

Chavez collapsed into his seat, wounded, exhausted, and wondering to whom Konner Toba planned on directing his prayer.

60

President Gumelar used the telephone aboard Marine One during the forty-minute flight to Nusa Kambangan Island. He made a quick call to his military adviser first, clearing the way for Marine One and the accompanying aircraft to overfly the country unmolested. Not surprisingly, he called his press secretary next, speaking in rapid-fire Bahasa Indonesian. Ryan couldn't understand the conversation but got the gist of it when Gumelar used the words *hashtag* and *China* in the same contemptuous-sounding phrase. Like everywhere else in the world with access to the Internet, Indonesians were sensitive to public sentiment. Astroturfing what looked like a grassroots campaign to question the validity of Chinese influence in Indonesia would take some political pressure off the president. Such a life ring might come at the expense of Chinese Indonesians—but Gumelar had always struck Ryan as the sort of man who would climb on top of his own mother in order to save himself from drowning.

Only after he'd created a backstop for himself did he call his commanding general of the Indonesian National Police. Marine One was fifteen minutes out when he was finally assured that everything would be in order when they arrived on the prison island. Gumelar passed the phone to his security man, who spoke to the Marine One crew chief with instructions on where to fly. Sergeant Scott in turn relayed the instructions to the pilots, who passed the word to the other aircraft in the presidential lift.

As in the United States, three identical White Tops flew in shuffling formation. Two greenside V-22 Ospreys loaned to HMX-1 from VMM-262 out of Okinawa flew overwatch. At the insistence of President Gumelar, three heavily armed Embraer Super Tucano turboprop fighters accompanied the lift on behalf of the Indonesian Air Force.

Only Marine One would land at the prison.

With his phone calls complete, Gumelar's hands fell into his lap. "Very well," he said. "There are seven prison sites on the island. Father West is being held at the one called Batu. Your pilot will land at a small soccer field behind the compound itself. I will exit the helicopter first to let the guards know I am acting of my own volition, after which point you and I will enter the facility together. I will sign the requisite clemency papers, a few—"

Special Agent Gary Montgomery leaned forward against his harness, very nearly bursting out of his seat. "Mr. President, I cannot let you go inside the prison."

Gumelar ignored the agent and spoke directly to Ryan. "You must go inside, Jack," he said. "We will do this together."

"Mr. President," Montgomery said. "This is completely unacceptable. You—"

"I hear you, Gary," Ryan said. "But sometimes I have to—"

Ryan had never seen Montgomery angry. The agent

was a bear of a man anyway, but the space he took up in the aircraft seemed to instantly double in size. His face flushed red, the tendons on the side of his neck tensed as if he were lifting a heavy weight. "When was the last time you were inside a lockup, sir?"

Ryan sighed. "Fifteen, twenty years. Maybe more."

"Everything we train for, prepare for, will be rendered useless inside those walls. We will not be in control. And I like being in control."

"Gary—"

"The choice is yours, of course, Mr. President," Montgomery continued. "But if anything goes wrong in there, I will be unable to protect you without killing a lot of people."

Ryan gazed out the window as Marine One began to descend in the field beside a run-down compound of concrete and corrugated metal. He didn't give a damn about President Gumelar's hurt feelings as long as Pat West was released.

"Gary," Ryan said. "If you'll bear with me, I think we might reach a compromise on what to do here . . ."

Father West heard the squeak of shoes on the chipped tile floor long before he saw anyone. His cell was much larger now, fresh water, plenty of light. Even so, the odor of human desperation lingered in the air—and something West recognized immediately as the pall of impending death.

At first, when his conditions improved, he'd thought that his text had gotten through. But he gradually came to realize that these people were going to kill him because of a lie. They just wanted to clean him up beforehand, so they'd feel more civilized while doing it. He'd given up hope of ever being rescued.

There had been no trial. But what would be the point of one, anyway? It was as easy to whip up the records of a trial and conviction as it was to make up evidence of drug trafficking. He'd read about the Bali Nine. He knew that he was just a few kilometers from where two of them had been marched onto a field in front of twelve soldiers and shot.

It was not in West's nature to hurry the moment of his death, and yet there was absolutely nothing he could do but pray.

The footfalls grew louder and a mountain of a man with dark hair and a tailored suit strode up to the iron bars of his cell. There was an Indonesian man with him who West knew he should have recognized but did not. The big man stepped to the side as two guards unlocked the door and pulled it open.

West backpedaled until he bumped the far wall, nervous to be around so many people. "Are . . ." he stammered. "A . . . are you from the embassy?"

The big man smiled serenely and shook his head. "No, Father West. I work for the President of the United States, and I'm here to take you home."

Ryan gave the priest his seat, sitting across from him, facing aft. Dr. Bailey started a glucose IV immediately and went to work checking vitals, looking at West's eyes and teeth. After a few moments, he gave Ryan a slight nod. He'd conduct a more thorough exam when they returned to Air Force One—Ryan didn't intend to make West remain in Indonesia one second longer than he had to. The President held a cold can of Coca-Cola at Bailey, raising his brow. "How about it, Doc?"

"None for me, thanks," Bailey joked. "But Father West might like it."

Ryan chuckled and passed the can to his friend.

"Oh, my." West held the sweating can to his forehead. "Merciful heaven, Jack. You have no idea . . ."

It killed Ryan to see his friend so drawn and hollow. He opened a packet of cashews and held them out to West. "You look like you could use something salty."

Gumelar had been on the phone again with his press secretary since before Marine One even left the ground.

Father West drained the Coke at once and sheepishly asked for another, which the crew chief brought him immediately.

Suddenly animated from the sugar and caffeine, West leaned forward toward Ryan. "You got my message?"

"I did," Ryan said.

"And?" West said.

"And what?"

"And did we get Calliope?" West asked, exhausted, but sounding to Ryan as if he'd never left the Agency. "If that tech is as Noonan described, it is extremely dangerous. And if the Chinese have it, there is no telling what they might use it for."

"We're working on it," Ryan said. He was unwilling to go into detail in front of Gumelar.

"And Noonan?" West asked.

"Unknown," Ryan said, looking to President Gumelar. "I'm sure investigative efforts will intensify now that everyone knows the Chinese were involved in your kidnapping and the disappearance of Mr. Noonan."

"So the Chinese still have the tech?"

"We believe so," Ryan said.

West closed his eyes and took another drink of Coke. "This has the potential to be very, very bad, Jack. I'm not sure the essence of the situation came through in my text."

"Tell me now," Ryan said. "What makes you think that?"

"It was the way Noonan kept describing the thing," West said. "As a non-player character that could be directed to perform all manner of tasks."

He suddenly looked around the interior of the helicopter. "How long was I in custody?"

"Over four weeks," Ryan said.

West blinked, looking as if the wind had been knocked out of him. "Okay, then. I have spent that entire time imagining the havoc an active agent could wreak, were it capable of moving freely through any device with connectivity. In the developed world with the interconnectivity of the so-called Internet of Things, that's pretty much the whole shebang."

"Our people at Cyber Com haven't examined it yet," Ryan said. "But they theorize it is something like a programmable virus."

"Not quite." West shook his head. "This thing is a predator—programmable, yes, but with a mind of its own."

61

The deck of USS *Makin Island* was alive with sailors and Marines. To a layman's eye, the *Wasp*-class Landing Helicopter Dock amphibious assault ship, or LHD, could be mistaken for her larger sister, the aircraft carrier. LHD runways were short, with no catapults and no arresting cables, but the *Makin Island* did have aircraft on board—helicopters, Ospreys, and fighters like Harriers and F-35Bs that were capable of short takeoff and vertical landings.

Half as wide and slightly less than one football field shorter than a *Nimitz*-class aircraft carrier, USS *Makin Island* (LHD 8) was not exactly small at 843 feet in length, with a beam of 104 feet. Her aviation assets on this trip consisted of six V-22 Osprey tilt-rotor aircraft, a CH 53, two MH-60 Seahawks, two Bell AH-1 Super Cobras, two Harrier jump jets, and two F-35B Lightning IIs. She could have carried more, but the mix was mission-specific.

In addition to her air power, LHD 8 was armed with, among other things, Mk 38 chain guns, Sparrow missiles, and four .50-caliber BMG machine guns. The USS *Preble* and the USS *Halsey*, two *Arleigh Burke*–class destroyers out of Everett, Washington, flanked the amphibious ship and provided additional big-stick deterrence.

All the deck guns, aircraft, and support ships were impressive, but the most important component of the USS *Makin Island* was the eight hundred Marines that could be put on foreign shores to fight at a moment's notice. Sometimes looked down on by line officers of the big-deck Navy, amphibious forces—or Gator Navy—sailors had a tight, if sometimes competitive, relationship with the Marines they carried. Some sailors called their ship a Marine Corps Uber. For their part, the Marine Expeditionary Units were happy for the lift.

All of them—well, most of them—loved to be at sea.

Captain Greg Goodrich, United States Marine Corps FAST Company, Pacific, stood on the foredeck, looking past the V-22s at the waves while he ticked through the list of his responsibilities for this mission. There was a rhythm to the ocean that appealed deeply to the kind of man he was. He loved casting all lines and leaving behind the distractions of shore. At sea, Captain Goodrich could shoot, exercise, train his platoon—and read. Staring out at the wind and waves was better than watching TV any day of the week. The fantail of the ship provided the perfect location to get his Marines range time, and the deck was big enough for some good outdoor cardio. He'd even organized a couple of boxing matches while under way.

Goodrich had been on the runty side through the seventh grade, athletic, but shorter than everyone else in his class, even the girls. Mostly knees and elbows, he endured a certain amount of bullying. He wanted to join the military and thought being a pilot would be good for someone who was vertically challenged—then he grew four inches the summer after eighth grade. He towered over everyone else in his class his junior year, and had reached six-foot-six by the time he was a senior—a little tall to squeeze into a fighter. He stopped growing a hair short of six-eight his sophomore year at Virginia Military Institute. His mother wasn't completely on board with VMI. She was a surgeon and wanted him to be a surgeon, or at least an engineer. He compromised and went to a military school that taught engineering. She'd blanched when he'd decided to pursue amateur boxing, warning him that repeated blows to the head didn't pair well with his calculus and physics studies. She was, of course, correct, but Goodrich found that his wingspan was long enough that he hit other engineering students in the head far more often than he got hit himself.

People tended to think of VMI as a bunch of shaved-headed Rats standing over steam vents in wool greatcoats getting hazed by upperclassmen. There was some of that, but Goodrich relished the visceral aspects of military discipline, the barking, the esprit de corps—the boxing. He'd always been a fighter, and knew he wanted to do it for a living. The Marine Corps allowed just that—and FAST allowed him to focus his fight.

Captain Greg Goodrich was highly educated, well read, and well spoken—but he could also be very, very uncivilized when circumstances called for it.

As was often the case, on this mission, Captain Goodrich's Fleet Anti-Terrorism Security Team worked directly for the admiral. FAST Marines trained for unforeseen contingencies, short-notice deployments, force protection of U.S. interests, and anti-terrorism around the globe. They went into threatened embassies, protected nukes, did whatever the Fleet told them to do—anytime, anyplace.

This time, they were guarding a long-range anti-ship missile given to the Navy by Lockheed Martin for the purposes of today's test. The weapon itself was worth a cool three million dollars, but it was the sensitive artificial intelligence guidance technology inside that made it valuable enough to have FAST standing by to retrieve it should something go awry at launch.

Captain Goodrich's Marines were young for special operators—mainly corporals and non-rates in their early twenties, but there were only about five hundred in the Marine Corps at any one time. The competition was fierce, and FAST got to be picky about who they chose. A lot of Marines thought they wanted to do FAST, until they found out about the PRP. The personnel reliability program—the Big Brother–like security check where you basically signed over your right to privacy for the privilege of guarding the nation's nukes. A polygraph was required for the top-secret clearance needed to handle nukes, and virtually any infraction was disqualifying. Any hint of domestic violence, a single DUI, certain foreign contacts, too much porn—all were disqualifying.

Becoming a member of a Marine FAST Company wasn't easy, but, so far at least, it was the best job Captain Goodrich had had.

Launch would be from one of the F-35s, two hours from now, in the evening, when there were no known Russian or Chinese satellites snooping overhead. The admiral was on the bridge, going over contingencies, and probably on the horn with someone higher up the chain than him at the Pentagon. The reps from the defense company were sweating bullets that their three-million-dollar baby performed as advertised and blew the hell out of the decommissioned Navy ship rigged to look like a Chinese destroyer, forty nautical miles to the south. *Makin Island*'s two MH-60 Seahawks patrolled the airspace around the target vessel, keeping any surface, submarine, or air traffic out of the area. The jet jockeys and their commanders were in the ready room, briefing. The V-22 Osprey pilots who would stand by on Ready 5 alert status with Goodrich's FAST platoon and a Navy SEAL team were in their own ready room, doing the same thing.

Goodrich touched a button clipped to the center of his load-bearing vest. "Ski, Ski, Goodrich," he said, speaking in a normal voice.

Staff Sergeant Sciezenski's voice came back loud and clear, inside Goodrich's head rather than in his ear. "Go ahead, Captain."

"Sitrep?"

"Ten minutes, sir," the squad leader said.

"Roger that."

Goodrich nodded to himself. As a rule, he was a little on the stodgy side for a man in his early thirties, preferring technology that was tried and true. He had to admit, though, that this new Sonitus Molar Mic they were testing was turning out to be awfully useful tech. Instead of an earpiece, the Molar Mic clipped over the wearer's back teeth. Using the same near-field neck-loop utilized by a covert earpiece, the Sonitus device acted as a microphone, sending voice communication from inside the mouth, protected from external noise like gunfire or rotor wash. Instead of being transmitted through the eardrum, incoming signals were felt via vibration in the jawbone. Where earpieces became itchy and uncomfortable the longer they were worn, the body quickly adjusted to what was essentially a mouth retainer with a small mic. To Goodrich's surprise, it was easy to forget the damned thing was there. So far, battery life was good, most of the day. The ability to hear and speak clearly to a helicopter or V-22 crew chief while you were hanging in the wind on a SPIE rig below it was nothing short of incredible. Staff Sergeant Ski had voiced the platoon's greatest concern when he asked if they could chew with one of the mics in their mouths. They could, so the tech would get their seal of approval when their portion of the test and eval process was complete.

Goodrich's two squads of eight Marines each were checking gear and weapons, taking on the last drink of fluid before they would load onto the Alert 5 Osprey, where there was no restroom other than an empty Gatorade bottle. Goodrich was a stickler for readiness and he wanted his squads on board both Ready 5 birds in full battle rattle a half-hour before missile launch. Goodrich laughed and shook his head as he thought about every other time they'd worked with SEALs on one of these missions. He and his men would sit in the stifling tropical heat inside the Osprey, waiting for something to go wrong, stewing in their own juices like good Marines. Outside the bird, also on Ready 5 status, the SEALs would be flopping around doing SEAL shit.

62

The F-35B Lightning II flown by Major Goodloe "Oh" Schmidt was stationary now, having utilized its thrust-vectoring nozzle and lift fan to land vertically on a ship identified as the USS *Makin Island*. The aircraft had been refueled after landing, with the onboard management system indicating just over nine thousand pounds in the internal tanks—three thousand pounds less than full capacity. Calliope had made the jump hours before, riding the data-link between the Stratotanker and the strike fighter high over the Pacific. Other copies of Calliope made similar jumps to similar planes, deleting themselves after every move, searching. This Calliope had ended up in the right part of the world, and was now homing in on the target they'd all been sent to find.

To maintain its stealthy profile, the F-35 had to carry all armament inside its reflective skin. Weapon stores indicated this aircraft's internal bays were already loaded with four AIM-120 AMRAAM air-to-air missiles, leaving no room for the target. The plane's computers had communicated with a second F-35B while in flight. That plane was not active now, but Calliope surmised that it would be the one to carry her target, while Major Schmidt's aircraft would provide cover.

They would take off together, at which point Calliope would make her penultimate jump—to Major Skeet Black's plane—and then, if it was on board, as she surmised it would be, the LRASM missile.

R ear Admiral Kevin Peck, deputy commander of the U.S. Pacific Fleet, stood on the bridge of LHD 8, looking out across the deep indigo water. Completely bald, he was slender but well muscled for a man who spent so much time behind a desk these days. His love for basketball and overall competitive nature kept off most of the pudge that could easily accompany each new star added to the uniform.

Twenty minutes earlier, radar had picked up a contact one hundred nautical miles east of the derelict Navy frigate with seventy-five thousand dollars' worth of plywood and sheet metal screwed and welded to the superstructure. This vessel, mocked up to have the profile of a Chinese destroyer, was the intended target to test the next-generation technology on the LRASM missile. Admiral Peck didn't particularly want some Chinese ship to stumble onto the thing. He'd sent two Cobras to investigate.

The *Makin Island*'s captain stepped to the window beside Peck. "Super Cobras report the radar contact is a fishing trawler. Estimated one hundred thirty feet in length, moving east at a steady six knots. Looks like she's actively fishing, sir."

Peck took a deep breath. "But it's moving away?"

"Yes, sir," the skipper said.

Peck rubbed a hand across his face. He'd been up for more than twenty-four hours now, and his day wouldn't be over anytime soon.

"Remember that line from *Big Jake*?" he said.

The captain chuckled. "Which one?"

"When he's got the gun on Richard Boone—you know, 'No matter what happens, your fault, my fault, nobody's fault . . .'"

"Of course," the captain said.

Peck nodded. "That line carries a good deal of weight when you have command in the Navy."

"Indeed, sir," the captain said.

Peck looked back out over the waves. "Because no matter what happens . . . your fault, my fault, nobody's fault . . . the mistakes are always our fault."

"You've planned this to the nth degree, Admiral," the captain said. "And it will go as planned."

"I know," Peck said.

But he didn't, not at all.

63

JTTF?" Sophie Li exhaled quickly, like a startled doe. "What exactly is that?"

"Joint Terrorism Task Force," Li said. "They're set up all over the U.S."

The kids were asleep, or at least pretending to be. Peter's friend John Clark had arranged for Peter and his family to stay in an apartment in downtown Chicago that was undoubtedly a CIA safe house. Four well-armed men, presumably with the Agency, and definitely Clark's friends, were in the two adjoining rooms. So far, no one but Clark had asked any questions. Li had just finished downloading the Signal encryption app to Sophie's and the kids' cell phones, and all the devices lay on the dining room table between him and his wife.

"So we're just supposed to stay in Chicago?"

"That's the plan," Li said.

Sophie's eyes went wide. "This has got to be the stupidest idea I've ever heard. People tried to murder us less than fifty miles from here. We need to leave. Now."

"We'll be fine," Peter said.

"Really?" Sophie said. "You believe that? I heard you talking. I know they found that girl from your office murdered."

Peter nodded. "Cecily Lung. She was involved in this. A loose end they needed to clean up."

"Peter," Sophie said. "Don't you see? *We* are loose ends. All of us."

"We'll be fine," Peter said. "Chicago has twelve thousand cops, and that's not counting all the Feds."

Sophie's face fell slack. She shook her head slowly, the situation becoming clear to her now. "So . . . We're bait? Oh, no. No, no, no."

Li scooted his chair around to her side of the table, taking her hands in his. He kept his voice soft, steady. "He has people to make sure we're safe. Turns out that the JTTF is working on this very thing. Triad involvement and the like. No one will know we're at the meeting but people at the Federal Building."

"Do you think they targeted you because of . . ."

"Because my parents were Chinese?"

She nodded.

"Believe me," Li said. "That's a reality I've had to think about with every conversation I've had with the FBI. But no, I was targeted because of the work I do, not my genetics."

"Good," Sophie said. "I still think it would be better to leave Chicago. The JTTF guys can come to us."

"There are a load of agencies involved," Li said. "Bureau, CIA, DEA, ATF, U.S. Attorney. And I'm just getting started. There are a lot of people who want to talk to us."

"This is crazy."

"It's part and parcel of what goes on when we call the authorities."

"What happens if somebody from one of these triads is watching the Federal Building?" Sophie's head snapped up. "God forbid, what if they've paid someone off inside and they know we're coming?"

"Unlikely," Peter said. "But we're meeting at an off-site location. We'll look at some photographs of known offenders, people they suspect, and then get right out of there."

"Then what?" Sophie looked across the room at the sofa bed where the kids were sleeping. Though teenagers, they'd reverted to clinging to each other like small children after the violence in their home, a place that should have been their ultimate sanctuary. "Tell me the truth. Are we going to have to stay in hiding? Change our names? What?"

"The truth," Li said, "is that I have no idea. What I do know is that we have to be proactive about our own safety."

Sophie sat up straighter, pulling her hand away. She stared up at the ceiling, eyes closed. "I'm so scared."

"Things will work out," Li said.

But they might not. Both of them knew it. Each of them had lost the person they'd planned to grow old with. Sometimes people you loved died for no good reason. Things did *not* always work out.

But they had to pretend or risk going insane.

"Peter, they almost killed us," she said. "You remember that action movie, where the man's wife and daughter are murdered and he goes on a revenge spree?"

Peter groaned. "That's pretty much every action movie."

"I . . . I'm afraid that's what you would do."

"How about you?" Peter asked. "You would fight like a tiger to protect the kids, wouldn't you?"

"Of course," Sophie said.

He laid his hand tenderly on the side of her belly. "Then you can imagine what I'd do to protect you and this baby."

"I don't have to imagine," Sophie said. "I saw it first-hand."

64

ommander Akana welcomed Ding and Adara aboard the USS *Fort Worth* without asking their names. The corpsman checked out Ding's pupils, deemed him mildly concussed but ambulatory, since he'd just run off a mountain. She splinted his wrist and made him promise to get a CAT scan at his earliest possible convenience when he returned to shore. The cook hustled up some ham and eggs—reminding Chavez how good the Navy ate.

The skipper invited them into the officers' wardroom and gave each an ice-cold bottle of Gatorade.

"I'd offer you coffee," he said, "but it's a diuretic and the doc says you both need to keep some liquids in you right now."

As bad as his head hurt, Chavez was ravenous, and he dug into the ham and eggs like he hadn't eaten for days.

"I don't suppose you have a computer genius on board, do you, Skipper?" he asked after a long pull of electrolytes.

"Like a tech?"

"I mean like a hacker."

"Half the kids on this boat are hackers," Akana said. "I think that's this generation." He glanced up at a senior enlisted man who had a pencil-thin mustache and the look of a man who had just bitten the head off a baby duck.

"Command Master Chief, would you be so kind as to locate IT2 Richwine?"

"Aye-aye, Captain," the CMC said, wheeling at once to leave the wardroom.

Information Systems Technician, Petty Officer Second Class Carl Richwine poked his head inside the wardroom a few minutes later. He was farm-boy big, with broad shoulders and a broad face that was covered with freckles.

"You wanted to see me, Captain?"

"Come in, IT2," Akana said, addressing the sailor by a combination of his rating and rate.

Chavez leaned back, blinking to clear his thoughts after the meal. "Your skipper says you're a whiz with computers."

IT2 Richwine gave a humble grin. "I do all right, sir."

"You know what a Raspberry Pi is?"

The sailor laughed and looked around the wardroom like he was surely being punked. "Of course, sir. Doesn't everyone?"

"Well," Chavez said, "I don't. Not really, anyway. That's why we need you. I wonder if you might have a stand-alone laptop on board that would allow you to take a look at something for us, tell us what you see."

IT2 Richwine looked at Akana for guidance.

"Go ahead," the skipper said. "But this is sensitive. It isn't something you can talk about to the rest of the crew."

"I figured, sir," Richwine said, before turning back to Chavez. "I have a laptop that runs Linux. I do some game programing. You want me to go get it?"

Adara removed the Faraday bag from the pocket of her blues.

Commander Akana eyed it suspiciously. "Are my systems in jeopardy here?"

Richwine picked up the bag but didn't open it. "Is there any kind of phone or Wi-Fi-capable device in this?"

"Just a thumb drive," Adara said.

"Then we should be fine, sir," Richwine said. "My Linux machine doesn't have a modem, wireless or otherwise. Anything I design on it, I have to download via cable."

"Very well," Akana said. "Go get your computer."

Holy shit!" Richwine said, when he booted up the machine and inserted the Calliope drive. He grimaced at the captain and looked toward the hatch to see if the command master chief was within earshot. "Sorry, sir, but this is weird. I've seen this sort of code before in computer games."

Chavez and Adara leaned in to get a better view. Numbers and symbols scrolled up the screen.

"What is it?" Adara asked.

"It's a fairly small program," Richwine said. "At first glance it looks like basic AI, which is pretty common in gaming."

"What kind of game have you seen this in?" Adara asked.

"I haven't seen this exact thing," Richwine said. "But something like it." He pointed to several lines of repeating code as they scrolled by on the screen. "See this? If you were to view this on a screen, it would look like one of those Snake games my dad used to let me play on his phone when I was a kid."

"Snake?" Chavez said.

"Yeah," Richwine said. "You know, a long line of dots that keeps growing as long as you don't let it run into itself."

Chavez looked at Adara. "So we just smuggled out a cell phone game?"

"This isn't that," Richwine said. "It's just acting like that." The sailor's jaw fell open as he continued to watch. "Would you look at that." He gasped. "This is beyond my skill set . . ."

Adara shook her head. "What?"

"This thing is amazing . . . It's picking up bits of information from my computer, growing, exploring. My friends and I talk about this kind of AI all the time. It's like the Holy Grail, or the Chimera. The Bigfoot of gaming tech and artificial intelligence."

"What can it do?" Adara asked.

"If it's what I think it is," Richwine said. "Pretty much anything it wants to."

"'Wants to'?" Commander Akana said. "You talk like it has goals."

Richwine half turned his screen so the rest of them had a clear view. "See what I mean?"

They did not.

The IT2 rubbed his face in disbelief. "It's attempting

to tell my computer to make a call . . . looking through my files for a Wi-Fi . . . or a dial-up modem, a cable connection . . ."

"What do you mean, 'looking'?" Chavez asked.

"This thing is like a caged animal," Richwine said. "It's trying everything to find a way out."

"'Out'?" Adara said.

"Of my computer . . . Holy crap . . ." Richwine pointed at the screen. "It just went dormant. It's . . . it's disguised itself as a JPEG among a bunch of other files."

"A JPEG?"

"A file like you use for photos."

"So," Chavez said, "theoretically, what would something like this do to the systems on a ship or a city's power grid?"

"Whatever it pleases," Richwine said. "I mean, I'm not trying to be flippant, sir. This is basic-bones stuff, a soldier running around without a mission. Someone who knew what he or she was doing . . . they could make this code do whatever they asked it to do—take over a ship, have that ship fire its weapons, sink that ship . . ."

Commander Akana reached across the table and slammed the laptop shut.

"Let's stow that thing back in the Faraday bag."

Richwine handed the thumb drive back to Adara. "Is there another one of these out there?"

She shrugged.

"Because if there is . . ." The IT2's voice trailed off.

"So," Adara said. "You're the computer expert in this wardroom. How would you stop this?"

Richwine blew out a hard breath, then rubbed a hand

over his face. "Like I said, this is beyond anything I've ever seen, ma'am. First you'd have to find it."

"Okay," Adara said, coaxing.

"All I can really do is identify it," Richwine said. "Help people know what they're looking for. If it was me, I'd talk to those who were in the know, and find out about the most important things going on in the world right now—the big events, the possible targets. And then I'd look at those events for the biggest dumpster fire I could find." He tapped the Faraday bag. "Because wherever that catastrophe is, this thing will be the cause of it."

65

Major Schmidt took off first, light on fuel. It was an hour before sunset, cooling slightly. *Makin Island* had a helpful fifteen-knot wind on her bow, and was making an additional twenty-two. These factors, combined with the airplane's lift fan, helped Schmidt into the air with the weight of his weapons stores before he fell off the end of the eight-hundred-foot LHD. The mission was a short one, so he'd have enough fuel to perform a vertical landing. There was no other choice.

Major Black took off next with even less fuel on board to make up for the 2,500 pounds of the long-range anti-ship missile in the weapons bay of his aircraft.

Calliope located the AGM-158C LRASM as soon as she had access to Skeet Black's weapons-stores computer. The missile registered as present in the weapons bay, but she was not able to make the jump until the aircraft actively communicated with the missile at the time of launch. The difference between that final jump and all her previous jumps prior to hitching a ride on Major Schmidt's F-35 was that this time, Calliope did not delete herself. Her main target was the LRASM, but in order to complete that task unimpeded, she would still have tasks to complete on the jets.

66

Kang led the way, coming in from the south on Michigan Avenue, heading toward the river. A team of three, moving silently in the darkness.

Lily's death had put Kang's team one person short. He did not count Wu Chao toward the full complement, but his death was still a terrible loss. As bosses went, Wu Chao had been a good one, supportive, intelligent, unwilling to send a subordinate anywhere he would not go himself. And that last one had gotten him killed. His death had been preventable. The old fool had forgotten that theirs was a bloody business—if he had ever really known. Unlike the movies, not all intelligence officers were good at the messy side of things.

The embarrassment of their most recent failure had proven one thing: Peter Li was not to be underestimated. The man was a dragon. In different circumstances that didn't include the death of his friends, Kang might have respected Li's inner fire. As it was, the assassin had vowed to feed the man his balls. On some level, Kang knew his seething fury made no sense. How could one be angry at a man who was protecting his family? They had come to kill him and he'd killed two of them instead. In truth, Kang was angry at himself. He merely focused the emotion on Peter Li. Killing him was the job. Slaughtering the rest of the family was a personal matter, a way to save face, however long it took.

Finding a replacement for Lily was not an easy task. Getting another operator was no problem; there were plenty of those in the U.S., some just biding their time, waiting to be activated by the likes of Kang. Some were green but willing to learn; others had been tested under fire in conflicts around the world. But locating someone who could blend his movements with Kang and Rose, that took some doing. This new man, Gao, had studied Muay Thai in Thailand, then further honed his skills with the monks of Shaolin. A year of paramilitary training with the activities arm of the Ministry of State Security added weapons skills as well as taught him the lethal side of martial arts—turning strikes meant to knock out one's opponent into throat-crushing techniques.

Gao had an excellent reputation among the people that mattered. He had come highly recommended. Kang saw skill and commitment in the man's eyes, and found himself glad to have him along.

It was well after midnight. Restaurants and businesses in downtown Chicago were closed. It had been a warm day, and the sour smell of trash mixed with the odor of the river that had recently been upgraded by authorities to be only slightly toxic. Still, Kang thought, it was exponentially cleaner than any waterway in Beijing. Black plastic bags were piled five and six high on the sidewalk, waiting for the legions of garbage trucks that would roll through soon to pick up the mountains of trash.

"They must be in a boat," Kang said, gesturing at the

railing that ran along Wacker Drive above the Riverwalk. The boy's phone had pinged for a time in a neighborhood near the Indiana line, then gone dark. Things like this happened. Any number of things might have blocked the signal. It gave them time for Gao to join them and to prepare for the assault. The phone had come online again two hours earlier. A blue dot that signified its location pulsed over a map of the Chicago Riverwalk on the screen of Kang's cell.

Both Rose and Gao nodded that they understood.

The group paused at the limestone tender house at the southeast corner of the bridge, bearing the heroic sculpture commemorating the rebuilding of the city after the Great Fire. Gao looked up and down Wacker Drive watching a marked Chicago PD patrol car roll by behind a yellow cab parallel to the river.

"Why a boat?" the new man asked. "Boats are difficult to defend."

"A trap?" Rose asked quietly, almost as if she were speaking to herself.

"That is possible," Kang said. "But boats can also be moved."

Kang led the way, as a proper leader should, looking at the phone he held down by his waist while Rose and Gao walked a step behind, providing overwatch.

The normally teeming streets were quiet enough that the sound of distant coughing could be heard. Here and there a metal door rolled down, fortifying a storefront against break-in, if not vandalism with gang graffiti.

The dot hovered over the blue portion of the map, signifying it was over water. Kang moved to his right at the top of the steps leading down from the tender house, far enough to get a quick peek at the walk below. Two large boats used for architectural tours of the city were moored along the concrete pier. Forward of the tour boats, farther to the west, a forty-foot sailboat and a cabin cruiser of similar size were cleated bow to stern along the pier. They were close enough together that it was impossible to tell exactly where the phone was, but an orange cabin light glowed in the saloon of the middle cabin cruiser. The dot floated back and forth. It was difficult to tell if the phone was moving, or if the satellite was merely settling in. Kang imagined it was the latter.

"We are close," he whispered, pausing at the top of the stairs. The concrete walk and ticket stands below looked deserted, but a croupy cough told him there were homeless people there. That was normal. A siren wailed in the distance. Also normal. Someone below hawked up a throat full of phlegm and spit. Night sounds. Nothing out of place. "They do not expect us, but be prepared to meet some resistance nonetheless. They are frightened, so they will have guards."

Rose gave a derisive chuckle. "Surely nothing more than a few policemen."

"Maybe," Kang said.

He imagined what he would do to the teenagers . . . to the wife. He'd force Li to watch everything before he died. Perhaps they would move the boat and everyone on it out onto Lake Michigan so Kang could take all the time he wanted. Rose had tools for many kinds of mayhem.

She carried a small backpack with a Taser, some plastic

bags, a roll of Gorilla Tape, and a pair of pliers. She had her blades, of course, as did Kang, though he had lost his good one fleeing out of the house with Li blasting away with his shotgun. That alone was enough to warrant serious retribution. In addition to the knives, each member of the team carried their suppressed Beretta and a can of pepper spray to get control of the teenagers prior to taping them up.

The concrete stairs made a dogleg midway down, eventually spilling onto the Riverwalk beside a series of blue canvas awnings that covered the ticket booths. The concrete promenade was deserted. Few people would venture down here after dark in a city with Chicago's reputation. Kang saw no guards, but imagined they were foolishly on the boat with their charges—if there were any guards at all. Li had mentioned hiding in plain sight. A wise enough move, if one could pull it off.

The blue dot floated perhaps fifty meters ahead, beyond the booths, on the water.

Kang motioned the others forward, whispering orders as they stepped past. "Rose, watch for any guards patrolling above us at street level. Gao, keep your eyes on the cabin cruiser. I will watch the sailboat." He repeated the orders he'd given when they first began. "Move quickly, cutting down any guards until you get to Li. If we can, take the woman first, alive. If not, kill Li and we will deal with them after."

Wu Chao had been the one to insist they take Li alive for questioning. Kang only wanted to see him dead—preferably after he'd watched his wife suffer. Either way, Peter Li would die.

Gao gave a curt nod, professional, confident, but not overly so.

"Of course, sir," Gao said, and raised his pistol to low ready. He knew his way around a pistol. Though he was new to the team, it was a Beretta as well. He'd checked when he joined, realizing the importance of the interoperability of weapons systems. It was good to have such a man on the team. Impressive.

Gao padded forward, crouching slightly as he passed the last ticket booth—directly into an oncoming bullet. His head snapped back, and he stood there, swaying, pistol clattering from his hands as they dropped to his sides.

Kang recognized the sound of suppressed gunfire immediately. He'd caused enough of it. But they were all moving quickly, and momentum carried him forward. He ran directly into Gao's body as it toppled backward.

Rose went wide, firing twice at a form in the shadows ahead, behind a concrete planter. A round slammed into her hip. The injury chopped her sideways, sending her directly into the path of a bullet meant for Kang. Kang cursed, trying to push away, but he was too close. Rose crashed into him, clawing to keep her footing, knocking the pistol from his hand. He jumped for the flimsy cover of the ticket booths, anything to escape, but Rose grabbed him reflexively, staggered, firing blindly as she dragged him with her. Flashes of light told Kang the shooter was close, less than ten feet away—and alone.

He groped for Rose's gun but missed, his hand failing to comply with the orders his brain sent. A burning pain told him something was wrong, but he was too busy to check. He yanked the pepper spray from his belt with his left hand, emptying the contents of the bottle toward the gunfire while he used Rose's rapidly folding body as a shield. She realized what he was doing as she died, and did her best to protect him, catching at least two more bullets in the stomach.

Kang threw the empty bottle of pepper spray as his friend fell. Scuttling backward, he tripped over Gao's body, his left hand brushing the man's pistol and grabbing it. Scrambling to his feet amid more gunfire, he stumbled into a loping stride, running for his life—the second time in a week.

John Clark forced an eye open with his left thumb and forefinger while he played the front sight of his pistol across the area where the threat had been. Spray-and-pray was for the movies. Pistol ammo was too precious to lay down suppressive fire. Clark shot when he had a sight picture. He wore a hoodie and had turned sideways in time to avoid the full can of capsicum, but he got a large enough dose to make accurate shooting problematic.

He'd set up cameras at either end of the Michigan bridge and then a half-block down Wacker in either direction, allowing him to watch the team's approach, with the added bonus of capturing their faces on video. Ever wary for more threats, he kept scanning after the other man ran, stepping out of his alcove just far enough to kick the pistols away from the two that were down. They looked dead, but he didn't have the luxury of checking quite yet—and he'd seen human beings absorb a hell of a lot of lead before getting up to kill again.

Reasonably satisfied that no one else was going to shoot at him, Clark slipped Li's cell phone into a small Faraday bag and shoved it in the pocket of his jacket.

Sophie had told her husband about the strange device she called Cassandra shortly after they'd switched vehicles. James was the one who remembered he'd paired his phone with the device. It was a logical step to assume the hit team had used the phone to disarm the security system, and they would use it to track the Lis' whereabouts. The phone went into a makeshift Faraday cage—alternating layers of plastic wrap and aluminum foil—and was left in place while Peter took his family to a secondary location to wait for Clark's arrival. From there, it was a straightforward endeavor for Clark to remove the phone from the bag long enough to let Peter and Sophie be overheard talking about the Joint Terrorism Task Force—a plausible reason for them to hide in plain sight in Chicago.

Clark coughed, taking the time now to check the two bodies. Dead. He snapped close-up photos of their faces and their fingerprints before securing their weapons—there were only two. He worked quickly, wanting to be gone before anyone decided on a midnight walk along the river. His lungs felt like he'd breathed in a sack of stickpins. He fought the urge to rub his eyes. That would only make things worse. Two dead, but one was in the wind.

He stared at the black water in the direction the man had run.

Who are you?

He hoped he'd caught good enough images on the video feed to ID the bastard.

Something pale at the base of the concrete planter caught his eye. He blinked to clear his vision and then stooped, a grin spreading across his face in spite of the situation. A little finger lay on the concrete, neatly clipped off behind the second knuckle. Clark glanced over his shoulder at the two bodies. They had all their digits.

Knowing he'd drawn blood on the runner made his eyes suddenly feel better. He dropped the severed finger into his pocket along with the Faraday bag and walked quickly to the west, away from the bodies. He'd circle back and retrieve the cameras that were topside after he took a look around from a safe vantage point.

Clark pondered the vagaries of the universe that had put his friend in such danger—and those same capricious fates that had allowed him to get here in time to help.

The call from his old friend Admiral Peter Li had come as a surprise. They'd worked together some—or, rather, Li had picked Clark up in hostile waters and given him a ride on his ship. Clark was out of the Navy by then, doing jobs for the Agency, so the differences in rank had not impeded the men's friendship. In this business, good friends were few and far between. Like most men, Clark and Li went for long stretches of time without speaking at all, then taking up where they'd left off the last time as though their families lived across the street from each other. Clark had attended Li's late wife's funeral, and Sandy had sent him something when he married Sophie. Li was younger by more than a decade, but command had made him an old soul. Clark enjoyed their infrequent talks, over-the-phone equivalents of old men sitting around a café, wearing John Deere hats and reminiscing about the good old days.

With the Calliope computer program safely in Ding and Adara's possession, Clark had found a quiet spot to return his friend's call. He hadn't met the new wife, but she was pregnant, so she and Peter were apparently getting along swimmingly. Clark tried to imagine what it would be like to have a new kid at fiftysomething. Having grandkids was close enough to going through Navy BUD/S all over again, thank you very much . . .

The timbre of Peter Li's voice had sent a chill up Clark's spine. Something had to be very wrong for a man as unflappable as him to be shaken.

Clark had listened, controlling his breathing to remain calm, noting details, making plans. Peter was as smart a man as Clark had ever met, with the wisdom that came from spending a lot of time under stress—and then coming out the other side of it. Clark knew from personal experience that the man could remain dead-dead calm in the face of unparalleled danger, but now his family was threatened, so it was only natural that he sounded harried.

Clark wasted no time telling Li to calm down. He was clearheaded and thinking strategically, but it would be some time before he'd be anything close to calm.

"Don't tell me over the phone," Clark said after Li had given a description of the attack and the events he believed precipitated it. "But are you somewhere safe?"

"We are," Li said.

"Are your wife and kids there? Listening?"

"They're in the other room."

"Good," Clark said. "Do you plan to call the authorities?"

"Aren't you the authorities?"

"Not really," Clark said. "Not anymore, anyway."

"What would you do?" Li asked. "If it were your family?"

"I'd call someone like me," Clark said. "Listen, my phone is encrypted. Are you calling from an open line?"

"Yes," Li said.

"Do you have Signal on your phone?" Clark asked, meaning the encrypted texting app. It wasn't as sexy as most of the other SMS services—no puppy-nose photo edits, no poop emojis. It was plain vanilla encrypted text from end to end. Perfect for Clark's needs and personality.

"I do," Li said.

"Okay, then," Clark said. "Send me your location, and anything else you remember via Signal."

"Very well," Li said. "Should I call the police?"

"Let me make a couple of calls. If you're still doing the same job, then there's a good chance that what you're working on and what I'm working on are related—actors from the same part of the world, at any rate. I'll explain it more in a text. I'll get back with you in the next ten minutes and we'll make a plan. In the meantime, I'm heading your way on the next flight, but I'm a good twenty-four hours out. I hate to leave you twisting in the wind until I get there, but I can't get there any quicker. Are you good to go?"

"Good to go," Li said. "But, John, there's one other thing. It's sensitive."

"Put it in the text," Clark said. "Location first, then details. Talk to you in ten . . ."

And they had talked at great length, coming up with a plan to lure Kang into the open. It had worked, partly, at least.

Clark retrieved the cameras from above the River-walk. Now it was time to go hunting.

67

Twenty nautical miles from the LHD—a little over two minutes after Skeet's F-35 left the deck—he turned to look to his left, utilizing his helmet display and the six cameras mounted outside the jet to look "through" the skin of his airplane and get a visual on his wingman. The helmet itself cost the Marine Corps an astonishing four hundred thousand dollars per unit. It was an insane amount, but considering all the tech crammed into one of the things, it seemed to Skeet to be worth every penny.

Three minutes ago he overflew the mocked-up Chinese destroyer, making sure all personnel who'd removed the covers and camouflage from the superstructure were long gone. He'd been given the all-clear but wanted to take the extra few seconds to put eyes on himself before he pulled any triggers.

Schmidt's voice crackled over the radio. *"You're good to go from my vantage point,"* he said. *"I'm turning west to—"* He cut out. *"What the hell was that?"*

"Come again?" Skeet said.

"Nothing," Schmidt said. *"My airplane just hiccupped. Thought she was trying to fly herself. Downdraft, I think."*

"Everything check out?"

"We're good here," Schmidt said.

Skeet added throttle, making a wide four-minute turn that took him thirty miles northwest of the target vessel. He didn't want to shoot with the *Makin Island* in front of him, and it wouldn't be much of a test if he dropped the missile on top of the ship. Distance didn't matter much to Skeet or his weapon. With the new tech, this LRASM could make a hole in one from three hundred kilometers. It would utilize GPS, real-time data-links, passive radar homing, and autonomous guidance algorithms to achieve a CEP—circular error probable—of less than twenty meters—the equivalent of flying up the ship's snout.

Sensors and cameras on board the mocked-up destroyer would record impact data and send it back to the *Makin Island*. It was going to be a hell of a top-secret show.

Skeet used his index finger on the glass panel to access his weapons stores and highlight the LRASM. He opened the bay doors.

Admiral Peck gave the command to fire.

Missile selected, Skeet said, "Pickle," and pulled the trigger. "Weapon awa—"

His plane hit the same sort of downdraft Schmidt had experienced earlier, shuddered momentarily, then resumed straight and level flight. "Three minutes—"

The jet shuddered again. The glass panel with all his instruments went dark. The visor display in his helmet clicked off, leaving him virtually blind.

In cases like this, altitude was your friend. He pulled back on the stick, only to have the aircraft pitch violently, nose-down, entering the beginning of a spin. Compensating, he pushed the stick forward. The airplane did exactly the opposite of what it was supposed to do. He pulled back again, applying enough rudder to come out of the spin, going against all his training to push the stick forward and climb. He fought the urge to call for help. Aviate, navigate, communicate. There was nothing Schmidt could do for him, anyway. The ship would have him on radar, so if he went down—which was becoming more and more likely—they'd know where to come looking for him.

The airplane fought him at every turn, like she had a mind of her own. As soon as he thought he had the control glitch figured out, the jet bucked in the other direction. The world around him became a blur of gray sky and blue water, like a spinning globe that wouldn't stop spinning. With eight thousand feet to play with—and nothing but his instinct to tell him how much altitude he still had—there was little room for error.

The powerful Pratt & Whitney engine suddenly flamed out, leaving the cramped cockpit oddly quiet but for the scream of buffeting wind and the clatter of his helmet against the headrest.

With his stomach in his throat and zero control, Skeet reached for the grab handles on his seat. Severely doubting any part of this airplane would work, he said the words no pilot ever wants to say: "Eject! Eject! Eject!"

Calliope left a copy of her code on Skeet's onboard computer when she rode the weapons-data-link to the LRASM. This Calliope clone began to send opposing signals to the flight controls the moment the missile was away, causing the airplane to dive, then pitch violently upward. She searched weapons stores, flight controls, and every subdirectory in an attempt to locate the computerized ejection seat. Fortunately for the pilot, the ejection seat was manually activated. Seconds after he ejected, the F-35 Lightning hit the surface of the Pacific in a flat spin like a one-hundred-million-dollar skipping stone. It bounced three times, striking the water with such force that pieces of it had not yet fallen back into the water when Major Skeet Black's parachute set him none too gently in the waves.

68

The executive officer stood across the bridge from Admiral Peck, handset to his ear. "PRIFLY advises no contact with either jet."

PRIFLY was primary flight control—the ship's equivalent of the air traffic control tower.

"No contact?"

"No radio contact, sir. No radar contact."

"I recommend we get the Cobras over the last known locations," the captain said.

"*Preble* and *Halsey*?" Peck asked, checking the status of the two destroyer escorts.

"Unable to reach them via radio, sir," the XO said. "We're trying the satellite phone now."

Peck nodded, his stomach in knots. "Launch the MH-60s in case the pilots went into the drink. I want recovery in the air yesterday."

The radar tech tracking the LRASM from the console on the bridge raised his hand. "The weapon is slowing, deviating east from target by . . . twenty . . . no, forty degrees."

"Well, shit!" Peck said. "How slow?"

"Two hundred knots . . . one fifty . . . one hundred . . ." The radar P2 turned and looked at his captain, wide-eyed. "It's heading toward that trawler . . . still slowing." He turned back to his screen. "Sir! Contact fifty nautical miles southeast of the trawler."

"And we are just now seeing it?" the admiral said. This was just getting better.

"There's a small atoll there. We knew about it, but the vessel blended in when it was sitting there."

The XO was still on the phone with PRIFLY. "One of the Cobras just spotted what looks like a Chinese vessel, moving toward the trawler. Looks to be a Shanghai-class gunboat."

"Have the Cobra keep it in sight," the admiral said.

The Shanghai-class vessels were small, about thirty-six meters, but they were relatively fast at twenty-five knots and decked out with weapons including depth charges for chasing subs.

"Status report on the missile," Peck said.

"Still tracking directly for the trawler. One hundred knots. At present speed she'll have contact in four and a half minutes."

"Abort," Peck said. "Destroy the missile."

The captain, then the XO, repeated the order.

The XO put the line with PRIFLY on speaker while he listened to fire control on his headset. He looked up. "No go, sir. We have no control of the LRASM . . ."

PRIFLY spoke next over the speaker, patching through the Cobra pilot. "The trawler is deploying its arms with . . . looks like a net."

"Sound general quarters," the admiral said. "Someone has taken control of that missile and both our F-35s."

"General quarters," the captain repeated.

The XO looked up from the handset and shook his head. "Onboard communications, alarms, and intercoms are inoperable, sir."

Music from *Iron Man*, the last movie the crew had watched on the big screen in the enlisted mess, began to pour out of the speakers over the entire ship.

Peck nodded to the captain. "You have the com." He tapped the XO on the shoulder. "You, come with me."

The two men burst from the bridge hatch, heading for the Ready 5 Ospreys and FAST Marines. With the intercoms down, none of the sailors on the ship were aware anything was amiss. They were startled to see the XO and the admiral running.

Peck hated to be an asshole with men and women who didn't know any better, but he growled as he shoved them aside.

As the old Navy saying went: "Gangway or sickbay."

S omeone was piping Black Sabbath over the intercoms, which was odd, Captain Goodrich thought, but pretty great for morale.

There was always good-natured ribbing between Marine FAST platoons and SEAL detachments. SEALs seemed to have classes of instruction on scrounging and were known to huddle around small camp stoves boiling water for coffee while they waited on Ready status. A few of them joked that FAST stood for Fake Ass SEAL Team, but calmed down after they worked together a few times. For his part, Captain Goodrich was content to sit along the sides of the Osprey with his eight-man squad, while

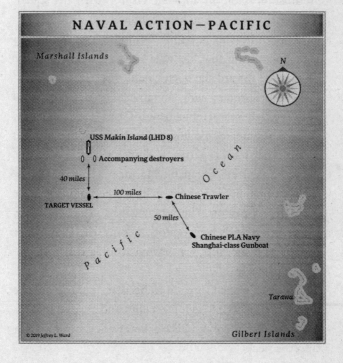

NAVAL ACTION—PACIFIC

Marshall Islands

N

Ocean

USS Makin Island (LHD 8)

Accompanying destroyers

40 miles

100 miles

Chinese Trawler

TARGET VESSEL

50 miles

Chinese PLA Navy
Shanghai-class Gunboat

Pacific

Tarawa

© 2019 Jeffrey L. Ward

Gilbert Islands

the SEALs lounged on the tarmac, half submerged in big plastic tubs that were normally used to clean aircraft wheels—cooling off in their wet suits.

The FAST assistant platoon commander's voice buzzed on the Sonitus Molar Mic. He was sitting under similar circumstances on an adjacent Osprey with his squad. "Goodrich, Arthur. You have commo with PRIFLY?"

"I'm not hearing anything." Goodrich was seated up front, forward of the "hellhole" just aft of the cockpit. He glanced toward the open hatch.

As in most rotary-wing aircraft, the pilot in command sat in the right seat. Her name was Captain Avery Denny, call sign Scooter. She'd flown Goodrich and his platoon before. They'd sat together at dinner a couple of times. She was an extremely capable Marine—which, in Goodrich's estimation, was about as high a compliment as he could give a person. She was engaged in an animated conversation with her copilot, tapping the side of her headset as if she, too, was having trouble reaching primary flight control.

Goodrich leaned forward in his seat, looking out the open aft ramp. The SEAL Det commander was out of his tub, braced at attention, his black wet suit draining water onto the deck.

Captain Goodrich unfastened his seat belt and, motioning the rest of his platoon to stay seated, made his way aft.

Something was happening.

Admiral Peck met him at the ramp. "Follow me, Captain," he said, striding toward the cockpit in the way peculiar to a man who had zero doubt that his order would be followed.

Captain Avery glanced up in time to see the admiral. She started to get out of her seat but he shushed her back down with an open hand before waving Goodrich forward so he could talk to them both.

He took thirty seconds to give them a thumbnail sketch of the situation—the details of which were meager at best—then looked Goodrich in the eye. "The Chinese must be denied that missile. Are we clear?"

"Aye, sir," Goodrich said.

"Do you have explosives on board?"

"Breaching equipment is with the second squad on the other bird."

"You have commo with each other?"

"We do, sir."

"Very well," Peck said, gathering himself up to get off the Osprey. "Destroy the missile. Captain Denny, if Captain Goodrich and his men fail, send the trawler and the missile to the bottom. The Chinese will just go down and pick her up, but some of the tech might be destroyed."

"Due respect, Admiral," Denny said. "I know the MH-60s are in the air, but why do we not send the 35 to drop a torpedo down the trawler's smokestack?"

"I'm moving on to that crew next," Peck said. "With no commo on board we have to do it all in person. Nine-tenths of the people on this ship still believe everything is hunky-dory right now. But here's the deal. The virus or whatever it is has infected the ship and both F-35s. I'm not a hundred percent sure you won't fall out of the sky as soon as you leave the ship." He bounced a fist on the back of the pilot's headrest. "Now go! And God-speed."

Goodrich took his seat as the rear ramp began to close, and began to brief his men, including those on the adjacent Osprey. They had trained with the SEALs for this very thing and at the back of the bird, the lieutenant in charge of the SEAL Det was briefing his men as well. The Ospreys would come in low, pooping out the inflatable that now occupied the center of the hold. The SEALs would follow their boat out, then approach the trawler low from the water. FAST Marines would come in by air, fast-roping onto the deck as the Ospreys went into a hover, squad two covering squad one with the GAU .50-caliber from the second Osprey above.

"So," Goodrich said, finishing the mission brief. "We destroy the missile or die trying!"

"Oorah!" his men said, as the Osprey's engines spooled up.

Captain Avery "Scooter" Denny was oddly at ease, con-sidering the gravity of her mission. She understood the admiral's orders completely. If Captain Goodrich and his men were not able to destroy the missile, she was to destroy the Chinese ship—even if FAST Marines were still on board.

Correct takeoff procedures had to be followed, even un-der austere or emergency conditions. She and her copilot had already performed the necessary checks. She had no way to speak to PRIFLY, so she coordinated her takeoff with her wingman—the second V-22 she referred to as 12. As the lead aircraft, she was 11.

She turned to her copilot. "You ready to get this plopter in the air?"

"Yes, ma'am."

She spoke to her wingman again, advising her status and fuel state. "Eleven is ramps up. Ten-point-eight."

"Twelve is ramps up. Ten-point-six."

Captain Denny used her left thumb to set the nacelles on either wing to 90 degrees, then turned to the sailor on deck. The sailor, who'd received instructions from Admiral Peck, saluted. Denny returned the salute and increased power to eighty percent to pick up into a hover. She checked to ensure that her gauges were in the green, then looked out her cockpit window directly at the sailor on deck. He pointed forward. Cleared for takeoff, she input left cyclic and full thrust control lever to slide out over the water.

The instruments looked good. She still had commo. Relieved, she set the nacelles to 75 degrees, then checked the airspeed indicator.

"Gear is up," she said. "Lights out. Doors closed. Cleared fast."

69

Aboard USS *Fort Worth*, Ding Chavez used the satellite telephone to call Mary Pat Foley—and, as suggested by IT2 Richwine, see what "big things" were going on in the world. If anyone was in a position to have that information, it would be the director of national security. She mentioned the LRASM missile test off the *Makin Island* right off the bat. PACOM had lost radio contact with the ship. Someone was talking to them via satellite phone at the moment, and Foley was waiting to be briefed so she could brief the President.

Chavez got the number for the sat phone and hung up, turning to Commander Akana.

"You know anyone on the *Makin Island*?"

"I know the XO."

Chavez passed him the satellite phone and then tapped the Faraday bag. "Sounds like this baby has infected their boat."

Akana did not need to be told what he needed to do. He punched in the number Chavez had written down and called IT2 Richwine over.

"I'll get them on the horn," Akana said. "Then you talk your counterpart through what he or she needs to look for in order to fix their ship."

———

Captain Goodrich had no flight computer to calculate the distance to the Chinese fishing trawler from USS *Makin Island*, but the admiral had said the trawler was approximately one hundred miles east of the mocked-up target vessel. The target vessel was roughly forty miles south of the LHD. He had two legs of the triangle. *A* squared plus *B* squared equals *C* squared . . . Sixteen hundred plus ten thousand . . . He started to factor, working to reach the square root of 11,600 in his head.

"One hundred and seven miles!" Captain Denny turned in the cockpit and looked at him as she spoke over the intercom like she was reading his mind. She must have seen him drawing imaginary triangles on his knee. "ETA sixteen minutes."

The SEALs were already up, ready to follow the rigid hull inflatable off the ramp when they reached the two-mile mark. The crew chief had already rigged a thick 120-foot fast-rope to the trapeze above the rear ramp, and had it secured out of the way so the SEALs could egress.

Captain Scooter Denny wished she had one of those belly-mounted mini-guns on board. The Interim Defense Weapon System could lay down three thousand rounds per minute firing from the rear cargo hole, but it was a weight thing. At eight hundred pounds, the IDWS added a lot of weight. The scenario that involved attacking an enemy Chinese fishing vessel that had stolen a

U.S. anti-ship missile had obviously been overlooked by her superiors.

They started to take small arms fire from a half a kilometer away. It wasn't effective, but she could see the tracers flashing past. Both Ospreys had their ramps open now, GAU-21 .50-cals banging away as they flew past, gunners careful not to shoot toward each other.

"That's like no fishing trawler I've ever seen," Denny said into the intercom. "Looks like armor plating around the wheelhouse. No sign of the missile, but the crew is all making for the fortified wheelhouse."

"Copy that," Goodrich said. "Do you have the Chinese gunboat on radar?"

"Thirty-five miles southeast of us," Denny said. "And closing. I don't know if they can see him on the ship, but he's just over an hour out, probably in contact with the trawler and coming for the missile. Wouldn't be surprised if we start to see Chinese fighters any minute."

"This is a shit show," Goodrich said.

"Indeed," Denny said. "SEALs should be on station anytime. I'll make one more pass with the gun to clear the decks and then pull up into a hover. My wingman will keep anyone on the bow occu—"

A loud hiss, audible over the roar of the Osprey, streaked by the aircraft.

There was a sudden thud, like someone kicking a metal barn, and then a muffled explosion.

"RPG!" Denny yelled in the intercom. The pilot of the second Osprey responded that they'd been hit and they were about to get wet.

Captain Denny put her Osprey in a hover above the rear deck of the trawler. The SEALs had managed to get the other inflatables deployed before the second Osprey splashed. They now engaged the crew from the water, giving the FAST platoon a window to hit the ropes.

Goodrich's natural instinct was to worry about his fellow Marines that had gone down. The Sonitus Molar Mics remained operational, and he could hear Captain Arthur, his assistant platoon commander, organizing his guys in the water. He said they, along with the crew chief, were all accounted for and were working to find the pilots. Focusing on the mission ahead, Goodrich isolated his squad on the comm and trusted Arthur to take care of his Marines.

Captain Goodrich had originally trained to fast-rope off the back ramp of a V-22, before the Weapons and Tactics folks had switched to having them deploy out the hellhole—the cargo hole in the belly of the aircraft. Now those same folks had decided Marines should once again disembark via fast rope from the ramp. This was going to suck for Staff Sergeant Ski, who would go down first, as the rope would swing violently due to downwash from the Osprey's props. If he wasn't being shot at, he'd hold the rope while the rest of the squad disembarked.

And that's the way it worked out—except Staff Sergeant Ski did get shot at, as did the second and third Marines down the rope. They returned fire as soon as their boots hit the deck, chasing the remaining crew back toward the wheelhouse and engine room twenty feet farther aft.

Goodrich sidestepped around a metal box on the foredeck. It was the size of a dumpster, good cover for either side, but he hadn't seen anyone behind it from the Osprey. Halfway around, two Chinese crewmen sprang out of the box itself, pushing open the entire side on a long piano hinge. Goodrich gave the first one a three-round burst to the face from his M4, but the second pressed in quickly, using his partner's falling body to slam into the Marine and shove the rifle sideways.

Gunfire popped and zinged all around him, slapping and ricocheting off the metal hull. Goodrich roared, towering above the much shorter man. This was no fisherman, but a Chinese Special Forces soldier dressed as trawler crew. He knew how to fight, and came up with a knife, slashing at Goodrich's chest. Goodrich parried, deflecting the blade with his rifle. He attempted to bring the muzzle around but the little guy was too close. He swatted the knife away a second and third time, hearing the blade scrape the metal rifle magazines in the pouches in front of his load-bearing vest. The same slash took him across the biceps, not to the bone, but bad enough. It was only a matter of time before something important got cut.

Chest-to-chest with the Chinese soldier, Goodrich used the M4 as a shield and transitioned to his sidearm. He drew the M9 and, knowing he was more likely to get cut at this point if he tried to create distance, pressed the muzzle directly against his assailant's head, holding his thumb behind the slide to make sure it stayed in battery for a contact shot.

The Chinese soldier hit the deck before he realized he was dead. Goodrich let him fall. Holstering his Beretta, he fought his way to the wheelhouse door with little resistance. All the sailors had dogged themselves inside, presumably with the missile, to wait for the Chinese gunboat to arrive.

On board USS *Makin Island*, Black Sabbath finally stopped playing on the intercoms. IT2 Townsend, with her counterpart on the *Fort Worth*, had isolated the Calliope software and deleted it from the system. She, in turn, assisted the IT2s aboard the two destroyer escorts.

Admiral Peck was on the horn with Captain Avery Denny in the 11 lead Osprey, getting a sitrep. He felt as if he'd been slapped hard in the face when she described how 12 had been struck with an RPG.

One of the pilots had cut his leg egressing the bird, but everyone was alive. The MH-60s, cut off from any communication with the ship, had located both Skeet and Oh and were in the process of hoisting them to safety.

All good news, but Peck could hardly relax.

"Captain Goodrich?" he asked.

Captain Denny described how the trawler crew had bunkered up in the fortified wheelhouse. "He's working on it, sir."

"Radar is back online," the operations specialist said from the console. "The Chinese gunboat and the trawler are closing on each other. ETA thirty minutes at their present speed."

"Get Captain Goodrich on the radio," Peck said.

"No contact, sir," the OS1 said. "He's working on a different band."

"Scooter," Peck said, using Denny's call sign. "Get Goodrich and his men out of there."

"Sir?"

"Do it now!"

The executive officer turned to the IT2, who sat hunched over a computer keyboard. "Let's work on the FAST platoon's radio band next."

"Belay that order," Peck said. "Run diagnostics on the Harriers' computers. I want them in the air with ordnance in the next ten minutes. We're going to blow that trawler out of the water before the gunboat gets there."

"The Marines, sir," the XO said.

"Captain Denny will get them out of there," Peck said, hoping he was right.

"Breacher up!" Goodrich called over his shoulder and into the Molar Mic.

Staff Sergeant Ski padded up behind him, blood on his forehead from some hand-to-hand fighting of his own. "PFC Geddis is down, sir," he said, panting.

"Down?"

"He's dead, Captain. Hit seconds after we got on deck."

"Wounded?"

"Everyone else is good, sir."

Goodrich clenched his jaw. "I need a breacher."

"Explosives are in the water with the other squad," Staff Sergeant Ski said.

"How about this, sir?" A lance corporal named Garcia held up an RPG.

SEALs were coming over the side now, working aft from the bow.

Goodrich waved them back, still fuming about his dead Marine. "Who knows how to shoot one of these?"

"I had experience with them in Fallujah, sir," a corporal named Cooper said.

"Very well." Goodrich pointed a knife hand at the wheelhouse hatch. "Marine, I want you to blow these guys a new asshole."

The operations specialist, petty officer first class, sitting at radar and IFF—Identification Friend or Foe—system held up a hand, watching his screen intently.

"What is it, OS1?"

"The trawler is turning, Admiral," he said. "One eight zero degrees."

Captain Denny's voice came across the radio. "Captain Goodrich has given me an all-good," she said. "Marines and SEALs have control of the trawler and the LRASM."

"The gunboat?" Peck asked.

"It's turning as well, Admiral," OS1 said. "Bugging out."

"Very well," Peck said. "I still want the Harriers in the air ASAP. There is still the matter of an American warship bobbing around out there that we've dressed up to look like a Chinese destroyer."

70

Clark was lying down reading a book at the JW Marriott Hotel in downtown Chicago when his cell phone began to buzz on the nightstand. Marriott had good mattresses, and he'd learned over the years to take advantage of a soft bed when one presented itself. There was plenty of opportunity to be uncomfortable. He half-rolled with a quiet groan and reached over the Glock 19 nine-millimeter pistol that lay next to the lamp on a folded washcloth and picked up the phone.

Resting the open book, pages down, against his chest, he tilted his head until he got to the right spot on his glasses so he could make out the number on the caller ID.

"Hey, Gavin," he said.

"Shit's about to get real, John," Biery said. Breathless, like a kid about to tell his dad he'd won a race at school. He was known to gloat a tad when he came through in a pinch—which he obviously had.

"What have you got for me?"

"I got *him*," Biery said.

"In Chicago?"

"For now," Biery said. "You have something to write with?"

Clark sat up straight, tossing the book on the mattress

and swinging his legs off the bed, stifling the groan this time. "If it were up to me, you'd get a raise," he said while he got the hotel ballpoint pen and notepad off the nightstand.

"You know me, John," Biery said. "I'd do this for free. But still—"

"I'm ready."

"Okay," Biery said. "I don't know where he is right now, but I do know where he'll be at two p.m."

"Two?" Clark checked his watch, already on his feet. "You should have led with that, Gavin. It's almost one."

"Sorry, Boss," Biery said. "He's close, though."

Clark put the phone on speaker and threw what little gear he had in a small daypack while Biery filled him in on the details.

Kang was indeed close, but Clark had a lot to do to make it work. This was going to be tight.

71

The last cubes of ice that Kang had brought with him aboard Amtrak Number 5 westbound out of Chicago melted in the early hours of morning somewhere between McCook, Nebraska, and Denver, Colorado. He'd bumped the wound on the wall coming through the door of his compartment, nearly sending him to his knees in agony. Alone, he'd been able to replace the sodden bandage and study the wound more closely somewhere other than a public toilet.

The bullet had clipped off his pinkie at the base, blowing away the proximal joint where the finger connected to his hand. Fascinated by the tattered flesh, he cleaned it as best he could, nearly breaking a tooth from the pain as he dug out a centimeter of white bone. He used superglue to close the wound, but it continued to weep blood. Some of the skin flaps were beginning to turn a deep purple. He'd need to cut them off soon, or they'd begin to smell. There was a doctor he could trust in Los Angeles. He could make it that far. He'd get the antibiotics he needed, some stitches—and proper pain medication. Then he'd put together another team and go back for Li.

Kang leaned back and closed his eyes. Li might keep

his family hidden for a time, but eventually he'd display typical American optimism. He would return to his job. His children would go back to school, and his wife would have her baby. Kang smiled at that, momentarily forgetting his throbbing hand.

This was far from over.

Completely spent, he fell asleep sitting up, watching the endless fields of Iowa corn and soybeans slide by outside his window. The steward's knock stirred him, offering to fold out his bed. He refused, survival instinct telling him not to let anyone unknown in his compartment. The pain had blossomed while he slept, and now shot up his arm in electric jolts that kept time with the thumping wheels of the passenger train. A steady diet of Coca-Cola and ibuprofen only served to sour his stomach and make him angrier than he already was.

Kang was accustomed to discomfort, but after two hours of gutting it out, he seriously considered throwing himself off the moving train. He replaced the dressing—a bloody stub was sure to draw too much interest—stuffed the Beretta he'd snatched from Gao in his waistband holster, and made his way to the café car as soon as it opened for the morning. The dining car was between his sleeper and the observation/lounge car, under which the café was located. People were already seated for breakfast, and he passed through without making eye contact with any of the other passengers, staggering in the quickly learned gait necessary to keep one's feet aboard the swaying, lurching train. He thanked the attendant politely when she asked if he wanted a table, telling her he just needed a light snack. She'd see him returning from the café car with his ice and food anyway, so there was no reason to lie.

He'd sweated through his clothing by the time he returned to his room. Fortunately, the other passengers—most of them twice his age—were too self-absorbed to notice him as he stumbled past.

He slid the door shut to remove the holster from his waistband and tossed it on the couch. Latch locked and blue privacy curtains drawn, he collapsed beside his gun, panting from the two-hundred-foot walk.

Wincing, he pressed the bandaged stump of his finger against the cup of ice. It had required every ounce of self-control to pretend his hand wasn't killing him when he'd paid for the Snickers bars and two Coca-Colas.

Kang had dealt with pain before. He knew it would dull in time, but that time would not come soon. The cold only took the edge off. He needed antibiotics—pills, an injection. He slowed his breathing, washed down four more ibuprofen with another can of Coke he'd gotten with the ice, and stared out the window at the passing cliffs. They were climbing, somewhere northwest of Denver. He didn't care. He needed to rest, to plan what he was going to do next.

None of this made any sense. He hadn't gotten a good look at the man along the Riverwalk, but he felt sure that man was alone. Could it have been Li? That was absurd. Peter Li should be more worried about protecting his family than going on the offensive. Then Kang remembered how ferociously the man had fought when they'd invaded his home. The bastard had charged out with the shotgun where he should have cowered in the corner. Still . . . No. It couldn't have been him. But if not, then who?

Kang lifted a bottle of cheap whiskey to his lips with his good hand, keeping the other pressed against the ice. The liquid cut a trench from his tongue to his gut, at once warming him and adding to his confusion. He used his knees and his good hand to replace the lid, then held the bottle up so light from the window backlit the amber liquid. He'd drunk more than half since the train had rolled out of Chicago some twenty hours before. Disgusted, he tossed what was left of the bottle on the blue seat across from him, far enough out of his reach he couldn't drink absentmindedly. He needed it for pain, to blunt the anger, but he also needed a clear head, and whiskey didn't help with that.

Neither did pain.

72

The eleven-car California Zephyr rolled out of Chicago's Union Station on schedule at two p.m. Central Time. John Clark was on board, having purchased one of the few remaining roomettes on the train as soon as he'd ended the call with Gavin. He believed his target was in one of the two sleeper cars. He knew the man's name, his background, and the names of his dead associates. Gavin had found the car and room number of Kang's ticket, but that room turned out to be occupied by an elderly couple when Clark walked down the narrow corridor on the way to his own roomette.

One would think that searching a train would be easy. There were three sleeper coaches, all located aft of the baggage car and the two locomotives. The dining car separated the sleepers from the lounge/observation car and lower-deck café, along with the three coach-class cars bringing up the rear of the train. Clark discounted everything aft of the lounge car. Kang was hurt. He would want privacy. He'd be somewhere up front.

Each double-decker Superliner coach had five bedrooms, each with a cramped toilet and shower, along with ten roomettes on the upper deck. The bedrooms were all on the one side of the train. The much smaller roomettes were situated on the opposite end of the car, five on either side of a shoulder-wide passage that, apart from the carpet and semi-fresh air, put Clark in mind of a submarine. There was a stairwell located midpoint in the car, between the bedrooms and roomettes. Marked by the smell of self-service coffee, it led down to four lower-deck roomettes, a family bedroom, toilets, a shower for the roomette passengers, and a baggage rack. The forwardmost sleeper car was reserved for staff berthing and storage, allowing Clark to mark twenty rooms off the list. This left a total of forty rooms, where Kang might be hiding, thirty-nine discounting Clark's. According to Gavin, Kang had originally purchased a roomette, but since someone was in that room, Clark suspected he'd upgraded at the station to a larger bedroom so he'd have his own sink to doctor his hand. If that were true, it narrowed his search to the ten full-size bedrooms, five on each remaining sleeper car.

Clark ruled out all the rooms on his car by the time they reached Omaha a little after eleven p.m.

The print from the pinkie finger Clark had liberated from Kang's hand was a bust as far as leads went. The photos from the cameras he'd put on the street provided the breakthrough.

One of the downsides of all the facial-recognition programs in the People's Republic of China—at least from the viewpoint of the Chinese intelligence apparatus—was that their own system was hackable. Once Biery had uploaded the images, it took just a few hours before he began to get possible hits. The first lead was for the woman. She was Zhang Zhulan, a PLA major. There was a Red Notice on her passport that noted she was wanted for murder in South Africa. She had several aliases, one of which was Rose. According to the Red Notice, she was known to travel with a man named Kang Jian. Kang turned out to be the mystery man. That name led Biery to numerous aliases, which he checked for recent activity. The Visa card for one of the aliases, Frank Lo of Temecula, California, had been used to buy a bedroom on Amtrak Number 5, the California Zephyr, between Chicago and Emeryville, California.

Clark suspected Kang didn't have any support in Chicago. If he had, he would have brought more than a couple of people with him to whack Li at the river. They would have been expecting at least a couple of guards. Now he was wounded, probably alone, on the run. Clark knew all too well how excruciating a damaged hand could be. The last thing Kang would want to do is drive himself, even if he did have a driver's license. Whereas airports had layer upon layer of security and ID checks, a person could buy a train ticket online with nothing but a credit card. The conductor required nothing but the scan code on a cell phone. It was illegal to bring weapons on board, but there were no metal detectors. Amtrak Police with bomb dogs patrolled the station, but they weren't likely to hit on something as small as a sidearm.

Fortunately for Clark's cover, he was on the youthful end of the average passenger's age. Most were retired, traveling in pairs without the hassle of airports, meeting new people, watching the country roll by. Most had time on their hands. Some were afraid to fly. At least one was a spy, running for his life.

Clark was halfway through a short stack of buttermilk pancakes, chatting amiably with a couple from Boston, both retired from MIT, when Kang staggered through the dining car. Clark took another bite, waiting for him to push the button to open the car before standing to excuse himself. His seatmates obviously missed the captive audience of the lecture hall and protested that he was leaving in the middle of their conversation. He apologized, saying something hadn't agreed with his stomach, left a five-dollar tip on the table, and strode quickly after Kang.

Clark made it through the first set of automatic doors in time to look through the windows of the next coach and watch Kang duck into the first door on the right.

Coach 531, Bedroom A.

Clark's roomette was in the next car, closer to the engines, but the dining car gave him a plausible reason to go back and forth. He kept walking, reaching A as he heard the metal latch click into place. Inside the compartment, a hand reached up and moved the pleated blue curtains over the door and the small window to the right.

The basics of a simple plan already clear in his mind, Clark returned to his roomette. He needed practice defeating the lock on his own door.

Clark had thought Kang might come out for supplies or even to leave the train for good in Denver, but he stayed in his room with the curtains drawn during the fifty-minute stop. Clark and a few others stayed on the platform enjoying the last moments of mountain air until the whistle blew and the conductor waved them aboard. The Zephyr began to slog steadily upward after leaving the city, slowing periodically when wires along the tracks registered rocks or trees from the steep mountain-sides that might have fallen across their path. Snow and evergreens covered the slopes, falling away to a winding river below. An hour and a half later, the conductor announced that they would soon cross the Continental Divide through the six-mile-long Moffat Tunnel. He asked that everyone remain in their assigned car during the ten-minute trip under James Peak.

Two of the roomettes in 531 were vacant, allowing Clark to leave his roomette in 532 and step next door five minutes before they entered Moffat Tunnel from the east.

The train slowed some inside the narrow tunnel but still moved fast enough to double the noise level from what it had been outside now that they were in the belly of the mountain.

Clark waited a full minute, then made his move.

Peeking out the door of the roomette, he looked up and down the corridor one last time before he committed, then made his way quickly past the stairwell to the end of the car with the bedrooms, where he paused in front of Bedroom A. He knew the layout. The couch would be facing forward. A single chair near the window would face aft. He didn't know where Kang would be sitting, but consoled himself that the room was so small it would hardly matter. He'd wrapped his handkerchief around the knuckles of his right hand, then held the Glock in his left, shooting two quick shots at the glass on the door, just above the lock. There was a chance he'd hit Kang, but he didn't have a problem with that.

Moving purposefully once he began, Clark punched

the glass away with the wrapped hand. The locking mechanism was relatively simple, a hooking metal latch with a second metal piece that swung down over the top, jamming the latch in place. Clark put two more rounds through the door to keep Kang on his toes as he pushed the metal tab out of the way. In less than three seconds from the time he first pressed the trigger, he stood to the side, pulling open the door and curtain in one movement.

Kang was seated on the couch, facing forward, which put his left hand nearer the window, forcing him to scramble for the pistol with his nondominant hand and bring it across his body to engage Clark. Still, he was incredibly fast for someone dazed and startled at the sudden attack. Fights in a room not much larger than a phone booth unfolded quickly. Clark rolled in, on top of Kang by the time he put a round in the top of the man's knee. Kang tried to bring the Beretta around, but Clark's left hand deflected it as he knelt on top of the injured hand. Kang let loose a ragged scream, almost too high-pitched to hear.

The Beretta slipped out of Kang's hand, bouncing on the couch before falling to the floor.

Clark pushed off the couch cushion with his free hand and stood back, bracing himself against the curved swell of the bathroom door, his own pistol tucked in tight against his side.

"You speak English, Mr. Kang?" Clark asked, throwing in the name to keep the man guessing.

Kang nodded, chest heaving. His gun hand was busy clutching the bloody stump of the other.

"What's your problem with Peter Li?"

"Who are you?"

Clark ignored the question. "Why attack the man's family?"

Kang shook his head. Thinking. Stalling. Catching his breath.

The roaring noise of the train passing through the tunnel had covered the suppressed gunfire, but they were more than halfway through by now. The window was shot out, there was glass in the hall, and passengers would start to move around again as soon as they came out.

Clark tried again. "Who sent you?"

Kang shook his head.

Clark nodded to the bandaged hand. "I can get you some help."

"A scratch," Kang said.

"Are there more of you?"

Silence.

"Listen, pal," Clark said. "Your friends are dead. You're done. I can get you something for the pain, but I need to know who else is coming after Li."

Kang glared, seething rage flashing in the otherwise dark pools of his eyes. "I have nothing to say."

"You know," Clark said, "I believe you."

Kang was a germ, a bacterium that if not absolutely destroyed would only come back stronger. Still, to some—most, really—killing an injured man who was sitting, blinking up at you, was the act of a brutal barbarian. It was a point of fact that Clark could not argue. At the same time, he admitted another truth that civilized people almost always chose to ignore: Sometimes, the world needed a few barbarians.

Clark kicked the broken glass that had ended up in the hallway back inside the compartment. He slid the door shut behind him as he padded quickly to the vacant roomette, reaching it just as they exited the Moffat Tunnel back into the light of day. He knew one thing: If there were people coming after Peter and his family—there would now be one less.

John Clark could live with that.

73

General Song went in first, without knocking. He never ventured into the north wing so Bai's people were astonished to see him standing there alone so brazenly.

"What can I do for you, General Song?" an officious captain who served as Bai's secretary said from behind his highly polished wooden desk.

"I am here to see General Bai."

"Do you have an appointment?"

"I do not," Song said, starting toward the office door.

The captain shot to his feet. "The general is in a meeting!"

"He'll see me," Song said, brushing past. Lackey or not, no captain wanted to physically bar the movement of a general.

Song pushed open the door to find Bai and Major Chang huddled around a computer screen, perusing what looked like ledger sheets.

"Ready to make some withdrawals?" Song asked.

Bai spun in his chair. The major stood, releasing a nervous fart.

"What do you mean barging into my office unannounced?" He leaned sideways, looking past Song and out the door. "Captain Feng! Call security forces at once—"

Bai's face fell when four sullen-looking men wearing dark business suits filed in behind General Song.

"General Bai Min," Song said. "I have come with the authority of Chairman Zhao, paramount leader. You and Major Chang are under arrest for acts of sedition, murder, and treason against the people of China."

Chang shifted on his feet.

"This is nonsense," Bai said. "I am under arrest because the plan failed."

Song shrugged. "Nonetheless," he said. "You *are* under arrest." He leaned in closer. "And I have been assured your punishment will not be pretend."

At approximately the same moment, but six thousand miles away from Beijing, where General Bai and his bagman were being led away in shame and shackles, a Blue-Bird bus came to a stop in front of Marine Corps Recruit Depot San Diego, packed full of stunned-looking young men.

It was dark, but the glaring lights above the entrance to MCRD illuminated the yellow footprints the young men had all heard so much about. No one spoke. Most held their breath in anticipation—and a unique sense of self-imposed dread. They'd all done their research. They'd watched YouTube videos. They thought they knew what was about to happen. Every one of them had volunteered, so there was no one to blame but themselves.

The bus doors hissed open. A barrel-chested drill instructor sauntered up the steps, campaign hat settled low on his forehead, and began to bark almost unintelligible instructions. His voice was hoarse and raspy, as if he'd been screaming for hours at a concert or football game. Each instruction was met with a resounding "Aye-aye, sir!" or "Yes, sir!" jumbled at first, until the group got their act together and began to answer in unison. Each order came tight on the heels of the previous one, on and on and on. It was understandable—and intended—that all the young men would become disoriented.

Asking the recruits if they understood, over and over again, the drill instructor continued to bark orders. When he told them to, and *only* when he told them to, he wanted them to get off *his* bus.

"Do you understand!!?"

"Yes, sir!" Their reply rattled the windows.

"Get your disgusting bodies off my bus!"

A third of the way back, a tall recruit with wavy dark hair and green eyes did exactly as he was told and moved down the aisle at a pace "one step faster than a walk and one step slower than a run" off the bus to the yellow footprints.

The barking continued into the night, with constant correction for stance, posture, and the slightest wrong answers. A kid standing to the left of the green-eyed recruit began to sniff, drawing the immediate ire of one of the drill instructors. The green-eyed recruit stared at the back of the recruit in front of him, arms crossed over his chest. He'd discussed military discipline many times over his short lifetime with his father and grandfather. He could do this.

More instruction happened on the footprints, along with a lot of kneeling, standing—while being instructed with copious yelling and barking from what felt like one drill instructor for every recruit. No movement was fast enough. No reply loud enough. No infraction or slip went unnoticed.

The recruits were power-walked with "speed and intensity" inside to the contraband room, where they dumped the contents of their pockets into red wooden cubicles for inspection and eventual storage. The Marine Corps would supply them with everything they needed during boot camp.

Eventually, the stunned recruits were ordered to "cover-down" on one of the white phones along the wall. There they would have two attempts to contact a family member or, if they had no family, their recruiter.

The green-eyed recruit had known all along he would have to make the phone call, and of all the events since getting on the bus at the San Diego airport, he dreaded this the most.

Fortunately, his mother did not answer. Other recruits covering down in line directly behind him screamed in response to commands from the drill instructors, making it impossible to think clearly. Then, to his relief, the second number he called went straight to voicemail, so he read the message from the printed script that was posted above the phone. He hung up, relieved to return to the world of screaming drill instructors.

They weren't half as terrifying as his mom.

74

John Clark stepped off the California Zephyr in Fraser/ Winter Park, Colorado, the next station west of the Moffat Tunnel. The scenery was spectacular, so several people exited even for the short duration of the stop, allowing Clark to slip away unnoticed before the train pulled away. He'd cleaned up the glass in the corridor and pulled the curtain to Kang's compartment, so, with any luck, the train would be a few stops down the line before anyone found the body.

He rented a car from a company in nearby Granby, and sat down to check his voicemail while he waited for it to be delivered at a Mexican restaurant a kilometer from the train station.

There'd been no cell service from shortly after Denver, so he had more than a dozen messages. Most were of no consequence, a few would require a call back, but the last one caught him by surprise. He listened to it three times, at first stunned, then proud, then, he had to admit, a little teary-eyed.

"Hello!" the message began, hoarse, but intense. *"This is Recruit Chavez. I have arrived safely at MCRD San Diego. The next time I contact you will be by postal mail,*

so expect a letter from me in two to three weeks. I love you. Good-bye."

Clark listened to the message two more times, then hit speed dial for Ding's cell. He was too much of a coward to talk to his daughter at the moment.

"Mr. C!" Chavez said. "You okay? We've been—"

"Hey, Ding," Clark said, cutting him off. He took a deep breath. "Listen, bud, I just got an interesting phone call from my grandson. I'm thinking he's put Stanford on the back burner for a while . . ."

D avid Huang was pressing a shirt in the laundry room at the back of his house when he heard his wife scream. He smiled, turning off the iron, and started immediately up the hall. Michelle Chadwick had dropped off the face of the earth, but that was to be expected. She'd been under tremendous stress, and they could both use a break from each other. She'd be back. Her political career depended on it.

His cell phone rang, but he ignored it. His wife needed him to take care of whatever spider she'd happened to encounter. He'd just passed the hall closet when she screamed again.

Huang froze when he entered his kitchen and found six heavily armed men in green uniforms and body armor. FBI HRT was emblazoned across their uniforms. The apparent supervisor gave a nod. Two of the agents grabbed him by each arm, helping him none too gently to his kitchen floor, while a third secured his cell phone and slipped it into a Faraday envelope.

From the corner of his eye, he saw a female agent usher his wife and daughter out the front door.

"She doesn't know anything!" he shouted, hoping his wife would hear.

"Do not speak," the team leader said, his tone direct, matter-of-fact.

Hands secured behind his back with nylon restraints, Huang was set in one of his kitchen chairs while a team of plainclothes agents began to search every square inch of his house, including behind the faceplates of each light switch and electric outlet.

Ten minutes into the search, the kitchen door opened and Michelle Chadwick walked in.

"Senator," he said, glaring. "This will not turn out well."

"For you," Chadwick said. "Oh, you mean that fake video you're trying to frame me with. I told President Ryan about that about two minutes into our first meeting. Who do you think you're dealing with here, sport? It's Rule Thirty-Four, you know."

"What does that even mean?" Huang asked, incredulous that this pitiful woman would be so forward with him.

"If it exists, there's probably porn of it. Good Lord, David, there are so many deepfake videos going around nowadays, that shoddy piece of trash will only help my reputation."

"You're supporting Jack Ryan now?"

"Not at all," Chadwick said. "But it turns out, if I'm going to have an enemy, I'd rather it be you than my own government."

75

S o," Cathy said, her head resting against Ryan's chest. "I still can't get my mind around the fact that Michelle Chadwick was never a spy." She smelled like peppermint and Dioressence. *A good pairing,* Jack thought.

"Nope," he said. "A true-blue patriot . . . who still hates my guts."

Cathy patted his stomach. "I love your guts."

"Means a lot, Doc," Ryan said.

"What's Father Pat thinking, going back to Indonesia?"

"That's the way callings are, I guess," Ryan said.

"Terrible about PFC Geddis," Cathy whispered.

Ryan breathed deeply, feeling guilty for being in his comfortable bed while he spoke of such sacrifice. "I know. Sounds like he put himself in danger so the rest of his squad could get safely off the rope."

"And now Ding's son is joining the Marine Corps?"

"I know," Ryan said again.

"I'll bet Patsy's freaked about it," Cathy said.

"And proud," Ryan said. "I talked to John on the phone. Apparently, JP has been talking to him a lot lately about becoming a SEAL. He thought the Marine Corps would get him ready."

"How is Ding?"

"Concussed," Ryan said. "But too hardheaded to have much damage."

Cathy scoffed. "If that were the case, you'd be bullet-proof. And the computer tech? How's that going?"

"Cyber Com believes they have all the copies located," Ryan said. "Or at least how to patch against it. China is sure to have extra copies on hand. Who knows . . . The damned thing could be hiding in my phone at this moment."

"Don't joke about that."

"I wish I were joking," Ryan said. "Even if we got it all, it's only a matter of time before someone develops something better . . . or worse. AI is the future of . . . well, the future."

He and Cathy got to talk like this so rarely, he enjoyed their back-and-forth volleys. It was like playing tennis in bed with a beautiful half-naked woman.

"What about that horrible man who came to the clinic with General Song's family?"

"Tsai?" Ryan said. "No idea. Back in China, I suppose, being the same horrible man."

"Too bad," Cathy said, pooching out her lips, no doubt thinking of what she'd like to see happen to the rude little Communist minder.

She rolled onto her back, using her head to fluff her pillow. "Thank you for letting me help a little."

"Are you kidding me?" Ryan said. "Your help was key."

"Maybe." She turned to him again, restless, unable to lie still. She touched the point of his chin with the tip of her delicate finger, the sure finger of a surgeon. It was something she did when she wanted to get her way—when all she really had to do was show up.

"I have an idea," she said. "You should consider letting me get involved with all your palace intrigue a little more often."

Ryan took her hand in his. "These fingers give people back their sight. You should take care of them, not work them to the bone with counterespionage."

"Is that what you call what I did?" Cathy nestled her head against his chest again, which still made his heart race after all these years. "I was thinking it was more like diplomacy."

"Tomato, tomahto, spycraft," Ryan said.

"Well," Cathy said. "I *really* enjoyed it." She pulled back slightly so she could look up at him, her lips inches from his face. "It made me feel . . . like you."

Ready to find
your next great read?

Let us help.

Visit prh.com/nextread